THE WHITE FEATHER KILLER

THE WHITE FEATHER KILLER

R. N. Morris

This first world edition published 2019
in Great Britain and the USA by
SEVERN HOUSE PUBLISHERS LTD of
Eardley House, 4 Uxbridge Street, London W8 7SY.
Trade paperback edition first published
in Great Britain and the USA 2019 by
SEVERN HOUSE PUBLISHERS LTD.

British Library Cataloguing in Publication Data
A CIP catalogue record for this title is available from the British Library.

ISBN-13: 978-0-7278-8885-3 (cased)
ISBN-13: 978-1-78029-606-7 (trade paper)
ISBN-13: 978-1-4483-0223-9 (e-book)

This is a work of fiction. Names, characters, places and incidents
are either the product of the author's imagination or are used fictitiously.
Except where actual historical events and characters are being described
for the storyline of this novel, all situations in this publication are
fictitious and any resemblance to actual persons, living or dead,
business establishments, events or locales is purely coincidental.

All Severn House titles are printed on acid-free paper.

Severn House Publishers support the Forest Stewardship Council™ [FSC™],
the leading international forest certification organisation.
All our titles that are printed on FSC certified paper carry the FSC logo.

Typeset by Palimpsest Book Production Ltd.,
Falkirk, Stirlingshire, Scotland.
Printed and bound in Great Britain by
TJ International, Padstow, Cornwall.

PART I
The Call to Arms

5 August–28 August, 1914.

HOW TO JOIN THE ARMY

Any man who is able to produce a satisfactory reference as to character may enlist in the Army.

The only requirements are the following:

He must be able to produce a satisfactory reference as to character.

He must be able to read and write.

Be within the limits of age, nineteen and thirty.

Be up to the physical standards for the particular corps he wishes to join.

A recruit who is slightly below the required standards, but who is otherwise considered desirable, may be accepted for enlistment as a special case.

Under the supreme crisis today men will be allowed to join under an entirely new condition.

Their period of service will be for "three years or until the war is over." The ordinary period is, of course, seven years with the colours and five in the reserve.

Men in the country who wish to enlist can obtain the address of the nearest recruiting station at any post office.

Daily Mirror, *Saturday, 8 August, 1914*

ONE

The day after war was declared, Felix Simpkins found himself on the edge of a crowd of men standing in the rain outside the recruitment station in Great Scotland Yard. The queue was four deep at its thinnest. It extended around the corner into Scotland Place, then on around the next corner into Whitehall Place.

By the time he arrived, the crowd had solidified into a single unyielding body. The mood was what the papers might describe as 'irrepressible'. Neither the constant drizzle nor their conspicuous lack of progress could dampen their spirits. They weren't intimidated by the looming mounted policemen in their dark capes penning them in against the wall of the old police station, keeping them out of the road so the traffic could pass.

Why should they be intimidated? They were not criminals. They had come here to do their duty. Even so, Felix thought it wise to give the horses a wide berth.

The unexpected crowds dismayed him, with their damp smells and cheery, long-suffering fortitude. They'd stand all day in the rain for their country, that was clear. Well, Felix didn't have all day. He only had half an hour for lunch. He'd have to be back at his desk by one thirty or he'd cop it from Mr Birtwistle.

Some of those who had already succeeded in gaining entry now shouted encouragingly from first-floor windows. A few were even perched on the windowsills, their legs dangling out as they smoked. They had the air of victors who had captured an enemy redoubt after a hard-fought battle. Exhilaration showed in their faces. And something else, a kind of amazement.

It was the realization that the world had changed overnight. And forever. That was what he could see in their faces. The realization that there was no going back.

Felix watched these men with a resentful, sullen envy. They were making light of the most momentous day in their lives. Didn't they know what it had cost him to bring himself here today? How long he had stood in front of the mirror, screwing up every ounce of his courage. And what hell there would be to pay with Mother!

It was all very well for them. They did not have Mother to contend with.

He realized that he was more repelled by these men than drawn to them. Their exuberance began to feel loutish to him.

They egged each other on with flickering smiles and eyes that flashed a fragile bravado. They steeled themselves with spitting. Quick-fire wisecracks delivered grimly out of one half of a downturned mouth were met with too much hilarity. From time to time, songs burst out, not all of which were patriotic, or even decent.

They excluded him with their half-turned backs and taut, dripping umbrellas.

It was unspeakably daunting.

Without realizing it, he was at that moment backing away from the queue of would-be recruits. In every face he looked at, he saw a knowing sneer, as if his failure of nerve at the last was what they had expected all along.

He felt the roar of something heavy and malign rearrange the air at his back. Out of the corner of his eye, he caught the black blur of a hurtling hansom cab tethered to the clatter of hooves. He jumped away from the disruption, almost out of his skin.

One of the mounted policemen saw the incident and attempted to steer his horse towards Felix. Felix was always nervous around horses, ever since as a child he had heard the story from Mother of a great-uncle who had been kicked in the head by a spooked horse while on holiday in Wales. Uncle Clar had never been the same again and had died from a stroke five years later to the day.

This one was a particularly large and unpredictable beast, over which its rider seemed to have little control. It was currently standing at right angles to the direction the policeman was encouraging it to go. Only when it was good and ready, with much snorting and flaring of its nostrils and twisting of its massive neck and baring of its big yellow teeth, did it finally consent to lift its hooves and shift itself. He could see the power in its muscles, barely held in by the shimmer of its chestnut coat. He had the feeling, inspired by something wild and wilful he detected in its eye, that it would rear up at any moment. He felt it held a grudge against its rider, which it would take out on any human that got in its way.

He supposed there would be horses in the army, in supply as well as in the cavalry. Of course, he had no intention of volunteering for the cavalry. Still, it would be impossible to avoid all contact with the animals.

But now the horse and its rider were looming darkly over him.

'You there! Stop being a bloody nuisance and get back in line.'

The policeman's coarse language shocked him. Really, there was no need for that. There was no need too for the horse's flank to swing towards him, forcing him back.

Felix attached himself loosely to the side of the queue. This provoked a chorus of protest from the men immediately behind him.

'I say, that's not on!'

'Bleedin' queue jumper!'

'Get to the back of the line, you cheeky blighter!'

Someone even laid hands on him, a quick shove propelling him back out into the street.

His arms flailed to keep him upright. There was boisterous laughter from the men in line. He felt the heat of a flush in his face. He turned sharply to see who had pushed him. A burly individual was squaring up to him with balled fists and a clenched face. Felix's heart tripped. He swallowed down the coppery taste of fear.

He ought to teach that fellow a lesson, he knew that. That was what the men watching him expected. But what was to be gained from it?

They were here to sign up to fight the Hun, not to fight amongst themselves.

'I'm sorry. My mistake. I didn't mean to. It's just, the horse, you see . . .'

The man regarded him with an angled head. 'What are you, some kind of nancy boy?'

There were sniggers of appreciation from the men around him. Felix felt himself blush again. It was a pathetic weakness and he hated himself for it. Just like a bloody girl.

He knew that he could not let this slur to his manhood go. Not in front of this audience.

He did what he had to do.

He swung a punch at the ruffian's head, catching him squarely on the nose. He heard a satisfying explosion of blood as the cartilage crumpled. Or perhaps he rushed at him and overpowered him, forcing him to the ground, squatting across his shoulders and hurling down multiple blows into his fat ugly face until it was a pulp. Or perhaps he contented himself with a huge gobbet of sputum which he launched into the bully's face. And like all bullies, the man was shown up as a coward himself, backing away at the first sign of resistance.

No. Of course. He did none of that, except in his imagination.

Instead, he did what he was compelled to do. He turned on his heels and walked away, away from another fight, and from the jeers that mocked his cowardice.

Why was it that whenever it came to any test of his character, however trivial, his nerve always failed him? He was a coward, that was all there was to it. A lousy, contemptible coward. He hid it from himself, but it came out every day, in a thousand small ways. In his fear of horses, of policemen, of crowds, of burly men, of Mr Birtwistle, of steaming kettles and scaffolding and countless malign things. Why, he even supposed he was frightened of the umbrellas some of the men were handling so carelessly! It was a wonder they hadn't had someone's eye out already.

Did he really think that he could just come along today and enlist? And so put an end to all his fears?

That if they gave him a uniform to wear he would be transformed from a coward to a hero?

He would reveal his true colours eventually. At a time when his funk might put other men's lives at risk.

So it was better really, more noble, more patriotic, not to enlist. There he went again with his convoluted self-justifications, his specious excuses and bad faith.

What was it Mother always said? 'Know thyself.'

She used it as a box to keep him in. But perhaps she was right. He was who he was and he could never escape that.

The rain did not let up as he hurried back to the office. If he didn't get a move on he would be late and he would cop it from Mr Birtwistle.

TWO

Of course, London was different now. There was a war on. A war was bound to change everything.

That was enough to explain the feeling of dislocation that Silas Quinn experienced as he walked the streets. The city belonged to the soldiers he saw everywhere, square-bashing in Horse Guards Parade, bivouacked in St James's Park, massing at Victoria Station.

London had the air of having placed itself at War's disposal. The pavements thundered with the harsh boot falls of an army on the move. It gave the place a new energy, a new purpose. A kind of glamour even, in which Quinn could not share.

But there was something indecent about it all too. It was almost abject, this surrender to militarism. An eager, blind and mindless fatalism.

He was walking along the Victoria Embankment. On the other side of the Thames, an untidy sprawl of cranes and scaffolding marked out the construction site of the new county hall. They had been building it for years, in fits and starts. Now, it seemed to have finally been abandoned for good.

Silas turned away from it to look up at New Scotland Yard as he passed in front of it. This was his place of work, from which he had been temporarily excluded. That was bound to make a chap feel out of sorts. Officially, he was on sick leave. It was for his own good, it had been explained to him. He had been under extraordinary stress. The last investigation had taken its toll on him, particularly as he had spent part of it undercover as an inmate in Colney Hatch Lunatic Asylum.

He needed to take a bit of time to 'put himself back together'. Or so Sir Edward Henry, the Metropolitan Police commissioner, had made clear.

But the listless empty days and sleepless nights had not restored him. On the contrary, he was now so discombobulated that he felt himself to be the cause of the city's strangeness.

The declaration of war had passed him by. It was fair to say he had had other things on his mind at the time. And now, it was as if he had passed from one bad dream into another.

Perhaps he wasn't ready to go back to work after all.

The test was to look up. Logic told him that there were no soldiers in the sky, no patriotic placards, or newspaper headlines. Nothing to remind him of the war at all.

The sky was eternally the sky. Constantly changing, but always itself. So if he felt the same sense of strangeness looking up, it proved that it came from within.

It was early evening, of the first fine day they had had for some time, the first to have any promise of summer heat. August had been a wash-out so far.

The sky was still bright, as if charged with electricity. It seemed to shimmer with a supernatural potential. And, yes, he thought it as alien and unwelcoming as a city under occupation. He looked directly into the setting sun, so that when he looked back towards the buildings of the Embankment, he could see only dark, looming shapes, devoid of detail. And so he did not see her approach, or rather he did not recognize her. Certainly he could not make out the smile that she brought him, which faded from her expression without his ever knowing it had been there. It was a pity, because she so rarely smiled.

It was almost as if he had not expected her. And yet this was the allotted time and she was the one he had come to meet.

'There you are,' she said flatly. No hint of the smile in her voice now.

'Oh, it's you. I'm sorry, I couldn't see.'

'Why? What's wrong with you?'

'I had been looking at the sky.'

'Oh, God.' With this exasperated aside, she fell back into the habit of mockery that was her usual mode with him.

It was only now, as his eyes adjusted, that he noticed the forget-me-nots on her hat. It was a pretty hat and he realized that she was pretty too. But with her ready sarcasm and flagrant eye-rolling, he had long believed that the only sentiment she entertained towards him was contempt. He was startled by the idea that she had made an effort for him.

He heard a female throat clearing itself, and saw for the first time that she was not alone.

'Oh, yes. This is Aunt Constance.'

A short, round woman came forward to present herself. She was wearing a pair of tortoiseshell spectacles, through which she scrutinized Silas closely. She offered him her hand, warily, as if she didn't trust him not to run off with it.

'Aunt Constance?'

'Yes. You didn't think I would come alone, did you? What kind of a girl do you take me for?'

Silas was about to say, 'I don't take you for any kind of girl.' But the warning glint in her eye deterred him.

'Lettice has told me a *lot* about you.' Aunt Constance offered this information in a tone that was on the disapproving side of ambiguous.

'Lettice?' It was only now that he realized he had never learnt her first name. To him she had always been Miss Latterly, the sentinel outside Sir Edward's office. 'Lettice Latterly?'

'What's wrong with that?' The brusqueness of her tone unnerved him. And yet he thought he detected a playful skittering in her eyes. It seemed she was pleased that he had grounds to mock her now.

'There's nothing wrong with it. Your parents had every right to christen you whatever name they wished.' He turned abruptly to her aunt. 'What has she told you?'

'Oh . . . oh . . . all sorts of things.' Aunt Constance was suddenly breathless and vague. He noticed that she backed away from him, as if something about his manner alarmed her.

'I told her that you've just come out of a loony bin. That's why she insisted on coming along.'

'Well, there has to be *someone* here!' Aunt Constance pointed out.

'Naturally,' agreed Silas. 'Did she tell you that I was there as part of a police operation, not as a patient?'

'Oh, but it wasn't a police operation, was it? Not an official one.'

Silas met Lettice's provoking hairsplitting with a dismissive shrug. 'It's over now at any rate.'

'There are plenty who say you should still be in there.'

'Lettice!'

He rather warmed to Aunt Constance to see how indignant she was on his behalf. Although perhaps it was more that she was afraid, alert to the danger that her niece's way of talking might provoke the lunacy in him.

'Is Sir Edward one of them?'

'Oh, you know that Sir Edward has always been your staunchest defender.' After a beat, she added, 'Against your many detractors.' She frowned distractedly and sniffed the air like a cat. 'Where are we going, anyhow?'

It was a good question and one to which he had given perhaps insufficient thought.

'I thought we might . . . eat?' But the realization that he would also have to pick up the tab for Aunt Constance made him suddenly less keen on the idea. She looked like she could pack it away.

'That's very *kind* of you.' Lettice gave the word a forceful emphasis, as if it were hard for her to say.

He remembered hearing talk of a restaurant on the Strand which celebrities were known to frequent. Among its regulars were a number of notorious criminals, which was how it had come to his attention.

'You don't mind walking, do you?'

Aunt Constance and Lettice agreed that it was a pleasant evening and a walk would be most welcome. Aunt Constance even went so far as to say, 'We might see some soldiers.' Her eyes shone brightly at the prospect. He could not discount the possibility that she would feel safer knowing that there were soldiers nearby.

They headed north. Silas and Lettice fell into step side by side and Aunt Constance, remembering her role as chaperone, dropped behind. Silas glanced back and caught her pretending to be very interested in the river. 'I'm sure this must be awfully tiresome for your aunt.'

'She gets a good dinner out of it.'

'Has she performed this function for you before?'

Lettice didn't answer, except to arch one eyebrow aggressively.

'I didn't mean to imply . . .' He left that hanging.

'What didn't you mean to imply?'

He opened his palm and grasped at nothing.

'You do know that I'm teasing you?' She watched his face closely. 'My God, you have no idea! How on earth you function as a detective I shall never know. I thought detectives were supposed to be skilled at reading people.'

'There are other skills.'

'Oh, you mean shooting people.'

'I . . . that has been overstated. By the press. In this last case, I shot no one.'

'Well done you.'

'It wasn't that hard. They don't allow guns inside Colney Hatch.' He surprised himself with the joke, and was gratified to see the merest twitch of appreciation on her lips, as if she were fighting down the impulse to laugh.

'I am surprised that, with your propensity for shooting, you have not thought of enlisting.'

'Sir Edward would not allow it. Essential occupation, you see.'

Lettice sighed heavily, as if disappointed. 'Do you think it will all be over by Christmas?'

'Is that what people say? I have no idea.'

'You sound as if you are not interested in the war.'

'I know nothing about it. They didn't let the patients see the papers in there, you know, in case it made us agitated. When I came out, there were soldiers everywhere. It's not that I'm not interested in the war. It's just that I can't quite believe in it.'

'Us?'

'I beg your pardon?'

'You said *us*. In case it made *us* agitated.'

He shrugged, unsure of her meaning.

'I thought it was supposed to be an undercover operation. *Us* implies you really did see yourself as one of the inmates.'

'You should be a police detective.'

'I should like to be.'

Silas smiled indulgently. 'I like your hat. It's very fetching.'

A veil of disappointment descended over her expression, closing her off from him. They continued in silence until they reached the Charing Cross extension terminus, where he timidly suggested they turn left away from the river.

She complied passively. He felt that he had lost her.

'I'm sorry,' he said. 'I'm not very good at this. I was trying to pay you a compliment.'

He could see the anger in her clenched jaw.

'You think it's ridiculous that I should want to be a detective.'

'It's not ridiculous. It's just impossible.'

'Because I am a woman.'

'I don't deny that you would be as clever as any male detective – cleverer than most, I'm sure. However, there are other aspects of the job for which a woman is simply not suited. How could you give chase to a violent criminal or indeed wrestle him to the ground? And then again, some of the sights that a detective is forced to confront are not suitable for feminine eyes.'

'You think our eyes are differently constructed to men's?'

'You know what I mean. It is not the eyes so much as the sensibilities, the nervous disposition . . . the female constitution is simply not robust enough. Besides, why would you want to expose yourself to such atrocities when there is no need? Any more than you would wish to fight in this war?'

'I am not afraid of danger.'

'You can only say that because you don't know what danger is.'

It was a moment before she replied. 'Well, perhaps I will start a female detective agency and show all you police*men* up. Like Sherlock Holmes does.'

The restaurant was on the north side of the Strand, next to the Vaudeville Theatre, where *Eliza Comes to Stay* was playing. Silas began to regret his decision as they waited for Aunt Constance to catch them up. The prancing Cupids that adorned the canopy above the doorway hinted at a louche and disreputable ambience within.

Aunt Constance read aloud the name over the menu board: 'Romano's? Is it foreign?'

'Italian, I believe.'

'Well, just so long as it's not German. We don't want to be poisoned.'

'The food, I'm told, is very cosmopolitan.'

Aunt Constance compressed her lips into a tight pinch of disapproval. Silas gestured for them to go inside.

The restaurant was long and narrow, and had the air of a place that had seen better days. A faded mural ran along one wall. It showed a wan and lifeless vista of a rocky coast and a sea so pale it was hardly there, like an invalid's dream. The rest of the decor had a vaguely Moorish feel to it, though its shabbiness counteracted any glamour that might have been intended. The waiters appeared either elderly and tired, or young and insolent. The clientele seemed suspicious and resentful, as if they had been got there under false pretences. Which was precisely how Silas felt.

Silas noticed a sprinkling of khaki here and there, officers enjoying a sullen last supper before the deprivations of campaigning.

One of the elderly waiters limped over with an air of distracted bewilderment and a moustache that looked like it was made of papier-mâché. He said nothing but raised both eyebrows in enquiry.

'Do you have a table? For three?' asked Silas.

'You have reservation?'

'Can't you fit us in?'

The waiter sized them up individually, as if their actual physical dimensions were the issue.

At the sight of Aunt Constance, his solid-looking moustache wobbled dubiously. 'I see what I can do.'

They watched disconsolately as he withdrew into the interior. Then they saw him called over by a man eating alone. The man was somewhere in his sixties. Something about him gave Silas the impression that he had been a regular at the restaurant for decades. He even speculated that he was the owner, having won the place in a bet. He was dressed impeccably, but this seemed to Silas to be compensating for some inner moral turpitude. The man and the waiter spoke briefly, while looking now and then in Silas's direction. The waiter gave a final bow of assent and hurried back to Silas.

'Please to come with me. You are the famous Quick-he-fire Quinn. Of course we have table.'

Later that night, Silas Quinn let himself into a hotel room in King's Cross. The single electric bulb flickered intermittently. When it was not on the blink it was thankfully dim, concealing in a discreet gloom the dust that filmed every surface and the large patches of damp that blossomed through the peeling wallpaper. But the darkness could not disguise the peculiar smells of a cheap hotel room. A faint smell of decay came from the fabric of the building. And, like a medium casting around for spirits, he sniffed some residual odour of every previous occupant, a patina of layered sadness.

He was only staying here temporarily until he sorted out more

permanent lodgings. It was out of the question for him to return
to his last address, although he had not officially given notice
there and his rent was paid up to the end of August. He must
write to his landlady, Mrs Ibbott, telling her of his intentions.
Also, his belongings were still there. He wasn't in a position to
collect them all yet, but there were one or two things he wanted
to pick up. A change of clothes would be useful. He couldn't
carry on buying things as he needed them.

He could not say why he had settled on a hotel in King's
Cross, except that it was cheap.

As he sat down on the bed, the springs whined like a wounded
animal and the frame bowed precariously. One of these nights it
would give way completely under his weight. A moment later
the whole room began to shake. He had identified two frequen-
cies of room shakes. This one was as harsh and wild as a tornado.
Often it was accompanied by the shriek of a steam whistle. The
other was deeper, slower in its build-up, and more pervasive in
the grip it held over the building. That was the Underground.

Sinking back on the bed, still fully clothed, he closed his eyes.
He could not say the evening had been a complete success. The
menu card had offered a bewildering choice of unfamiliar dishes,
all listed in French, which seemed odd given that he had assumed
Romano's to be an Italian restaurant. He had ordered a *zéphir
de poussin*, which he suspected of being some kind of chicken
dish, though he could not be entirely sure. He had not wished
to reveal his ignorance by asking the waiter for guidance, instead
allowing himself to be enticed by the romantic-sounding name
of the dish. A dangerous system for ordering food, he realized.
Lettice had opted for *goulache*. Aunt Constance took a long time,
shaking her head and tutting, before enquiring of the young waiter
who now attended them: 'Do you not serve *English* food?'

'If you have any special requests, I am sure Chef will be happy
to oblige.'

Special requests and obliging chefs sounded expensive to Silas.
He watched nervously as Aunt Constance came to her decision.
'Very well, I'd like a pork cutlet.' *Could have been worse!*

'*Côtelette de porc*, of course. Perhaps some *pommes frites* to
accompany?'

'What the Devil is that?'

'Chips.'

'Why didn't you say so?' She handed back the oversized menu with a flourish of satisfaction.

It was left to Silas to select something from the wine list. He wished that he had Sergeant Macadam with him. He would have known what to order. In the end, Silas plumped for a wine which at least excelled in economy.

The wine, a claret, arrived quickly, along with some bread rolls and curls of butter. He weighed the massive butter knife in his hand and judged its haft substantial enough, when wielded with sufficient force, to crack a child's skull. He proposed a toast to good health and sipped at it in an exploratory way. The wine was insipid, which was probably the best that could be hoped for in the circumstances.

His efforts to rekindle the conversation were met with little enthusiasm by Lettice, who still seemed cross with him. The arrival of a group of army officers, evidently drunk, drew their attention.

'They ought to be ashamed of themselves,' volunteered Aunt Constance. 'They should think of the example they set. Isn't that right, Inspector Quinn?'

'They are just boys really, if you look at them. I am not surprised they need a shot of alcohol to fortify them for what is to come.'

'Dutch courage? Is that what it is?' demanded Aunt Constance. 'Perhaps a coward would need artificial stimulants to strengthen his nerve, but a real man would not.' The remark seemed to be directed at Silas as much as the drunken soldiers.

The food when it came was revelatory, or at least his *zéphir* was. He hadn't known what to expect. But nothing had prepared him for this frothy mousse that melted on his tongue with an explosion of flavour that was both elusive and satisfying. He suspected that it was a clever way of making a little bit of chicken – or whatever it was – go a long way. At any rate, he couldn't imagine tasting anything more exotic or sophisticated. Lettice seemed less pleased with her dish. She ate very slowly and asked for some water to counteract the spicy flavour. He was most concerned that Aunt Constance should enjoy her cutlet and chips. She viewed the dish suspiciously when it arrived, flicking the parsley garnish away with the tip of her knife. But on the first mouthful she pronounced it 'adequate', so that was all right.

His resentment, which at first he had not been aware of, had built slowly over the course of the evening. It seemed especially humiliating to be in the midst of so many couples, so clearly not married, engaged in intimate *tête-à-têtes* around them. Lettice Latterly was not a child. And it was insulting to him, the imputation that he could not be trusted to behave like a gentleman without the presence of some gruesome old biddy. Well, perhaps gruesome was unfair. But Aunt Constance did cast rather a shadow over the table.

The consequence was that he grew more tongue-tied and charmless as the evening went on. By the end, it was a relief to pay the bill and be out of there. He was left wondering what on earth had possessed him to invite Miss Latterly out for the evening in the first place. No doubt he had done it when the balance of his mind was disturbed.

He had walked them to Waterloo, from whence they took their train to Wimbledon. So, she lived in Wimbledon and her Christian name was Lettice. But really, apart from the fact that she had some extraordinary ideas about female detectives, that was all he knew about her.

Then, just when he had been ready to turn away and put the whole thing down to experience, he caught her half-apologetic, half-teasing smile through the grimy carriage window.

THREE

Felix Simpkins returned to the recruitment station in Great Scotland Yard every lunchtime for the next two weeks. Although the numbers fluctuated day by day, after Lord Kitchener's call for volunteers on 7 August there were generally more men than even on that first day. It must have been a streak of masochism that brought him back so many times. Every day he told himself that this would be the day he would enlist. And every day, he failed. There was always some excuse that let him off the hook: Mr Birtwistle's growing desperation, they were snowed under with work, he couldn't spare a single one of them; Mother's fears and tears, her hysterical pleas, how could he think of abandoning her, with her weak heart it would kill her; and then there was the rumour he had heard that there was no point enlisting as it would take at least six months to train up the raw recruits and the war would be over before they were needed.

Deep down he knew that they were all equally specious. Every time he failed to enlist for one reason, and one reason alone. Because he was a coward.

This realization came to him anew, and with a fresh flush of shame, each time. And each time he vowed that this would be the last occasion. He would not subject himself to this humiliation any more.

He remembered back to a time in his school career, when he had somehow landed a part in the play. He was the third or possibly fourth senator in *Julius Caesar*. He learnt his one line and conscientiously attended every rehearsal, even the dress. But at the last minute, on the day of the opening night, he had been struck down with a mysterious belly ache. The pain was real, he was sure, and it was Mother who had kept him at home for three days, which just happened to be the extent of the play's run.

It was awfully bad form to let the other chaps down, not to mention Mr Lomax, the master who was producing it. He was pretty sure he had protested. Pleaded to be allowed to go to school. Or possibly he had known it would be to no avail. Mother had said, 'If you are ill, you are ill.'

If only he could see one thing through. One bold deed. And enlisting in Kitchener's army would be the most splendidly bold deed of all.

The ranks of men waiting in line seemed to sense his cowardice. If they looked at him at all, it was with a quick dismissive glance, before they puffed out their chests and stood tall. In the glow of the warm, approving sunlight, they appeared cleansed, sanctified even. Whatever sins they had committed up to this point were wiped away. They stood immaculate and pure now.

As he turned away, he felt the weight of a pitiless depression possess his heart.

That afternoon, back at his desk in the sunless offices of Griffin Mutual in Holborn, Felix felt every heavy tick of the big clock on the wall like a hammer blow on the fragile carapace of his self-esteem. He did not even dare to lift his head to look around at his fellow clerks, their backs bent in meek and uniform compliance.

It was partly shame that inhibited him. But also, he accepted bitterly, fear. If Mr Birtwistle caught any of them looking away from their ledger book he would come down on the slacker like a ton of bricks.

He was destined to live out his life on that high perch, without once having done anything notable, not even having the courage to look up at the clock.

He looked at his work without understanding it. The numbers jumped off the page and swam into a blur. He felt a balled wad of misery pushing its way up through his throat, his mouth clamped tightly to hold it in.

His vision cleared for a moment, enough for him to see a drop of moisture land heavily on his page of workings. Instantly, a second drop landed beside it. *And so, tears now!* He allowed himself a sly glance at his colleagues on either side. They were as engrossed in their own work as he always imagined them to be. His humiliation was no less intensely felt for all that it was private.

The shudder of a suppressed sob wracked his jaw. He took out his pocket handkerchief and dabbed the page, smudging the ink in the process. Of course! Was he stupid as well as pathetic?

Heat flooded into his face. Mr Birtwistle was ever so particular about neatness. Felix tried to over-write the smudged numbers, but the nib of his pen churned up the soggy paper almost to the point of wearing a hole in it.

By the time the bell rang at five o'clock, Felix had worked himself up into a state of dread and panic. It was just like that time in the third form when he had snagged his hand on the point of a 2H pencil he had sharpened with a scalpel to a dangerous acuity for Geometry. The pencil had broken his skin and he had become convinced that his blood had been poisoned with lead from the pencil. He had fainted in the middle of double Maths.

He fled the office with his head down, into the tide of humanity on High Holborn.

He had no clear idea where he was going, or where he wanted to go, except that he did not want to go home. He could not bear to face Mother. She had a damnable knack of making him feel worse about himself. And yet in many ways this was all her fault, for it was she who had effectively put the kibosh on his joining up. It was better if he didn't see her just now. He couldn't answer for the consequences if he did.

Before long he found himself in the back streets north of Covent Garden. The day was still warm, drawing people out of their dilapidated lodgings, hungry for the last few hours of light – or for something more tangible. With a jolt of apprehension, he realized that he had wandered into the Seven Dials district.

There was a dingy public house in the middle of the terrace. It looked more like a condemned ruin than a place of entertainment. A group of soldiers spilled out of it, taking the evening by storm. They attacked their beers with a grim determination, as if they had been ordered to get drunk. Their glee was a fierce, angry glee of shouted insults and threatening postures.

They squared their shoulders and clogged the pavement with heedless arrogance. One or another might tap his mate to make way for a pretty girl, or any female actually. The manoeuvre would be effected with exaggerated courtesy. For the likes of Felix, of course, not one of them would give way, and so he was forced to navigate his way around them. He naturally gave them as wide a berth as possible.

He marvelled at the women who launched themselves towards this glut of Tommies, responding to their loutish attentions with flirtatious smiles and encouraging remarks.

Did they have no shame?

He realized that quite possibly they did not. More than likely they were prostitutes. Certainly no decent girl would expose herself to such blandishments, in such a place. No decent girl would be seen in Seven Dials at all.

It was then that it struck him. The reason he had been unable to sign up. He was a virgin. He did not want to die a virgin. It would be as if he had died without ever having lived.

All he needed to do was go with one of them and then he would be ready to give his life for his country.

He latched his hopes on to one girl in particular, whose face seemed kinder than the rest, as if she had not yet lost all potential for human sympathy. He thought he detected humour about her eyes, which were not quite so stupefied and avid as her fellows'. He could not guess her age. Perhaps she was not as young as she wished to appear. Or perhaps, he speculated with a thudding heart, she was younger than was strictly legal.

He swallowed on a suddenly dry mouth. This was a new kind of fear.

If he could go through with it, if he could approach her, proposition her and take her to some stinking alley to do whatever it was men did with prostitutes, if he could conquer this one fear, he could conquer anything.

But he could hardly breathe now. He found himself panting like an overheated dog. He was a dog to be contemplating such an act.

What would Mother say?

It was this thought that decided him.

He began to walk towards the girl.

As he approached her, the signs of sympathy that he thought he had detected evaporated from her face. She was engaged in some kind of coarse badinage with a group of Tommies. There was nothing subtle or clever or charming about any of it. The laughter that it provoked was beastly.

Felix thought of turning back, but steeled himself to stand about a pace to one side of her. But whatever words he had thought he would say deserted him.

He could only stand there, as mute and useless as a boulder.

At first she didn't notice him. Then the soldiers she was with fell silent and nodded in his direction, pulling faces of exaggerated respect as they hid their smirks behind their pint pots. There was only the odd guffaw to give away their sarcastic intent.

'Looks like you've got an admirer, miss!' said one of them, to a round of sniggers.

She turned at last to face him, making no attempt to hide her disappointment. ''Ere,' she said. 'Does your mother know you're out?'

The soldiers greeted this devastating witticism with ugly laughter. They were not laughing so much because they thought it funny; they were laughing because it insulted him. They were seeing him off with their laughter.

Once again, Felix felt his face flood with heat. How shameful it was always to signal his humiliation like a girl.

He turned sharply and hurried away from their mockery, tears pricking his eyes.

FOUR

D CI Silas Quinn stood once again on Victoria Embankment, looking up at New Scotland Yard.

He was dressed in an overcoat, a brand-new ulster, and a bowler hat. The coat was his trademark. His last ulster had been taken from him and burnt at Colney Hatch Lunatic Asylum. By that time it was in a terrible state anyway, filthy and ripped, no longer the symbol of a brilliant police detective.

It was a warm day in late August. Despite the heat, it had seemed important to him to wear the ulster today. It would signal to his men that he was back and that he meant business.

A group of uniformed bobbies came out of the entrance. They seemed cocksure and heedless, sealed off from him in their camaraderie. Quinn drew himself up self-consciously, expecting them to recognize him. They passed him by without a second glance.

The building had always inspired powerful emotions in Quinn. He knew the story of the 2,500 tons of granite that constituted its lower stories. It had been quarried and dressed by convicts. That seemed both fitting and cruel, as if criminals as a class were being co-opted into their own prosecution.

His gaze swung upwards to the roof, where his own department was housed, in a single cramped attic room.

What if his sergeants, Macadam and Inchball, greeted him with the same indifference that the bobbies had shown? No, he could not believe that of them. They had stood by him, for all the grounds he had given them to question his authority. At the thought of their loyalty he felt overcome by an emotion that threatened to unman him before he had set foot inside. He dabbed away the moisture that was welling in his eyes.

He carried a rolled-up copy of the *Daily Mirror* beneath one arm. He opened it up and read the headline, as if to distract himself from his doubts:

BRITISH MARINES PREPARE TO DEFEND OSTEND:
"READY AND ANXIOUS TO MEET THE GERMANS."

The photograph below it showed men dug in, peering over a trench 'on the lookout for Uhlans' in the words of the caption. It was difficult to judge what each of the Tommies in the picture was feeling. One man's expression was either resilient or apprehensive, Quinn could not decide. Whichever it was, it was certainly alert. The headline seemed to suggest that they were eager for the fight. And yet, one also had a sense of what was at stake.

Of course, it was all a set-up. There were no Uhlans about to come over the horizon towards them just at that moment. The photographer would not be positioned where he was if an assault was expected any time soon.

Even so, the headline and the photograph chimed with Quinn's own mood – or at least with what he felt he should be feeling.

The time that had been allotted to him for his recovery had come to an end. Therefore he had to assume that he was recovered. Certainly, he was bored of doing nothing. Reading daily in the papers about the massing troops and imminent battles had begun to convince him that the war was something more than just a bad dream. The reports had instilled in him a restless craving for activity of some kind.

He folded the newspaper and tucked it under his arm.

His footsteps echoed from above and below as he climbed the concrete steps to the Special Crimes Department. It gave the effect that he was both being followed and following another. He also had the sensation that the stairs would go on forever. He almost believed they had added another flight in his absence, a mysterious flight of infinite extent.

By the time he reached the third floor, his calves were beginning to ache.

The last investigation had taken its toll on him. What made it worse was that it all seemed to be for nothing.

He had to shake off such thoughts. The long ascent helped him do that. He was climbing away from his old self, with its negative attitudes, towards a brighter future.

He snorted contemptuously at the fanciful turn his thoughts had suddenly taken. Where did he get these ideas? he wondered.

No brighter future awaited him. Just more of the same, three big men crammed into a room that was too small for them, too hot in the summer, too cold in the winter, banging their heads every time they stood up too sharply from their desks. The only good thing about the room was that it at least encouraged them to get out and do some real policing.

More of the same, with the extra work that the war and the new laws brought in under the Defence of the Realm Act would inevitably entail. They had already questioned, before the war, whether they were becoming a branch of military intelligence. He was sure that that would be the case even more now. There was a war on. They all had to do their bit.

The corridor in the attic was at the apex of the roof, so that it was possible, just, for a man of average height to walk along it without stooping. Most of the rooms off it were used as store rooms, stuffed with old administrative files that no one had looked at for decades or surplus equipment, forgotten and gathering dust. There were one or two civilian support offices up here. The only active service department was the SCD.

The door was unmarked. Those who needed to find it knew where it was. But strangely, now, after his prolonged absence, he began to doubt his memory. Was this really the right door? Was there even an office there at all?

The doorknob felt alien and resistant in his hand.

Neither Macadam nor Inchball were at their desks. The room was airless and dusty.

Quinn noticed that the coat-stand was missing. The chair had gone from behind Macadam's desk. All the desks, including his own, were piled up with files and folders. Someone was already beginning to use the room as a dumping ground.

Perhaps his sergeants had been seconded to another unit in his absence. That would make sense. But still, that was no excuse to start treating the room as if he were never coming back.

He would get to the bottom of this.

He pushed the files off his desk, letting them spill their contents as they fell to the floor with a startling din. Whoever had put them there could sort them out.

He sat down behind his desk and reached for the telephone. But before his hand got there, it started to ring.

He put the earpiece to his ear and heard a female voice: 'Sir Edward will see you in his office immediately.'

It was her voice, Lettice Latterly's. He recognized it despite the thinness of the signal and the crackles that overlaid it.

That was all she said before hanging up. She gave him no opportunity to respond.

There was a world of recrimination and disappointment in her simple message.

'How are you?'

She did not look up from her typewriter at his tentative enquiry. 'You're to go straight in.'

'Is there something wrong?'

'There is a war on. Is that not wrong enough for you?'

'No, I meant . . . with you.'

'We don't have time to discuss this now. He's expecting you.'

At last she looked up, but did not meet his eye. She took in his appearance and frowned. 'Aren't you hot in that?'

'In what?'

'Your coat.'

'Someone took my coat-stand.'

'I don't know anything about that.'

'And there are files and all sorts of rubbish in the office.'

'Nothing to do with me.'

'I don't know where Macadam and Inchball are.'

At last she looked at him properly. Her look was not unkind. 'You had better go in. You can leave your coat with me if you like.'

'It's all right. He will have to take me as I am.'

'Oh but he's not alone.'

'He's not?'

'No.'

'Who?'

'Some chap called Kell.'

'Who's he?'

She shrugged. 'And the assistant commissioner.'

'Thompson?'

'Yes.' She gave him just enough time to take all this in, then added: 'And Sir Michael Esslyn.'

Esslyn was a Whitehall mandarin whom Quinn had once encountered in a previous investigation. His brush with this powerful man, although it had not resulted in any charges against Esslyn, had been enough to earn his enmity. 'What's going on?'

'I told you. A war.'

*   *   *

'It's gone way past that, I tell you!'

Pale light flared in the clouds of tobacco smoke that filled Sir Edward Henry's office, partially obscuring the face of the man who was speaking as Quinn came in. He recognized the voice, however, as Sir Michael Esslyn's.

Quinn could detect the sickly narcotic scent of Esslyn's brand of opium-laced Egyptian cigarettes, which he had once smoked experimentally himself.

But there were other smells too, pungent and noxious, and more smoke in the room than could have been produced by one cigarette. He could also hear a faint rasping sound, which came and went in regular waves.

'Ah, there you are, Quinn.'

Through the smoke, Quinn was able to make out the silhouette of Sir Edward Henry, the commissioner of the Metropolitan Police, seated behind his desk. Two men were seated in front of the desk. He recognized one as Esslyn. The other was a man in beribboned khaki, with the green band of an intelligence officer on his cap. He too was smoking a cigarette, although his seemed to have a vaguely medicinal smell. This must be Kell. Assistant Commissioner Thompson stood by the window, looking out at a view of the Thames and puffing away determinedly on a briar. He turned at Sir Edward's greeting and blew a lungful of grey smoke towards Quinn as if to blot him out. Kell did not look up. He seemed to be absorbed in weighty thoughts. Quinn could not be sure whether Esslyn was looking at him or not. It was a disturbing sensation.

The only one of them not smoking was Sir Edward. He looked distinctly green about the gills.

Sir Edward gestured impatiently for Quinn to sit down. There were two vacant seats. One next to Esslyn, the other facing him and Kell. Either Quinn would align himself with these men, or place himself in opposition to them.

He preferred to remain standing, identifying himself with the other man of action in the room.

Sir Edward's brows contracted in disapproval, as if this were further evidence of Quinn's incorrigible eccentricity. 'The feeling is, Quinn, that you have been operating rather too independently of late.'

'With respect, sir, the SCD is an independent unit. You set it up that way yourself.'

'Circumstances have changed. There's a war on, in case you hadn't noticed.'

'So people keep telling me.'

'Well, then. We all have to pull together. There have been times, Quinn, when your independence has bordered on insubordination. You have jeopardized other operations with your disregard for procedure. We all know what happened with your last investigation.'

'Fiasco, more like.' Esslyn tapped the ash from his cigarette pointedly.

Assistant Commissioner Thompson shook his head, a gesture of incredulity as much as anything. 'You're a loose bloody cannon, Quinn.'

Sir Edward gave the impression of being swayed by these last two remarks. 'I'm closing down SCD.'

Quinn was surprised by the strength of his own reaction. He felt like an adolescent raging against the unfairness of the world. 'You can't . . .'

'I already have.'

'What about my men?'

'Macadam and Inchball have been absorbed into CID.'

Thompson, under whose jurisdiction the CID came, gave a terse nod.

'I have persuaded Assistant Commissioner Thompson to accept you too as an officer under his command.'

'But I answer directly to you, Sir Edward.'

'Not any more. That was an anomaly. An indulgence on my part. The time for indulgences has passed. We must bring you back into the fold, Quinn. Greet you like the prodigal son. With a fatted calf and all that. There shall be much rejoicing. You know the verse. Luke, 15:7. "Joy shall be in Heaven over one sinner that repenteth, more than over ninety and nine just persons, which need no repentance."'

'What of my special warrant?'

'That is terminated. You will operate within standard command structure from now on. You will do as you are told, in other words.'

Sir Michael Esslyn drew deeply on his cigarette with evident satisfaction. 'Now that is settled, we should get on with the matter in hand.'

Quinn felt that nothing had been settled. But he calculated that he had no allies here and that the game was already lost. He had too much pride to give them any further indication of the extent to which they had hurt him. Besides, he was curious. What, precisely, was the matter in hand?

Sir Edward affected a conciliatory tone. 'Do you know Major Kell, by the way?'

Kell looked up with a mildly pained expression. The man had the face of the more intelligent type of professional soldier. Reassuring in its rugged decisiveness, but not without the capacity for imagination or sympathy. It was the face of an adventurer, or possibly even a soldier-poet. But there were signs of conflict and even suffering there.

'You've heard of MO5(g) Section?' continued Sir Edward.

Quinn gave a slow, uncertain nod. He had heard rumours.

'The major basically runs the show.'

Quinn was not immune to the heart-quickening thrill that came from any brush with the intelligence services. He was aware of the privilege of being admitted to such a conclave. Secrets would be revealed and he would keep them, that went without saying. But it made him complicit too.

'Kell?'

The intelligence officer accepted Sir Edward's invitation to continue with a distracted nod. He seemed to be gathering his thoughts. But after a moment, Quinn realized he was struggling to gain control of his breathing. The faint rasping sound he had heard when he came in was Kell's asthmatic wheezing. Kell took one final drag on his medicinal cigarette. His speech was punctuated by frequent breaks as he tried to catch his breath. 'Thank you, Sir Edward. I'll keep it . . . brief. This war will not just be fought on the fields of Belgium and France. Our enemies are here . . . in this country, in this city, right now as I . . . speak. They are determined to use every means within their power to defeat us and destroy us. They do not all speak with thick German accents, eat sausages and wear . . . lederhosen. Some of them are born in this country and may have half-English parentage. It is not even beyond the bounds of possibility that they have recruited English . . . men to their cause. Their influence is . . . everywhere . . . invisible but . . . felt. We cannot say that they do not have their stooges placed in the highest positions within our major institutions, the judiciary . . . the Church, the fourth estate, the civil . . . service, military command, even . . . here.'

'I say,' objected Sir Edward.

'Present company excepted, of . . . course. Their first priority is to commit acts of sabotage and violence. Beyond that, they have a wide-ranging remit to spread fear and . . . despondency wherever they can. Their aim is to undermine public morale so that there is pressure on the government to . . . sue for peace.'

'And so? What has this to do with . . .' Quinn stopped himself saying 'Special Crimes', 'me?'

Esslyn's aristocratic drawl came out from the misty obscurity that was his face. 'For the duration of the war, the entire policing of the capital falls under the overall direction of military intelligence.'

'Everything? Even moving on tramps and collaring pickpockets?'

AC Thompson strode over to stand in front of Quinn. 'It's quite simple.' He pointed his pipe at Quinn. 'You must look for the hidden hand behind everything.'

'That is the essence of my method.'

Thompson grunted sceptically.

'Just to be *clear*,' said Esslyn. He gave the word a brittle emphasis that suggested shattering glass. 'The hidden hand that you are to look for – and find – is the hand of the enemy. German spies and agents.'

'But isn't that rather to predetermine the outcome of an investigation before even a crime has been committed?'

'Are you doubting that our enemies will try to harm us?'

Sir Edward cut in, leaving Sir Michael Esslyn's question unanswered: 'I want you, Quinn, to act as liaison officer between CID and MO5(g). You will receive briefings from Major Kell or his proxy and, in consultation with the assistant commissioner, you will ensure that they are efficiently executed by the appropriate officers. You will report back daily to MO5(g) on the progress of these cases.'

'Liaison officer?' Quinn could not keep the contempt out of his voice.

'It is a job of vital national importance. That should be enough for you.'

So that was it. They had taken away his department and hemmed him in behind a desk. The purpose of the whole charade became clear to him. Sir Edward could have delivered the *coup de grâce* without the others present. They were there simply to see that it was done, knowing that the commissioner had a weak spot when it came to Quinn. It was not a confidential briefing at all. It was a private audience to a knifing, and he was the victim.

At last the smoke cleared in front of Sir Michael Esslyn's face. He was smiling, the thin, lipless smile of a snake.

FIVE

A fine-grained summer dusk was slowly seeping down over the sky.

Felix could hear the piano through the open sash window: Bach's Sonata in F Major played with the usual mixture of enthusiastic attack and wishful imprecision. It brought back unhappy memories of his own childhood. How many years had Mother persisted in her project to make a musician of him, standing over him as he willed his fingers to find the right keys? All those hours of practice, all those sunny afternoons that he had missed out on, wasted. His fingers always let him down.

Eventually, she had given it up as a bad job. She must have known the truth, that he had no talent, right from the beginning, but such was her confidence in her own powers as a teacher that she had persevered long beyond the point where either of them were getting anything from it.

He had progressed to Grade 6 in the Trinity College examinations, but no further, and never achieved anything higher than a Merit. He was capable of a certain mechanical proficiency, but that seemed to upset her more than his mistakes. He had no touch, she complained. No feeling. No soul.

He remembered the time his tears had dripped on to the keys, causing his sweaty fingers even more trouble than usual. It was soon after that that she had relented. She had made it clear that she was releasing him from the torture of continuing with the piano because it was too painful for her to listen to him play. What he wanted did not come into it.

Mother's voice cut through, silencing her pupil's uncertain

performance with three heavily accented syllables: 'No, no, no!' The pained exasperation, the angry incredulity that anyone could be so incompetent, was all too familiar to Felix.

He felt for the young musician, but at the same time was relieved that someone else was bearing the brunt of her displeasure.

He descended the steps to their front door, passing the partially subterranean window, and let himself in, closing the door behind him as quietly as he could.

Felix and Mother occupied five rooms in the basement of a large house on Godolphin Avenue, off the Goldhawk Road. It was just the two of them. His father, who was never spoken of except to be held up as an example of male perfidy, had run out on them when Felix was a baby. Felix could not remember him at all. There was one photograph on the mantelpiece in the piano room of Mother and his father together on their wedding day. Mother kept it for social and professional reasons, as evidence of her propriety. When asked about 'Mr Simpkins', she would assume an expression of infinite sadness and regret. If her inter-locutor took from this that her husband was dead, she did not disabuse them. She invariably dressed in black, giving further credence to the myth of her widowhood.

For all Felix knew, his father *was* dead. Never once had the man tried to contact him. Or if he had, the letters had not reached him.

When he was younger, from time to time he had found himself standing in front of the photograph staring into the black pinpricks that represented that unsmiling stranger's eyes. He was trying to will an authentic memory of the man into being. But there was nothing. He couldn't even recognize himself in his father's face, not even as he grew older. The man in the picture had a thin face, almost ascetic – or the secular equivalent of ascetic, put-upon. His own face was puffy with plump cheeks quick to blush, a small mouth, weak chin, protruding forehead and slightly bulging eyes that gave him the look of a baby with wind.

He wondered, had he known his father, whether they would have had anything in common at all. They seemed to share the same solemnity of expression. Something shifty and distrustful about the eyes. Even on his wedding day, his father looked like he was casting about for a way out.

Of course, according to Mother, Felix had inherited a host of negative attributes from his father, his stupidity, his laziness, his deceit and, most of all, his selfishness. Mysteriously, he had failed to inherit any compensatory virtues from her.

What had brought his parents together, Felix could not imagine.

The couple had never divorced and, despite her contempt for him, Mother had kept her husband's surname. At least it served her well now, disguising her German origins.

The door to the parlour was closed. Behind it, the young pupil was having another run at the phrase that had earned Mother's opprobrium. This time, in response, she barked a sharp, 'Better!' Felix acknowledged a pang of jealousy. He did not think, in all his life, in any endeavour he had set himself to, he had ever been able to earn a 'Better' from Mother.

He took off his shoes and padded softly to the kitchen at the back of the house. He tested the weight of the kettle before lighting the gas ring beneath it. There was a loaf of bread on the table. As always, he was hungry when he came in. He cut a slice and buttered it, devouring half of it in a few quick bites. He held the rest of the bread in his mouth as he put a spoonful of tea in the teapot. Then he took off his suit jacket and hung it on the hook on the back of the door. Mother would have something to say about that. It spoilt the line of his jacket not to use a hanger. But what was he to do? She didn't like it when he hung it over the back of a chair either, as it made the place look untidy.

As soon as he heard the lesson ending, he would retrieve his jacket.

The kettle began to whistle. Still with the bread between his teeth – it was getting precarious now and could break at any moment – Felix took the tea towel drying on the range to lift the kettle over to the teapot.

Just at that moment, the kitchen door opened.

'Felix! What are you doing?'

The remnant of bread dropped from his mouth into the open teapot. He fished it out with one hand as quickly as he could, splashing hot, buttery tea everywhere. The steaming kettle was still in his other hand. He crossed back to the range to put the kettle down, but the soggy mess he carried in his other hand fell apart and dropped all over the kitchen floor.

'You imbecile.'

'Sorry, Mother.' Felix used the tea towel to wipe the slops up.

'I didn't hear the lesson finish.' In fact, he could still hear the piano being played.

'Leave it! Leave it! Leave it!' Mother was screaming at him now. He bent his face away from her, unable to look at her.

Felix stood up, unsure what to do with the soiled tea towel in his hand.

'You make everything worse. You make a bad thing, then you make it worse.'

'Sorry, Mother.'

'Sorry, Mother.' Her mimicry brought the heat to his face.

Felix fixed his gaze on the floor, as if he might find some scraps of sympathy there between the bare wooden boards. He still could not bear to look at Mother. Besides, he knew too well what he would see. Mother was small and birdlike in her frame and face. But she was not delicate in the way birds were normally thought to be. Birds, Felix knew, were wild, untameable creatures. They had savage claws and pointed beaks that could peck out your eyes. They ate bugs and worms. Their song was not the sentimental accompaniment to Nature's splendid tableaux, but a fierce, self-driven cry for survival.

Birds were just another thing that Felix was afraid of.

No, there was nothing delicate about Mother. The smallness of her body had often struck him as the result of distillation. She had been reduced to her essence. And that essence was bitterness.

She gave out a squawk that a parrot would have been proud of. 'What is your coat doing on the back of the door?'

'I am sorry, Mother.'

'Will it pain you so much to keep your jacket on until the lesson is finished? What if my pupil had seen you, or his parent? Did you think of that? I have come in here now for a glass of water for the boy. What if I had sent him in to fetch it himself?'

Felix couldn't see what was so bad about a boy seeing him without his jacket on. But he knew to keep this thought to himself.

'You have no idea! How hard it has been for me to keep house, to keep this, our life, together. How hard I have had to work to pay the rent.'

He might have objected that this was rather unfair. Since he had found his position at Griffin, he had contributed to the household expenses. He also knew that she had some income from investments that her father had set up in her name.

She seemed to sense which way his mind was running. 'It is my name on the paper. It is my house. While you live here you will obey my rules. We must show people we are respectable. They will not bring their children here if they do not think I am respectable.'

'Yes, Mother.'

'And why do you not use a plate when you eat bread? Have I brought you up to be a savage?'

'I was hungry.'

'Greedy savage. Imbecile. So like your father. And look at this mess that you have made.'

'I'm sorry. It was an accident.'

'Will you clean it up? Of course you will not. You are a man. You are like all men. You are useless and dirty and good for nothing.'

'I will clean it up, I promise.'

'No! You will make it worse. You always make it worse. Leave it! I will clean it later.'

She took a glass from the dresser and ran the tap. Felix stood with his head hanging, his hands behind his back.

'How I ever let your father touch me, I will never know. All my problems have come from that. If I knew then what I know now – no! It is poison! The male sperm is poison. It is the root of all the evils that afflict womankind. If it was not for male sperm we would not have menstruation. You are a vessel filled with poison. You disgust me. You must keep it in! You must keep the poison in. If ever you infect another woman with your poison, I will never forgive you. Why can you men not keep it in? Tell me you will never do it. It is disease and it is death. And the women who would let you do this, they are traitors to their sex. They are whores. Worthless whores.'

At last, her tirade came to an end and the water was switched off. But only when he heard her footsteps recede and the door to the parlour open and close did he dare to look up.

SIX

Quinn found himself in the midst of a large, busy department, surrounded by men whose days were driven by a purposeful energy in which he could not share. A thick masculine scent permeated the room. It was the smell of men under stress. There was camaraderie, but it was camaraderie shot through with a merciless instinct for survival. Every joke had at its kernel a brutal and wounding truth.

From time to time he caught sight of his former sergeants across the vast floor of the department. As far as he could tell, they had been split up. But they threw themselves into their new roles with admirable vigour. Each of them had welcomed him back in their own way: Sergeant Macadam with the heartfelt assertion that Quinn was a better detective than any other man in the CID and it was shameful the way he had been treated; Inchball with the simple monosyllable 'Guv', accompanied by a terse nod.

The echoing clamour around him made it hard to concentrate. But then it struck him that he didn't really have anything much to concentrate on. Meetings took place without his being invited. The promised briefings from MO5(g) seemed to bypass him entirely. If he were to spend his days doing nothing, he felt that there would be no one there to hold him to account. In fact, he rather got the impression that everyone would prefer it that way.

One lunchtime he joined the queue in the canteen behind two plain-clothes detectives, who were otherwise unknown to him.

'He always was a mad bugger,' he heard one say.

'God knows how he got away with it for so long.'

'The commissioner gave him too much rope.'

'You know what they say. Give a man enough rope . . .'

'We might see that yet. His old man . . .' But at that point, his companion nudged him with a sly nod in Quinn's direction.

'No, please, go on,' said Quinn. 'I'm interested to know what you have to say about my father.'

'What makes you think we was talking about you?' asked the nudger.

'You need to get a grip,' said the other. 'Otherwise they'll be carting you off to that place again.' His mate guffawed appreciatively.

Perhaps he should give them something that would confirm their worst suspicions about him. Bang their heads together, or tip over a table. In the end, he was happy simply to nod towards the serving counter. 'You'd better move along now. You're holding up the queue.'

They turned their backs on him with a pair of vulgar sneers.

SEVEN

'**M**r Simpkins!'

The pen shook so much in Felix's hand he had to put it down for fear of spattering the ledger with ink. The glances he received from the other clerks were those given to a condemned man by his fellow convicts on the day of his execution. There was some sympathy, but mostly relief that they were not the one summoned. They were not bad fellows. They at least made an effort to disguise their schadenfreude. Yes, he knew the word. Mother wasn't just German. She was the embodiment of that particular emotion, though sometimes he suspected it wasn't just other people's misfortune she took pleasure in but her own too.

Felix slipped off his stool and took a moment to straighten his clothes and brush himself down. He pummelled his hair flat with the palm of one hand. 'Coming, Mr Birtwistle.' He made the announcement under his breath.

Mr Birtwistle, the head clerk, was looking down at his desk as Felix let himself into his office. Felix had a clear view of the top of his boss's head with its few strands of black hair plastered across a gaping expanse of glistening skin. There was something both comical and obscene about this pathetic attempt to mask the scalp. It was such an odd combination of vanity and miscalculation. Felix found it humiliating on Mr Birtwistle's behalf, as if his boss had appeared before him naked from the waist down.

Felix coughed to announce his presence, in the hope that

Mr Birtwistle would look up and he would not have to confront
the disconcerting sight any longer. But Mr Birtwistle was intent
on studying the workbook that lay open on his desk.

At last he repeated 'Mr Simpkins', but not in the same angry
bellow as before. Now Felix heard his name expelled in a kind
of weary sigh. But any thought that Mr Birtwistle had relented
was dispelled by the grim expression on his lantern-jawed face
and the hatred in his eyes when he looked up.

'Is this your handiwork?'

Mr Birtwistle pushed a ledger book across his desk. Felix saw
the smudged workings from yesterday.

'Yes, Mr Birtwistle.'

'Would you care to explain yourself?'

'Explain?'

'What is the meaning of this?'

'I . . .'

'What caused this catastrophe?'

'I . . . Mother . . .'

'Mother?'

For a split second, Felix was tempted to say that she was dead.
Much as he would have welcomed that event, he restrained
himself. 'Mother has not been well.'

'I don't see what . . .'

'I'm very worried about her.'

'What?'

'I was . . . yesterday afternoon . . . I'm afraid I became upset.
The thought of losing her, you see.' Felix dabbed one eye with
the knuckle of his hand.

A look of disgust came over Mr Birtwistle as it dawned on
him what had caused the smudging. 'You . . .? Oh.'

'I am very sorry, Mr Birtwistle. It's her heart, you see.' Felix
was beginning to feel quite light-headed. He had to stop himself
from adding, 'She doesn't have one.' He had to get a grip. There
was a danger he might burst into hysterical laughter, as easily
as tears. Such a display was the very last thing he wanted to let
slip in front of Mr Birtwistle.

'See to it that it doesn't happen again.' Mr Birtwistle laid a
wooden ruler diagonally across the offending page and drew a
line through it in red ink. 'You will have to do the whole page
again. Naturally, you will be docked a day's pay for yesterday.

Consider yourself lucky that I don't give you notice. If we were not so short-staffed, there would be no question.'

Felix thought it rather unfair of Mr Birtwistle that he did not mention the many hundreds of immaculate pages that Felix had produced in the fifteen months he had worked at Griffin.

He took his ledger without complaint and returned to his perch amid the shy, sideways glances of his colleagues.

On Saturday afternoon, Felix joined the crowds at Shepherd's Bush Market.

No one expected anything of him here. He could be who he liked, anyone but Felix Simpkins, the pathetic coward who couldn't go through with a single resolution. As far as anyone in the crowd knew, he was on his way to a recruitment station right now.

To his ear the cries of the costermongers seemed to have a harsher, more desperate edge than before the war, as if there was more at stake than the price of veg. The men were not competing for sales, but fighting for survival. Even so, he welcomed the clashing shouts. It was a sign of business as usual, defiantly so. What did it matter if the Germans occupied Brussels if beets were still being cried on a London street market in August?

At the outbreak of war, there had been shortages in the shops, to which Mother had contributed with her frantic stockpiling. She had bought up all manner of supplies – butter, sugar, bacon, flour, cocoa and her beloved coffee – which he had been obliged to carry home for her, loaded like a pack animal. Shops were left as devastated as a field stripped by locusts, except the locusts in this case had the appearance of respectable housewives. Felix had felt ashamed of his part in it. But what could he do? What Mother wanted, Mother got.

All that had settled down now. The emptied shops had gradually been restocked, if not to their former levels then at least to a degree which the middle classes could contemplate without undue alarm. Yes, some imported goods, like tinned pineapples and raisins, would be harder to come by from now on. But there was a war on. One had to expect some hardship.

In the aftermath of the most severe shortages, prices rose. It was a simple question of supply and demand. Certain customers everywhere had shown their willingness to pay over the odds for essentials. That was the way the world worked. It was unfortunate but inevitable that some would be priced out of the market. For them it was as if the shortages had never ended. Even Mother felt the pinch, and contemplated the dwindling of her treasured provisions with a grim, hard-eyed apprehension, as if she were afraid not of her supplies running out, but of what she might do when they did.

Felix liked to look at the barrows bursting with vegetables of all sizes and colours. They rewarded his gaze with a comforting sense of plenty. He moved through the wafts of fresh-baked bread, the mouth-watering savour of meat pies, past the silver gleam of fish stalls and the smell of blood and slaughter from the butchers. His senses were overwhelmed. It took him back to a simpler time, a time of infantile appetites and pleasures, when his relationship with the world was uncomplicated by experience. It reminded him that he was alive.

He wanted to immerse himself in the market even more, to be consumed by it. To become part of the bustling mass which pulsed through the market like its lifeblood.

Put simply, he was driven by the impulse to buy something. It almost didn't matter what. To buy something for himself, which would compensate him for all the setbacks and failures he had endured.

It was most irksome of Mr Birtwistle to dock his pay, but Felix had few expenditures, apart from the contribution he made to the household expenses. He was able to put aside a little each month, which he was saving for a rainy day. Perhaps he would take a holiday. To Switzerland, perhaps. The idea of an Alpine hike appealed to him immensely. And Switzerland's neutrality made the prospect even more attractive. Of course, one couldn't get there without going through France, which was possibly dangerous. He hadn't considered the details. It didn't have to be Switzerland. There were some marvellous walks to be had in the Lake District, he didn't doubt.

A chap could feel the war was a long way away standing on the banks of Lake Grasmere, surrounded by the fells and forests of Cumbria.

Or perhaps he would follow through on his adventure of the other night. This time he would go to a music hall, to the promenade. He had heard that that was where a man went to pick up a girl of a certain kind. He tasted the gaseous tang of anticipation.

He kept his savings in a tin box under his bed. That morning he had taken the money out and counted it, all £1 17s 11d. It was never quite as much as he hoped it would be, but still a tidy enough sum.

He didn't know how much it would cost to purchase the services of a lady of the night. He would be surprised if it ate too much into his nest egg. Or perhaps something else might catch his eye. And so that morning he had transferred the money to an envelope, which he now felt bulging against his chest in his inside jacket pocket.

He found himself standing outside the shabby exterior of a junk shop. The window was crowded with mismatched items of furniture and cracked bric-a-brac, chipped candelabras, a stuffed heron in a glass cabinet and a black-spotted mirror in a lacklustre gilt frame. If these were the best the shop had to offer, then it did not say much for what was inside. But Felix noticed some small nude figurines amongst the tat. He knew nothing about antiques, but they seemed to him to have been executed with some skill. The curves and lines of the figures possessed an alluring delicacy. The sculptor had imbued the cold, grey marble with something of the quality of living flesh. The figures represented some species of mythological females, unnamed goddesses or nymphs, or possibly sirens, enticing him into the shop. There might be more of the same inside, perhaps even more indecent. If he could not bring himself to pick up a real girl, he might at least take home a statue of one. Of course, he would have to keep it hidden from Mother. She had a principled horror of him 'spilling his seed' which he had no wish to provoke.

It took a moment for Felix's eyes to adjust to the interior. Muddy oil paintings by obscure artists began to emerge from the darkness. Loitering ghosts lurked in the corners, plaster mannequins dressed in dusty clothes from the last century, a suit of armour and a medical student's skeleton. Oppressive wardrobes loomed over him on every side, while a gang of unruly dining chairs blocked his way. Cabinets and tables jutted out to snag him. Overhead, tarnished chandeliers hung like ornate crystal stalactites, laden with danger for the unwary. There were clocks everywhere, all stopped at different times, and more examples of the taxidermist's art, a strange, inert menagerie set free amongst the assembly of secondhand objects. This was the plunder of interrupted lives, pilfered from the houses of the dead, the remnants of countless midnight flits, and possibly even the booty of actual larceny.

He had stumbled into a bargain basement Aladdin's cave.

The air smelled musty and stale. Felix had the sense of small creatures scuttling away from his feet.

At first he didn't see the man seated behind the large, leather-topped desk, or perhaps he saw him, but took him for another of the curiosities on sale. The man was dressed in a black morning coat, dusted with a faint patina of something white and possibly luminous. His face was dominated by momentous side-whiskers, giving him something of the appearance of a character from Dickens. He was a stout man – the side-whiskers seemed designed to detract from the corpulence of his face – who seemed well suited to the sedentary life. He was, in fact, sitting very still, reading an old olive-coloured volume, which had evidently been taken from one of the bookcases that added to the clutter. It was only when he turned the page that he revealed his presence among the living.

Grateful for the man's indifference, Felix made his way towards the back of the shop.

Here he found rails of secondhand clothes. Boxes of shoes littered the floor. A shelf of hats drew his attention. A silk topper teased a smile to his lips.

Felix looked back towards the man at the desk, who was still engrossed in his book. Gingerly, as if he were transgressing some unwritten rule, he picked up the top hat and put it on.

He found a tarnished mirror in which to admire the effect. It fitted him admirably, though there was the problem of what to do with his ears. Maybe he should dress like a toff when he went to the promenade to pick up a girl. He should go the whole hog and get a cane and a cape while he was at it.

He returned the top hat to its place and scanned along the other headwear. He was intrigued to see a collection of military caps and helmets, including some spiked Prussian ones. And on one of the rails nearby he found a collection of khaki field tunics and greatcoats. He took off the jacket he was wearing and tried on one of the tunics at random. It engulfed him. The cuffs extended a good inch beyond his fingers. The shoulders flapped loosely around his own. Felix found it hard to imagine the individual who could fill this uniform.

The second tunic he tried on was more like it. He turned back to the mirror as he finished buttoning up the last of the five brass buttons. It was still not a perfect fit, but better than the last one. It just needed taking in an inch or so. Failing that, he could bulk himself up by wearing a pullover underneath it.

Yes, the effect was not too bad at all. Passable. It was a private's uniform. It did not seem to have been worn. Felix could not help wondering how it came to be in the shop. Perhaps the owner had died before he had a chance to serve and his impoverished family had been forced to get what they could for it. Times were hard for many, after all. Somehow that didn't quite add up, but he was reluctant to probe the tunic's history too deeply.

He rooted through a pile of combat trousers until he found a smallish-looking pair. He held them up against his body. Perhaps a little on the large side but no matter. That was what braces were for.

Felix was excited now as he picked out a cap from the shelf. The oilskin lining gripped his scalp tightly, but a second cap came down comically over his eyes. He opted for the first. He would have preferred it if the regimental insignia on the front had matched the metal badge on his tunic collar, but he didn't suppose anyone would notice that – unlike an ill-fitting cap, which would stick out like a sore finger.

He took off the tunic and gathered his selections together.

The man behind the desk did not look up from his book.

'I say,' began Felix nervously. 'How much for all this?'

It was a moment before the shopkeeper treated Felix to the most cursory of glances. 'Ten shillings.'

'Ten shillings? That's rather steep, isn't it?'

'It's all authentic War Office issue. Brand new. Never been worn.'

'It's for a play, you see. I'm in an amateur dramatic group. We're putting on a production. I'm in charge of the wardrobe. We don't have much money.'

At last the man put down his book. He regarded Felix with undisguised contempt. He even contrived to have his right eyebrow ascend with slow, deliberate scepticism. 'Take it or leave it.'

'I'll take it.'

'Do you have puttees?'

Felix frowned.

'You bind them round your calves.'

'Oh yes, I see.'

'You can't do the play without puttees. The audience won't buy it.'

'How much more would that be?'

'I'll throw them in for an extra sixpence.'

'Very well.'

The man rose from his seat at last. 'And what about a gun?'

'A gun?'

'It's a question of verisimilitude.'

'You have guns?'

'Antiques. But adequate for theatrical purposes.'

'So they don't actually fire?'

'I dare say I can find you one that does, if it's important. For the play.'

Now that he had been roused, the man moved with surprising sprightliness, given his size. He unlocked a cabinet and took out a small leather case which he placed on the desk in front of Felix. He unfastened the buckle of the case, revealing the object of interest. It was forged from a dull grey metal. Just by looking at it, Felix had a sense of its dense mass, which seemed far in excess of its size.

The man took out the gun and aimed it nonchalantly at Felix. 'It's an old one, but the basic Webley service revolver hasn't changed much over the years.'

Felix felt his heartbeat quicken. There was something darkly pleasurable about being in the presence of this deadly weapon, even if it was pointed at him. He had no doubt the gun wasn't loaded, but it was laden with the potential to wield death. 'How much?'

'I can let you have the whole lot, uniform and gun, for a guinea.'

The man carefully turned the gun around, offering Felix the handle. It was even heavier in his hand than he had imagined it would be. But as soon as he touched it, he knew that he must have it.

PART II
Dreams of Flight

31 August–2 September, 1914.

THE INFLUENCE OF A GIRL.

The Interesting Romance of a Love that Conquered.

"'There is nothing in human life more unfortunate than that
a man should be without a woman's influence.'"

    Begin this fine story today: previous chapters contained
in synopsis.

Daily Mirror serial, Monday, 31 August, 1914

EIGHT

Adam Cardew had seen the bird return to the same bush several times now. It was a small brown bird with stripes on the side of its breast. When he got home he would look in his copy of J. L. Bonhote's *Birds of Britain and Their Eggs* to see if he could identify it. Was it possible that it had a nest in there? It was rather late in the year, he thought, for that, but not impossible. Some birds continued nesting into September. He should like to have a look inside the bush, next time the bird went away.

Adam liked to come to the Scrubs after school, not just to look at birds. Even more thrilling was the prospect of catching sight of some activity from the great hangar. He remembered coming here with some of the chaps from school to see the arrival of M. Clément-Bayard's dirigible No. 2 from France. The notable event had occurred on a Sunday. He had got out of church by feigning a stomach ache. His father was suspicious but Adam had managed to induce vomiting by drinking a tumbler of salt water and poking his finger down his throat. The results had been spectacular, beyond anything Adam could have hoped for.

His mother had pleaded his case. Her most persuasive argument was that he might have something contagious which would infect other members of the congregation. It was decided that his mother should stay behind too, in case he wanted for anything. This almost scuppered his plans. But he had read enough Boys' Own Adventures to know what to do.

He told her that he thought the best thing was if he slept it off, so please not to trouble herself with looking in on him. If he needed anything he would call out. Then he stuffed some pillows and extra blankets down the centre of his bed. The effect was spiffing. With the curtains drawn and the light out it would fool anyone, particularly his mother, whom he took for something of a fool. And anyway, it was more than likely that she would be lying down in a darkened room herself with one of her famous heads.

His mother was a good soul, too trusting by half. Good people were always easy to deceive, he had noticed.

Admittedly, it was not as satisfying as getting one over on his father.

It would not have surprised Adam to learn that his father was the Devil incarnate. That would be ironic, to say the least, as his father spent his life warning people against the Devil and all his works. The Devil laid snares for the unwary everywhere. In the moving picture shows, the music halls, in books and advertisements. It was the Devil's way to entice you in with pleasures and idleness, to lead you off the path of righteousness, which was no easy path to walk. And before you knew it, you would find yourself burning in the fires of Hell, condemned to eternal damnation.

The Devil this, the Devil that. It was all his father talked about. Adam would have laid money on it that he mentioned the Devil more than he mentioned God. Though naturally gambling was one of the things his father expressly forbade.

It would be typical of the Devil if he had been masquerading as a Baptist pastor and Sunday school teacher all these years, attacking and condemning all the sins that he secretly approved of, and so tempting you into committing them by bringing them ever to your attention. Adam saw that this method worked particularly well in his own case. He hated his father. Inevitably he was drawn to disobey him. If his father had wanted to make a sinner of him, he could not have chosen a more effective way to do it.

Back then, when he had gone to look at the airship that Sunday, his hatred for his father was not so firmly rooted. Adam thought of his father then simply as an obstacle to be overcome.

So he improvised the decoy in his bed, tiptoed downstairs and let himself out of the house with a burglar's finesse. It was typical of Adam – of the Adam of those days – that he gave no thought to how he would get back in without his adventure being discovered.

All that mattered was that he got to the Scrubs in time to meet his pals and see the arrival of the fabled airship. Through a peculiar failure of imagination, he thought that the excitement he felt witnessing this historic event would somehow mollify his father's rage.

There had been men in the crowd, men there with their sons

– indeed, some of his pals had their dads with them – men who outwardly looked every bit as respectable as his own father. Not low-class types or drunkards or degenerates or hooligans. But men with kindly faces and friendly smiles. Men who put their arms around their sons' shoulders as they pointed out the approaching aircraft. Men who cheered and clapped and even threw their hats into the air.

Surely his father would see that there was nothing wicked, let alone sinful, in this?

His elation stayed with him all the way home, even after he took leave of his pals and their equally excited fathers.

It stayed with him as he mounted the steps to the front door. Only as he was about to ring the front door bell did he remember that he was not supposed to be out at all. Not only that, he had lied to his father. Not only that, the lie had been told so that he could play the wag from church.

He still felt a flush of shame now, not for having gone on the adventure, but for failing to think it through sufficiently. He should have left his bedroom window open so he could shimmy back in up the drainpipe.

But perhaps the window was open after all? At any rate, he stood a far greater chance of success if he tried to gain entry from the rear of the house.

The family lived at the end of the street. There was a side entrance to the garden through a wooden door in the wall. But the door was kept locked. Fortunately a large plane tree grew out of the pavement nearby, its branches hanging over into their garden. It was possible to clamber up between the wall and the tree.

He let himself down carefully over the other side, hanging by his fingers before dropping the last three or four feet to the ground. A rhododendron plant broke his fall, and was flattened in the process.

He stood glued to the spot for several moments, sure that someone must have heard the rustling of foliage. But the house was silent. His father and Eve must be back from church by now. He knew that he had been longer at the Scrubs than he had intended.

A quick glance up at the back of the house revealed that his own window was closed. Not only that, no drainpipe or pipe of any kind approached it. But the window to the room next to his, his twin sister Eve's room, was partially open, and a drainpipe passed right by it. Adam could not believe his luck.

If Eve was not in her room, then perfect. No one need ever know about his transgression. But even if she was there, he felt sure that she would not betray him. True, she would then have a hold over him, which she was bound to exploit, but that would be a small price to pay to avoid his father's wrath.

He rubbed his hands and took a run at the drainpipe.

Adam was wiry and strong, but also light. His was the perfect physique for shinning up drainpipes. So much so that he wondered why he did not do it more often. Above all, he was – or had been at that stage of his life – quite fearless. He was not daunted at all by the prospect of clinging on and hoisting himself up, hand over hand, feet testing for toeholds, shins squeezing tight to grip the pipe.

He felt the pipe shift, just as his head drew level with the windowsill. He clenched his muscles and held on even tighter to pull himself up the last few feet. The gap in the window was not big enough to squeeze through and it would be tricky opening it without help from inside.

Adam extended his right arm and swung the other arm out to clutch the windowsill. It gave him the chance to look inside and see if his sister was in her room.

She was. But so was his father.

They were sitting on the edge of the bed. Their heads were bowed as if in prayer. But they were not praying. He knew this because their palms were not pressed together. In fact, it was not clear at first what their hands were doing. One of his father's hands was out of sight. It seemed to be thrust into Eve's dress, which was bunched up around her thighs.

His other hand . . . Adam could not process what his other hand was doing. Because before he could think about what his father's other hand was doing, he had to first confront the sight of that part of his father that he had never thought to see. That part he had been taught to abhor and deny in himself. But his father was not abhorring it or denying it. He had it out in the open, exposed and sticking up, in the state of sticky-up-ness that that same part of Adam was most mornings, and the very exist-ence of which brought only shame and mortification.

And now he realized with horror what his father's other hand was doing. It was enveloped around Eve's hand, pulling it towards that part of him which must be denied and abhorred. And that part of his father was twitching horribly.

Now Adam really was going to gag in earnest.

But he could not look away. Why could he not look away?

It was only when his sister's hand gripped that part of his father that he had never thought to see, and had gripped it in such a way that suggested she knew what was expected of her, it was only then that he could no longer look.

It was then that his muscles had given up their clenched clinging on to hope, sanity and the windowsill.

The impact of the fall was barely felt. Whatever pain he experienced would eventually pass. It was nothing next to the indelible damage caused by seeing.

After a moment of dizzy blackness – if only it had been an eternity! – he came round and vomited all over himself. He had a thumping headache, and the knowledge that one ankle at least was completely shot.

Adam remembered little of what happened in the immediate aftermath of his fall. His mother's screams drew his father out. And the horror and disgust and rage that his father focused on him meant nothing to Adam.

He merely closed his eyes to block it out.

From that day, his father lost all moral authority over him. Let him punish Adam all he wanted, let him spew forth spittle from his bloodless lips, let him thump the black Bible with a clenched fist, let him lay the same fist across Adam's ear, let him strike him with the bone-handled cane that he used for such purposes . . . it made no difference to Adam.

Perhaps that was why he came back to the Scrubs, every day after school if he could. It was to go back to that time before. To a time of innocence, when the world was still capable of being enlivened by the appearance of such a prodigy as an airship, like a harbinger of hope, as if hope were still a possibility.

Adam looked back to the bush to see it shiver as the small striped bird took flight from it.

It was the opportunity he had been waiting for. He began his lurching step over to the bush. His broken right ankle had never properly healed. It was slightly crooked and nagged him with a continual twinge, which was worse when he walked. It was his penance. God's punishment, his father called it, for the sins of mendacity and defying the Sabbath. *And what about your sins?* he had wanted to scream back. But never did.

He had never said a word about what he had seen to anyone, let alone his sister. To talk of it would have been to acknowledge the reality of it.

But it was simpler than that. He could not imagine what he would say to her. In some moments, he blamed her. His anger was as much for her as his father.

But in a deep part of him, he knew that she had not been a willing participant in what had been enacted within the frame of her bedroom window. Then his anger was all against himself. Because he had not had the courage to intervene and save her.

The pain was ringing like a small bell by the time he reached the bush. That was manageable. It was when it went off like Big Ben that he really felt it. Would his gammy ankle keep him out of the army? It was something he worried about often. There was no question that he would enlist when he was old enough, if the army would have him. He had heard of chaps lying about their age. But he did not want to give the recruiting sergeant any other excuse to turn him down.

Adam pulled back a branch and peered inside the scrubby bush. There it was, the nest. And there, sheltering within it, four pure, perfect eggs, tiny and fine, like bubbles of chalk. They were the colour of the sky on a tremulous spring day, but speckled like a young girl's eye.

It turned him about inside to look at them. It almost healed him.

He picked one up, holding it lightly between forefinger and thumb. His hand trembled at the delicacy of the shell protecting the life within.

Dare he take it home, to compare it to the pictures in J. L. Bonhote's *Birds of Britain and Their Eggs*? But he knew that the colours in that book were not quite natural. Any picture there would be an insult to the weightless miracle he was holding.

Even just to hold it was a feat of virtuosity akin to walking a tightrope.

Something welled within him. It was a wordless emotion, as heavy as a bag of wet sand, as hard as a stone.

He felt it in the tensing of his forefinger and thumb as he crushed the innocent egg between them.

He looked down at the viscous mess on his fingers. The fine strands of an aborted creature smeared like something he might have picked from his nose.

He felt no grief, no guilt, no shame. Only amazement at the vast emptiness of his heart.

NINE

For a moment, Mrs Ibbott seemed startled by his appearance on her doorstep. He could have sworn her eyes even bulged in their sockets.

'Inspector Quinn! What a pleasure it is to see you looking so well!'

Quinn knew a lie when he heard one. 'There's no need to call me Inspector.'

'Are you not with the police any more?'

'I am, but . . . I'm not here on police business.' He could have added, *and besides, it's Chief Inspector*, but thought better of it. 'I wrote to you? I think you must have received my letter because I believe you wrote back? I have it here, your letter.' He reached into a pocket.

She waved the letter away. 'Of course, yes! Come in, come in!'

But Quinn hesitated, as if he wanted to give her one last chance to slam the door in his face. 'You said that it would present no difficulties to you – nor anyone else – if I were to call. And so . . .'

'Oh, Inspector. I said more than that, I think. I believe I said it would be a pleasure to see you. That we all were very anxious on your behalf and that we wanted nothing more than to see you again.'

At last her expression caught up with her words. Her smile was touched by a genuine if troubled sympathy.

Quinn frowned. He found it difficult to believe her words, or accept her sympathy. And he was troubled by that 'all'. Had they *all* been talking about him? Given the circumstances of his departure from the lodging house, it would be absurd to imagine that they had not.

'I wanted to apologize . . .'

'Please, *do* come in, I insist.' There was an urgency to Mrs Ibbott's voice. She cast a nervous glance over Quinn's shoulder, then settled an imploring look on him.

His former landlady was a stout but tidy woman, who kept her person as impeccably as she kept her house. She dressed in dark, sombre colours that suggested a deep respectability, but which failed to hint at the essential amiability of her personality.

Quinn nodded.

Mrs Ibbott seemed to become suddenly self-conscious as she stepped aside to let him in. 'You'll have to forgive us. I have given Betsy the day off.' It was as if the oddness of her opening her own front door needed an explanation. 'Her brother has enlisted and she wished to see him before he goes off to join his regiment.'

'If it would be more convenient for me to come back another time . . .?'

'Not at all! I didn't mean that . . . I merely meant, you must forgive us.'

The house was just off the Brompton Road. He had lived there for the last six years. It must have suited him. It was strange to step across the threshold now as a visitor rather than a resident. So many times he had sneaked in like a thief. It wasn't always out of consideration for the other residents. He had to admit that he had got into the habit of solitude, and so his clandestine ways were to avoid being invited in to join the other lodgers in the drawing room. One of the things Mrs Ibbott liked to do was bring her guests together for social evenings. Quinn had a horror of such occasions.

She led him into the drawing room, where her daughter Mary was reading a novel. Mary looked up and flushed red to the roots of her hair when she saw Quinn.

'Hello, Mary,' said Quinn. He did not attempt a smile.

Mary sat open-mouthed, unable to answer him. The novel dropped from her hands on to the floor.

'Mary, make yourself useful, my dear. Go and make us some tea, will you? Bring some fruit cake too.'

'Why do *I* have to do it?' Mary Ibbott could not take her eyes off Quinn. She was watching him like she might watch a large spider, or some other unpleasant and unpredictable creature.

'Well, you know we have no Betsy today. So unless you wish to stay here and entertain Inspector Quinn while I go . . .'

Mary ran from the room as if from mortal peril.

'There's really no need to go to any trouble,' said Quinn.

'Nonsense,' said Mrs Ibbott, bidding him sit down with a gentle tilt of the head.

After a moment of constrained silence, they both began speaking at once.

'I wanted to say . . .'

'You gave us quite . . .'

Quinn gestured for his landlady to go on. She demurred.

'Very well,' said Quinn. 'My behaviour was unforgivable.'

Mrs Ibbott cut him off. 'We understand that you were ill, that you have been ill. That you were not in control of your actions.'

'No. My apparent breakdown was part of an investigation I was conducting.'

'I don't pretend to understand. But I think you are not being honest with me, with yourself.'

It was Quinn's turn to be startled. 'What do you mean?'

'I think there was nothing *apparent* about it. You suffered a genuine collapse. If I did not think so, I would not now allow you in my house.'

Quinn stood up. 'Then I must go, immediately. I will send for my things when it is convenient to you.'

'Sit down, Inspector. I don't care what you say happened or what you think happened. I know suffering when I see it. And you were suffering. Just like a typical man, you cannot admit it, so you have invented some story about I don't know what. You prefer to claim that you were pretending to have a breakdown, rather than admit that you actually had one. That's . . . well, I hope you will forgive me, Inspector, but that is utter poppycock!'

'I cannot forgive myself for what I said . . .'

'Exactly! If you were to admit that you were genuinely out of . . . that is to say, that your mind was . . . that you were ill . . . then you would be *obliged* to forgive yourself, as we all have forgiven you.'

'All? You have *all* forgiven me?'

'I am sure I speak for everyone.'

'I don't see how you can. Mrs Hargreaves . . .'

'Mrs Hargreaves forgives you.'

'And Mr Hargreaves?'

'Don't you worry about Mr Hargreaves.'

'But there can be no question of my coming back here. To live.'

'I don't see why not. If you wish to. You are up to date with your rent.'

'It is not simply a question of rent, is it, Mrs Ibbott? This is more than a business to you, it is a . . .'

'It is my family.'

'Yes.'

'And you are part of that family.'

The interview was not going as Quinn had planned. He had not planned on a stab of emotion that threatened to unpick the stitches that were holding him together. He had not planned on crying.

TEN

M ary Ibbott shuffled her feet, making slow progress back from the kitchen. She had overfilled the teapot, so every slight deviation from the horizontal caused tea to spill out of the spout and slop about in the tray. The strain of holding the tray level was most trying. Her wrists ached. The china cups rattled in their saucers. And the harder she tried to keep the tray steady, the more it shook.

It was most inconsiderate of Betsy to take the day off, forcing Mary to play the skivvy for her mother. And to be waiting hand and foot on *that man* was the last straw. Wait till Mr Hargreaves discovered he was back! There would be hell to pay.

Mr Hargreaves! She ought to say Corporal Hargreaves. Little had they known he was a corporal in the territorials and was set to join his regiment the very next day. How distinguished he looked in his uniform. And how brave he was. Mrs Hargreaves was a very lucky woman and no mistake. Mary wondered sometimes if she truly appreciated quite how lucky she was. It wasn't just that Mr Hargreaves was handsome – he was ever so witty too. He always had a twinkle in his eye and a special little wink for Mary, like they were conspirators against the rest of the house.

She couldn't believe old Quinn had the nerve to come back. Mary was simply bursting with the news of his return. She longed to tell Mr Hargreaves, but failing that, she simply had to tell someone.

Mary heard voices on the landing above. It was Appleby and Timberley. Their voices were low, but intense, as if they were having an argument in whispers.

She thought of the two young men with a certain indulgent scorn. She was fond of them, but they really were chumps. And mere boys compared to Mr Hargreaves. It was rather embarrassing how they both doted on her so. Perhaps she oughtn't to lead them on the way she did, playing one off against the other, when she was really interested in neither of them. But it was their own fault. They couldn't tell when she was ribbing them. They were very clever and all that, and she had to admit they did make her laugh, but such chumps, it really had to be said. There was no other word for it.

They must have heard the rattling of her tray because their furious little tête à tête came to an abrupt halt. One by one their faces appeared, peering down at her from the landing above. They really did look quite ridiculous.

'What ho, Mary!'

'Is that tea? *And* fruit cake?'

'It's not for you two chumps.'

'I say, Mary, that's rather harsh of you, you know.'

'Who is it for then?'

'It's for Mr Quinn. Or should I say Inspector Quinn?'

'Quinn?'

'Quinn!'

The two of them yelped the name simultaneously, one in wonder, the other excitedly.

'Yes.'

'Is he here?'

'Now?'

'Yes. He's talking to Mummy in the drawing room.'

'Good heavens!'

'Good old Quinn!' This was Timberley's rather more surprising response to the news. His excitement played havoc with his asthma, setting off a coughing fit, which he stifled with his handkerchief.

'What do you mean, good old Quinn?' objected Mary. 'He's a horror!'

'Oh, I rather like Quinn,' said Timberley, examining the contents of his handkerchief with a distracted frown. 'He's an odd cove, I'll grant you. But a decent chap deep down. And he is something of a celebrity, you know. A bona fide hero. Quick-fire Quinn of the Yard!'

Mary was having none of this. 'A hero? That's not what I'd call him. You saw the way he carried on with Mrs Hargreaves.'

'I say, Mary,' put in Appleby. 'I don't think there was any *carrying on*, as you so salaciously put it. I rather think it was just a misunderstanding.'

'He practically declared his undying love for her. In front of her husband! And *everyone*!'

'That was unfortunate, I grant you,' said Timberley. 'But I think, well . . . you know he was admitted to Colney Hatch soon after?'

'Exactly! He's a lunatic!'

The door to the drawing room opened and her mother peered out severely. 'Mary! What on earth are you doing out here?'

'I've brought the tea, Mummy.'

'Well, bring it in. And stop . . . gossiping.' Mrs Ibbott projected a disapproving scowl up the stairs at Appleby and Timberley, causing them to scatter as if under enemy fire.

ELEVEN

Mary set the tea things down with a final clumsy jolt that sent another spurt of tea sloshing out.

'That will be all, Mary,' said Mrs Ibbott tersely.

'I am not the maid! I am your daughter!' With that, she stomped from the room, slamming the door behind her.

'I do apologize,' said Mrs Ibbott, after a moment in which she sought to regain her composure.

But the door opened almost immediately and Mary stomped back into the room to retrieve her novel. The door was slammed a second time.

'I don't know what to do with that girl, I really don't.'

'She's young,' said Quinn.

'That's no excuse. I am sure I have not brought her up to be so ill-mannered. And sometimes, well, I despair. She is in danger of making a positive fool of herself over Mr Hargreaves, you know.'

This was a difficult subject for Quinn, who, it could be argued, had made a positive fool of himself over *Mrs* Hargreaves. He gave a vague gesture of solicitude.

'He's all she ever talks about. Quite besotted, she is. Thank heavens Mr Hargreaves is leaving us tomorrow. Perhaps then we shall get some peace.'

'Leaving? The Hargreaveses are leaving?' If Quinn had wanted to keep the note of keen interest out of his voice, he did not succeed.

'*Mr* Hargreaves is. He's joining his regiment. He's in the territorials, you know. Mrs Hargreaves is naturally most anxious on his behalf, although she is equally proud that he is answering the call of duty. Mind you, I don't think they are likely to send the territorial regiments out to Belgium though, are they? They will leave that to the professional soldiers. That's not to say he won't be required to risk his life in defence of England, should the Germans invade. We can only pray that it will not come to that.'

'I feel that I ought to apologize to Mr and Mrs Hargreaves in person.'

'Do you think that's wise? Would it not be better for us all to put the incident behind us, to carry on as if it never happened.'

'But it did happen.'

'There is no need to torture yourself over it, Inspector.'

'I really do wish that you wouldn't call me Inspector.'

There was a beat before Mrs Ibbott asked, in a voice that brimmed with emotion: 'May I call you Silas?'

'If you wish.' Quinn's response was hurriedly careless, as if it didn't matter to him what she called him. And yet even he

could not deny her use of his Christian name represented a new
level of intimacy. He was no longer her tenant. Did that mean
he was now her friend?

'You know, Silas, I have not forgotten your kindness to a
certain lady who used to live here.'

'Ah – I would rather we did not talk about that.'

'You don't wish to talk about the good that you do, but you
insist on picking away at your . . . mistakes?'

'It's not a question of that. The whole business with Miss
Dillard is still rather painful to me.'

'She was a very unhappy woman. Your kindness to her, I am
sure, was a rare light of warmth and comfort in the darkness of
her existence.'

Before he could answer, the door to the drawing room was
thrown open, and a man in khaki uniform burst in. Hargreaves.

Quinn put down his teacup and rose to his feet. It was not
intended to be a threatening gesture. On the contrary, he meant
to signal his respect. But he only succeeded in provoking
Hargreaves to raise his fists in a boxer's guard.

'So, it's true! What a bloody nerve!'

'Mr Hargreaves!' protested Mrs Ibbott, rising to her feet and
putting herself between the two men. 'Kindly watch your
language! You're not in the barracks now.'

At that moment, Celia Hargreaves rushed into the room. 'Jack,
stop it! Don't be a fool!'

She was quickly followed by Appleby and Timberley. A
moment later, Mary completed the gathering.

'So I'm the fool, am I? That's what a man gets for defending
his wife's honour.'

'I am so sorry,' said Mrs Hargreaves, flashing a pleading look
towards Quinn.

'Don't apologize to *him*! He should be the one apologizing to
us,' protested her husband. He had dropped his guard, but was
jabbing the air aggressively with an extended forefinger.

'That's precisely why I am here,' said Quinn. 'To apologize
to both of you. To everyone. You are right to be angry, Hargreaves.
I should not have said the things I said. Needless to say, there
is no truth in any of it.'

He should not have done it, but he could not help himself.
He looked in her direction, for the merest sign of

disappointment on her face. Was this why he had come back, after all, to look at her?

'Why did you say it, man? Good God, what were you playing at?'

Quinn looked imploringly towards Mrs Ibbott.

'Mr Hargreaves, the important thing is that Inspector Quinn acknowledges that he made a mistake. We must all put it behind us and move on. If Mr Quinn is to come back to the house . . .'

'Over my dead body!'

Celia Hargreaves let out a shriek of distress. 'Jack, how can you say such a thing? When you are about to . . .'

'I didn't mean it like that.'

'It is not up to you to whom I let my rooms,' Mrs Ibbott pointed out.

'I am about to go off to war and you are proposing to bring this adulterer into the house, leaving my wife alone, unprotected, a prey to his vile attentions.'

'Mr Quinn is not an adulterer. I think we can all acknowledge that no impropriety of any kind occurred. Words were said, I grant you that. However, they were said while Mr Quinn was under the influence of a mental imbalance, from which he is now recovered.'

'Is that what he says? Is that right, Quinn? Your mind was unbalanced?'

'I cannot explain why I said the things I did.'

'Cannot or will not? You said them because you meant them. You used the pretence of a breakdown as a screen to hide behind. So that you could make love to my wife and then claim that you didn't know what you were doing. Meanwhile, if your advances were met with anything other than the disgust they merited, you would take that as encouragement to continue.'

'No one regrets more than I what I said.'

'You have no idea what damage you've done.'

'I am sorry. I am sorry. I can only say it again. I am sorry.'

'You're pathetic.'

Quinn turned to his landlady. 'There are a few things I wish to collect now, then I will send someone for the rest of my belongings.'

Mrs Ibbott did not answer. She merely bowed her head in resignation.

*   *   *

His bed, his armchair, his desk, his wardrobe, his chest of drawers and his one bookshelf were all exactly as he had left them. It was strangely wearying to look at them.

It was tempting to lie down on the bed but he felt that that would be an imposition. It was no longer his bed, after all.

He took down the suitcase from the top of the wardrobe and laid it open on the bed. It was dispiriting, actually, how few possessions he had. Perhaps he would even be able to take everything away in the suitcase.

There was a knock on the door. He opened it to let Timberley in.

'I say, I'm awfully sorry you're going, Quinn.'

'It's for the better.'

'Well, I think it's a bad show. It was simply spiffing having a famous detective about the place. Old Hargreaves is such a boor, you know. I don't see what difference it makes to him. He's going to be away with his bally regiment.'

'That's precisely why I cannot stay here.'

'Well, the old place won't be the same without you, Quinn. That's all I can say.'

Quinn was surprised to hear this information.

Timberley went on: 'I don't like it when things . . . change around me. It upsets me. I didn't like it when . . . when Miss Dillard died.'

'Of course not.'

'I didn't like it when the Hargreaveses came. I mean, Mrs Hargreaves is a decent sort, but he . . . well, you know what I think of *him*. He's taken to going around in his uniform all the time, you know, preening himself like a blooming peacock. Rubbing a chap's nose in it.'

'I beg your pardon?'

'Well, it's difficult, you see, for Appleby and me. We're young and everyone expects us to enlist. But it isn't so simple, you know. I envy you, Quinn. You're a policeman. No one will say, what are you doing here when you should be at the front? Everyone accepts that we must have policemen. But really it's no different for Appleby and me, in a manner of speaking. Not *exactly* the same, I admit. But there aren't many people who can do what we do. We are specialists. I know we rather appear to be bumbling fools, but we are both very highly thought of in our fields. Our supervisor has made it known that he simply cannot afford to lose us. Some would say it's not essential war work. But it's important, is it not? It's part of our civilization. The Natural History Museum is a national institution. It must continue. In a way, that's what we're fighting for, isn't it?'

Quinn looked into the young man's eyes, trying to find there what he needed to say.

Timberley angled his head as if he were trying to identify birdsong, and a wistful smile played across his lips. 'When I was a boy, one Christmas I got a cap gun in my stocking. It wasn't what I wanted. Not what I really wanted. What I really wanted was a magnifying glass and a tray for pinning my specimens on. But that year all the other chaps had cap guns, so that's what I asked for. What I really wanted, I suppose, was to be like the other chaps. On Christmas Day, I duly opened up my present. I knew what it was, of course – my parents weren't the sort not to get a chap what he'd asked for. But when I finally had the wrapping off and saw it in its box, I remember I felt this awful disappointment inside me. A kind of emptiness. I mustn't have been able to keep it off my face, because my mother, bless her, looked very worried. "What's wrong," she said. "Isn't that what you wanted?" "No," I said. "It's perfect!" I ran around for half an hour firing off caps. I rather think I pretended I was a daring police detective, you know. At the end of Christmas Day, I put it back in its box and never took it out again. I still have it, you know. In mint condition, it is. I suppose the moral of the story is, *to thine own self be true*, or some such. I should have had the courage to ask for what I really wanted. I imagine you liked to play with cap guns when you were a boy, eh?'

'I had a toy stethoscope, I seem to remember. For many years, I thought I would follow in my father's footsteps. He was a doctor.'

Timberley did not seem to hear what Quinn said. 'It's damned awkward though. Mary – you know, Miss Ibbott – well, you know I'm rather fond of her. Mary says she could never marry a man who failed to do his duty. It's not just Mary. All the girls think like that, you know. Well, I'm doing my duty, Quinn. It's just that my duty is to stay at the Natural History Museum.'

'What does Mr Appleby say?'

'I think Appleby's going to enlist.' Timberley made the pronouncement bitterly.

'Thereby giving him the advantage with Miss Ibbott?'

'Yes.'

'I am not sure how to advise you, Mr Timberley. Your supervisor cannot forbid you from enlisting, if that is your genuine wish. If it is not, then I would advise you to remain in your post. But to join up merely to win the favour of a pretty girl . . .'

Quinn noticed Timberley's face was suddenly flushed. 'Are you suggesting that I'm reluctant to fight?'

'That wasn't what I said.'

'I'm not a coward, Quinn.'

'I misunderstood. I thought you wanted my advice. I'm sorry.'

Timberley bit his lip. 'No, I'm sorry. This beastly war has set my nerves on edge. Everything has changed. The whole world has changed. And there's nothing we can do about it.'

For a moment, Timberley became absorbed in his own thoughts.

Quinn looked down at the suitcase on the bed. 'If you will excuse me . . .'

Timberley snapped himself out of his reverie. 'Of course. I'll leave you to it. I just wanted to say, I'm sorry you're going, that's all.'

The young man was gone. Quinn heard him coughing on the landing outside his room for a moment before the sound trailed off downstairs.

Quinn crossed to the wardrobe and took out a small tin box hidden away in the bottom beneath a pile of folded blankets.

The tin was almost weightless, and yet he knew that it contained the heaviest freight imaginable: the story of his father's infidelity.

He had read every letter but one. He had read his father's declarations of love to another man's wife, a woman Quinn had never known. He had been forced to confront his father's delight in the intimate details of their physical love. Worse than that, he had read of his father's avowed willingness to abandon everything – by which he meant his family – to be with the woman he loved. In this way, Quinn had learnt of the person who meant more to his father than he did.

The only letter he had not read was the one that his father had written shortly before his death, after he had lost his beloved mistress to a particularly unpleasant form of cancer.

This was the letter that would settle once and for all the question that had troubled Quinn all these years.

He placed the tin box unopened in the case. He quickly covered it with a towel, and various items of underwear.

TWELVE

E ve Cardew was pulled along by the crowd on Goldhawk Road. She had to keep her step in pace with those around her, otherwise she would fall and be trampled. She felt that the heart of the crowd was as pitiless as her own.

There was something welcome – almost blissful – about this surrender of individuality. She felt part of something purposeful.

She had been sent out by her mother to buy some pork chops for tea. As usual, Mama had retired to a darkened room to lie down. The last maid, Mildred, had given notice weeks ago, muttering something about how she couldn't be doing with all the praying (amen to that!). Her father had said that he would find someone through the church, but so far, nothing doing. Eve smiled a private smile at the thought of his failure. He couldn't understand it. What was wrong with these people? Were they afraid of a little good honest toil?

When the war had broken out, Eve had felt a quickening of her pulse. If she had been a man she would have enlisted. Not because she wished to defend the Empire, or Belgians, or for any patriotic reasons. She had allowed herself to be whipped up into a frenzy of anti-German hatred by what she read in the papers. She fantasized about horrific atrocities committed by faceless soldiers. At times, she put herself into these fantasies as a victim. She would imagine herself surrounded by a gang of slobbering, brutalized Germans. They would paw at her and rip her clothes off, then take turns in raping her. After they had sated their brutal appetites they took out long knives and began to carve pieces of her flesh away from her body. They always started with her breasts. She willed herself to feel pain, even as she imagined the blade cutting into her skin and the blood beginning to gush. But, of course, there was never any physical pain. Just the longing for it.

What swept her along with the crowd was her sense that the people around her were driven by the same toxic mixture of fear, glee and hatred as she was.

The papers had been full of the latest German crimes in Belgium. Priests threatened with death if they did not ring the bells to celebrate German victories. The mayor of a small town and ten other prominent citizens had been rounded up and held as hostages to ensure the good behaviour of the townsfolk. At every act of insurgence, one of them was executed. Not everything made its way into the papers. There were rumours of babies spiked on bayonets. Of old men struck down in the street. And of rapes, always the rapes. Of nuns, of nurses, of milkmaids and schoolgirls.

The pace of the crowd picked up. Voices rose to an excited clamour. It was hard to distinguish what was being said, but the anger was unmistakable. Then one man she could not see started to chant: 'Filthy Bosch! Filthy Bosch! Filthy Bosch!'

The cry was taken up. Eve herself felt the thrill of it in her throat. They matched their step to the rhythm.

With the heavy accent on *Bosch*, the chant sounded like the beating of a giant pair of wings. The mass of people had become an avenging angel.

All at once the crowd seemed to fragment, and Eve experienced a pang of grief, afraid the energy around her was beginning to dissipate. But it was simply that a cluster of youths had broken away and were engaged in some absorbing activity of their own. Their shouts competed with the chanting. She went over to see what they were doing. Mama would have been horrified to see her keeping such company. The thought gave Eve immense satisfaction.

She saw that the youths were tearing apart a wooden pallet that one of them had found on the pavement. They were stripping off lengths of wood that they brandished like weapons, claws of rusty nails protruding from one end. They laughed with savage delight as they hefted the planks.

The pallet was torn apart in seconds. A few remnants of wood lay scattered on the ground. Eve threw down her shopping basket and picked up a handy-looking chunk. The laughter of the youths redoubled, but not in mockery, in delight.

'She's a game 'un, awrigh'!'

'Who you gonna wallop with that? The bloody Kaiser?'

'I know who we can wallop!' cried one of them, a scrawny boy who couldn't have been older than eleven. Either that, or malnourishment kept him small for his age. His eyes stood out large in his grimy face. 'There's a bloody Hun butcher's around 'ere somewhere.'

'I know where it is,' said Eve.

She led the boys along the street. Word of their intent quickly spread. Within minutes she was at the head of a surging mass, many of whom were armed with lengths of wood and even bricks and half bricks that they had scavenged from somewhere.

The chant now was 'Smash it up! Smash it up! Smash it up!' The Filthy-Boschers had all been converted to Smash-It-Uppers.

She felt herself enlarged and enlivened by the energy behind her.

It was a strange, intoxicating feeling, not without a faint flickering of guilt. They bought their chops from Egger's every week, and she herself had visited the shop many times. Her mother used to take her there as a child, in the days when she used to do her own provisioning. Eve remembered the smell of the shop. It was an unpleasant smell, but there was something about it that she wanted to get to the bottom of. She remembered Herr Egger as a big, round, jolly man, who always tried to make her smile with some joke she barely understood because of the funny way he spoke.

Sometimes he sang German songs to her. She had no hope of understanding the lyrics, but the melodies seemed to suggest a wistful longing for a faraway place. He had a surprisingly sweet and high-pitched voice, which was strangely at odds with the smears of blood on his apron. He was always chuckling and winking, and sometimes he even found little sweets or treats for her. There was no doubt Herr Egger had taken a shine to Eve.

The Eggers had a son, who was a few years older than Eve. Every now and then, if his son was there, Herr Egger would call for him, 'William! Come here and say hello!' William would come solemnly out from the back and mumble a few words while staring at the sawdusted floor. 'One day, they will be married, no?' Herr Egger would suggest to Mama. '*Ja*? *Gut, ja*? Then you will never want for pork chops, Frau Cardew.' This was the worst joke of all, as far as Eve was concerned. Herr Egger would laugh so much the tears would come to his eyes.

She remembered feeling sorry for the boy. She knew that he no more welcomed this teasing than she did.

William was a grown man now. He had followed his father into the business and stood beside him now behind the counter in identical butcher's aprons and straw boaters. His mother was there too, smart and prim in a dark matronly dress. All three looked anxiously out. William conferred for a moment with Herr Egger. He seemed to be urging his parents into action. But his father's expression was confused, as if he could not comprehend, let alone believe, what was happening in the street outside. But it was clear that William had grasped the crowd's intent immediately.

Herr Egger seemed suddenly very old. She had always thought of him as a big man, a kind of plump, jolly giant, the archetypal butcher, even to the mutton-chop whiskers. But now he seemed shrunken, almost frail.

She saw the reality of the situation dawn on him. His jaw dropped, he stood aghast, slowly shaking his head, staring in blank despair at the angry crowd outside. His face went an unhealthy grey colour.

At that point, William took charge of the situation. He ushered his parents, and what customers there were, into the back, then rushed to bolt the front door. That was the moment the first brick was thrown. It hit the large glass pane in the very door William was busy locking.

The glass shattered. William's face and hands were immediately streaked with blood. Aghast, he looked into the crowd, as if demanding an explanation. It was confusion more than fear that she saw in his face. And when his gaze found her, it was something else, something personal and recriminatory.

An unexpected restraint seemed to come over the crowd, as if they were suddenly abashed. Undoubtedly, violence is easier to contemplate in the abstract, but when the human face of your victim is there before you, it takes a special kind of savagery to go through with it.

Then Eve realized that they were in fact waiting for the signal. And that it had fallen to her to give it.

She was in control of them. Their energy flowed through her. And William's fate was in her hands.

'No more bricks!' she cried.

There were grumbles of dissent from the crowd. She sensed her power over them waning. The grumbles turned to shouts.

'Bloody filthy Bosch!'

'Robbed us blind all these years!'

'Leeches!'

'Shouldn't be allowed!'

Eve felt herself jostled from behind. For the first time she was afraid that they might turn on her.

But really they were so stupid. They had misunderstood her earlier caution.

She climbed up on the low windowsill at the front of the shop and turned to address them.

'Listen! If you smash the windows, you'll spoil the meat. That's all. We want the meat. We're hungry. Our children are starving. It's the Germans' fault, with their beastly blockade, sinking our ships. It's only right that we should take Fritz's meat. He's profiteering from it anyhow. Putting his prices up so none of us can afford it. What does he expect? But if you smash his windows now, we can't eat the meat. Take the meat, take as much meat as you want. Then smash the windows!'

The crowd appreciated this, rewarding her with cheers and laughter. They immediately set about following her directions.

By now, William Egger had bolted what was left of the door and fled out of sight. But it was a simple matter to reach through the broken window and undo the latch.

The rabble flooded into the shop.

Eve jumped down and stood back from the turmoil. She looked up at the first-floor window, where she saw William Egger glowering down at her, his face still dark with his own blood.

She kept looking at him as the smashing began, and the cries of the mob rose to a frenzy. A moment later, she heard the first blast of a policeman's whistle.

Then she remembered what old Mr Egger had once said about them one day getting married. She was still looking up at William Egger when she began to laugh.

PART III
Purity

3 September–5 September, 1914.

BRITAIN'S HERO ROLL OF 10,345.

Corrected Casualty List of British Soldiers Who Fell in Battle.

MORE OFFICERS' NAMES.

The Press Bureau last night published a further list of casualties in the Expeditionary Force, bringing the total casualties issued up to date to 10,345.

Details of the casualties are as follows:

KILLED

Officers	....	54
Other ranks	....	179

WOUNDED

Officers	....	135
Other ranks	....	941

MISSING

Officers	....	181
Other ranks	....	8,855

Total officers killed, missing, wounded 370
Other ranks killed, missing, wounded 9,975

Grand total of casualties **10,345**

Daily Mirror, *Friday, 4 September, 1914*

THIRTEEN

S ilas Quinn looked across the floor of the CID room. Everywhere he looked, officers were busy about their jobs. He had the impression that every single one of them was studiously avoiding his gaze. But in his more rational moments, he accepted that they simply had a lot on their plates.

He appeared to be the only one there who had nothing particular to do. Reports landed on his desk, which he was required to read, in order to assess whether there was any aspect of the case that needed to be passed on to MO5(g). But it was down to others to do the actual police work.

Quinn being Quinn, he could not help reading the statements and reports and coming to his own conclusions about the investigating detective's conduct of the case. He saw the tricks that were missed, the leads that went unexplored, the potentially key witnesses who were not interviewed, not to mention the flawed evidence, or even the total lack of evidence in some cases. Of course, it was not in his remit to challenge these shortcomings. But Quinn being Quinn, he did not let that stop him.

As far as Quinn could tell, the new emphasis on supposed German agents was a godsend to the lazier elements within the detective force. Now they didn't even have to go through the motions of fitting up a likely villain. They could simply mark the case file as SFA – 'Suspected Foreign Agent', in effect shifting the file off their own desk on to Quinn's. That would have been fine if Quinn had then had the latitude to investigate the case himself, but he was only required to assess the credibility of that conclusion and brief his contact at MO5(g), Commander Irons, on any that passed muster.

Commander Irons had the appearance of a games master at one of the better public schools, except that his face was strangely immobile, so much so that Quinn half-wondered if it was paralyzed. But no, it was merely that Irons was consciously straining not to give anything away in all their interactions. Perhaps he was new to intelligence work, and had not yet acquired that habit

of practised insouciance that Quinn had noticed in the best
agents. The trick, you see, was to put your interlocutor at their
ease, to appear to be garrulous and indiscreet, in order to draw
forth indiscretions from the other. But Irons was as taciturn as
he was facially inexpressive. Perhaps, with such men, there were
layers of dissimulation, which they could put on depending on
their audience. With Quinn, Irons saw no reason to be anything
other than his granite-faced, tight-lipped self.

They met in a nondescript room in the Admiralty, which at
least gave Quinn the opportunity to get up from his desk and
leave the building.

Some of the files Quinn handed over would be taken from
him and he would never hear of them again. With others, he
would receive direction which he was to pass on to the senior
officer in the case. Occasionally he might be required to set up
a meeting between Commander Irons and the team. His presence
was not required at these meetings.

There was no denying that Quinn found his reduced role
demeaning.

Looking at the backs of his colleagues, hunched and tensed,
he felt a pang of envy.

He was suddenly aware of a presence at the side of his desk.
He turned to see his former sergeant, Macadam, patiently waiting
to get his attention.

Quinn sat up in his seat. 'Macadam? What can I do for you?'

'Good afternoon, sir.'

At that moment, Sergeant Inchball drew up alongside Macadam.

'Both of you?'

'Guv.' Inchball offered the greeting tersely. He avoided looking
Quinn in the eye.

'We just wondered how you were getting on, sir?' offered
Macadam, somewhat uncertainly. 'It can't be easy, what with the
SCD being closed down and all.'

'It's a diabolical liberty, that's what it is,' was Inchball's view
on the matter.

'We just wanted to let you know, we are here . . . if you
need us.'

'I'm sure you have duties of your own already. I wouldn't
dream of imposing on you.'

'I wasn't talking about in an official capacity, sir.'

'In what capacity, then?' Quinn's voice brimmed with alarm.

'Oh, he would be difficult, wouldn't he!' cried Inchball. 'You need some friends in 'ere, doancha?'

It was a startling thought. He did not disagree with what Inchball had said. It was rather that he had never thought of it in those terms before.

'Some of the fellows are . . .' Macadam broke off delicately to consider his words. 'Rather vexed by your . . .'

'Vexed?'

'Some of them are exceeding vexed, sir, if you don't mind me saying so.'

'What has got them so vexed?'

'Your . . . well . . . how shall I put it?'

'They don't like the way you're always making them look like fools, guv,' said Inchball with a chuckle.

'I don't mean to,' said Quinn simply.

'*We* know that, sir. But the way they see it, it's not your place to be . . . offering your opinions on their conduct of their cases.'

'I'm only trying to help.'

'They don't welcome your help, sir. They haven't asked for it. They don't want it.'

'Bloody interfering bugger.' Inchball added quickly: 'That's what they call you, guv.' He held up his palms in a placatory gesture, to make it clear that these were not the words he would have chosen.

'I know it's hard, sir, when you see . . .'

'Incompetence?'

Macadam winced at Quinn's choice of word. 'Mistakes, shall we say?'

'Exactly. Mistakes.'

'Different methods, perhaps. Perhaps that would be a better term? The thing is, sir, the way some of the fellows see it, this isn't your job.'

'Ain't you supposed to be looking out for Germans?'

Quinn ignored the question. 'What would you have me do?'

'It's not our place, sir.'

'Look, guv, we know you're in the right, Mac and me. That ain't the point. The point is this. Watch yer back. Keep yer head down. Wait it out. Don't make waves. Not yet. Bide yer time. That's the sensible thing to do, if you ask me.'

'We've heard rumblings, sir. There's a faction out to get you. They're waiting for one slip up, then the knives will be out.'

'How high up does it go, this faction?'

'You've ruffled quite a few feathers, sir. Inspectors, DCIs. But the types who have the ears of those even higher up.'

'They want me out, do they?'

'Yes, sir.'

'Well, I was thinking of leaving anyway. Perhaps I shall apply for a commission. In the artillery. I think I would quite enjoy firing big guns at the enemy.'

'They fire back at you, from what I hear, guv.'

'It would be no fun if they didn't.'

'Don't let them win, sir. It's like Inchball said. You're in the right. If officers like you go, then . . . well, what hope is there for the decent coppers?'

'Still, I don't understand what you expect me to do. Stay in the force but do nothing? People keep telling me there's a war on.' Quinn picked up a file from his desk. 'Take this case . . . you heard about the riot at the pork butcher's in Shepherd's Bush?'

'The Bosch butcher of Bush?' Macadam must have sensed Quinn's astonishment. He had the decency to look abashed. 'That was how it was reported in the papers, sir.'

'I don't see that it is a matter for puns. A man died.'

'You mean the butcher?' Inchball bristled defiantly. 'One less German to worry about, that's what I say. Besides, geezer had heart attack is what I heard. Weak heart, could have happened any time.'

'Oh, you don't think the attack on his premises had anything to do with it? His son was badly hurt in the melee, according to the report.'

'Badly hurt? I don't think so. A few scratches. Serves him right, the bloody Bosch.'

'The deceased gentleman was a naturalized citizen. His wife is English. His son was born in this country. Is English.'

'Half English.'

'The law recognizes him as English. And we are servants of the law.'

Quinn opened the file and glanced distractedly down at the contents. 'Well, the lead investigating officer, one Inspector Leversedge . . . do you know him?'

'He's a protégé of DCI Coddington's,' said Macadam.

That was all Quinn needed to hear. 'Why does that not surprise me? Friend Leversedge has even marked down this case as SFA. Presumably he thinks that the German butcher himself instigated the riot in his own shop? For what purpose is not made clear. Though the motive in these cases is always the same. To spread despondency and panic among the civilian population. It seems this can be used to explain any crime or misdemeanour, from common assault to shoplifting. Or possibly Inspector Leversedge imagines that the pork in the shop was poisoned? And that the looting was deliberately incited in order to spread the contaminated meat amongst as many people as possible? As for the man's death, no doubt he engineered that too to throw the police off the scent.'

Inchball and Macadam said nothing, sunk in thoughtfulness as they considered Quinn's words.

'So tell me, what am I to do with such a case? If I hand it back to him, I will be resented for insisting he does his job properly. If I pass it on to MO5(g), I will be taken for as big a fool as him.'

'Chuck it in the bin!' was Inchball's radical solution. 'Who gives a damn about a German sausage butcher? They ought to give the looters medals.'

Macadam did not agree. 'It's a question of public order. We can't have people smashing up shops and stealing things, even if it is a German shop. Before you know it, you'll have anarchy on the streets of London.'

Inchball pulled a face. 'You can't blame people though, can you? I mean, there's a war on. They wanna do their bit, don't they? Besides, the riot was broken up as soon as the bobbies got to the scene. I tell you something. There ain't a man here as would bring a single one of those looters in, even if 'e could find 'em. That's your first problem. I mean, who's gonna squeal? Pardon the pun.'

Quinn frowned. Which pun needed pardoning was not immediately obvious to him. 'The case does present difficulties. Especially as the family of the pork butcher refuse to press charges, presumably to escape further harassment.'

'There you go!'

'If that's the case, I can understand why Leversedge wants to kick it into the long grass,' conceded Macadam.

'And so my desk is the long grass now, is it?'

The two sergeants' embarrassed silence was eloquent enough.

Quinn closed the file with a heavy sigh. 'It's still our duty to uphold the law. No matter what the nationality of the victim.'

Macadam and Inchball cast anxious glances about, as if Quinn had just given voice to a dangerous heresy and they were afraid that he might have been overheard.

FOURTEEN

P astor Clement Cardew stood on the top step at the entrance to Shepherd's Bush Baptist Church looking down at the mass of people assembling on the pavement of Shepherd's Bush Road. He recognized faces among the multitude. (As God was his witness, that word was no exaggeration today. It was a veritable *multitude*.) Some were regular churchgoers, others were lapsed members of the congregation whom he had not seen for years. His family were there, of course, his wife Esme, and the twins, to whom he had given the first names in the Bible, Adam and Eve.

But many of those he saw were unknown to him, strangers for now, whom he was glad to welcome to his church, and who, by the warmth of that welcome, and the eloquence of his words, and with God's blessing, would become his brethren in Christ. Perhaps he had crossed paths with some of them in the past. There were many, adults now, who must have passed through his Sunday school classes as children. He would not remember them, but they would remember him. He took comfort from the sure and certain knowledge that he had instilled in them the Word of God, which, though it may have lain dormant for many years, had now come into glorious life.

Pastor Cardew smiled with satisfaction. It was good to see the errant return to the fold, and indeed to see so many people milling about in readiness to enter the church. But it was not just the numbers of the throng that gratified him. It was the spirit evident among so many of them. He could sense their excitement. They were eager for admittance.

At first Cardew had been astonished by the increase in the size of the congregation at the outbreak of war. But really, it was not so surprising. The war had brought people back to God. It had been good for business, he might almost say. There was no blasphemy in the joke. Humour was the yeast that leavened the conversation of men, and when that conversation was godly, so too was the humour. If the heart was true, the wit would always be pure. Besides, it *was* his business to bring his flock to salvation. And like every good preacher, he understood the value of a good metaphor. You could compare God to the farmer, perhaps, who produces the food that nourishes His people. Therefore, the minister may be thought of as the grocer who distributes this food to the hungry. Except, of course, the food is salvation. So his business is salvation. There could be no disrespect in a homely metaphor.

People were on the steps now, passing either side of him into the church. He smiled and nodded as he looked into the faces of those approaching. Some he greeted by name. To others, he merely said, 'You are very welcome.'

A middle-aged woman and a girl who appeared to be her daughter stopped in front of him. 'Hello, Pastor Cardew. You probably don't remember Mary, do you?'

Mary pulled at her mother's sleeve, widening her eyes in embarrassment. 'Mummy!'

Cardew looked down at the girl. The face was vaguely familiar, allowing for the passage of years. But it was more than just her physical appearance that he recognized, it was the way she had of playing the coquette. Pretending to be too bashful to look him in the eye, her eyelids fluttering over a yearning gaze, lips pursed as she held in check lascivious thoughts. That faint blush on her cheek that suggested the heat of passion. They were all Eve's daughters, born knowing how to use their wiles to entrap men. Born temptresses.

'Of course, she was much younger when she used to come here for Sunday school. That was when we used to live on Melrose Gardens. My George was still alive then, of course.'

'Mary . . . Abbott, isn't it?'

'Ibbott, in point of fact.' The mother, Mrs Ibbott, corrected him mildly with an indulgent smile. 'Silly name. My George's fault, I'm afraid. He was a good man otherwise. But he would insist on having a name no one could remember.'

'Ibbott, that's right. I do remember, of course.'

'See, I told you he would, Mary!' Mrs Ibbott beamed. 'We saw the notice in the paper, and I thought, that's Pastor Cardew! So I said to Mary, Mary, you remember Pastor Cardew.' To the pastor she added, confidentially, 'We're at a difficult age, you know. All these men in uniform. They do tend to turn her head somewhat. So . . . when I saw what you were doing here today, I thought, well . . . I thought, yes!'

Mary Ibbott, he calculated, must be about the same age as his own children. Which would have meant she was in the same Sunday school class as them. The realization provoked a complex emotional reaction, the simplest way to deal with which was to have her out of his sight.

And so he repeated, 'You're very welcome.'

Taking their cue, Mrs Ibbott and her daughter moved on.

Pastor Cardew surveyed the milling crowds again, blocking out the image of Mary Ibbott and all the dangerous memories that it provoked, as he tried to resume his earlier train of thought.

Today they were not here for a service, so perhaps the numbers were deceptive. But they were still here – to continue his earlier terminology – on God's business. And he was confident that any who came for today's meeting, even if it were secular in nature, could be made to consider the necessity of returning for worship on the morrow.

It was fear that led them back. The world had suddenly become a dangerous and uncertain place. A drastic shift in perspective had brought Death into the foreground; the dim figure on the horizon, drifting in and out of sight, had become an insistent, looming presence, so close its stinking, clammy breath could be felt on the back of the neck. Sons and brothers, husbands and fathers, in answering the call to the colours, had brought this dark stranger into the family. Not only that, there was fear of air raids, and invasion. The prospect of Death was imminent and omnipresent.

In Cardew's mind there was no difficulty in a belief that was born out of fear rather than love. It did not matter to God what led each one of them to Him. The old phrase for a good man was God-fearing. And so fear always had a part to play. It tempered the believer's faith, like fire tempered steel, making it harder and more resilient. It showed too the miracle of God's compassion, for it allowed Him to give comfort to those who were afraid, and through the agency of His Love, to convert their cowering fear into towering strength, the abiding strength that only comes from the knowledge of eternal salvation.

'O death, where *is* thy sting? O grave, where *is* thy victory?'

And so it thereby followed that the war must be God's Will.

Cardew was put in mind of Romans, 11:33. 'O the depth of the riches both of the wisdom and knowledge of God! How unsearchable *are* His judgements, and His ways past finding out!'

There was no truer verse in the Bible. Or, as Cowper had paraphrased it in his hymn: 'God moves in a mysterious way, his wonders to perform.'

Behind him now, inside the church, his church, preparations were in place for an extraordinary meeting. Men in khaki were putting up a table bearing their pamphlets and placards and other propaganda. And this was with Cardew's consent. Jesus had driven the money-changers from the temple. What would his reactions have been to the presence of recruiting sergeants? Pastor Cardew was in no doubt that the Son of God would have approved. The Bible exhorted the faithful to fight the good fight. And did a further verse, Zechariah 10:5, not say, 'and they shall fight, because the LORD is with them, and the riders on horses shall be confounded.' The riders on horses were without doubt the Prussian military machine. *Mutatis mutandis*, and all that.

The soldiers had – rather cleverly, Pastor Cardew thought – enlisted the services of a pretty young woman to draw the attention of the young men in the audience, as well as to elicit the sympathies of other females, and in general to instil in all the youth the correct attitude towards the war. She would be dispensing the various items after the speeches.

Pastor Cardew would address the assembly, welcoming them all to his church. Alongside him on the platform would be celebrities from the wider nonconformist movement and public life in general.

Cardew could not deny that it was the presence of such luminaries that had drawn the crowds today. They had even attracted the attention of a representative of the press. Some fellow named Bittlestone from the *Clarion* had turned up. He had been especially interested in Mrs Ward, naturally, and made much of how the meeting had brought together two ladies who had until recently been on opposing sides of the suffrage question. It was all for the good of the cause, Cardew didn't doubt, even if the journalist was rather dismissive of his own contribution.

Still, it was not vain pride that encouraged Pastor Cardew to believe that, locally at least, his name counted for something. So too did his position. His endorsement of the event, his willingness to hold it in the church, would have swayed many who might otherwise have shunned it as an exercise in blatant militarism. His presence was essential for the success of the meeting, and gave it its moral core.

For this was to be no ordinary recruitment rally. The notices that had appeared in various newspapers, paid for by contributions from a number of eminent members of the church, spoke of 'THE DEFENCE OF PURITY' and a 'WAR AGAINST IMMORALITY'.

This was the fruit of his own particular genius. He had been party to discussions with certain high-ranking soldiers, who also happened to be avowed Christians. They had expressed to him, in the most compelling terms, their concerns about the calibre of recruits that Kitchener's drive was attracting. They spoke of criminals who joined the army only to escape the long arm of the law, so that they might be able to continue their thievery elsewhere. Of men who had no compunction in persuading girls to sleep with them – on the usual understanding – and then abandoning them with child, but without fulfilling their promises of marriage. Thus the war would produce a whole generation of illegitimate children, which would only exacerbate the moral decline already in evidence. Then there were the men who resorted to prostitutes. With the consequent problem of venereal disease. Such men thought nothing of coming back on leave and infecting their innocent wives or even sweethearts with the filthy contagion.

On top of all this was the general physical weakness, not to mention intellectual deficiency, of many rank-and-file soldiers.

And so a need was recognized, a most urgent and vital need, to recruit good Christian soldiers. The leaders of all churches and denominations must come together and urge the young men in their congregations to do their duty. There was a difficulty here, he acknowledged, in that Christianity was first and foremost a religion of peace. How many times had he himself preached the lesson of Matthew 5:39? 'Whosoever shall smite thee on thy right cheek, turn to him the other also.'

But there could be no turning of the other cheek with the Kaiser.

It came down to a battle between good and evil. And the battle was real, and it was being waged constantly, all around them.

He saw his own son come up the steps towards him. There was something shifty and underhand about the youth now, exacerbated by his halting gait. As usual, he refused to meet his own father's gaze.

Ever since that Sunday four years ago when they had found him sprawled in the garden with a shattered ankle, the trust had gone between them. His blasphemous lie had been discovered.

He had called down God's punishment upon himself.

Cardew averted his face just as Adam approached.

Cardew saw his wife coming up the steps now. She was looking steadily at him, her gaze wary rather than confrontational. Her eyes were moist and pink and puffy. No doubt she had recently been crying. It was never long since she had been crying. Or long until the next cry. It would break her heart to have Adam go off and fight. Perhaps the boy's ankle would save him. God truly did work in mysterious ways, for He had punished Adam for his sin with a crippling injury, but that injury might well turn out to be his salvation.

Cardew acknowledged Esme's gaze with an imperious uplift of the head. This provoked a self-pitying sniffle from her as she walked past him into the church. It was the strongest form of protest that she ever allowed herself.

Pastor Cardew looked for his daughter Eve in the streams of people passing either side of him. But somehow, as she always did these days, she managed to make herself invisible to him.

FIFTEEN

Three steps behind Mother, Felix Simpkins hung back while she stopped to exchange pleasantries with Pastor Cardew. It had not been Felix's idea to come along today but Mother had been insistent. Purity was one of her manias, having suffered so much because of her one lapse from that impossible standard.

Of course, he didn't see why he should be dragged into it. Every now and then, however, it paid to go along with her lunatic ideas. It would buy him a few days of peace and relative freedom. And the alternative was one of her raging tantrums.

Besides, when he had seen Pastor Cardew's name on the advertisement, Felix had experienced a kindling of interest of his own. He remembered Pastor Cardew from his childhood, when Mother had gone through a brief but intense religious phase. The Cardews had brought their two children to Mother for piano lessons and she had been quite taken by the charismatic pastor. Though not a Baptist herself, she was piqued enough to attend a service and had become, for a time, a regular celebrant, with Felix in tow of course. She had even played the organ for the occasional service, when the usual organist was indisposed.

With her characteristic maternal authoritarianism, she had, without consulting him, enrolled Felix in the pastor's Sunday school, which he had been forced to continue attending even after her own interest had waned.

Strangely, this loss of interest seemed to come as soon as Mother had been baptized. The idea of the ceremony had exercised a fascination over her. He remembered that she had talked of little else at the time. The drama of it appealed to her. Her imagination was gripped by the commitment of whole-body immersion. She was even a little afraid of it, and had asked Pastor Cardew if anyone had ever drowned being baptized. But the pastor had reassured her that every precaution was taken.

Felix felt too that Mother was attracted by the symbolism of cleansing. She had always talked so much about how dirty everything was. He was a dirty boy. London was a dirty city. Men all had dirty minds. Looking back now, he thought she must have hoped that the ceremony would in some way wash her clean – and not just her but the whole world.

But now, seeing the way she made a fool of herself in front of the pastor, gushing and simpering as she asked after his children, her former pupils, Felix realized with nauseating certainty that Mother's interest in the Baptist Church had been tied up with her interest in its minister. Perhaps that was why she had been so keen to come along today, after she had seen his name in the newspaper.

A slow smirk formed on his lips. He could not think of Mother in this way except through the prism of contempt. She must have made quite a fool of herself. Felix shook his head to dispel the thought of it.

In the years since then she had flirted with other denominations and religions, returning for a time to the Roman Catholicism of her childhood, before settling more or less on Theosophism, or an interpretation of it that Felix didn't doubt was peculiar to her. It was a peculiar enough thing to begin with, but Mother was perfectly capable of overlaying it with misunderstandings and stupidities of her own.

Felix peeked shyly over Mother's shoulder at Pastor Cardew.

Cardew was older now, of course, though still a powerful presence. His once-black hair was sprinkled with silver shards. His face was lined and drawn. There was a new hesitancy to his manner that Felix did not remember, a slight wariness in his greeting, which seemed to contradict the forceful confidence with which he had a moment before possessed the threshold to the church. Felix had to admit this might just have been the effect Mother had on people.

Felix had never really understood anything that Pastor Cardew had tried to teach him. It had always seemed that the pastor assumed he already knew the most important things, that the biggest questions were already settled. The questions that most preoccupied Felix – what did God look like? Where did he live? And if God was good, why did he let bad things happen? – were never addressed by the pastor, and Felix didn't have the courage to raise them himself. But it didn't matter. He enjoyed drawing pictures and colouring them in with wax crayons. Most of all, he enjoyed the stories. Even if he was humourless, Pastor Cardew possessed a deep, resonant voice and could imbue his readings from Blackie's *Scripture Stories for Boys and Girls* with a lively sense of drama.

But the real reason why Felix had never really objected to going to the Sunday school was the presence in the class of Pastor Cardew's daughter, Eve.

She had been a pretty little thing, with gleaming black locks, a cupid mouth and big, serious eyes that took everything in. For some reason she had taken a shine to Felix. She had pressed little folded pieces of paper into his hand with messages such as 'I love you' and 'Will you marry me?' written in earnest, oversized letters in pencil. He had to admit that he had not always responded well to her attentions. The notes had at first shocked him. As had her invitation, whispered hotly into his ear while her father's back was turned as he wrote out the words to the Lord's Prayer on the blackboard, for Felix to kiss her. In fact, it seemed not so much an invitation as a command, and when Felix failed to obey, Eve took matters into her own hands and pressed her lips lightly on to his in such a way that it set his heart fluttering.

The incident had not been missed by their classmates, who immediately let out scandalized shrieks (the girls) and peals of mocking laughter (the boys). Felix had felt the colour flooding into his face, so that when Pastor Cardew turned round to see what all the fuss was about, Felix's face shone out like a beacon of guilt. Eve by now was sitting primly in her seat with her best butter-wouldn't-melt face on.

Pastor Cardew had homed in on the one boy who evidently had something to hide. 'What is it? Felix? What's going on?'

But Felix, of course, could say nothing.

'Well, settle down, everybody. And know that whatever you have done, God sees it, even if I do not.' The pastor was looking directly at Felix when he said this. 'And if you have transgressed, God will mark it down against you. And one day you will be called to give an account of all your sins.'

With very little encouragement from Felix, Eve persisted in her campaign of billets-doux and whispered amorous propositions. He was invited to hold her hand, to carry her books, to draw her portrait and sit for his own. He was given sweets and apples and conkers and marbles, gifts which he never reciprocated, but which despite that showed no signs of coming to an end. Felix's initial shock gave way at first to embarrassment, then to a kind of wonder.

He found that he began to look forward to Sundays. When he was in her presence, he felt a kind of pride in himself, that he had somehow won the undying love of this strange, intense girl. The fact that this love was, as far as he could tell, unearned ceased to trouble him. At any rate, it was better than the teasing and downright bullying that he endured at day school, where the only attention he got from his fellow pupils was a knuckle ground into his scalp.

And when he was not in her presence, he often caught himself thinking about her. Was he in love? He did not think so. He looked upon her rather as a puzzle he had yet to solve.

Then, one Sunday, he unfolded a larger piece of paper than usual and read upon it her most shocking message yet:

> *Dearist Felix,*
> *Meet me in the Scrubs at 4 o'clock. There is a plase near where the airships land where my brother and his pals have bilt a den out of branches and things. For we must run a way. A Great Evil has come in to my life you would not believe. I will tell you all later. You are my Saviour. We will live in a cottige with flowers and hens. I can do sewing. No one will find us. I love you and will love you forever. You are my only hope. If you do not come I will kill myself.*
> *Your Darlin Eve*

He had folded the note up and pushed it deep into the pocket of his short trousers.

Needless to say, he did not make the rendezvous. It was not so much the hints of danger and the threat of suicide that put him off as the one sentence 'I love you and will love you forever'. He was used to Eve's declarations of love. So long as he could think of this love as something momentary and therefore essentially whimsical, he could look upon it with equanimity, if not enthusiasm. But the prospect of its continuing indefinitely frankly terrified him. Besides, he rather had the feeling that things had gone a little too far.

For the whole of the next week he had been terrified that Eve would go through with her wild threat. On the following Sunday he had been so sick with apprehension that he had even vomited up his breakfast. He had hardly slept at all the night before. And what sleep he had managed had been dominated by a terrible nightmare in which he tried to revive a dead Eve, whose tiny, husk-like corpse exploded into a shower of dust at his touch. He had breathed in the dry particles of dust and was overcome by a feeling of suffocation, at which point he woke in a fit of urgent breathlessness.

All the same, he had forced himself to go to Sunday school

that day. It was possibly the bravest thing he had ever done, although it did not feel brave at the time. It was simply that he knew he would be unable to go on with his life until he had reassured himself that she was still alive.

She was. But it was clear that he was dead to her. From that day on there were no more notes, no more fervid whispers, no more hot, clandestine hand-holding. He did not go back to Sunday school the week after, or ever again.

'And is that Felix I see behind you?' Pastor Cardew's bass tones drew him back to the present moment.

Felix stepped forward. As usual, he felt the ridiculous heat of a blush in his face, prompted no doubt by the course his thoughts had just taken. The past was invariably humiliating.

'Oh, yes,' said Mother. 'I have brought my Felix with me. We must instil a love of purity into our young men in order to preserve our young women, I think.'

'Quite so,' agreed Pastor Cardew. 'You are both very welcome. I hope you will find the meeting suitably uplifting. I see you are not yet in uniform, Felix. Perhaps some religious scruples are holding you back? I understand if that is the case. Pacifism would seem to be the natural calling of a young Christian man. However, you will be interested to hear, I think, what one of our speakers, Sir William Robertson Nicoll, has to say. He is a church minister, but I vouch that he is more effective in rallying troops than any recruiting sergeant.'

'Felix cannot join the army,' said Mother bluntly. 'I will not permit it.'

Pastor Cardew was taken aback. From the look of disgust on his face, Felix knew that he was thinking about Mother's nationality.

'I cannot possibly survive without him,' she went on.

'But if it is his duty?'

'His first duty is to his mother. And, besides, I know the ways of soldiers. They are not the ways of my Felix. Felix is a good boy.'

Good boy indeed! I'm not her bloody dog!

But still, he had to admit it was so rare to hear Mother say anything positive about him – rare? It was unheard of! – that Felix felt a surge of pathetic emotion, part pride, part gratitude, both of which were immediately swamped by self-loathing.

'And you, Felix, what do you have to say for yourself? You cannot hide behind your mother's skirts forever, you know.'

'Is Eve here?' He had not known he was going to ask the question, and now that he had blurted it out, he felt a fool. The blood rushed into his face again.

Pastor Cardew was thrown by the question too. 'Eve? I . . . yes . . . she is here, of course.'

Felix flinched away from the pastor's frown and ducked past him to go inside the church.

SIXTEEN

Eve sat on the wooden seat next to her brother. Neither spoke. She looked up at the balcony which ran around the church. It was filling up fast. This being a Saturday afternoon, and not a church service, the mood of the audience was unfamiliar. It was lively, excitable even. There was a buzz of anticipation going round.

The noise distracted her from the normal run of her thoughts, and for that reason she welcomed it.

Who were these people? How did she come to be sitting in the midst of them?

She looked at them with a kind of blank fascination that was close to horror. She felt that there was a real possibility that she might stand up on her seat and scream.

Do you know what he did to me? She could feel the words forming in her throat, a clenched fist of meaning punching up her windpipe, choking her.

It was not the first time she had experienced the urge. Usually it came upon her when her father was in the middle of a sermon. She would find herself fixated on his hands, watching as they formed the gestures that gave emphasis to his pious words, scything the air, grasping at meaning, spreading to beseech, coming together in prayer. It was as if she were unable to let them out of her sight for fear that they might touch her again. Those hands were the focus of her loathing and hatred. They were the focus of his hypocrisy too, which made her hate them even more.

Once they had settled into their routine – it would always happen on a Sunday afternoon, after church and Sunday school – it had surprised her how normal it became. She always knew that it was wrong. And she always felt a sickening tension as the moment approached. But that tension was released and relieved by the attention he paid her.

She hated him for that. And she hated her body, her treacherous body, which betrayed her by responding to his attentions.

There was nothing left in her life, in the world, that she did not hate.

His hands were always firm, but never rough. He never hit her or threatened her with violence. He might guide her hand and plead in hot, husky whispers with her. What might have happened if she had not obeyed, she did not know.

To her shame, she had never tested this. She had never once pulled back from his compelling grip. Had not even tried to.

And so the sin was hers. The blame was all on her. She could not claim that he had coerced her. For she had never once tried to resist him.

The last time he came to her was that Sunday of Adam's fall.

Since then, he had hardly spoken a word to her, except such as were necessary for the functioning of their household. When she caught him looking at her, there was as much hatred for her in his gaze as she felt towards him.

Or was it fear? Was he afraid that she would one day speak of what had passed between them?

She realized that she had a kind of power over him now. And that shocked her, because she welcomed it. She realized that she had it in her power to punish him – to destroy him, even – for what he had done to her. All it would take was for her to climb up on her seat now and give voice to the words that had come to her a moment ago: *Do you know what he did to me?*

Except she knew that no one would believe her. She would be thought hysterical. They would say the pastor's daughter had gone mad. She would be carted off to spend the rest of her days in Hanwell Asylum.

The speakers were coming on to the platform now. Pastor Cardew was fussing around them. There was an old, grey-bearded man in a ridiculous uniform, with tasselled epaulettes at his shoulders and an old-fashioned bicorne hat on his head. A row of big medals stood out on his chest. He looked like something out of a children's picture book. For all the comicalness of his appearance, an unaccountable sadness came over Eve when she looked at him. He was rather slight of build, she thought, and he seemed to be puffing himself up with his medals and his uniform and his hat. As he strode on to the stage, he struck a pose of deliberate resoluteness, as if this was how he imagined a great general should walk. Or perhaps he was an admiral? The hat struck her as somewhat nautical and she remembered that an admiral was to be one of the speakers.

His face was stern and urgent. He swept the audience with a heavy scowl before taking his seat.

Next to him was a handsome woman of middle years. She looked younger than Mama (who was forty-five), but it had to be admitted that Mama had aged badly, what with her headaches and being as she was a martyr to her nerves.

This woman had a kind, engaged face, with an earnest, slightly anxious expression that made you think she always thought very hard about things before coming to her opinion. Was she the suffragette or the anti-suffragist? Eve wondered.

Probably the suffragette, because the woman next to her had much more the air of self-regard that you would expect from a celebrated authoress. Yes, that must be Mrs Humphry Ward, who was most definitely not a suffragette. Eve had not read *Robert Elsmere*, largely because Pastor Cardew recommended it so enthusiastically. Older than her fellow woman on the platform, with her grey hair neatly tied in a tight bun, Mrs Humphry Ward was too severe in her expression, too much the ageing bluestocking, to be thought handsome. However, she dressed with a certain elegance that testified to the success of her books.

Last in the row was a man with a high domed forehead and a drooping moustache. Like everyone on the platform, Eve could only think of him as old. There was no denying, however, the youthfulness of his expression. And he moved with quick, energetic decisiveness. You would say that he was eager to get on with things. She imagined this was an impression he gave, whatever he was engaged in.

The panel was all seated now, and Pastor Cardew was consulting his notes for the last time. The buzz of anticipation intensified and Eve gave a quick glance behind her to assess the

size of the audience. It was a full house. There were even people
standing at the rear. Up in the gallery, the front row was straining
forward to get a better view. Eve imagined the balcony collapsing
under their weight and the whole lot of them falling down on to
the crowd below. She could almost hear the screams of panic
that would ensue.

If the balcony fell on her and killed her, she believed she
would welcome it. She would welcome even the pain that it
would entail as being her due. Of course, it was easy to say that.
Perhaps in the event, she might feel as much terror as anyone,
and find herself equally unwilling to give up her hold on life.
But somehow she knew that her imagining of the catastrophe
was a form of wishful thinking. She was eighteen years old and
all that she craved for was to die in a freakish accident.

She could hear Pastor Cardew's voice from the platform, calling
the meeting to order. The din of chatter faded.

Eve brought her gaze down slowly. She was in no hurry to
turn to face him.

In fact, she took one last look at the row behind her. A face
had caught her attention. A young man who seemed to be looking
fixedly at her. She realized immediately who it was. For though
it was many years ago that they had known each other, the
essential qualities of his face had not changed. And besides, he
was sitting next to his mother, Mrs Simpkins, her old piano
teacher.

How dare he look at me!

Of course, it was a long time ago, and they were both very
young. Children, silly children. But still, he had no right to look
at her. She had made a fool of herself, perhaps, in that business.
But he had done something far worse. He had failed her, betrayed
her even. The memory of it – the memory of how she had once
felt about him – brought a quick flush of embarrassment to her
cheeks, which she saw mirrored in the sudden flood of colour in
his face.

She glared back at him, then turned away. She would never
make the mistake of feeling like that about anyone again.

She could not avoid looking at the man who was speaking
any longer. His face was a mask of respectability and responsi-
bility. The face of a man who had answered a higher calling,
who had given himself over to serving his God, and the people

who worshipped that God. The face of a public man. He was talking, no doubt impressively, no doubt rousingly, about the fight ahead. 'Yes, the country is at war now,' he was saying, 'against Germany and her allies. But there is a greater war that is always being fought, in which we are all foot soldiers. Every man, every boy, every woman, every girl. Every one of us, no matter our age or sex. This is a war that requires constant vigilance. And courage, yes, courage indeed. But a different kind of courage to that manifested by Tommy Atkins on the front. This is the courage to face up to the Evil One, to stare down the Tempter, and say *No!* Thou shalt not lead me astray.' He was staring right at her as he said this. And the hatred in his eyes had never been clearer.

Now was the time, if she was ever going to do it, to get up on her seat and shout out those words that were clumping and clenching inside her: *Do you know what he did to me?*

'But you see, here is the thing. What we find is that these two wars are in fact one and the same war. And in them, we are fighting the same enemy. So he who would join me in the fight against Satan, must join also in the fight against Germany. It is the same fight. And he who would fight against Germany, why, it is only right and proper that he should join in the fight against Satan! Which is why we are here today, and why I am delighted to welcome our panel of distinguished speakers. On the continent of Europe our soldiers are battling to defend the tiny nation of Belgium against the might of the German militarist state. It is the same as if you or I were to defend a young virgin against the vile assault of a brutal rapist. I am a man of God, a man of peace, but I would not hesitate to take up arms to defend that virgin. And God would see that it was the right thing for me to do. I know that Sir William has much to say on this very subject, so I will cut short my remarks on this now and leave it to his greater eloquence. I would only say one more thing. You are all here today because you understand what is at stake in this war. What it is that our enemy threatens. We are defending the most precious possession we have as a nation. And that is the purity of our young people. I say people because I believe that the purity of our young men is as vital to our nation's health as the purity of our young women. We must have pure young men to preserve the purity of our girls. You cannot have one without

the other. We need soldiers for the war in Belgium. There is no
question. But we need soldiers who are pure at heart, otherwise
our very cause is sullied. Every grain of wickedness and sin
that finds its way into the heart of just one of our soldiers
contaminates and weakens the morale of the whole army. This
is how the Devil works. When he tempts a soldier to indulge in
vice of any kind, he is like the termite eating away our house.
And that is how we will be defeated. Therefore, give us soldiers,
yes, but give us Christian soldiers. That is what I say.'

Pastor Cardew drew his remarks to an end and called upon
Sir William Robertson Nicoll, whom he described as 'a luminary
of the nonconformist movement', to address the audience. There
was warm applause and some cheering, which at first startled
and then disgusted Eve, when she realized that it was meant for
her father. She glared at the most enthusiastic applauders. Did
they not recognize a hypocrite when he stood in front of them?

Sir William spoke with a soft Scottish accent, which belied
the intensity and indeed ferocity of his oratorical style. His eyes
shone with a zealous gleam. He began with a direct call to arms:
'I call on all nonconformists who can fight to enlist without delay.
That nonconformists are neither cowardly nor incapable when
called to a righteous war the glorious name of Oliver Cromwell
sufficiently attests. That this is a most righteous and necessary
war cannot be contested.' The directness of his message seemed
to take Pastor Cardew off guard. He shifted uneasily in his seat.
But when he saw how warmly the audience responded to Sir
William's tone, he began to relax. 'We are fighting for our very
life as a nation. We are fighting for our children as our fathers
fought for us. It is the men who will go off to fight but the
women and girls among us can play their part too. And their part
is to encourage those of their menfolk who can fight not to shirk
when it comes to their duty. It is those women and girls who
must be defended, and so they have the right to insist on their
defence. We are honoured to have here with us today, the two
founders of a movement which began in Folkestone just a few
days ago. I refer, of course, to Admiral Penrose-Fitzgerald and
Mrs Humphry Ward, whose idea it is to have young ladies
dispensing white feathers as a badge of dishonour to those young
men who refuse to answer the call to arms. It is my fervent hope
that we will succeed today in enlisting as many young women

to that cause as we do men to the colours. There are, I believe, on a table at the rear of the church, envelopes already prepared with a quantity of white feathers for those of the fairer sex here today to take and use as they see fit. For the Order of the White Feather there will soon be no room in our land.'

This rousing sentiment was met with a full-throated cheer. Eve found herself joining in the applause. She could not resist a sly look back over her shoulder.

He was still looking at her. Had he been staring at her the whole time? Naturally, he looked away as soon as he saw her eyes on him, but the flood of pink across his face betrayed him. Ah yes, she remembered his frequent blushes and how they had once endeared him to her. She had seen them not as a weakness, but as a sign of his sensitivity and vulnerability. Perhaps they were partly responsible for her decision to invest her trust in him, and even to love him. She might now dismiss what she had felt then as not really love at all, but something strange and inexplicable and even grotesque. She was just a child, a silly child, even if not an innocent one. But it had not felt silly or childish at the time. It had been something huge and intense and overwhelming. It had felt real. And it had given her hope.

And he had let her down.

SEVENTEEN

Eve could not wait for the meeting to end. She only half-attended to the remaining speakers, although now and then, something they said cut through and reached her. For example, when Florence Conybeare declaimed, her voice trembling slightly but still forceful, that for her it was an issue of a woman's freedom. Purity, she believed, was synonymous with freedom. There was something in this, Eve thought. Hadn't her purity been snatched from her? And with it, her control over her own body. But more than that, she was now a prisoner in an existence which she had no hand in shaping. By maintaining her purity, and refusing to debase herself with sexual intercourse, a woman asserted her right to self-determination. Mrs Conybeare (for she was a married

woman) conceded the necessity of sexual contact for the purposes
of reproduction, but deplored its occurrence in any other circumstances. She called upon men to exercise self-control. Eve could
not help looking at Pastor Cardew. And, of course, he was nodding
his head in sanctimonious agreement.

She concluded her remarks by exhorting men and women to
come together to defend the great and noble ideal of women's
purity. 'If this must be done on the field of battle, then so be it.
If our menfolk must shed blood and lay down their lives to defend
this vital principle, then I say that there can be no nobler death.
And to the women here today, especially to those of my sisters
who marched beside me in the battle for suffrage, I say this.
Now is the time to join in a new fight. We cannot, by law, take
up arms in this battle. But we can do something else. We can
arm ourselves with Admiral Penrose-Fitzgerald's white feathers
and use them to drive our menfolk to do their duty by us.'

She received a reception of almost unanimous warmth, with
even some cheers and foot-stamping. It must have been an unusual
experience for a suffragist, Eve thought, whose meetings were
normally disrupted by opposing protesters and the police.

Next it was the turn of the admiral himself. He took off his
funny hat and placed it on his seat as he stood up. Eve had an
image of him sitting down on it after his speech, having forgotten
it was there. She held her hand over her mouth to hide her sniggers. Before beginning his remarks, Admiral Penrose-Fitzgerald
glowered at the audience fiercely, seeking out, she thought, the
young men who were not in uniform. She hoped he found Felix
Simpkins and sent his piercing gaze into his coward's eyes. His
clipped speech was peppered with stark warnings. 'The time for
words has passed. Now is the time for action. The nation is at
crisis point. The Empire is under threat. We stand poised on the
brink. Our fate is in the balance. Defeat or victory. This is no
time for shilly-shallying. There can be no place for skrim-shankers.
The enemy are barbarians. Be in no doubt. The fairer sex is in
peril. Purity must be defended. Every man who can must answer
the call. To fight. Men's duty is to fight. Women have a duty too.
To urge them on to the fight. The answer, white feathers.
Show them the feathers. Shame them into fighting.'

In the event, the admiral remembered his hat before taking his
seat, which Eve found strangely disappointing.

The final speaker, Mrs Humphry Ward, was more eloquent, but in essence her sentiments did not differ so much from Admiral Penrose-Fitzgerald's. She had the gift of presenting everything she said as a story, and so she engaged Eve's wandering attention more than the others had.

First there was the story of how the admiral had visited her to discuss ways in which our country's womenfolk might be enlisted in the war effort. They both agreed that women had a crucial role to play. In times of peace, a woman's part was to act as a civilizing influence on men, to temper their worst instincts and bring out the best in them. To provide comfort, support and companionship. It was true that a woman's inclination was to all things soft and gentle and pleasing. But this was a time of war. And war was most definitely not soft and gentle and pleasing. So women must put aside this role, and take up another. This was what she and the admiral had decided, apparently. Who came up with the idea of the Order of the White Feather, she could not say. The admiral was kind enough to say it was her idea. Certainly, she had reminded him of A. E. W. Mason's novel *The Four Feathers*, from whence their inspiration came.

That set her off on another story about the time Alfie, that is to say, Mr Mason, the author of the book in question, had visited her to tell her of his idea to create a detective who would be the very opposite in every way of Sherlock Holmes. She could not claim any credit for the creation of Inspector Hanaud of the Sûreté, but she remembered talking to him of a recent visit she had made to Paris and noted how his eyes had seemed to spark with the fire of genius as he listened to her.

Story followed upon story. Until she told the story of the young man who had forgotten his duty, who had fallen into soft and idle ways, who did not want to go to war because war was a frightful bore, and because it would take him away from his sweetheart. For, yes, this young man was in love. But fortunately, the object of his love remembered her duty, even if he did not remember his. She returned his blandishments and lover's words with a gift that some might think strange: a single white feather. The whiteness of the feather reminded him of her purity. The lightness of it reminded him of her vulnerability. The many fibres of it reminded him of all those who were depending on him. The effect on the young man was galvanic. He rushed off to enlist

that very instant. All it took to remind him of his duty was that
strange token from the girl he loved.

After the speeches there was a huddle of excited girls around
the table at the side of the stage. A young woman who not so
long ago might have been knocking policemen's helmets off
their heads was handing out the envelopes of white feathers. She
seemed to be enjoying herself immensely, doing her best imper-
sonation of a market hawker, even if it was a hawker with a
distinctly plummy accent: 'Get your feathers! Get your white
feathers!'

Eve pushed past her brother to get to the front of the queue.
'Good show! That's the ticket!' said the erstwhile suffragette as
Eve snatched up an envelope.

She could no longer see Felix Simpkins anywhere. He and his
mother must have slunk off as soon as the meeting came to an
end.

Eve barged her way through the clogs of people milling in the
side aisles. As she went, she took out one of the feathers and
hid it in a clenched fist, pushing the envelope into one of the
pockets of her coat. Mama had once sewn up her pockets because
she didn't like Eve putting things in them. She claimed it spoiled
the line. But Eve had simply unpicked the stitches. Some rebel-
lions were easier than others, and though they might go unnoticed,
they still afforded a secret satisfaction.

At last she made it to the main entrance and burst outside.
She caught sight of the two of them as they reached the bottom
of the church steps.

'Felix!'

He turned round sharply at her cry. She noted the transform-
ation in his face when he saw her waving to him. His face lit
up. He beamed at her. It was perfect.

His mother looked up too. It took a moment for the angry
scowl in which her face was set to lift. Eve could see the woman's
emotional gears shift as she put on her habitual mask of socia-
bility, a simpering smile with fluttering eyelids. It was horribly
affected and insincere.

The two of them waited for her to catch them up.

She kept her hand with the feather in it clenched at her side.

'Eve,' said Felix, as she stopped in front of him. 'How good
to see you.'

'Shall we not shake hands?' she asked.

He held out his hand. She clasped it with both of hers, transferring the hidden feather into his palm.

'There. That is for you,' she said, before leaving them speech-less at the bottom of the steps. She ran off along Shepherd's Bush Road. She did not, as yet, have any clear idea where she was running to. But she did not look back. She did not see him stare at the weightless insult in his palm. She did not catch the mute, uncomprehending appeal he cast towards his mother. Nor the resettling of an angry scowl on his mother's face.

She did not see him slip the feather wordlessly into his pocket.

PART IV
White Feathers

6 September–11 September, 1914.

A THOUGHT FOR TO-DAY.

> Sound, sound the clarion, fill the fife!
> To all the sensual world proclaim,
> One crowded hour of glorious life
> Is worth an age without a name.
> *Sir Walter Scott.*

Daily Mirror, *Monday, 7 September, 1914*

EIGHTEEN

S ergeant Macadam looked down at the body on the ground. He had seen worse, but still, a dead body is a dead body. And this one was young. Had probably been pretty too before someone crushed her nose and covered her face in bruises.

He heard a burst of laughter and looked up. DCI Coddington and his crony Inspector Leversedge were sharing a joke.

The two of them had already blundered in and trampled all over the crime scene. Even Inchball – who was not the greatest at the forensic side of the job – knew better than that.

'What you worrying about, man?' Leversedge had said. 'This is a public place. All sorts of people come through here. Especially today, Sunday. No point worrying about footprints, if that's what's bothering you. There'll be too many to make sense of.'

It was true, they were on Wormwood Scrubs, which was one of the most popular commons in London. However, the killer had chosen a secluded area of the Scrubs, a small triangular clearing surrounded by overgrown bushes towards the southeast corner. Most people kept to the paths and open fields. Perhaps the odd dog might wander in here, followed by its owner if it failed to respond to the usual whistles. Or it was the ideal spot for a game of Hide and Seek. Only, any children who played Hide and Seek here today would find more than they bargained for.

It was more than likely that the last person to have walked here, before the individual who found the body, would have been the killer.

None of this seemed to matter to Leversedge and Coddington, who were now blithely lighting up, with their backs to the crime scene. They were watching the comings and goings at the Royal Naval Air Station base. The big doors were in the process of being opened. Perhaps they would catch sight of an airship. It might even be brought out and take off.

Macadam shook his head. They were like children, easily distracted. And lazy, too. No doubt they would throw their dog ends into the undergrowth when they had finished smoking.

If only DCI Quinn were here.

Macadam imagined bringing his old governor up to speed.

'Do we know who she is?' Quinn would say.

'Eve Cardew. Aged eighteen. Daughter of the minister at Shepherd's Bush Baptist Church. Pastor Clement Cardew.'

'When was she last seen alive? By whom?'

'Yesterday, Saturday, the fifth of September. Last confirmed sighting was fifteen thirty, or thereabouts. There was a meeting at her father's church, which she attended. She was seen there by a number of people, but disappeared straight after. She did not return home and the family became concerned. Her father and brother, one Adam Cardew . . .' Macadam could imagine the governor's questioning eyebrow hike at that – Adam *and* Eve? '. . . went out to look for her. Father returned after three hours, without success, deeming it more useful to comfort his wife and alert the police. Adam did not return until after eleven p.m., having discovered her body here.'

This would no doubt arouse Quinn's suspicions. 'What made him think of looking here?'

'Apparently, this was a place they used to come when they were children.'

'Cause of death?'

'We're still waiting for the medical examiner. But there are no obvious wounds other than the bruising to her face and the broken nose. My guess would be that she was suffocated. Someone pressed down with considerable force to block her mouth and nostrils.'

Macadam tried to think what Quinn would do now. No doubt he would examine the ground for clues.

Some scraps of wood, a bit of torn tarpaulin and a yard of corrugated iron were propped up in the apex of the triangle to form a makeshift structure, an abandoned children's den perhaps, or the sleeping quarters of a tramp. The corrugated iron was rusted away in parts, the wood rotten and weathered, soaked through with countless storms, the tarpaulin in tatters. It gave every appearance of having been there since time immemorial.

The body lay in a line with the den, its head pointing towards the entrance.

There were no signs of the body being moved. It seemed a fair assumption that she was killed here.

He scanned the ground. He had the feeling of something snagging on his vision, so crouched down to look more carefully at the surface of the undergrowth. There it was. A single white feather, a few yards to the right of the body. Macadam glanced quickly at Leversedge and Coddington as he contemplated drawing their attention to the feather. He could imagine what they would say. 'A feather? What of it? There are birds around here, aren't there?'

Macadam took out his notebook and made a sketch of the crime scene, indicating the position of the feather relative to the body. He then produced a pair of tweezers and an envelope, items he was never without, and deftly picked up the feather, transferring it to the envelope.

He imagined Silas Quinn watching him as he worked, nodding quietly with approval.

But his old boss would go further than that, he knew. The dead always exercised a fascination over Quinn, and in every investigation he would spend time staring into the face of the victim, usually when they were laid out naked on a marble slab in the morgue. Quite why he did it, Macadam could not guess. Was he trying to bring about some kind of communion between the living and the dead, willing them to give up their secrets?

If so, it was a little too mystical and unscientific for Macadam's liking.

But still, Quinn was the best example of a detective that Macadam had to model himself on, so he gave it a go.

Her eyes were open. Staring straight ahead. She was looking whoever killed her in the eye. Reproachfully, as if storing up resentment. But fearlessly too, he would have said. From which he might tentatively conclude that the killer was known to her.

Her attacker was probably a man. No way of knowing for certain, of course, but it was a valid assumption given the way she had been overpowered, and the brute force that it must have taken to snuff out her life.

The medical examiner would tell them if she had been raped, but the arrangement of her clothes did not suggest it. Her skirt was not pulled up. The buttons on her light summer coat were all fastened. It was a strange rapist who tidied up his victim's clothing after killing her.

Her hair wasn't even in disarray.

Perhaps he had intended to rape her, but had accidentally killed her in the struggle.

Had she not cried out for help?

There was something about this, something not quite right, something that Silas Quinn would get to the bottom of in no time. This was right up Quinn's street, and no mistake.

Macadam looked across at the airship hangar, which was surrounded by a wire fence, topped with barbed wire. It must have been thrown up when the navy took the station over. The consequence was that there would have been few members of the public passing that way, and most of the men from the base would have been inside the hangar. Scrubs Lane ran on the other side of the bushes, and beyond that were the railway tracks, together forming the dividing line that cut Little Wormwood Scrubs off from the main parkland. Perhaps a train had gone past at precisely the moment of the attack, drowning her screams in its clatter? All things considered, it was not unfeasible that she had cried out but no one had heard.

Macadam turned back to examine the dead girl's face more closely.

Her mouth was open, no doubt in an effort to gulp in air.

She seemed about to cry out. As if she now regretted her earlier reticence. But it was too late now, of course.

Macadam felt the presence of someone standing at his shoulder. A quick glance confirmed there was no one there. He turned back to the body. That sense was still with him. He liked to think of it as Quinn, watching over him, making sure he didn't put a foot wrong.

Good Lord! The fellow wasn't dead. He could always go and consult him back at the Yard. He felt sure his old governor would take an interest in this case, especially as Leversedge already had it in mind to mark the file SFA, a decision which Coddington had approved. 'It makes sense, doesn't it?' Leversedge had insisted. 'What with the airship base right there. Poor girl stumbles on some German spy about his business and he's done her in. One for the military intelligence chaps.'

Perhaps they were right. But it was stupid – and lazy – to jump to the conclusion so quickly, before they had conducted their own investigation.

Again, he returned to the question: *What would Quinn do?*

But the dead girl refused to commune with him. The livid bruising on her face merely made him feel queasy, and he felt there was something vaguely indecent about her mouth being open like that. Leversedge and Coddington had made a smattering of ribald comments about it. If it ever got out how some coppers spoke about the dead, there would be a public outcry, and quite right too.

But he had to admit, he could not take his eyes off that mouth.

Perhaps the killer had felt the same way about it? Certainly the bruises around the nose and mouth, and the supposed method of dispatch, suggested a degree of fixation. It looked almost as if he had been trying to block it. Perhaps she had tried to scream, and it was his over-energetic efforts to silence her that had killed her.

If she had been killed by a foreign agent, wouldn't he have simply shot her, or cut her throat? He would have come armed with some weapon, for sure.

The fact (if he was right) that the killer had smothered the life out of her with his bare hands suggested that the whole business was improvised, unforeseen. Perhaps the result of a terrible accident.

Macadam dropped down to his haunches to get a closer look at her mouth. He took the tweezers out of his pocket and gently probed the small emptiness between her lips. It felt like a transgression, of course it did. He knew he should not be interfering with the body like this. In some ways, he was committing as serious an offence as Coddington and Leversedge had with their clodhopping about. Worse, perhaps, as this felt like a violation. But they had forced him to it. He could not leave it to them to manage the evidence in this case.

He pressed the flat of the tweezers down gently on the tongue. Rigor mortis had already set in, as he should have expected, given the likely time of her death. It always starts in the eyelids, spreading to the muscles of the jaw soon after. And so the tongue had become a resistant slab. He did not try to force the mouth, but instead moved round to kneel on the ground at the crown of her head so that he was looking down on to her tongue at an angle, at the same time allowing as much sunlight as possible on to her face.

He gasped when he saw what was lying there, almost on the

tip of her tongue: a single white feather, identical to the one he had found on the ground a moment before.

He resisted the impulse to remove the feather. It was enough that he knew it was there.

He took out his notebook to record his find and make a sketch of the position of the feather on the tongue.

He heard a twig snap, the stirring of foliage somewhere behind him to his left.

Macadam stood up slowly and pocketed his notebook and pencil. He looked over at Coddington and Leversedge. They were still watching the hangar. The big doors were open now, and a number of men in naval uniforms were milling about the entrance.

The thing to do was to take yourself by surprise too. To lull the other into thinking you weren't on to them, and then pounce.

He swung round in the direction the sound had come from. A figure, a man in uniform, khaki, not navy blue, was crouching in the bushes – not five yards away – watching him closely. The soldier remained as still as a plaster mannequin. There was something almost absurd about it. The two of them so close, close enough to have a civilized conversation without raising their voices, and one of them acting as if he were invisible.

The other fellow's face was partially hidden by branches. The strain of holding still caused the bush to tremble. From what Macadam could see, the soldier was young. His eyes, which peeped through one of the many gaps in the scrubby foliage, were fixed warily on Macadam. He struck Macadam as an unlikely soldier, but no doubt Kitchener's recruitment campaign had attracted a fair number of unlikely soldiers to the colours.

They stood looking at one another for some moments. Macadam even had time to take in the details of the brass badge on the soldier's cap. He recognized it as the flaming grenade of the Royal Fusiliers. It was just one of those scraps of knowledge he had picked up along the way.

It seemed to fall to Macadam to break the ice. 'I say, I wonder if I could have a word with you?'

The young man's eyes widened with alarm. He looked like the proverbial startled rabbit. An instant later, he was gone, leaving the scrawny branches shivering in his wake.

Macadam stomped through the bushes to give chase. A low wooden fence marking the perimeter of the parkland slowed him down even more. As he clambered over it, he saw the soldier run out across Scrubs Lane, narrowly avoiding the path of an oncoming collier's cart. Evidently, he was more afraid of an encounter with Macadam than of being trampled by a dray horse.

Macadam was cut off by a Model T speeding in the opposite direction. The driver honked his horn three times but did not slow down.

This gave the soldier enough time to scale the eight-foot chain-link fence that ran alongside the railway embankment. Macadam watched helplessly as the man dropped to the ground on the other side and disappeared into the thick greenery that grew there.

As he reached the other side of the lane, there was a sound like the bough of a dead tree cracking. At the same instant, it felt like an invisible assailant had punched him in the shoulder with a steel-gloved fist. Macadam looked down and saw a flower of blood blossom on his jacket.

He felt the unconscious tension that kept his body upright loosen its hold on his legs. They were all of a sudden all over the place. And the air was nowhere. He gasped in shallow breaths. His lungs lit up with a silent roar of pain. His heart went into spasm.

He sat down on the ground and tried to catch his breath as he felt his shirt front grow heavy, wet, clinging.

NINETEEN

Mary Ibbott came running into the drawing room waving a copy of the *Clarion* in front of her. 'Mummy! Mummy! Have you seen this?'

Mrs Ibbott was almost afraid to ask what it was that had caught her daughter's eye this time. Mary had taken to scouring the paper every day for news of Mr Hargreaves' regiment. Mrs Ibbott had pointed out that he hadn't even left the country yet, but was still at training camp.

This reasonable observation, which was intended to soothe, had provoked floods of tears. 'But why doesn't he write to me?'

'Naturally, he doesn't write to you, Mary. It would be very

wrong of him to write to you. He writes to his wife. And so, all we need do is ask Mrs Hargreaves, if we are ever desirous for news of Mr Hargreaves.'

'Oh, but she won't tell me anything. She hates me!'

'Mary! How dare you say such a thing? It's nonsense and you know it.'

Mrs Ibbott had hoped that taking Mary to the Purity Meeting would calm her down somewhat. With any luck, it would restore in her a sense of propriety, though some days Mrs Ibbott had to wonder if her daughter had ever possessed such a thing. That's why she had been so keen for the pastor to speak to Mary, though she had to admit that the interview had been somewhat disappointing. Admittedly, Mary had behaved rather rudely, hardly saying a word to the pastor, barely looking at him, her face as miserable as sin the whole time. But Pastor Cardew had seemed distracted too. His remarks were rather vague and inconsequential.

The meeting itself had turned out to be a very different affair from what Mrs Ibbott had expected. She had not realized there would be so much talk of the war, and so many military gentlemen in attendance. And she did not like the fact that there had been a suffragette on the platform, as Mary had informed her with glee. She had no argument with the aims of the suffrage movement. She considered it to be a matter of simple common sense that if a woman was expected to obey the laws of the country she ought to have a say in who made those laws. 'Men know best' was not a formula she ascribed to but neither was she convinced that the best way to get men to change their minds about this or any other matter was to go about throwing yourself under horses.

It seemed that some at least of those women who had formerly agitated for female suffrage had now put that struggle to one side in the national interest, which was of course commendable. But Mrs Ibbott was not sure she could wholeheartedly approve of all this business with the white feathers. Granted, we needed men to fight in the war. But there was something rather nasty about it, she thought. What good was it shaming a man into doing the right thing?

She certainly didn't like the enthusiasm with which Mary had seized upon the wretched things. 'I shall give one to Timberley and one to Appleby!' she had cried, delightedly brandishing her little store of feathers.

'You shall do no such thing,' Mrs Ibbott had commanded.

'But why should Jack risk his life when those two cowards stay here counting their beetles or whatever it is they do?'

'Mr Hargreaves to you, I should think! And it is not for you to comment on what our gentlemen guests do or do not do. Do you hear?'

'But Mummy . . .'

'There is no *but Mummy* about it! If I hear that you have given one of those beastly feathers to Mr Timberley or Mr Appleby, I shall . . . well, I don't like to say what I shall do but I wouldn't like to be on the receiving end of it.'

Mary had pouted sulkily, clutching the envelope to her chest jealously, as if afraid her mother would snatch it away from her. But Mrs Ibbott was content that her daughter was sufficiently warned.

When they had got back to the house after the meeting, she had reminded her daughter: 'You are to leave Mr Timberley and Mr Appleby alone, is that clear?' Mary had taken off her toque and hung it up without comment, before thundering upstairs to her room. They had barely spoken a word for the rest of that day, or the next. When it came to bearing a grudge, Mrs Ibbott had to hand it to her daughter. At the same time she knew that Mary's seeming rebelliousness was simply her coming to terms with the fact that she would in the end comply with her mother's wishes. And Mrs Ibbott was wise enough to give her space to play out her pet.

Now it was Monday morning and Mary had come rushing in excitedly, their quarrel evidently forgotten. 'Look! She's on the front page!'

'Who is? What on earth are you talking about, Mary?'

'Eve Cardew. Pastor Cardew's daughter. She's been murdered!'

No, this couldn't be right. The girl had got it muddled, surely. But that was a picture of Eve reproduced on the front of the *Clarion*. And there was a picture of Pastor Cardew too, so there could be little doubt that the girl shown was Eve Cardew. But surely it was some other girl the headline referred to, some other parson's daughter: PARSON'S DAUGHTER FOUND DEAD IN PARK.

But no, the article confirmed it. The body of Eve Cardew had
been discovered in Wormwood Scrubs Park. The police suspected
foul play.

It was only now that Mrs Ibbott noticed the heading in slightly
smaller type beneath the main headline: POLICE DETECTIVE
SHOT. FIGHTING FOR LIFE.

'Oh, but Mary . . . this is horrible!'

Her first thought was that it was Silas Quinn. But it was some
other name in the account.

Mrs Ibbott could hardly take in what she was reading. First
there was the death of Eve Cardew. That poor girl. Although she
had to admit that her last memory of Eve was of her pushing
past them to get to the table where they were handing out the
envelopes of white feathers. She knew no good would come from
those damnable feathers.

'It says here that she was last seen alive at that meeting we
were at!' Mary's eyes widened in horror as she read the newspaper account.

'How awful!'

Mary shuddered. 'I always knew there was something funny
about that man.'

'What are you talking about, child?'

'Her father. He used to give me the cold creeps, I tell you. I
wouldn't be surprised if he done it himself.'

'Good heavens, Mary!' Mrs Ibbott told herself that it was
the shock of the discovery that had somehow set Mary off on
this regrettable raving. 'You must be very careful what you say,
dear. Especially when it comes to accusing people of things
like this, when there is no basis whatsoever. Pastor Cardew is
one of the most . . .' Mrs Ibbott paused to find exactly the right
word that would do justice to the pastor's goodness, '*saintly*
men there is.'

'He used to lick his lips when he looked at you.'

'But he can't have had anything to do with . . . this. It's simply
unthinkable.' Mrs Ibbott snatched the newspaper off her daughter.
'No, no, no. It says here that the police suspect the murderer
was a German spy whom Eve inadvertently interrupted as he
was gathering information on the RNAS base in Wormwood
Scrubs. There, you see, it's not Pastor Cardew.'

Mary pursed her lips sceptically. 'They say that, but what do they know? The police always get it wrong. That's why they need Sherlock Holmes to solve all their cases for them.'

'Oh, Mary, don't be ridiculous. I wonder if I ought to write to Inspector Quinn?'

'Write to old Quinn? Why would you do that?'

'Well, he may want to hear from people who were at the meeting on Saturday. We were among the last to see Eve alive, you know. We may have something important to say.'

'But I thought you said it was a German spy? If it was a German spy, what has the meeting got to do with anything?'

'That's for the police to decide. There may have been something about Eve's behaviour that might shed light on her death. She was awfully keen to get at those feathers, if you remember.'

'Yes, and I saw her give one to a chap outside the church.' Mary grinned at the memory. 'You should have seen his face.'

'Well, there, you see . . . if she's so all-out for the war, who knows, she might even have challenged the German spy when she found him. She was evidently a rather headstrong young lady, so perhaps . . .'

'Perhaps she mistook the German spy for a shirker and tried to give him a feather!'

'Oh, well, that is an interesting theory.' Mrs Ibbott returned to scouring the newspaper account for details.

'Who shot the policeman?' Mary wondered. 'Does it say?'

'No. It doesn't say very much about that, except that he is in a critical condition. That sounds jolly like a German spy to me, shooting policemen and everything.'

Mary's face suddenly lit up with excitement. 'Mummy! We should do it! We should solve the crime! We'd make a spiffing team, you know.'

For a brief moment Mrs Ibbott shared her daughter's enthusiasm. And then the absurdity – and danger – of the proposal hit her. 'This isn't a game, Mary. Someone's been murdered. And the police are getting shot at. Besides, we know nothing about solving crimes.'

'How hard can it be? If old Quinn can do it, anyone can!'

The child's youthful arrogance was provoking. 'No, we must leave it to the professionals.'

'Oh, you're no fun!'

At first, Mrs Ibbott thought that Mary had offered this rebuke

in a spirit of joshing. But then she saw the tears welling in
her daughter's eyes. A moment later, Mary ran from the room,
slamming the door on the way.

TWENTY

A line of ambulances was parked on Hammersmith Road
outside the West London Hospital. Quinn watched as a
stretcher was lifted out of the back of one of them, on
which lay a wounded soldier, still in his bloodstained and muddy
uniform. His face was wrapped in bandages, which were discol-
oured by the seeping matter from his wounds. The porters carried
him with great care, keeping the stretcher level, avoiding any
sudden movements, but at the same time moving with practised
speed. A doctor and several nurses were in attendance, supervising
the arrival of the wounded. It was an impressive scene. Quinn
was struck by the preciousness of the fragile body around which
they were all huddled. So much human activity to preserve one
life.

He turned to Sergeant Inchball, who was by his side. The
grim-set pallor of Inchball's face mirrored Quinn's mood.

Quinn tilted his head towards the entrance of the hospital.
Inchball nodded and the two men went in.

Macadam was being cared for in a private room just off the Acute
Ward. A soldier, presumably from MO5(g), stood on guard at
the door.

'They're taking no chances, I see,' muttered Inchball.

A ward matron, with a cap and apron so brilliant white and
starched that it almost skinned their eyes to look at her, came
out of Macadam's room. She challenged them with forbidding
disdain.

Quinn produced his warrant card.

'We have enough to contend with here with all the war
wounded without you policemen going around getting yourselves
shot.'

'How is he?'

'I shall ask the surgeon to speak to you. Mr Carter-Minton.'

Quinn felt chastened, and more than a little cowed, simply by the consultant's name.

All the same, the matron allowed them to go in.

Macadam lay propped up in bed with his eyes closed. Quinn was shocked by how grey and drawn his face looked. Something had been sucked out of him from within. His breathing was shallow and rapid; he seemed to be fighting for every breath. Other than that slight but desperate movement, his body was appallingly inert. His arms lay at his sides on top of the covers, as if they had been placed there.

Quinn felt a spreading blankness come over him.

It was left to Inchball to ask, in a barely audible murmur: 'What the Devil, Mac?'

A tremor flickered across Macadam's face, converging on one corner of his mouth, twitching it up into the suggestion of a smile. He flexed the fingers of his right hand. It could have been a reflex reaction to some unconnected nervous stimulus. Or it could have been an attempt at a wave.

'The governor's here too.'

'Hello, Mac.'

The sound of Quinn's voice seemed to revive Macadam a little. With a tremendous quivering struggle that put Quinn in mind of a carnival strong man straining at dumbbells, his eyelids began to lift. The injured man's eyes were revealed, swivelling like the glass balls in a doll's head.

His lips parted with a soft *puh!* that might have been an attempt at speech.

'Take it easy, old chap,' cautioned Inchball.

The eyes closed again. Macadam's mouth fell open and his breathing became louder and more erratic.

To Quinn, it seemed that their visit had done more harm than good. 'Perhaps we should leave him?'

But there was an answering movement from the bed. Macadam's head stirred in a minuscule side-to-side motion.

He managed to smack his lips once or twice and then his hoarse, rasping breath coagulated into a sound that seemed to carry in it some semblance of articulation. It was a difficult sound to listen to, being as pathetic as it was heroic. Quinn touched Macadam gently on the shoulder to quell it. Macadam's eyes opened again, this time with a desperate energy. His gaze locked on to Quinn pleadingly.

'Very well, old man.'

Quinn leant down and put his ear next to Macadam's mouth. He tapped him again on his arm encouragingly.

'What did he say?' demanded Inchball as Quinn straightened up. Macadam slumped down into his pillows after the effort of communication.

'White feather.'

Inchball gave vent to a violent oath. But before he could explain the meaning of his outburst, they were joined at the bedside by a man in a tweed suit, with a neatly trimmed beard and a gruff, no-nonsense manner. 'I hope you're not agitating my patient.'

'Your patient, my sergeant. I am Detective Chief Inspector Quinn of the Yard.'

'The poor fellow's not on duty now. For God's sake, cut him some slack. He took a bullet in the chest, you know.'

'How bad is it?'

'It's never good having a bullet shot into you, you know. Especially in the thorax. But, all things considered, he was lucky. It narrowly missed his heart, which is something. But the right lung has sustained severe damage. On top of all that, he lost a lot of blood.'

'He'll be all right, though?'

'He's not out of the woods yet but we're doing what we can. Draining the chest cavity to relieve the pressure on his lungs. Keeping a close eye on him. He's a fighter, I should say. Scrawny, lean, but tough.'

It was strange to hear Macadam described in those terms. Macadam was the self-taught intellectual, eager, curious, full of enthusiasms. A sensitive man, even, someone who would take a slight to heart but was always quick to forgive. Scrawny, lean, tough seemed to be describing a piece of meat rather than the man Quinn knew.

Macadam was not one to run in and take a bullet. Not that he was a coward. He had proven that on countless occasions.

Just that he was not a fool.

'Has he said anything to you about who shot him?'

Carter-Minton's eyes widened in outrage. 'Why the Devil would he say anything to me? He was under anaesthetic most of the time that I spent in his company. And I have made it clear in my instructions that he should be discouraged from speaking to anyone for the time being.'

'There are things we need to know, that only he can tell us.'

'Yes, yes, it's always the same with you policemen. But it will have to wait. The patient's survival is my priority. I have no objection to you sitting quietly with him and letting him know that you are there. But I shall tell Matron to throw you out if she sees you questioning him.' Carter-Minton gave a sharp nod, as if he were head-butting an imaginary antagonist. Then, with a slightly startled look in his eyes, left them to it.

Quinn looked down disconsolately at Macadam. If anything, the sergeant's breathing seemed more ragged than before. Every breath took its toll as it rattled through him.

'I wonder if Coddington and Leversedge have been here to visit him?'

Inchball gave a sardonic snort. 'Do you think?'

'What was it you were about to say? Before the doctor came along?'

'What?'

'I told you what Macadam had said and you looked like you had seen a ghost.'

'Nah, it's nothing. Just that I was given one of those blasted things this mornin' on the way in to the Yard. Some little chit of a thing handing them out when I was walking through Trafalgar Square.'

'Do you still have it?'

'I should say not! I sent her away with a flea in her ear, I did. Chucked the blasted feather away. Why should I hold on to a thing like that?'

'Why did she give *you* a white feather?' Quinn was genuinely confused. He knew that the white feather was meant to be a symbol of cowardice, but the idea of someone giving such a thing to Inchball was absurd.

'Have you not read about it in the papers? Some admiral started it all off in Folkestone. It's meant to shame young blokes into enlisting. The white feathers are chicken feathers, you see.'

Inchball made a noise like a clucking hen. 'She took me for a coward, that girl. The cheek of it! I gave her a piece of my mind, and no mistake.'

Quinn looked again at Macadam. There were questions he was desperate to ask him. But for now they would have to wait.

TWENTY-ONE

M ary Ibbott let out a curious sound, halfway between a snarl and a sob, as she threw herself down on her bed. The bedsprings creaked back at her sympathetically. Mary felt she wanted to cry, but the tears would not come. She buried her face in her pillow all the same. She often had the feeling that she was living her life under the gaze of a hidden watcher. Perhaps it was a relic of her years at Sunday school, an unconscious belief in God that Pastor Cardew had somehow instilled in her, after all. It left her feeling that she was an actor in a play. But the scenes never came off quite as she wanted them to. And the set decoration was positively tatty.

She felt herself over-heating. On top of that, the feather stuffing made her nostrils itch. She turned over listlessly on to her back and let out a loud sneeze. Aggh! She hated sneezes!

She opened her eyes to confront the unsatisfactory props and backdrop of her life. The insipid wallpaper with the twee posies of lilies of the valley. (Mary had once declared it to be her favourite flower, a passing whim now memorialized forever on her wall. She loathed the despondent drooping things.) The clashing chintz of the curtains, bedspread and armchair. The fussy lace covering on her bedside table. The china ornaments that she had once thought sweet, but which now struck her as infantile and embarrassing.

She wanted to smash them all up. To tear down the curtains and rip away the wallpaper.

She thought of the satisfaction it would give her, and the outrage it would provoke in her mother. She gave a little smile.

Maybe it would be worth the trouble.

Or maybe there was an easier way to get her own back at her mother.

There was one relic from her younger days that she could still tolerate, a wooden box with twelve drawers. In it she kept such items of jewellery as she possessed, together with other treasures and trinkets small enough to be housed within its tiny compartments.

The box was made of mahogany, inlaid with marquetry fleurs-de-lis on the top. When she was a child it had seemed to be such a sophisticated object, the kind of thing a lady would have to keep her secrets in. Each of the drawers was capable of being locked by a Lilliputian key. It was an operation of great delicacy and skill to insert the key into the lock and turn it.

She pulled out the middle drawer of the bottom row, revealing her hoard of white feathers. The feathers sprang up eagerly as if they had been waiting for release. She picked out two and pushed the rest down so she could close the drawer again.

Mary now opened one of the drawers in her dressing table. Rummaging through a hair-tangled melee of brushes, combs, brooches and hairpins, she pulled out a set of letter stationery, which she had bought herself from a shop in the Burlington Arcade with a half-crown her wealthy Aunt Leonora had given her last Christmas. She had got it especially for secret correspondence. Not even Mummy knew of the stationery's existence.

She took out one of the envelopes and slipped the feathers in before sealing it.

Should she address the envelope? There was no need, she decided. Those who received it would know it was meant for them.

Now she stood with her ear against the door, straining to hear over the thump of her own heart.

She bent down and unfastened the cloth uppers on her two-tone brogue boots, ten buttons each boot. She was immensely attached to the boots and liked to wear them at every opportunity. But the occasion demanded a certain degree of stealth. The heels would produce a tell-tale clatter.

Mary opened her bedroom door and tiptoed out on to the landing.

Timberley and Appleby lived on the floor below. It was morning. They would be getting ready to leave for work. There was a risk that they might come out just as she was executing her mission.

Of course, she could wait until they had left the house. But that would require too much self-control. She had conceived the plan to do this. She could tolerate no delay in executing it.

She reached the landing below and listened at their door. She could hear whistling. It was probably Appleby. How dare he whistle when Jack had gone off to fight and he was shirking here!

It was done in a moment, in less than a moment. A quick stoop and the envelope was pushed under the door, then she turned and ran upstairs again, her heart beating in time with her padding feet.

TWENTY-TWO

Quinn pushed open the door to Coddington's office without knocking.

Coddington looked up from behind his desk. His prodigious moustaches trembled like the whiskers of a startled walrus.

'Ah, Quinn, old chap! How are you?'

'Don't give me that old chap guff. What the Devil were you thinking, letting Macadam get shot like that?'

'Whoa, now! I did not *let* him get shot, as you so charmingly put it. He had his orders, which he disregarded. He was to watch the body and make sure no one approached it or tampered with it. My instructions were clear. He was not to move from that spot. If he had obeyed my instructions, he would not have got shot.'

Quinn doubted that Coddington had ever given any such orders, but he let that go to point out: 'And a possible suspect would have got away.'

'All he had to do was blow his whistle.'

The failure to blow the whistle was a mistake. And it was not like Macadam. Quinn suspected Macadam had as little faith in Coddington and Leversedge as Quinn himself did, and had preferred to trust to his own initiative. Perhaps he had not considered himself in danger. There must have been something about the suspect that had lulled Macadam into a false sense of security. Even the best coppers make mistakes.

Naturally, Coddington was quick to make personal capital of it. 'I put it down to poor training by his previous CO. I can't begin to tell you what bad habits those ex-SCD officers have got into.' Coddington shook his head sadly. 'I can't do a thing with them.'

'They're better officers than you'll ever be, Coddington.'

'Is that so, DCI Quinn? Well, thank you for sharing your opinion with me, but you really must excuse me. I have work to do. Proper police work. Not just writing notes in the margins of other chaps' reports.'

'I need you to share with me everything you have on the murdered girl.'

Coddington threw back his head and let out a curious rasping sound. It was a moment before Quinn realized he was laughing.

'Oh, you're a card, Quinn. A real card.' Coddington's great display of amusement turned into a sudden expression of grave concern. It was quite a performance. 'But, no, you're serious, ain't you?'

'One of my men is lying in hospital.'

'Sergeant Macadam is one of my men, I'll have you know.'

'And that's the reason he got shot.'

'Get out of my office, Quinn. You will see the file at the appropriate time. Which is to say, when you can't do a fucking thing about it.'

Quinn held his ground for a moment longer, wondering whether there was anything else he might be able to say to bring Coddington round. But the arrival of Coddington's crony, Leversedge – 'Everything all right here, guv?' – persuaded him to leave it. It was hard enough talking to one idiot, he decided.

'I wish to see Sir Edward.'

Miss Latterly took her time in looking up from her typewriter. Her gaze was blank and unfocused. She looked round Quinn and through him, before finally acknowledging his presence with a frown.

'That won't be possible.'

'I am willing to wait, if he has someone with him at the moment.'

'He'll not see you.'

'Ah, so you do know who I am. I thought for a moment—'

'Why wouldn't I know who you are?'

'I don't know. You seemed not to recognize me.'

'Well, it has been a long time since I saw you.'

Quinn waited a moment before trying to explain himself. It was never going to be an easy undertaking. 'I . . . know that I . . . should have . . . spo—'

'No! You can't come here, now, like this, and start . . . no!'

'No.' He saw her point. 'I should have come before.'

'If you have come here to see Sir Edward, you have not come here to see me.'

'I have been afraid.'

She looked at him in disbelief. 'Of me?'

'No. Of myself.'

'This is ridiculous. And nonsense. And I won't have it. I simply forbid you to—'

'I have been on my own for so long.'

'And that's the way you like it, is it?'

'No. But . . . I don't think I would be any good at living any other way.'

'What on earth does that mean? Any other way!' She was contemptuous.

'I admit it . . . I was to blame . . . I backed away . . . Because . . .'

'I forbid you to talk of it!' The force of her anger was shocking. He flinched away from her glare. In a barely audible whisper that nevertheless snapped hold of his attention, she added: 'Here.'

He turned a look of appeal on her. 'Where then?'

'I don't know!'

'We could try again. A . . .' Quinn gave a nervous nod to indicate a vast range of possibilities. 'But . . . would Aunt Constance have to come?'

'No.'

He didn't know whether that 'No' was a refusal of his invitation or a reassurance that Aunt Constance would not be there.

'If you're saying all this just to get to see Sir Edward . . .'

'No, that's not it at all.'

'It won't do you any good. You report to Assistant Commissioner

Thompson now. That's what he said. Whatever you might want to say to Sir Edward, you should take to the assistant commissioner.'

'Sergeant Macadam has been shot.'

'Yes, I heard. I'm sorry.'

'I want to be put in charge of the investigation.'

'Sir Edward can't help you. His hands are tied. This war has got everyone jumpy. And I hate to say it, but at this moment in time, your enemies are more powerful than your friends. The only way you'll get what you want is if your enemies wish it.'

'My enemies have me right where they want me.'

The look she gave him softened. If it was not enough to give him hope, it at least encouraged him to believe that she was not one of those enemies.

TWENTY-THREE

St James's Park had been turned into a military camp. A squadron of soldiers was being put through its paces by a hoarse NCO. In another part of the park, bloodcurdling cries went up as trainees lunged at sandbags hung from makeshift wooden frames with fearsome bayonets. Officers with their canes tucked under their arms strode purposely about everywhere. There was the sense of a tremendous effort being made – an effort to keep busy while waiting for the real action. Every order was barked at full voice. Every boot came down with a decisive stomp. Steps were hurried. Eyes were eager. The air crackled with the energy of fighting men held back from the fight.

Quinn and Inchball walked in silence. Five minutes earlier, Quinn had caught his former sergeant's eye and signalled for him to meet him outside. Inchball's nod of acknowledgement had been minimal.

They came to Horse Guards Parade, where a marquee had been erected to deal with the rush of men to enlist. The recruiting office at Old Scotland Yard was struggling to cope. There were reports of men waiting eight hours without being able to get in. Even now there was a long line of men queuing outside the marquee.

The two police officers stopped for a moment and watched.

'I've been thinking,' said Inchball.

'You're going to enlist?' said Quinn.

'I don't see how I cannot.'

'It's that feather's got to you.'

'No. I was already thinking about it before she gave it me. After the news came in of Mons. Our boys are dying in their droves out there. I can't stand by.'

'You have a duty here.'

'What? Enforcing DORA regulations? Teaching the public how to queue at bus stops?' This had indeed been a duty that some bobbies had been called upon to fulfil.

'I was thinking more of Macadam.'

'I haven't forgotten about Mac.'

'Well?'

'I won't do anything until we've caught the bastard who shot him.'

'It's going to be up to you, Inchball. You know that, don't you?'

'Me?'

'I don't hold out much hope of Leversedge and Coddington cracking the case, do you?'

'You can't leave it to them, guv. You're going to have to take it over.'

'I can't get near it. I'm what you might call *persona non grata*. They're edging me out.'

'But Mac was your sergeant!'

'Cuts no ice. He's not my sergeant now. I want you to get yourself on the case.'

'That shouldn't be a problem. They're pulling in officers left, right and centre. One of our own goes down, it's what happens. Then there's the foreign agent angle.'

'That still the line they're pursuing?'

'Only line they've got.'

'Have they spoken to the family?'

'They've taken statements. Nothing significant has come to light, as far as I know. Family's in a terrible state, as you'd expect. It's hit them like a bolt from the blue. Mother's in bits. Has been since the girl went missing, from what I hear. Father's trying to hold it together but I'm told the strain's beginning to show even on him. She had a brother too. Twins, they were, apparently. It's hit him specially hard. He's the one who found her, see. So, you can imagine. Father's a Baptist minister. Pillar of the community and all that. Not the sort of family this kind of thing happens to. That's what people are saying.'

'What family is?'

Inchball looked at his former boss closely without answering.

'I need you to be my eyes and ears on this.'

Inchball nodded.

'I can't just sit around waiting for them to share the file when it suits them. By then it will be too late. Leads will have been lost.'

'Whatever you need.'

The red-faced screams of a sergeant major drilling some ragged squaddies into shape drew their attention.

Inchball consulted his pocket watch. 'Are you heading back?'

'You go. It's better we're not seen together. Better for you. Besides, I have an appointment.'

The two men nodded, one in confirmation, the other in appreciation, and went their separate ways.

Quinn took his seat in the nondescript room in the Admiralty.

'I need to speak to Kell.'

Commander Irons let out a deep sigh. 'That's not how this works.'

'I was told my contact would be Kell.'

'No. You were never told that. You *might* have been told that your contact would be Kell or A. N. Other intelligence officer.'

'I have not seen Kell once.'

'There has been no need. I tell Lieutenant-Colonel Kell everything that he needs to know.'

'I thought he was Major Kell?'

'He's been promoted.'

Quinn shook his head in frustration. 'What is the point of all this?'

'Our work has a vital role to play in the war effort.'

'One of my officers has been shot.'

'Yes, I heard about that. My understanding was that he was a *former* officer of yours.'

'I have to be put in charge of the investigation. You need to tell Kell that.'

'The allocation of officers within the CID is a matter for the police authorities alone.'

'You could make it happen, if you wanted to.'

'It's outside our bailiwick.'

'There are briefings occurring to which I am not invited. MO5(g) and the CID are working together without me.'

'And what? They are talking about you behind your back? Listen to yourself, Quinn. Do you know what you sound like? You sound like a man who has just come out of a lunatic asylum. My advice to you: stop thinking the world is against you. That it's you versus every bugger else. It's not. It's us versus Germany. You have a role to play. Play it.'

'I can be useful to the investigation.'

'You're not a soldier, are you? Never have been?'

'No.'

'Thought not. A soldier doesn't question his orders.'

'I'm a policeman. A detective. A detective questions everything.'

'There is a war on, you know. That's all that bloody matters, when it comes down to it.'

Quinn took a moment to consider Irons' point of view. He suddenly saw that as far as the authorities were concerned, it didn't matter who'd actually killed Eve Cardew, or even who had taken a potshot at Macadam. What mattered was whether the crimes could be used to manipulate public sentiment against the Germans.

There was no room for detectives in war.

But still. It was not in Quinn's nature to let this go unchallenged. 'My understanding is that the officers investigating the case are pursuing the theory that this is the work of a foreign agent. A German spy, I suppose.'

'It's an eminently valid theory.'

'There is no evidence for it.'

'That's the police's job. To find the evidence.'

'We usually approach cases with more of an open mind.'

'Really? You don't just round up the usual suspects, pick the likeliest and fit him up for it?'

'Other officers may employ such methods, I do not.'

'No? You're far more likely to shoot the suspect dead before he is able to answer whatever questions you may have to put to him.'

'You're a soldier. You know how it is.'

'It's not for me to teach you your job, Quinn. I'm sure you're a perfectly decent detective. But you have to understand, the world does not revolve around you. There are other concerns at work here of which you know nothing. Of which you can never know. You are a cog, and a cog's job is to rotate when subject to external force. Is that understood?'

Quinn turned his head sharply as if he had been slapped. He stared in mute appeal at the blank wall opposite.

TWENTY-FOUR

Timberley looked down at the fine white feather in his palm. If he didn't look at it, he wouldn't know it was there, so weightless and insubstantial was it. A thing of nothing, spun from nothing. And yet when he looked at it, the weight of it was unbearable. He felt its cold, dark gravity somewhere inside him, oppressing his heart with a burden of shame. He did not think *how could she have done this?* He did not think she was cruel. His only thought was the one that he gave voice to now: 'We have to do it. And we have to do it today.'

'Of course, I agree, without question.'

'We'll go together. Enlist in the same regiment. That will be bully.' Timberley sensed some constraint – reluctance even – in his friend's demeanour. 'What is it?'

'Nothing . . . only . . . I had thought of applying for a commission.'

'Well, of course, you must do whatever you think is best for you. But I think it's nobler somehow to serve in the ranks as a regular soldier. I don't think I'm officer material, Appleby. But if some chap tells me what to do, I'll do it all right.'

'No, yes, you're right.'

'Besides, I can't put it off any longer. If you want to apply for a commission, go ahead. I shall not. I intend to become a soldier today.'

Timberley saw the look of calculation come over Appleby. He knew what he was thinking all right. It all came down to one question. Who would steal a march on whom when it came to Mary?

No doubt she would look favourably on an officer. But applying for and receiving a commission would take time, and was by no means a certain endeavour. The one who enlisted today would gain the immediate advantage. There was also the romanticism of the gesture to be taken into account. For a young man of good background, from a good public school, Oxford-educated to boot, to volunteer to serve as a regular soldier in the ranks was akin to joining the Foreign Legion.

Appleby must have come to a similar conclusion. 'You're absolutely right. We'll go today. No moment like the present. That's what I say.'

Timberley was glad. On the whole, he would rather have his friend there with him. And if they could get themselves in the same battalion, so much the better. 'I say, Appleby, this isn't about Mary, you know.'

'God, no!'

'Well, in one way it is, I suppose.' Timberley felt himself blush. Some truths were hard to own up to. 'I mean, I know she was the one who shoved these damnable things under our door.' He continued to stare fixedly at the feather. 'I do so hate the idea of her . . . contempt. That is to say, I would prefer to know that she held me in some esteem. But it is too late for that, I fear.' Timberley broke off and was lost for a moment in silent contemplation. 'No, really, I'm doing this because I believe it is the right thing to do.'

'Yes, me too.'

Timberley slowly raised the hand holding the feather, as if he were lifting something of great value or weight. 'I have no . . . expectations. No hope. It is all the same to me whether I live or die. And so, I might as well fight.'

'There's no need to be so glum about it, Timbers, old chap.'

'I'm not glum, Apples. But one may as well face up to what one is getting into. And why.'

He slipped the feather into the breast pocket of his suit jacket.

*   *   *

It was rotten luck. But his beastly asthma flared up on the way to the recruiting office. The shortness of breath and the harshness in his lungs set off a coughing fit that left Timberley hot and weakened. The handkerchief he held in front of his mouth was sodden with mucus.

Timberley felt the first tightening of his chest when they called in at the Natural History Museum. Appleby reckoned it was only fair to give old Gahan notice of what they were intending. Besides, they couldn't just not turn up for work.

Several rooms in the basement of the museum were given over to the Department of Entomology for storing specimens and carrying out research work, dark, subterranean chambers which seemed somehow appropriate for the study of exotic beetles. The Endopterygota room was an Aladdin's cave for entomologists; each specimen tray glistened like a tray of gems in a Hatton Garden jeweller's shop. Sunlight never penetrated the walls. The exclusively artificial lighting gave the room a curious, almost magical atmosphere, as if it were a realm cast under a fairy spell. It was easy to become engrossed in one's work there, and lose track of time and what was happening in the outside world. The air was charged with a vertiginous energy. The dark wood tables were washed with a silvery glow. Their gravity and substance evaporated. On one of them, a tray of pinned specimens lay open. The beam from an electric light appeared to be transfixed by the garish colours of the beetles. It seemed to be communing with them, seeking to draw them up into the air. And they were on the cusp of taking wing.

An Irishman in his early fifties, Charles Gahan, Keeper of the Department of Entomology, was unexpectedly emotional. 'My boys! My boys!' he cried. 'For I think of myself as something of a father figure to you both. I must say, it is a sad day for me, but also a proud day. I confess, I was of the mind that you would better serve your country by staying here and dedicating yourself to your work; you, Mr Timberley, with Chrysomeloidea; and you, Mr Appleby, with your research into the diversity of Cupedidae. But reading the reports in *The Times* the other day has changed my mind. And when the lists came in, those terrible lists of the wounded and the missing and the dead, well, then I realized I could not be so selfish and keep you to myself. I must let you go if it came to it. And today, I see, it has come to it.'

His eyes were dewy as he shook their hands, holding on to them for as long as possible with both his hands and only letting go with great reluctance.

'You have my blessing, of course you do.'

It was at that point that Timberley felt the ratcheting sensation across his chest and the breath went from him as suddenly as if he had been punched in the solar plexus.

Emotion overwhelmed him. He told himself it was a mixture of pride and love and honour, if honour could be an emotion. But there was also a slight nagging sense of something that might have been disappointment. Had he secretly wanted Gahan to try to talk them out of enlisting? Was that part of their motive, so far unacknowledged, in coming to see their supervisor? Of course, they would have resisted his entreaties, but it would have added even more to the poignancy of the moment. And, who knows, he might have swayed them.

The acknowledgement of that shameful hope was another ratchet on the chain that was wound around his chest. Mary had been right to give him the feather. It was no more or less than he deserved.

He found it impossible both to speak and continue breathing. A chair was brought for him and he was encouraged to sit down.

'Are you well enough to do this?' asked Appleby. 'Perhaps we should wait a day?'

Timberley shook his head. 'Today,' he managed to wheeze.

The medicinal cigarette he smoked on the top deck of the number 9 bus gave some short-lived relief, but a second attack of coughing nearly finished him off.

At the sight of the crowds of men milling on Horse Guards Parade, the tightness in his chest returned. There was something humbling about it, so many men with the same intent: to sign up to fight for their country. At the same time, it was the moment that their intentions became reality.

They had to stand in line for two hours before they made it into the marquee. Timberley took advantage of the delay to smoke a couple more cigarettes, although he had to abandon the second as it provoked another bout of coughing.

They were given a critical once-over by a red-headed sergeant major, who did not seem overly impressed by the sight of them, nor by the sacrifice that their presence implied. It seemed to be all the same to him whether they joined the army or not, which Timberley had to confess he found rather discouraging. He had imagined that they would be welcomed with open arms and lavished with rapturous praise. Instead, they were told to sit at one of the long tables to fill in the forms he gave them.

When Appleby raised his hand to say they had finished their forms, the sergeant major answered him sarcastically, 'Aren't you the clever one!' which Timberley had to say he found unnecessary. But he supposed there was a point to the fellow's rudeness.

Eventually, they were told where to go to see the doctor for the medical examination. Timberley felt a fresh spike of abrasiveness inside his lungs.

He let Appleby go first and watched nervously as his friend was weighed and measured. He then read rows of letters of diminishing size off a card, before having his chest listened to through a stethoscope.

'You'll do,' pronounced the doctor, signing him fit to serve on his form. 'You can wait there for your friend, if you like, then you can both be sworn in together.' He turned blandly to Timberley. 'Your turn now.'

The doctor's concerned frown at Timberley's audible breathing was the first sign that all was not well. The second was that he chose to listen to Timberley's lungs before he did any of the other tests. 'Have you seen a doctor about that?'

'About what?'

'Well, you're wheezing quite atrociously, you know.'

'It's a spot of asthma. It's never too bad. This morning perhaps a bit worse than usual. But . . . uh . . .' Timberley was unable to finish the sentence.

'I'm terribly sorry, but I can't sign you fit. Not only that, I recommend that you see your own doctor at the soonest opportunity. Do you have a cough with it?'

'Not usually.' But his treacherous lungs gave the lie to his assertion and he began coughing again.

'Any sputum with the cough?'

As the question was asked, Timberley held his already damp handkerchief in front of his mouth. There was no point denying it now. He closed his eyes and gave a barely perceptible nod.

'Any blood in the snot?'

Timberley shook his head, his eyes still closed.

'Let me see,' demanded the doctor.

Reluctantly, Timberley held open the handkerchief.

One sinister strand of red, like a fibre from a frayed ribbon, lay in the dead centre of the cotton square. 'In all honesty, I have never seen that before.'

'I'm sorry, but we can't have you in the army. You understand, of course.'

Timberley squeezed his eyes closed tightly. When he opened them, he felt the sting of tears.

'Bad luck, Timbers,' said Appleby quietly.

Timberley did not want to discuss it. Luckily, Appleby was sensitive enough to realize this, or perhaps it was simply that he could think of nothing to say to his friend.

And so they rode back to the Natural History Museum in silence. Appleby thumbed the shiny new shilling in his pocket, resisting the temptation to take it out and look at it. He contented himself with imagining how it would glint as he held it up to catch the sunlight.

When they got off the bus outside the Albert Hall, Appleby at last ventured to say: 'You should take the rest of the day off, you know. You really don't seem well at all, old man. I dare say Gahan would understand.'

'No, no. It's nothing.' And indeed his asthma attack seemed to have passed now that the crisis had been reached. 'I think it's only fair to let old Gahan know that I won't be leaving him after all.'

'I'm sure he'll be—'

'Don't say it.'

Gahan was surprised to see them back. 'What's this?'

'I failed the medical,' said Timberley bluntly. 'So you're stuck with me for a while longer, I'm afraid.'

'Your asthma, was it?'

Timberley nodded.

'And you, Appleby?'

'Oh, I'm in. They didn't have a uniform for me but I've sworn the oath and taken the shilling.' He contrived to make it sound as though he were the unlucky one. 'All that's left to do now is wait for the call-up. May as well make myself useful in the meantime, what?'

Gahan gave Timberley a sympathetic smile, pitying really, before drifting away back to his work in quiet embarrassment.

'You shouldn't have listened to me. You should have applied for a commission as you originally intended.' Timberley's resentment had turned into a despondent fatalism. If Appleby was going to get the girl, he may as well do so as an officer.

'No, this way is better. I . . . I just wish to serve.'

'How noble you sound.'

'You would have been the same.'

'How she will despise me now.'

'No! She's not like that! She's . . .'

'You mustn't tell her.'

'What?'

'About the reason.'

'Your asthma, you mean?'

'It's not asthma, Apples. Didn't you see the look on that doctor's face?'

'You don't know. You have to get it checked out, as he said.'

'Yes, yes . . . all in good time. I don't want her to know, though. I don't want her to think me more of a weakling than she already does.'

'Then what will you say to her?'

Timberley shrugged. 'Let's say it was my eyesight. I don't want her pity, you see. I'd rather have her contempt than her pity.'

'But that's . . . ridiculous!'

'Promise me, Apples.'

Appleby's discomfort showed in a deep frown. 'It doesn't seem quite fair, you know. As if you're testing her. Provoking her to be . . . cruel.'

'Do you think she will be cruel?'

'Not if she knows the truth.'

'It won't matter. I won't hold it against her. In a way, I sort of think I deserve it.'

Appleby shook his head, still not convinced. 'It rather smacks of bad faith, if you ask me.'

Timberley snapped: 'I just don't want her pity! Don't you understand?'

After a moment of shock at the force of Timberley's outburst, Appleby's expression became sealed off and distant. Something had struck home. The rift that now existed between them; the one who would go away to fight, and the one who would stay at home. He took his leave with a minimal nod, grim, silent and wounded.

Timberley immediately regretted his temper. But he knew that he would never be able to apologize for it. Indeed, he wondered if he would ever be able to look his friend in the face again.

And the thought of seeing Mary that evening appalled him.

PART V
Arrest

14 September–16 September, 1914.

PATRIOTISM is a splendid thing, and I would be the last to belittle it, but I do think it might take another form than badgering poor inoffensive Germans just now.

I know, and have known (by sight) for some years, an old German who keeps a little tailor's repair shop in our high road. A more inoffensive man there could hardly be, and he certainly does not look over-prosperous.

Yesterday morning I was told, and saw, that "patriots" had shown their disapproval of his nationality by absolutely wrecking his place the night before. The poor old man was staring at his broken windows and torn blinds with an absolutely bewildered air, and the grins of passers-by did not help him.

If these enthusiasts are so filled with the martial spirit, let them go and enlist and find some outlet in serving their country by fighting a worthy foe. These poor fellows cannot help their nationality, and probably most of them would be Englishmen to-morrow if they could.

NOT PRO-GERMAN.

Letter to Daily Mirror, *September, 1914*

TWENTY-FIVE

'This is for you!'

Leversedge hefted a large sack on to Quinn's desk with a gleeful disregard for anything else on it. It landed with a soft thump.

'What's this?'

'Tip-offs. The assistant commissioner wanted you to have them.'

'Tip-offs?'

'Letters received from members of the public reporting the suspicious activities of suspected German spies.'

'And what am I supposed to do with them?'

'You can stuff them up your arse as far as I'm concerned.'

By the time Quinn had formulated a suitable riposte, Leversedge was gone.

Sergeant Inchball came over. 'What you got there, guv?'

Quinn took out his penknife and slit the top of the sack. He pulled out a sample letter, opened it and began to read: '*The man who is renting the house across the road from us at number 27 is a German spy. I have seen pigeons make a beeline for his house and depart again soon after. He moved in on the day the war was declared. If that ain't suspicious I don't know what is. He comes and goes all hours. I seen the light go on and off in his bedroom three times last night. Like as not he was signalling. We live on the ridge of a hill so the signals could be seen for miles I shouldn't be surprised. I have heard of German spies signalling to the fleet in the North Sea.*' Quinn looked across at Inchball and raised an eyebrow. 'The address given is Tulse Hill. Do you think you can signal to the North Sea from Tulse Hill?'

Quinn pulled out another letter.

'You're like Jack Horner with his plum puddin'!' observed Inchball.

'*On Tottenham Court Road, I saw a woman with a foreign accent bend down and address a German sausage dog. She was petting it and stroking it for a long time and talking to it in a very quiet voice. I couldn't hear what she said but I think it might have been foreign. She had every opportunity to attach a message to the dog in some way. I could not see for sure but why was she talking to it for so long? She then went into a cafe where they sell foreign pastries.'*

Inchball gave a loud guffaw at that. 'Give me five minutes with that sausage dog and I'll get the truth out of it.'

Quinn drew another letter out of the sack and glanced at it distractedly.

'Oi, guv, I thought you might like to know. I got myself on the investigation, like you said. And, erm, I've had sight of the ME's report.'

Quinn looked up, suddenly alert. He dropped the letter he had been scanning and nodded for Inchball to go on.

'Asphyxiated, she were. Signs of pressure applied to her chest. Broken ribs. Bruises to her face. Her nose was in a right state. The cartilage was detached and pushed in. Probably some fella sat on her, he thinks, and forcibly covered her mouth and nose to suffocate her. Poor mite.'

'Any sign of sexual activity?'

'She wasn't raped, if that's what you mean. She wasn't a virgin either.'

'Anything else?'

'He found a small white feather in her mouth.'

'I see. And what are they making of that, Detectives Coddington and Leversedge?'

'They say she could have breathed it in on the air, for all they know.'

'It was placed there.'

'Of course it was. What do you suppose it means, guv?'

'It means the killer wanted to send a message.'

'Just like the fella at number 27 switching the light on and off?'

'In a manner of speaking, yes.'

'One other thing, guv. You'll be glad to hear Mac's on the mend.'

Quinn felt a wave of relief. 'Has he been able to say anything more about the man who attacked him?'

'He's been able, but he won't, is what I'm hearing.'

Quinn leant forward in his seat. This was not like Macadam at all.

Inchball nodded, acknowledging Quinn's surprise. 'He's refusing to talk to Leversedge and Coddington. Insists there's only one detective he'll talk to.'

'Who's that?'

'You, of course, you ninny! Who did you think it was?'

'I've heard nothing of this.'

'Of course you ain't. They ain't gonna give you the satisfaction. They're saying Macadam can't remember, not that he won't say. They'd rather have the case turn to shit than have you solve it for them. Besides, what does it matter? They'll haul in the first sausage-eater they find and pin the girl's murder on him. In the meantime, they want me to work on Mac to get him to say what he saw.'

Quinn cast a wary glance across the department. Coddington and Leversedge were ensconced in Coddington's office with the door closed. 'Do they not think that I will visit him in hospital? As a friend.'

'It doesn't occur to them to do it. So they do not see why you should.' Inchball gave a wry smile. 'One other thing, guv. I'm not the only officer on the team what thinks they're a waste a' space. You got more friends in CID than you realize.' With that, and a conspiratorial wink, Inchball moved on.

For some reason, Quinn found that last revelation more troubling than reassuring. If he had friends, why did he not know who they were? The conclusion was that it would be damaging to the career of any officer who openly supported him.

Quinn consulted his pocket watch. It was an hour before the end of his shift, but he was left to his own devices so much these days that no one would notice – and certainly no one would care – if he took himself off early.

Quinn held out the bag of Cox's Pippins that he had picked up at a fruit stall just outside the hospital. 'There were no grapes to be had.'

Macadam gave a minimal tilt of his head towards his bedside table, where Quinn deposited the gift. Nothing more was said about it.

Macadam was still propped up on a bank of pillows. It appeared that he had not moved since the last time Quinn had seen him. Possibly he was no longer capable of movement. His face was every bit as grey and drawn as before. If anything he looked weaker and sicker than before, with dark crescents smudged in heavily under his eyes. He appeared exhausted by his recent brush with mortality. It seemed to have added ten years at least to his age.

'You certainly gave us a scare,' said Quinn, taking a seat at the bedside.

'I was a bloody fool.'

Quinn could not help rippling one eyebrow in surprise. The oath was unlike Macadam. 'You're beginning to sound like Inchball. Then there's your recent insubordination. What's this I hear about you refusing to talk to anyone except me? Are you sure you didn't sustain a blow to the head in the incident?'

'Well, what's the point of telling them anything? What they don't understand, they ignore. You know about the feather in her mouth?'

'Yes.'

'I spotted that.'

'Yes, I know. You tried to tell me about it, I think.'

'They said she could have breathed it in!'

Quinn gave a non-committal shrug. 'It's possible, I suppose.'

'Please! You know that she was at a meeting earlier on the day she was murdered? They were giving out envelopes of white feathers to young ladies there.'

'You think she was killed by someone who was at the meeting?'

'I'm not saying that, sir. But here's the thing; I found another feather on the ground nearby. What do you think of that?'

'I think it's very interesting.'

'Here's what I think. She took the feathers there with her. We can assume she took a packet of the things at the meeting.'

'Do we not know?'

'Well, they haven't asked, have they? They don't think it's important. There are lots of birds in Wormwood Scrubs, they say. A passing feather could have blown into her mouth on the breeze just before she was killed. I mean, did you ever hear such nonsense?'

Quinn thought carefully. 'I cannot say that I have.'

'Apparently Leversedge heard of it happening to an aunt of his once. So there you have it. That must be what happened.'

'Very well. Let's assume she took the feathers there.'

'Well, don't you see, sir? Maybe she tried to give it to her murderer and he didn't like it. So he killed her. Shall I tell you why he didn't like it?'

'Why?'

'Because he was a soldier.'

'I don't understand.'

'The man who shot me was in uniform, sir. He's a private in the British army.'

'I still don't understand. In fact, I understand less. If he's a soldier in uniform, why did she give him the feather?'

'Well, he was in uniform on the Sunday. She was killed on the Saturday. He might have been in mufti that day. It's an easy mistake to make. She sees a soldier out of uniform and assumes he is a shirker.'

Quinn pursed his lips. 'I don't know, Macadam. It doesn't make sense to me. If you were a soldier and some girl gave you a white feather, wouldn't you just shrug it off? You might be annoyed, angry even. But you wouldn't kill her for it.'

Macadam appeared crestfallen. He sank back perceptibly into his pillows. 'You're right of course, sir. How could I be so stupid? I just got carried away, lying here in this bed, stewing in my own juices. I was so sure Coddington and his pal were the fools that I made an even bigger fool of myself.'

'Can you give a description of the soldier who took a potshot at you?'

'He was very young, I remember that. He seemed little more than a boy. Must have been eighteen or so, I would say. Fresh-faced, slight of build. I'd be surprised if his face had felt the razor much as yet. His uniform didn't fit him so well. A bit loose on the shoulders, but maybe that's to be expected. He looked fright-ened more than anything. I would not have supposed him capable of shooting anyone.'

'It is always when they are frightened that they are most dangerous. You didn't happen to notice what regiment?'

Macadam's face lit up. 'I did! I'd forgotten that I did, but I did. I got a good look at his cap badge while we were staring each other out through the bushes. Royal Fusiliers, it was.'

'That's good. We can make enquiries at the regimental head-quarters. A young man such as you describe must be a recent recruit. Perhaps we could even arrange a line-up, when you are fit enough.' It sounded simple enough, and it gave Quinn some satisfaction to think that he knew something Coddington did not. His satisfaction was short-lived, however, as an unwanted thought clouded his optimism.

'What is it, sir?'

'We'll have to hope he hasn't been shipped out to the front already, or off to a training camp somewhere in the country. If you knew you were about to be shipped out, it might make you more trigger-happy. The war is a great way for criminals to evade justice.'

'Damn! I'm sorry, sir. I should have said sooner.'

'It's not your fault, Macadam.'

'But perhaps I should have agreed to speak to Inspector Leversedge, after all. He would have jogged my memory like you did.'

'I doubt it.' Quinn fell silent. He was pondering how best to proceed. If it did turn out to be a serving British soldier who had murdered Eve Cardew, it would not play well in the press. It was not the narrative his contacts in MO5(g) were looking for.

Another thought suddenly occurred to Quinn. 'Tell me, did you see the gun?'

'No. When he shot me, he was hidden behind the bushes that screen the railway tracks.'

'But if it had been a rifle you would have seen it before then?'

'A rifle? It wasn't a rifle. It was a revolver, according to the chaps in forensics. They have identified it from the bullet they pulled out of me as a .455 calibre Webley service revolver. Why did you think it was a rifle?'

'Well, you said he was a private. A private would be armed with a rifle, if armed at all. The Webley service revolver is an officer's weapon. What on earth was a private doing with that?'

'Perhaps he stole it.'

It was an interesting suggestion. After all, if the man was capable of murder, he was surely capable of lesser crimes too. Quinn was about to make the point to Macadam when he noticed that the sergeant's eyes had fallen closed. He listened for

Macadam's laboured breathing to settle into the regular rhythm of sleep before stealing away with a backward, wistful look at the bag of apples.

TWENTY-SIX

Quinn dined in a Lyons teashop on Pentonville Road, close to his hotel. He had made little effort to find a permanent place to live. In some ways, despite its obvious shortcomings, the hotel suited him. And the longer he stayed there, the more it suited him. You can get used to anything eventually, he told himself.

He dined alone, of course. Quite often, he chose exactly the same dish on the menu: the mutton pie with Russian salad. He might briefly fantasize about bringing Miss Latterly here. He could see them sitting opposite each other, chatting easily about all manner of strangely unspecified things.

Before he knew it, he had finished his meal, so he supposed he had better go back to his hotel.

He drank the last swill of cold tea from his cup and left money for the Gladys. The same amount he left every night.

The evening was coming on. The darkness that would soon engulf the streets was beginning to make its presence felt. For now, it was just a sinister potential hanging in the air.

With the outbreak of the war, the tops of the glass globes on the street lights had been painted black. As a consequence, the nights were darker than anyone had ever known. Quinn couldn't help but see it as a policing issue. A new realm of licence and transgression had been created. Shadows congregated within shadows.

Quinn walked into an invisible cloud of cheap scent, the first intimation he had of that second population that came out to possess the streets at sunset, drawn by the cover of a rapidly expanding night.

A street girl stood on the corner of Pentonville Road and Caledonian Road. As he drew closer, her face contorted into an expression of exaggerated lasciviousness. She twirled a tatty, folded parasol on her shoulder, all the time pouting and smiling and fluttering her eyelids like some kind of mechanical coquette. She began to move her body towards him in a series of shimmying sways, in which she seemed to invest every ounce of her femininity.

Quinn found the performance more alarming than alluring; it was so patently artificial.

'Fancy a good time, darlin'?' As soon as she had made the overture, she immediately collapsed into a fit of cackling. Quinn had never seen someone fall about with laughter before, but that seemed to be what he was witnessing now. He didn't know what the joke was.

Quinn came to a halt in front of her, as if he were going to answer her question one way or the other. Why should he not go with her? Why should he not, for once, open himself up to such an experience?

She must have read his thoughts as she intensified her efforts to win his business. She pressed herself against him. Her voice was now a husky whisper in his ear. 'My, you're all wound up like a clock spring, ain't you? I'll bet you'll go off like a bloody geyser.'

Was it really possible that he was about to go with her? Only minutes ago he had been eating a perfectly ordinary pie in an unexceptionable teashop, surrounded by stolid, decent citizens who could not have suspected into what depths of depravity he was about to plunge himself.

And how would he face Miss Latterly, Lettice, if he went through with this? It would seal the end of any hope of a future between them. For she would know. And even if she didn't know, he would. And that would be enough to stifle their relationship. His guilt would mute him. He would withdraw even further from her for fear of giving himself away. He would find himself more alone than ever.

But his body so ached for the release the prostitute had promised. And the pressure of another human against him, unfamiliar and unsolicited, sent a jolt of something like electricity through him.

And at least with the prostitute there would be no Aunt Constance to contend with.

She began to grind her groin into his thigh.

Quinn made no response, except to reach slowly into the inside pocket of his ulster to take out his warrant card.

'What you got there?' The woman pulled back to look. The crest of the Metropolitan Police Force glinted in the failing light. The playfulness and promise went from her posture. A sour expression settled over her face. With her heavy layer of slap, she reminded him of a tragic clown, made up for laughter, but wearing a frown. 'Are you going to arrest me?'

'I ought to.'

'Why don't you then?' Her look became contemptuous now. 'Are you one of them dirty cops what expects it for free? A girl got to eat, you know.'

Quinn's mouth was suddenly dry, as if filled with feathers. He pocketed his warrant card and moved on.

The hotel was on Caledonian Road. It was indicated by a sign in the window which read simply HOTEL. The window was filmed in soot and grime so the sign was difficult to read, especially at night when only a single dim light illuminated the reception lobby.

He collected his key from the desk. The room number, 217, was engraved into a greasy piece of wood that had been darkened by the manipulations of countless grubby fingers. He was fastidious enough to handle it only by the metal ring that connected the key to the wood.

It was the kind of place where if you looked down you would see threadbare rugs and black dust gathering on the skirting boards. If you looked straight ahead, or to either side, you would see peeling wallpaper and black fungal stains. If you looked up, you would see the corners of the rooms hung in cobwebs. The husky carcasses of flies, and the occasional bee, accumulated on every windowsill. The lace curtains in the windows were grey. You were not advised to move them. To do so would disturb the dust which gathered in the netting, in the spaces between weft and warp. The cloud that arose would set you coughing for days. If you did not have a weak chest when you came here, the chances were you would by the time you left.

In the light of his recent encounter, Quinn had little doubt that it was the kind of place where a prostitute would bring her clients. He supposed it was possible to rent rooms by the hour and doubted the sheets were changed between guests. To be fair, he had not passed any women who looked like prostitutes on the stairs. As for the men, he supposed that any one of them might be a punter. The step was always hurried, the glance shifty.

The only evidence he had for this libellous supposition was that of his ears. He would lie awake and hear the sound of coming and going on the stairs throughout the night. From time to time there would be fervid whispering too, or even incoherent drunken cries and joyless laughter. And the clincher: the sound of beds thumping against the flimsy walls, which could be heard at all hours.

These sounds would be strangely amplified in the quiet hours of the night. Quinn would feel himself to be under assault, as if the couple in the next room who were frenziedly working their way towards climax would at any moment come crashing through the wall.

The room was in semi-darkness, the only light a square of dying luminescence where the window was.

And after all, he knew every inch of the room without having to look at it. He knew where the sagging bed jutted out to catch his shins with its rusting iron frame. He knew where the one seat was, a wooden object so singularly devoid of comfort just looking at it induced a weary ache deep in his bones. He knew where the wardrobe with the door that wouldn't shut loomed. Every joint of it was out of true, and if you pushed it with your finger it would tilt a good half-inch from side to side. One side of it was given over to drawers. It had taken him some time to work out that the wardrobe had to be leaning over to the right for him to push the drawers home, yet leaning to the left to pull them out.

Between bed and wardrobe there was barely room for him to stand. To move into his room, he had to turn sideways and edge his way in like a crab.

He fumbled to light the gas. The flickering glow flooded into every corner with an intrusive eagerness. Quinn took off his ulster and hung it in the wardrobe. He went through his usual ritual of repeatedly closing the wardrobe door and fiddling with the lock. Eventually, he managed to get it to stay shut. But as soon as he sat down on the bed it swung open with a mocking creak.

Quinn gave vent to a profanity, which somehow allowed him to move on. He took off his bowler hat and placed it on the seat of the chair.

It did not do to examine too closely the path that had led him to this place. It was an exercise akin to picking away at a scab. But he knew that he had come here for a reason. And if it had not been this hotel, it would have been another very similar.

This was the kind of room you came to to read your father's suicide letter.

Every night he had pulled out from under his bed the tin box that contained his father's correspondence to his mistress, Louisa Grant-Sissons. He had read every letter except the last, the one written after Louisa's death. As he had not read it, he did not know for certain what it contained, nor that it was indeed a suicide note. But he had read the narrative of their affair laid out in the letters that preceded it. The postmarks revealed the sequence in which they had been written. This was the last, dated *7PM 16 JLY 1899*, the day of his father's death.

As he held the letter in his trembling hands, a weight of emotion expanded within him, pushing out with intolerable pressure against his ribcage. He felt a vice tightening on his heart and lungs. He gasped for air. The gasping turned into sobs. Heavy droplets of grief fell from his eyes.

TWENTY-SEVEN

I know you will never read this, my love, but that does not matter, because soon we will be together and I will be able to say all the words I long to say to you myself.

There are those who would say that we were sinners while we lived. And so, if we are united in death, it will not be in Heaven. But wherever you are, my love, will be Heaven for me, if I am able to be there with you.

But I am not religious in the conventional sense. If I have a faith, it is the faith that something of us endures after death. Where it endures, or how, I know not.

I know too that after death we will be united.

And what will unite us is that love we shared while we were alive.

For if there is a deity it is not some grey-bearded old man perched on a cloud, but rather a beautiful naked woman borne aloft on a scallop shell. Yes, I am a worshipper of Aphrodite, I confess it!

Love is the force that drives all living things. It is the surge that propels the sap to rise in spring. It is the fire that blazes in the heart of existence. It blazes green in every blade of grass. It blazes silver in the sunlit waxen leaves of an evergreen tree. It blazes red in the blood of every man and woman.

And so it will be our love that saves us. And a God of Love cannot but be moved by such a love as ours. And whatever else we did, whoever else we hurt, they will be as nothing next to our love. And know that in loving one another we did a great good thing. A pure good thing. And the God of Love will treasure us and celebrate us and love us for that. And she will forgive us those lesser sins, for she cares not one iota for them.

Am I raving, my love? Perhaps I am. Raving and raging.

Ever since you were so cruelly taken from this world, I have been raging in a pit of black despair. The only relief I have from this is the thought that I will be reunited with you in death. Soon, soon, my love. And that you will be whole again when we are together.

The hand that I held so often in mine will be restored to your body.

I have kissed each finger of that hand.

I have felt its gentle touch against my cheek.

I have followed its beckoning crook.

Do you remember when you held your forefinger playfully against my lips to silence me? Had I spoken too intemperately? Perhaps I had complained about your husband or the family ties that bound me. You always were my conscience.

Or perhaps I had begged too importunately for your caresses.

You always said I was in too much of a hurry.

Well, you were right. And I cannot wait any longer. I must hold your hand in mine again, and soon.

Soon, soon, my love, we will be together.

I am a doctor. A man of science. Do I truly believe that we will be reunited after death? It is not the scientist in me that believes this. It is the lover.

And if that lover is proven to be a deluded fool, and all that awaits me after death is nonexistence, then so be it. A nothingness with nothing in it is preferable to a world with everything in it but the one person that I love.

To feel nothing, to know nothing, to be nothing for eternity, is better than to endure another moment without you.

And so I am resolved, my love. I will be with you soon, or I will be nowhere.

Tonight I will inject myself with five grains of morphine. It will be a blissful death. I will sink into your arms, your two arms that I know are waiting for me.

Until we meet, my love. Soon. Soon.

TWENTY-EIGHT

The main CID room bustled with the appearance of activity. All Quinn saw was men who didn't know what they were doing pretending that they did. Anger and frustration showed in the clash of raised voices as they marshalled the rabble of suspects they had pulled in for interrogation. Most of these were registered foreigners already known to MO5(g). Naturally, the men who had been brought in protested their innocence, loudly, and in accents that did not help their cause. The CID detectives shouted back, and sometimes jostled or even struck them. There might have been purpose to it, but the purpose had nothing to do with solving any case. The chaos that it was their job to keep at bay was closer to the surface than usual.

As soon as he could, Quinn signalled to Inchball.

Five minutes later they were back at Horse Guards Parade. All at once they were engulfed by a company of soldiers on bicycles, heading south in loose formation along Horse Guards Road. There were about a hundred of them, Quinn estimated, each one whipping past at a nifty lick. It took several minutes for the entire column to pass, the stragglers pedalling hard to catch their comrades. The whole thing had the air of an outing. It did not seem like men preparing for war. The soldiers on their bicycles struck Quinn as unspeakably vulnerable. Their jauntiness as they sped along had a hollow ring to it, as if each man knew he was heading towards his death but had sworn not to tell his fellows. Quinn could not shake off the image of a shell exploding in their midst and of the mangled wreckage of bicycle frames and bodies that would be left in its wake.

He waited for the cyclists to pass entirely before speaking. 'I've spoken to Macadam.'

'And?'

'It was a soldier, that is to say a man wearing the uniform of a private of the Royal Fusiliers.'

'Good God! Are you sure?'

Quinn nodded. 'He got a good look at the cap badge. You need to tell Leversedge, I suppose.'

'He won't like it. He and Coddington are working on the theory that it's a Hun spy.'

Quinn let the observation go without comment. 'It might be advisable to get an artist down to Macadam and have him produce some kind of sketch of the suspect. Macadam said it was a young man, a recent enlistee most likely. Then take that down to the regimental HQ, show it around and see if it rings any bells. Time is of the essence. If he's a serving soldier, he could get transferred out at any time.'

'They won't like it coming from you. Coddersedge, I mean.'

Quinn smiled at Inchball's name for the two-headed hydra of incompetence. 'No need to tell them. Say you heard it from Macadam yourself.'

Inchball's expression grew pained. 'That won't wash. If I heard it myself, why didn't I take it to them first thing?'

'What does it matter? The important thing is it's a definite lead. It's got to be better than hauling in Germans off the street. You'll just have to make a clean breast of it. A further thing you should know, our soldier shot Macadam with a Webley. Likely as not stolen from an officer. There's a chance he could be a deserter.'

'Or a German agent!' suggested Inchball hopefully. 'In disguise.'

It couldn't be discounted. 'If that's what it takes to get them to do their job, then why not? First things first. Talk to the regiment. At least rule out it's not a serving soldier. It's called policing, you know.'

'You don't have to tell me.' Inchball's voice was spiky with impatience. But Quinn knew it was not directed against him.

Commands shouted and responses shouted back assailed their ears. An artillery piece was discharged. Quinn assumed it was a training exercise, the ammunition blank. Even so, it brought the idea of war closer.

The two men nodded grimly. Inchball took off at a brisk pace, heading back to the Yard to share the new information with his superiors. Quinn lingered for a few minutes more, watching soldiers square-bashing in front of him. His gaze was almost wistful. The idea of swapping the frustration and murkiness of police work for a life of soldiering was beginning to appeal to him.

As he approached New Scotland Yard along Richmond Terrace, Quinn was surprised to see Mrs Ibbott looking up at the building, her face set in determination. With her was her daughter Mary, whose expression somehow managed to be both daunted and sullen.

Quinn called out to his former landlady. 'Mrs Ibbott, what are you doing here?'

She turned to him with a look of confusion, which evaporated when she recognized who had accosted her. Her face lit up. 'The very man we have come to see!'

'You have come to see me? But why?'

Mrs Ibbott looked about her warily, as if she were afraid they might be spied upon. 'Is there not somewhere we might go?'

'We could go inside, if you wish.' Quinn looked at Mary. The girl stood with her head bowed. She seemed to be shivering, and he would have said she was on the verge of tears. 'Or we could find a teashop, if you like? It's rather busy today in CID.'

Mary flashed a look of grateful relief at him. 'It's all a waste of time. I don't even know what we're doing here,' she cried.

Mrs Ibbott was stern. 'Nonsense, Mary. You know very well why we are here. You agreed with me that it was the right thing to do.'

'Well, it's only that now we are here it all seems so . . . silly.'

'Why don't you let me be the judge of that? We'll have a nice cup of tea and a chat, and if I decide the matter needs taking further, then you may leave it to me to do so.'

Mother and daughter looked up at him with identical smiles, appreciative, yes, but also somehow vindicated, as if what he proposed was no less than what they expected.

'And so you were at the meeting too?'

Mrs Ibbott and her daughter nodded in unison. They were seated at a table in the back corner of the Lyons teashop on Parliament Street.

'And you saw Eve Cardew there?'

Mrs Ibbott took a sip of her tea. 'We certainly did.'

'Am I to take it that you know her? And the family?'

Mother and daughter exchanged a quick conferring look. Mary nodded for her mother to speak for both of them, before tucking into the iced bun that Quinn had ordered for her. 'We do.'

Quinn sat back thoughtfully. 'I'm very glad that you came to speak to me. Perhaps you could explain how you know the Cardews?'

'Well, many years ago, I used to worship at that church. And Mary went to Sunday school there. Eve Cardew and her brother attended at the same time. It was because we knew Pastor Cardew that we decided to go to the meeting.'

'You decided, you mean.' Mary's words came out through the wadding of iced bun that she was still chewing on.

'Mary! Manners.'

'And how did she seem when you saw her that day?'

'She was so rude!' exclaimed Mary, who had by now swallowed the mouthful of iced bun. 'She barged through to the front of the queue so she could get her hands on some feathers, then pushed everyone out of her way as she rushed out.'

'She was in a hurry then?'

'I should say so!'

'Did you see her leave the church?'

Mrs Ibbott gave a broad smile that indicated just how happy she was with Quinn's question. 'We saw her outside the church. There was a young man on the steps.'

'Felix,' added Mary.

'Felix?'

'He used to go to Sunday school with us. Eve Cardew was soft on him, if I remember rightly. But she always was a queer fish.'

'In what way?'

'Oh, all hoity toity and full of herself. But for some reason she fixed on Felix. God knows why.'

Quinn had his notebook out now. 'Felix . . .? You don't know his surname?'

'I can't remember! It was all so long ago. Mind you, seeing them together that day brought it all back. Reminded me what a horror she was.'

'Did she have any friends at Sunday school, apart from Felix?'

'I should say not. She was a very peculiar child. Everyone was a little bit afraid of her. That's why she's stuck in my mind so much, I think. I can't remember a thing about anyone else who went there.'

'What about her brother?'

'I remember she had a brother. I think they were twins, weren't they? But I don't really remember him at all.'

'So you saw Eve and Felix together outside the church?'

'Yes. That's why she had been in such a rush. She wanted to catch him.'

'To catch him?'

'So she could give him a feather!' Mary's words had a verse-like lilt to them, as if she were explaining something patently obvious to a simpleton.

'And then what happened?'

'She ran off. He had a face like thunder. And the next thing we know, she's been murdered.'

'And you think this Felix had something to do with it?'

'Don't you?'

Quinn pinched his lower lip between the thumb and first two fingers of his right hand. 'Why did she give him the feather? Has he not enlisted?'

Mary shrugged. 'He certainly wasn't in uniform that day. And he was with a woman who I think was his mother – and she had a German accent!'

'And these feathers? People were queuing for these feathers, were they? Girls, that is? Young women?'

'I should say so!'

'You took some yourself, I suppose?'

Mary became suddenly shamefaced. She picked up what was left of her iced bun and bit off a prodigious mouthful, such that she was unable to speak for the foreseeable future.

Quinn turned to Mrs Ibbott inquiringly.

'I do not approve of the feathers.'

Mary gave a jerky shrug of her shoulders as her jaws continued to work on the bun.

Quinn tapped the page of his notebook with the tip of his pencil. 'Thank you. What you have told me is very interesting.'

'Are you going to arrest Felix?'

'I will pass on the information you have given me to an officer who is investigating the case. I am sure he will want to talk to this Felix chap once we have been able to track him down. Do you think Pastor Cardew will know him?'

'Most certainly.' Mrs Ibbott replaced her teacup in its saucer with emphatic force. 'I saw the pastor talking to Felix and his mother before the meeting began. They seemed to be on familiar terms.'

'Excellent. It should not take too long to get to the bottom of this.' Quinn could well imagine how Coddington's and Leversedge's ears would prick up at the news of the mother's German accent. Perhaps he would withhold that detail. Perhaps he would not pass the lead on at all. It was possible that Mrs Ibbott and her daughter had got themselves worked up over nothing. Was it a lead, or simply tittle-tattle? Having said that, there was the fact that a feather had been found inside the victim's mouth. That seemed to suggest that the feather had some significance in the case. But was it a strong enough motive for murder? He had to admit he had encountered murderers who had killed for less. It all depended on the psychology of the fellow receiving the feather. One man might be able to brush the whole thing off as nonsense. For another, it might be a wounding humiliation that he could not get over, or forgive. Especially if he had conceived some kind of violent passion towards the girl.

Mrs Ibbott gave a nod of satisfaction. 'I felt that it was our duty to say something. I don't want to get anyone into trouble if they have done nothing wrong. However, that poor girl is dead and someone killed her.'

'That's very true, Mrs Ibbott.'

Mrs Ibbott's demeanour grew perceptibly more relaxed. She gave a sigh and helped herself to some more tea from the pot. 'So, Silas, how are you?'

The question – and the use of his Christian name, which of course he had sanctioned – took Quinn off his guard. He gave a flustered, 'I am very well, thank you.'

'Have you found somewhere permanent to live yet? I trust you are not still living in a *hotel*?' It was clear from the emphasis Mrs Ibbott placed on the final word that she did not approve of hotels. She tilted her head back and sniffed. It was a disdainful gesture that made Quinn suspect she knew very well what kind of a hotel he was staying in. At any rate, she knew that it was in King's Cross, as she had forwarded correspondence to him. No doubt she did not approve of King's Cross, any more than she did hotels.

'I . . . I find that it suits my needs at present. I have not yet found anywhere more permanent.'

Mrs Ibbott appeared to be unimpressed by this information.

Quinn was reluctant to say more, for fear of placing Mrs Ibbott in a difficult situation. He did not want her to feel responsible for his accommodation difficulties. 'I wish to take my time,' he said at last. 'So that I may find somewhere as amenable as my last abode.'

Mrs Ibbott took the compliment with a little smile. 'You know, if it was up to me, I would have you back like a shot.'

Her position, he thought, had subtly changed since the last time they had discussed this. Then she had been ready to defy Hargreaves and prepared to have Quinn stay on. She would permit no one to dictate to her who might or might not be a guest in her house, he seemed to remember. Now it seemed her hands were tied, presumably because of Hargreaves' resistance.

Perhaps aware of this, she clarified the situation for him. 'With Mr Hargreaves away with his regiment, it would not be honourable to renege on the understanding we came to – with your agreement, I think.'

'There's no need to explain,' said Quinn.

'I do wish you would find somewhere respectable, Inspector. In a nice neighbourhood.'

'I shall apply myself to the task as soon as . . .' The sentence trailed off. Quinn was unable to think of anything preventing him from doing what Mrs Ibbott had urged. 'But now, I am afraid you must excuse me, for I fear I must be getting back to my desk. There is no rest for the wicked, they say. Well, the same is true for those whose job it is to curtail them.' Quinn surprised himself with this remark. It was almost a witticism.

Mrs Ibbott gave him a curious look, as if she was thinking he was not quite himself.

TWENTY-NINE

B y the time Quinn got back to CID, the chaos that had been beneath the surface before had burst out into open uproar. He managed to catch Inchball's eye.

'All hell's broke loose. There's been a tip-off. Via the telephone. From a member of the public. Saw the dead girl's picture in the newspaper and recognized her. Coddersedge are all set to make an arrest.'

'Who is it?' Quinn's heart began to race, a reflex reaction to the prospect of the chase closing in on a suspect. Even if he were not directly involved, he could still feel the excitement vicariously. He wondered if it was this Felix person that Mrs Ibbott and Mary had told him about. Or perhaps it would turn out to be a soldier from the Royal Fusiliers. In either case, he couldn't help but feel disappointed. It would have helped his cause if he had been the one to point the investigation in the right direction.

'Remember the Bosch butcher in Bush?'

'What of it?'

'She was only there. Eve Cardew. Egging the crowd on. Ringleader, is the word what was said.'

Quinn's brows contracted as he tried to make sense of this. 'But she's a girl.'

'That's why it was so notable.'

'What has it to do with her death?'

'The old man died, di'n' 'e? The pork butcher. Well, he had a son. The son was there, in the shop, when the riot happened. Got injured in the fracas, if you remember. Well, here's the thing –

according to our tip-off, he was seen looking daggers at Eve Cardew. It was a very nasty look indeed, according to our witness. Like he meant to do her harm and no mistake.'

'It's rather flimsy.'

'It's a motive. And it's good enough for Coddington.'

Quinn gestured around him at the tumult. The suspects who had been brought in earlier were protesting even more vociferously than before. In one corner of the room, a man was being truncheoned into submission. Handcuffs were being clapped on all around.

'They got wind of it, di'n' they? One of ours must have let it slip that we were all set to feel the collar of one of theirs. You could say it di'n' go down well.'

At that very moment, DCI Coddington himself came barrelling towards them. His eyes were lit with a triumphant glee. 'So, you have heard the news, Quinn. We have our man.'

'You don't have him yet, I think.'

'Perhaps you would care to come along and see the arrest being made. It will do you good to observe a proper police operation in action. You might learn a thing or two.'

Quinn swallowed down the urge to say, 'I doubt it.' The truth was Coddington's proposal appealed. Only one thing deterred him, and that was the fact that Coddington was wearing an identical ulster overcoat and bowler to Quinn.

But he found that he could not resist the thrall of action.

Coddington was leaving nothing to chance. As well as a horse-drawn Black Maria to hold the suspect, there were two police cars crammed with CID officers and a wagon lined with two ranks of uniformed bobbies.

Quinn rode in the second of the cars with Inchball and learnt from him that Coddington had also contacted the local police station so that they would send officers round to the pork butcher's shop on Goldhawk Road in order to contain the suspect until the men from the Yard arrived.

'All to pick up one man?'

'If he's our man, he's a dangerous bugger. He's already taken a potshot at one of ours.'

'Did you not tell them what Macadam said? About his assailant wearing a uniform?'

Inchball heaved a shrug that lifted Quinn from his seat, so tightly were they squeezed in. 'All this was kicking off, so he didn't want to hear it.'

'This is a waste of time.'

'It might be. Or it might not be. That's the thing, ain't it, guv, you never can tell. You gotta look into everything. You taught me that. You can hardly blame Coddington for following it up. We'll talk to this sausage-eater, and if he has an alibi we can rule him out.'

'In the meantime, the soldier who took a shot at Macadam may well have been transferred out.'

'It's a question of resources, guv. We can't pursue every lead.'

'No. It's a question of stupidity.' There were other officers in the car, more or less loyal to Coddington. Quinn felt them bristle at his criticism.

The contingent from the local station were already in place. A fresh-faced plain-clothes detective introduced himself as Inspector Driscoll and glanced in wide-eyed confusion between Quinn and Coddington, each dressed in identical ulster and bowler.

Quinn suppressed the instinct to take charge. This was Coddington's op, after all. And if it all fell apart, as Quinn was confident it would, on Coddington's head it would be.

Coddington stepped in front of Quinn. 'DCI Coddington.' Leversedge hurried over to stand shoulder to shoulder with his mentor, blocking Quinn from Driscoll's vision completely. 'And this is Inspector Leversedge,' continued Coddington.

Quinn moved to one side to see Driscoll frown at the panto-mime that had just been enacted. All credit to him, he didn't let it throw him off his stride. 'The suspect is inside. As instructed, we have not attempted ingress. We have secured the front and rear of the premises. He can't escape.'

Coddington nodded his approval. Quinn left them to it and turned his attention to the shop. The shutters were down on the windows. A large chipboard panel had been nailed into the frame of the door. Someone had painted the words 'BOSH SCUM' over it.

'There's your motive, Quinn!' Coddington's grin as he came over was insufferable. 'Revenge. His father's dead, his business ruined. And he blamed Eve Cardew.'

It was strange, Quinn thought, how important it seemed to be to Coddington to secure Quinn's approval. 'But what else is there to link the two of them?'

'What else do you need?' It was a rhetorical question, thrown out with the confidence of an unimaginative man. But there was something, a tremor in Coddington's glance, that hinted at uncertainty behind the bravado.

'I thought the theory you were pursuing was that she disturbed a German spy as he was watching the airship base on Wormwood Scrubs?'

'You have to be willing to modify your theory as new evidence arises. I'm surprised you don't know that, Quinn. It's basic detecting. But then again, nothing about you should really come as a surprise.'

'What I do know is that the man who shot at Macadam was wearing a military uniform – that of a private in the Royal Fusiliers. So unless the dead butcher's son has recently enlisted, he was not the one who shot Sergeant Macadam.'

Coddington's face flushed with emotion. Whether it was anger or embarrassment, there was no way of knowing. 'When did you find this out?'

'Last night.'

'And you didn't think to inform me?'

Quinn had no desire to drop Inchball in it. 'You have made it clear that my assistance is not welcome or necessary on the case. I had resolved to look into it myself, and if my enquiries resulted in anything material, I would of course pass it over to you.'

'I don't need your help, Quinn. But neither do I want you working against me. Which is what you're doing here.'

Inspector Driscoll came over. 'My men are awaiting your instructions, sir.'

Coddington fixed Quinn with a narrow glare. 'I know what you're trying to do, Quinn. And it won't succeed.' To Driscoll, he added: 'Get an axe to that panel on the door.'

The axe was wielded by a burly copper who gave his helmet to a mate to hold. The first blow landed with a dead thud. The blade sank deep into the soft chipboard, so that the copper struggled to retrieve it. It came out with a sudden creak that sent the axe swinging dangerously in his hand. A few of his fellows cried out in warning and protest. A moment later, just as he was sizing up for the second stroke, the door was opened from within. A young man in a dark suit stood framed in the doorway. His expression was both defiant and wounded. It was a face of great misery, crumpled, hopeless, grieving, to say nothing of the multiple cuts and grazes that marked it.

He looked at the axe-wielding policeman with consternation. 'What do you lot want?'

'Are you William Edgar?' shouted Coddington.

'Nah, I'm William Egger, ain't I?' It was typical of Coddington to have got the man's name wrong.

'Don't get clever with me, sonny.'

'Ain't no need for this, you know. If you'd just knocked on the door, I would have let you in. Now look at the damage you've done. It was bad enough when that rabble came round and started throwing bricks and stole all our meat and all.' Egger shook his head forlornly.

Coddington was striding towards him, brandishing a pair of handcuffs. 'William Egger, you're under arrest for the murder of Eve Cardew.'

'Murder? What you talking about?'

It took Egger a moment to weigh up the situation. He must have seen something in the eyes of the men gathered there outside his dead father's shop. He must have seen their muscular bodies tense and flex in preparation for closing in on him. He must have sensed the coming of the command that would seal his fate. His eyes, already hopeless, grew desperate. He slammed the door to. Quinn heard the lock turn, a bolt slide into place.

'That went well,' was Inchball's muttered wry aside.

Coddington caught Quinn watching him. 'An innocent man would not seek to evade arrest.' Quinn had the impression that Coddington was trying to convince himself as much as anyone else.

'No, but a frightened man might.'

Coddington stuck to his theme. 'An innocent man has nothing to fear.'

'Do you really think that's how he sees it, after what was done to his shop? After what happened to his father? He might have expected to look to the police for protection. Instead, he finds we have come to arrest him. Put yourself in his shoes, Coddington.'

With perfect equanimity Coddington nodded for the policeman

with the axe to resume his assault on the panel. Again Quinn detected that tremor of uncertainty in his eyes. 'Truncheons out, men!' he shouted, his voice suddenly hoarse and strained.

The axe was the kind used by firemen, long-handled with a massive blade, as sharp-edged and merciless as sunlight in an empty sky. It was a serious weapon, professional and deadly.

It was mesmerizing to watch the axehead bear down. It made short work of the flimsy panel. The rhythm of the blows was steady and merciless, although the timbre of the hacking modulated as the chipboard broke into smithereens.

The bobby stood now with his legs apart, the axe held in front of him in both hands. His pose said, *Anything else you'd like me to smash?*

Now with his truncheon in hand, Coddington stepped forward and peered gingerly into the ragged gap created. Leversedge was right behind him, so that when Coddington stepped unexpectedly back, he trod on the other man's boots.

'What the Devil are you playing at, Leversedge?'

'Sorry, guv. I thought you were going in.'

'That's not the procedure. You know that. I was simply having a look-see so that I can direct operations more efficiently. I'm the commander. The brains. I don't do the heavy lifting.' Coddington cast a sly look at Quinn. 'Inchball.'

'Yes, sir, DCI Coddington, sir.' Inchball clicked his heels and gave a salute. Quinn could only believe it was meant sarcastically.

'Take as many coppers as you want and get him.'

Inchball pointed to a handful of uniforms. They quickly mustered into a line behind him. One hand on his bowler, he ducked his head down and led the way in through the wreckage of the chipboard panel.

A tense moment stretched into a tense quarter of an hour. Quinn kept his eye on Coddington, who was getting twitchier with every minute that went by.

Eventually, one of the constables popped his head out of the ragged hole in the chipboard panel. 'Beggin' your pardons, sirs, but he's asking for DCI Quinn.'

'Who is?' Coddington's eyes bulged in outrage.

'The suspect, sir. He's saying he'll only hand himself in to the famous Quick-fire Quinn what he's read about in the papers.'

Coddington's jaw was trembling now. His nose twitched into

a snarl. His eyes narrowed as he flashed a look of focused hatred in Quinn's direction. Quinn realized this was a man close to breaking point.

'Believe me, Coddington, I no more want this than you do.'

'Bollocks.'

'Surely the important thing is that we extract this fellow without anyone getting hurt? If that is what you wish to accomplish, then I place myself at your disposal.'

'I see what you're doing here, Quinn.'

Quinn suppressed a groan. 'I'm not *doing* anything, Coddington. Other than trying to make myself useful.'

'You want to take the credit.'

Quinn resisted the temptation to say that he was not convinced there would be any credit. 'If I go in, it will be on your orders. The credit will be all yours.'

Quinn could see the calculations taking place behind the other man's eyes.

'And if anything goes wrong, I'll be the one in the firing line.'

A look of dull cunning dawned across Coddington's face. He impelled Quinn into the butcher's shop with a callous nod.

THIRTY

Quinn stepped through into a shuttered darkness. What light there was gatecrashed in behind him, prurient and blinking. A pungent odour filled the gloom, the heavy, hanging air of blood and meat. The smell felt oddly familiar to Quinn, like an unhappy homecoming.

The constable who had beckoned him in stood alone in the middle of the shop.

'Where's Sergeant Inchball?'

'This way, sir.'

The policeman lifted the flap to the marble counter and stood aside for Quinn to enter. 'They're in the back, sir.'

There was a door to one side. Quinn opened it on to an over-furnished parlour typical of a well-to-do family, for the most part conservative and conventional. Here and there, little flashes of individuality jumped out. A painting of a pied pig with large ears hanging down over its face. Another pig, this time cast in brass and with a set of wings on its back, was mounted on the wall as if in flight.

Pride of place was given to a dresser displaying examples of Dresden china, the only indication of the dead man's Germanic origins that Quinn could see.

The room was incongruously bright and cheery after the shop, and even more incongruously crowded with policemen. A woman in a black dress sat on a divan, assiduously dabbing at a dampness that would not go away beneath her eyes. The pork butcher's widow, by the looks of her. An English matron from the stolid, respectable mould.

Her son stood on the hearthrug with his arms crossed and legs spread in a defiant pose, facing off the policemen.

He looked up at Quinn's entrance. 'Is this 'im?'

Inchball confirmed Quinn's identity.

'I thought 'e would be more . . .' William Egger broke off, squinting at Quinn in dissatisfaction.

'What?'

'I dunno . . . *dashing* or something.'

'Why did you ask for me, Mr Egger?'

Sergeant Inchball cut in. ''S'my fault, guv. I told 'im you was 'ere.'

'I wanted take a look at you, di'n' I? You're famous, ain't ya?'

'And now that you have?'

'I ain't killed that girl. It was 'orrible what she did. And it killed Dad, you know. She killed 'im, as sure as if she'd fired a gun at his heart. But I di'n' kill 'er. What kind of a monster do you think I am?'

'I don't think you're a monster at all.'

'She used to come in the shop, you know. When she was a little girl. Dad would make an almighty fuss of her. That was 'is way. He loved those people. They was 'is people. All those people, all those people what came 'ere and smashed our windows and stole our meat. He thought they were 'is friends. Look what they did. Look what she made 'em do.'

'I think the best thing you could do is come with me to the station. You can tell your side of the story. We can get this whole thing cleared up.'

'Ain't I under arrest? That bloke out there . . .'

'Don't you worry about him. If you're telling the truth, you have nothing to fear. There has been a tip-off from a member of the public. We are obliged to look into it. If you come in voluntarily, it will be better. Trust me.'

'The police did *nothing* when it all kicked off. There was a copper there but he did nothing, I tell you. He just stood there and watched.'

'I'm sorry.'

'I ain't a murderer. I ain't even German. I was going to enlist. Now how can I, with Dad dead and Mum all on 'er own? She needs me 'ere, she does.'

'Come and say all this to the officers investigating the murder. It will help your case.'

William Egger went over to his mother and knelt down in front of her. 'What do you think, Mum?'

His mother dabbed her eyes with her handkerchief and nodded.

Egger stood up and turned to Quinn. 'Let's go then.'

Quinn gave a brief nod of assent. The hand of one of the uniforms came down on Egger's shoulder. Egger tensed as the copper yanked his arm up to clap on the handcuffs. 'Go easy! I said I was coming, didn't I?' He glared at Quinn.

'It's all right,' said Quinn. 'There's no need for handcuffs. Mr Egger is cooperating.'

The copper blew out his cheeks. Then his face settled into a crestfallen look, as if he had been cheated of a privilege he had every right to expect.

PART VI
A House of Grief

16–17 September, 1914.

THEY THOUGHT HE WAS A SPY.

An eminently respectable journalist friend of mine, who went to St Albans yesterday to see how the Territorials there were enjoying themselves, had an amusing experience, which, however, shows how thoroughly the authorities are guarding against spies. He had taken a note or two, when unexpectedly he was tapped on the shoulder by a corporal and challenged as to his business.

Inquired Before Released.

"I said I was a reporter," he told me, "and I was thereupon marched off to the nearest guardroom between four soldiers. I was kept there for about half an hour, and then marched to the City Police Station, where enquiries at my office established my identity and I was allowed to go. There was some good-natured chaff between the corporal in charge of the escort and the police inspector, who asked him if I looked like a German."

Daily Mirror, *Wednesday, 16 September, 1914*

THIRTY-ONE

Outside the interview room, Quinn did his best to convince Coddington of Egger's innocence.

'I don't believe he did it. It doesn't fit with anything else we know. The soldier who shot Macadam. The white feather in the victim's mouth.'

Coddington's prodigious moustache twitched impatiently. 'What's the white feather got to do with anything? You're always trying to complicate things, Quinn. You get bogged down in irrelevant details. What it comes down to is this: we have a motive. That's good enough for me.' The familiar look of stupidity masquerading as cunning flashed across his eyes. It seemed that Coddington had thought of the clincher. 'If he's innocent, why did he resist arrest?'

Quinn stifled a groan. You really never got anywhere with this man. 'He didn't resist arrest. He cooperated.'

'He shut the door on us.'

'He panicked. Then, when I'd had a chance to talk to him, he came voluntarily. We didn't even have to cuff him.'

'And whose stupid idea was that? Don't you know anything about procedure? What if he'd turned nasty?'

'He didn't.'

Coddington shook his head. 'You're a bloody liability, Quinn.'

'We need to follow up the lead of the soldier Macadam saw. Talk to the CO of the Royal Fusiliers. Find out if they have had any deserters.'

'Are you trying to tell me how to run my investigation?'

'I'm trying to help. I'll do it if you don't have the men. I don't want you making a mistake, Coddington.'

That was clearly the last straw as far as Coddington was concerned. His moustache trembled with rage.

The door to the interview room swung to in Quinn's face.

Quinn found his former sergeant at his desk. 'What the Devil are you doing there?'

Inchball sat up, flushing at the injustice of Quinn's accusatory tone. 'Well, they won't let me in there with 'im, will they?'

'What about that sketch? We need to ID that soldier. Or have you forgotten?'

Inchball sprang to his feet. 'I'll get on to it.'

Quinn knew that he had no real authority over Inchball any more, but old habits died hard. Judging by the speed Inchball dashed off to find the police artist, it seemed that was true for both of them.

'I need your help.'

Miss Latterly – Lettice – looked up from her typewriter. Her look was anxious, concerned – and sincere. She must have detected something in Quinn's voice that caused her to put aside her usual armoury of spiky irony. Whatever she had heard was evidently confirmed by her impression of his demeanour. She sat up, took notice, and said nothing.

Quinn flashed a persecuted glance about him. He dropped his voice to an urgent whisper. 'I need you to go into Coddington's office. There's a case file in there. I need you to look at it for me. If I do it, they'll see. You can go in there and they'll assume you have a reason.' Again his eyes flicked warily from side to side, on the lookout for his enemies.

Lettice got to her feet without demur. For a split second, Quinn was startled by her compliance. And then it seemed the most natural thing in the world. Perhaps it really was this simple. All he had to do was show her that he needed her and she would come to his aid.

'I'd better bring something with me. Some papers. There's this. A memo from Sir Edward which he wants circulating to all the senior officers.'

She was a bright girl. He hadn't thought of that: a cover.

'I can give some to the other officers and then go into his office.'

'We have to be quick though. I don't know how long we have.' Quinn explained what he needed her to do. Just once, in a few brief words. She nodded once, understanding fully. Taking in the gravity of it too.

Then they walked in silence back to CID. There were things Quinn wanted to say to her, and possibly things she needed to say to him. But now was not the time. The urgency of their shared endeavour bound them together as no words could.

They split up before they got to the department. Quinn went ahead and sat back down at his desk. Lettice came in a few minutes later. She did not look at him. Not even when she dropped a copy of the memo on his desk. Quinn tried to watch her without looking at her, looking in every direction except where he sensed she was, aiming to catch sight of her as his gaze swept distractedly from one part of the room to another. In between such glances, he had his head bowed over the sack of mail that he had been given to sort through. As he pulled each letter out, he cast a seemingly bored glance about him. If anyone sought to meet his eye, he would not flinch away.

He saw her just as she disappeared into Coddington's office, and was careful not to let his gaze linger, instead returning his attention to the bottomless sack.

She needed to be quick. Everyone in the department had seen her. What Quinn had to hope was that she had become invisible to them now. They had registered her and forgotten her, so that if she needed more time to find the information that Quinn wanted from Coddington's office, then no one would grow suspicious. The arrest of William Egger helped. Most of Coddington's detectives would be thinking about the breakthrough in the case. They would be excited, distracted, complacent. They wouldn't give a second thought to the female secretarial worker going about her business, unless it was to speculate unpleasantly about her. That was the danger. Quinn knew what a lot of dirty-minded bastards they were. He'd heard the banter, seen the leers and picked up the rumours of coppers abusing their positions to extort sexual favours from women. Miss Latterly was an attractive young woman. She would be a natural target for their smutty interest.

Quinn cast a slow, sweeping gaze around the room.

There was the possibility – a possibility almost too painful to acknowledge – that news of his liaison with Lettice had got about. He knew how policemen liked to gossip. The place was a rumour mill. Perhaps they had been seen out together. Or someone had overheard their fervid whispering outside Sir Edward's office. That would make her an object of suspicion to Quinn's enemies. And God knew, there were enough of those about.

Quinn looked back down at the pile of letters on his desk and picked one out. Feigning some kind of vague investigative purpose, he held it up to the light to examine it. In the process of lowering it, he was able to sneak a look at Coddington's door.

She had still not come out. Quinn's heart began to pound. This was taking too long.

He was powerless to act. And that made it intolerable. The anxiety of just sitting and watching was far more stressful than any active police operation he had been engaged on. He should never have involved her in this.

Suddenly the sound of bellowing laughter alerted Quinn to the return of the Coddersedge hydra. His pulse rate spiked and he glared desperately at the door to Coddington's office. Coddington and Leversedge were making brisk progress towards it. There was no chance to cut them off without arousing suspicion. Better to let her brazen it out. The chances were she would hear their voices and leave the office nonchalantly, making some remark about just dropping off a memo from Sir Edward. They might be suspicious if they had heard any rumours about him and Miss Latterly, but otherwise it was a natural enough occurrence.

Coddington and Leversedge made it to the door of the office and stopped to continue their conversation.

She had to come out now. If she took any longer it would be obvious that she had been snooping in there.

But still she did not come out.

Coddington disappeared inside his office.

Quinn waited for the inevitable fireworks. They did not come.

Gradually his heartbeat returned to its normal rate. He stared fixedly at the letter in his hand but could make no sense of it.

Then he shook his head in disbelief, as his shoulders shook in laughter and relief.

THIRTY-TWO

B rick-built and suburban in their scale and vision, the properties on Wallingford Avenue were more modest than the three-storey stuccoed town houses that dominated the Ladbroke Grove area. They were pleasant enough all the same, and presented a front of quiet domesticity. The sunlight glinted benignly on their bay windows. Their front gardens were well tended, competitively so perhaps. And behind the benign bay windows and the tidy front gardens, ordinary English lives were lived out. Lives of uniformity, composure, convention and restraint.

Elsewhere, in the bigger, flashier houses, the rich and servanted classes might indulge in their racy pastimes and let their jealous passions run wild. Here the worst that could be imagined of one's neighbours was the coveting of another man's gardenias, or perhaps going hatless on a warm Sunday afternoon.

And yet into this west London Eden, the most terrible of crimes had intruded.

The glints on the windows no longer seemed so benign. The universal compulsion for tidiness was revealed to be a mask.

Quinn looked down at the address written on the scrap of paper that Lettice had given him.

He had to admit, she had surprised him. She had handed the address over nonchalantly, with the merest flick of an eyebrow, her old ironic amusement back in place. She knew, of course, that he had underestimated her. And it evidently gave her the greatest pleasure to see his confusion.

'I didn't see you come out.'

'Well, I did. Obviously.'

'Yes. You must have been very quick. I was worried.'

'You needn't have been.'

'You did well. Very well.'

'Thank you.'

'I had no right to involve you in this.'

'No, probably not. But I did it because I wanted to.'

'Still, I . . . There was probably another way to get this. I should have . . .' He should have asked Inchball was what he should have done. But he had noticed Coddington watching his former sergeant even more closely than before. And so he had put Lettice at risk.

'Don't spoil it now.'

'Spoil it?'

'You chose me. To help you. Don't spoil it by wishing you hadn't.' Her tone had lost its playfulness.

At that point, the door to Sir Edward Henry's office had opened

and Sir Edward himself had come out. Quinn discreetly pocketed
the piece of paper.

Sir Edward seemed startled to see him. 'What are you doing
here?' The commissioner did not wait for an answer. 'No, no,
this won't do. You don't report to me any more, Quinn. You
know that. You report to Thompson now. I can't speak to you.'
With that – and a recriminatory glare at Miss Latterly – he had
retreated back inside his office.

And they had instinctively looked at one another, Quinn and
Lettice, and laughed, the sniggering laughter of naughty
schoolchildren.

Quinn came at last to the house. It was at the end of the
terrace. The front garden was a little less well tended than its
neighbours. The windows had their curtains drawn and somehow
seemed to absorb the gleam of sunlight without benefiting from
it. That was all to be expected, perhaps.

The door was opened by a woman perhaps somewhere in her
forties. She was dressed in black, her dark hair tightly pinned
up, with a few loose strands of wiry grey sticking out. These
stray hairs gave her a look of impending derangement, as if they
were lines drawn around her head to represent the silent scream
of her thoughts. Her face was drained of colour, except in the
eyes, the whites of which were raw, while there were dark
smudges of exhaustion around them. She was exhausted by grief,
as if grief was all she had to offer and it was never enough. She
gave the impression of being a woman out of her depth, but then
who wouldn't be in these circumstances?

Quinn held out his warrant card. He may as well use it, even
if he were not here officially. 'Mrs Cardew?'

'No. My sister is . . . indisposed.'

'Yes, quite. I understand. I wonder if I may speak to Mr Cardew
then. Pastor Cardew, as I believe it is.'

'Has there been news? Have you found the man who did it?'

Quinn thought of William Egger, and of Coddington's self-
satisfied conviction that he had his man. 'No.' It would be cruel
to answer otherwise.

The woman stood to one side to allow Quinn to enter. 'Who
could have done such a thing? Poor Evie. Poor, poor child.' The
emotion that was evidently only just held in check burst through.
Ready tears streaked from her eyes. A convulsive sob shook her

as she turned hurriedly away from him, as if to hide something shameful. Quinn had a glimpse into the life they must have been living inside this house since the murder. Uncontrollable weeping, questions asked that had no answers, no expectation of comfort or solace.

She left Quinn to close the door behind him and led the way into the house. He had walked in the wake of violent death before. Often, as now, it presented an incongruously mild face. This house, the walls hung with homely decorations, paintings of Bible scenes, scriptural verses embroidered in needlepoint, was in its fundamentals unchanged since the murder. They kept the curtains drawn now, so that a mournful pall had settled over everything. But here in the hall, light streamed in through the panes in the front door. It showed the dust gathering where once it might have been chased away. There was a stale, airless atmosphere, as if the building was holding its breath. The aunt who had let him in was thin and drawn, as if she had reduced her nourishment to the minimum.

Quinn guessed that she had come to take care of her sister and her family. But the impression he had was that she was barely able to take care of herself. They might have benefited from a maid. He presumed they lacked the resources.

She showed him into the front parlour, which was cast in a gloom that the electric light failed to dispel entirely. The empty chairs were arranged in a desolate grouping, as if they had given up hope of ever being sat upon again and had resorted to each other's company.

He saw the aunt shake her head as she closed the door on him, an involuntary tic, a gesture of denial, of refusal to accept the unacceptable, of hopelessness that could not be articulated any other way, the negation of all hope. It was perhaps as well that the girl's mother was indisposed. He could not imagine facing her grief.

He was left alone with the loud tick of a grandfather clock in the corner, meting out the heavy seconds until eternity. It was an ugly object, domineering and stubborn in its insistence on the relentless passage of time. Around the room, he saw more evidence of the family's faith. A simple wooden cross was mounted above the fireplace, stark and minimal. On another wall he saw a painting of a lamb. And on the sideboard, he found a modest Bible open at the Book of Matthew. A ribbon marker lay under chapter five, verse four: 'Blessed are those who mourn, For they shall be comforted.'

Quinn sensed the presence of another in the room and turned to see a man of middle years, dressed in a dark suit, wearing a shirt collar and tie. His hair and beard were greying and dishevelled. You would say that he was a handsome man; his good looks had survived the evident pain that he was suffering, perhaps had even been enhanced by it. He looked more like an actor than a minister, although perhaps, thought Quinn, those two professions were more closely related than many suspected. Both required that mysterious quality known as charisma.

'My condolences,' said Quinn, holding out his hand. 'I am Detective Chief Inspector Quinn of . . .' Quinn hesitated. He had been about to say *of the Special Crimes Department*. 'Of the CID.'

The pastor took Quinn's hand in both of his, as if he were offering comfort to Quinn. '"The Lord giveth and the Lord taketh away."'

'It must be a great comfort to you, your faith?'

'It is more than my comfort. It is my rock. Do you have no faith yourself?'

'Once, perhaps.'

'I spoke to your colleagues. They told me that the man who did this is probably a German spy.'

'That is one theory.'

There was a beat, a tense beat, before: 'There are others?'

'There are always many theories.'

'Which, I suppose, means you are no closer to catching the man who did this?'

'Where do you think . . . where do you *believe* she has gone?'

'Who?'

'Your daughter.'

'She is dead.'

'Yes. And you are a man of faith. So, do you believe she is in Heaven?'

The pastor hesitated. His eyes narrowed as he assessed Quinn. 'That is a strange question for a policeman to ask. Is it relevant to the investigation?'

'I don't ask it as a policeman but as a man. A man who wants to believe but cannot. My father committed suicide. I suppose it was about that time that I lost my faith. I don't know. Or maybe it had already happened. Certainly I lost my mind. Your sister-in-law, I met your sister-in-law.'

'Yes. Gwyneth. What about her?'

'She seems to have taken it very badly. Your daughter's death. I would say. I don't know. But that's how she seemed to me. Raw.'

'Yes, of course.'

'She doesn't have the same faith as you?'

'I suppose not.'

'And your wife, Mrs Cardew . . . how is she taking it?'

'How do you think?'

'It must have been a tremendous blow to her.'

'To all of us.'

'But you have your faith.'

'I don't quite see what you are driving at.'

'"O Death, where is thy sting?" That's from the Bible, isn't it?'

'The Book of Corinthians.'

'My governor, Sir Edward Henry, is forever quoting the Bible at me. He's a very Christian man. A good Christian. Forgiveness . . . surprisingly perhaps, for the commissioner of the Met . . . forgiveness is something he places great store by.'

'Is there any particular reason why you have come here today, Chief Inspector?'

'I wished to offer my condolences.'

'Which you have done.'

'And to tell you that we are doing all we can to find your daughter's killer.'

'I should hope so.'

'But you didn't answer my question, you know. Do you believe she is in Heaven? With God, in Heaven? That would be a great consolation if you could believe that, I would imagine. A great comfort.'

'Wherever she is, it is God's will.'

'That is enough for you?'

'More than enough.'

'And my father . . . a man who killed himself? It is a sin, is it not, suicide? Where do you think he is?'

'God is compassionate. He may forgive us our trespasses.'

'As we forgive those who trespass against us? The Lord's Prayer. I remember it well. It is ingrained in my memory. Even though I have not said it since I left school.'

'Would you like us to say it together?'

'Perhaps not now.' Quinn took a moment to gather his thoughts. 'You know the pork butcher's on Goldhawk Road? Egger's?'

'I know of it. I think we get our pork chops and bacon from there. Herr Egger died, I believe.'

'Yes, there was a riot at the shop. My colleagues have arrested William Egger – he is the son of the man who died.'

'I don't quite . . .'

'They have arrested him for the murder of your daughter.'

'I see.'

'The theory is that Eve was there at the riot and, in fact, played a part in instigating it. And that William Egger, holding her somehow responsible for his father's death, and the damage that was done to the shop, took his revenge by murdering her.'

'You speak as if you do not concur with the theory?'

'Well, to begin with, it came as the result of an anonymous tip-off. I am always suspicious of anonymous tip-offs. And in the current climate, a tip-off directed against a person of German or half-German parentage makes me even more suspicious than usual. You understand?'

Cardew nodded distractedly.

'Does that sound like Eve, your daughter? Do you believe she could have whipped up this crowd to loot the butcher's shop?'

'She always was a wilful child.'

'So you do not discount it as impossible?'

'I believe my daughter was capable of many things.'

'That you would not approve of?'

'I will be honest. There is little point in being otherwise.' Cardew paused, looking Quinn directly, unflinchingly in the eye. 'She had a sinful nature.'

'Your daughter?'

'It is painful for me to admit it. But I am trying to help you. That is why I think it better to be frank.'

'I see. I have had another . . . lead, you might call it. On the day of the Purity Meeting, she was seen giving a white feather to a young man who was there with his mother. His mother, I understand, had a German accent.'

'Felix, you mean?'

'That's right, yes. Felix. You know him?'

'Felix Simpkins. You don't suspect Felix? His mother is a little . . . eccentric, but . . . Well, I suppose you must have your reasons.'

'He had a motive.'

'You mean the feather? Surely that's not enough to . . .' Pastor Cardew trailed off thoughtfully.

'Humiliation is one of the most powerful emotions there is.' Quinn grew reflective. 'As is shame.'

'But to kill?'

'What would you consider a sufficient motive?'

Cardew thought for a moment. 'Self-defence. Or the defence of your country against an aggressive enemy bent on your destruction.'

'That's why you held a war rally in your church?'

'Do you think there is some incongruity there? Our nation faces a mortal peril.'

'Self-defence takes many forms, does it not? A man may feel himself threatened in numerous ways.'

'I am not sure what you mean.'

'What was the relationship between your daughter and this youth, Felix?'

'There *was* no relationship. Except to say that they both attended Sunday school together. But that was a long time ago. And other children did too.'

'So it's not true that Eve and Felix were at one time close?'

Cardew pinched the bridge of his nose. It was a gesture of profound weariness. 'Close?'

'Perhaps she confided in him?' Quinn watched the pastor carefully. It seemed that he had been hit by a fresh wave of emotion. Grief was like that. It came at you when you least expected it.

'I don't think so.'

'Still, I would like to talk to Felix. Do you happen to know his address?'

'The twins used to go to his mother for piano lessons. That was years ago. But they lived on Godolphin Avenue then, just off Goldhawk Road. As far as I know they still do.'

'You don't remember the number?'

'Adam will know.' Cardew turned, as if to leave the room. 'I'll go and ask him.'

'Ah yes, your son. Would it be possible for me to speak to him?'

Cardew stopped with his hand on the door. 'Is that really necessary?'

'He was the one who found your daughter, I believe.'

'Yes, he did. And he has not got over the shock of it.'

'I understand.' Quinn fixed Cardew with a steady gaze. 'I would not ask if I did not consider it necessary.'

Cardew trembled with a conflicted tension, as if he were torn between nodding his assent and shaking his head in refusal.

THIRTY-THREE

The young man shuffled into the room, dragging his feet, or perhaps just one of them, avoiding eye contact, his face a ghastly grey as if he was about to be sick, or just had been. The resemblance to his father, who was right behind him, was marked. Adam Cardew looked like a stretched out, younger version of the other man. But it was as if in that stretching out, all the strengths of the original model had somehow been spread a little too thin. Adam was not as strikingly handsome as his father; his chin was weaker, his eyes more evasive, his overall demeanour sullen rather than forthright. Fiery constellations of acne erupted across his cheeks. Somehow you could never imagine his father suffering from acne. And Adam lacked that mysterious quality that marked Pastor Cardew out as a leader, a teacher, a shepherd of souls. It might have been self-belief he lacked, or a belief in anything. He held himself stooped and seemingly tensed in a permanent flinch. Of course, all this may have been simply grief, or shock. But Quinn had the sense that there was something else on display here.

He was dressed in cream flannels, the turn-ups floating a good inch above his ankles, with a woollen vest over a white shirt, a cravat tied at the open neck.

For all that he lacked his father's charisma, Adam struck Quinn as an interesting young man, more human, more sympathetic, more complex somehow than his father.

Quinn held out his hand. 'Hello, Adam.'

'Hello. Are you the policeman?'

'That's right. I'm Detective Chief Inspector Quinn of the Special Crimes Department.' The words were out before Quinn realized they were no longer strictly true. He let them go uncorrected.

'I've heard of you? Have I? I think I have?'

Quinn shrugged as if that was not important. But it was true that he had wanted to impress the boy, even intimidate him.

'Father says you want to ask me something.'

'Shall we sit down?' Quinn consulted Pastor Cardew. 'Would that be all right?'

Quinn detected a tension in the pastor's demeanour, between wariness and a desire to appear cooperative. 'Make yourself at home.'

Quinn waited for Adam to sit down before taking a seat opposite. Cardew remained standing at the edge of the room, a spectator.

'Your father tells me you used to have piano lessons?'

Adam appeared bewildered by the question. 'I thought this was about Eve?'

'It is. We're anxious to speak to Felix Simpkins. He's the son of the lady who used to teach you and your sister piano, I believe?'

'You think that Felix killed Eve?'

'We know that they spoke at the Purity Meeting at your father's church shortly before your sister disappeared. Quite possibly Felix was the last person to speak to her before she died.'

'Felix didn't do it.'

'How can you be so sure?'

'Because I know Felix.'

'You don't think he's capable of murder?'

Adam shook his head dismissively. 'He's not capable of filching a bird's egg.'

Quinn watched the boy closely. 'Sometimes you think you know someone and it turns out you don't know them at all.'

Adam said nothing. But Quinn noticed a strange look pass between him and his father, bitter and accusatory on Adam's side; thoughtful, uncertain on his father's.

'Of course, I'm sure you're right. We would just like to talk to him.'

'We used to go to Mrs Simpkins' house on Godolphin Avenue. They had a flat on the ground floor. 12a. I can see the house number in my mind's eye.'

Quinn made a note of the address.

'If that will be all?' Pastor Cardew cut in smoothly. 'My son has been under tremendous strain, as you can imagine. I don't want him upset any more.'

Something like a sneer spasmed across Adam's mouth. He didn't seem to value his father's protection very highly. 'Oh, it's all right, Father. Besides, we don't want the detective thinking we have anything to hide, do we?' Again a strange, dark look from son to father.

'Why should he think that?' Pastor Cardew's deflection was coolly done, but Quinn sensed the faintest tremor of unease brimming.

Adam contented himself with a sly and humourless smile, the meaning of which only he knew.

Quinn waited until this particular exchange between father and son was played out. 'You were the one who found her – Eve.'

'Yes.'

'How did you know where to look for her?'

Adam seemed startled by the question. 'I didn't. I looked everywhere I could think of.'

'But there. That particular spot in Wormwood Scrubs Park. What made you think of looking there?'

'It was somewhere we used to go. When we were children. I once made a den there with some chaps from school. It's still there.' There was a note of boyish pride in his voice.

Quinn scribbled the detail in his notebook frantically. 'It must have been a good den. These chaps, was Felix one of them?'

'No!' There was a note of disdain in Adam's reply.

'So he didn't know about this place?'

'Eve might have told him, I suppose. They were very close at one time.'

Quinn turned a probing stare on Pastor Cardew, who maintained a look of unruffled composure, as if his son's revelation had not proven him either a liar or a fool.

'What about your other friends? Were any of them close to Eve?'

'What do you mean, *other friends*? Felix wasn't my friend. He was Eve's friend. He was always too much of a mummy's boy for my liking. I don't know what Eve saw in him. But Eve always did have strange tastes.' The merest flicker of something in his eyes this time.

'But these other chaps. Were any of them interested in Eve?'

'I shouldn't think so.'

Out of the corner of his eye, Quinn sensed Pastor Cardew stir. 'Why not?'

'She used to scare them off. Too intense. Too weird. Too Eve.' Adam broke off and glared at Quinn, as if the policeman had just made an indecent suggestion.

'Thank you. You've been most helpful.' Quinn rose from his chair and stood for a moment, waiting for Pastor Cardew and Adam to acknowledge the end of the interview. But the two of them were lost in their own thoughts.

THIRTY-FOUR

The address Adam had given him was a good half-hour's walk away. The threat of rain hung in the air. Quinn felt it as an extra layer of pressure in his head. If the threat was made good, so be it. He had his trusty ulster on. If anything, the rain would be a relief. He wondered if that was how the chaps at the Front felt about it.

At last he came to the house on Godolphin Avenue. It was a large, prepossessing building in a street of similar properties, four storeys including the basement and an arch-windowed gable floor. All the windows were dressed with white stone architraves, in keeping with the pretensions of the original owners. A set of grand stone steps led up to a monumental front entrance, mounted with a small brick-built balcony. The entrance to the basement flat was tucked away below this to one side.

Quinn descended the steps to the basement and yanked the mechanical bell-pull, the answering clang coming after a split-second delay. He could hear no further sound from inside, no sign of anyone stirring to answer the door. After waiting a minute or so, he rang the bell again, this time pulling it continuously.

Eventually he heard footsteps slapping irritably on a tiled floor. He kept ringing, even as he heard the latch turning. As the door opened, a foreign-accented woman's voice cried out, 'All right, all right already, I hear you!' Quinn released the bell-pull, which retracted in on itself with a snap.

The force of her voice had led him to expect someone larger. But her presence was nevertheless impressive, despite her lack of physical stature. She occupied her place in the world with a performer's confidence, and there was something uncompromising about her appearance. She demanded you look at her, and met your gaze with unblinking candour. Her face was strong, with a wide jaw and prominent forehead. She was dressed picturesquely for the time of day, in something like an evening gown, black, with a décolletage neckline that exposed more of her chest than Quinn wished to see. She wore her very blonde hair in Alpine plaits. But the lines around her eyes and mouth told you she was no adolescent Heidi. Her expression was compressed into a hostile glower. 'Who are you? Why are you not Felix?'

'I beg your pardon, madam. My name is Detective Chief Inspector Quinn of New Scotland Yard.' He flashed his warrant card.

The woman let out a shriek. 'And so, you have come to arrest me, have you? A poor defenceless woman.'

'But why should I want to arrest you?'

'Because I am German. I have lived in this country for over twenty years. I married an Englishman. I pay my English taxes. I have a son who has abandoned me, and you come to harass me because I am German! Where is your pity? Have you no shame?'

'In fact, it was about your son that I wished to speak to you. Felix Simpkins. You are Mrs Simpkins, I take it?' Quinn cast a pointed look back over his shoulder. 'May I come in?'

'You will not arrest me?'

'I promise you that I will not.'

Despite this assurance, Mrs Simpkins continued to protest:

'Since when is it a crime to be born in one country and not another? Surely you must judge a person by what is in his heart, not where he is born? If you look into my heart, you will find it is very English. God save the King! I hate the Kaiser with a passion, do you hear me? The only thing I will say is that my husband was a wastrel. But I do not hold that against all Englishmen. But you! You hear one single thing bad against some German fellow and you will say that all Germans are monsters! How is that fair, I ask you?'

'I assure you, Mrs Simpkins, your nationality is of no interest to me.'

'You say that now, but the time will come when you will hunt me down like a rabid dog.'

For a moment, the force of her expression robbed Quinn of a response. He stood on the doorstep with his mouth gaping. It was this more than anything that seemed to incline her to relent. She opened the door fully for him to come in.

She led him into a room that was practically filled by a grand piano. There was space only for a couple of rather basic armchairs, placed awkwardly on either side of the chimney breast, slightly recessed from one another. Once they were seated, Quinn found that he had to lean forward to face Mrs Simpkins.

'So this is where you give your lessons, is it?'

'Of course. You are a very good detective, I think. What was it that gave it away?'

Quinn smiled. 'You taught Pastor Cardew's children, I believe. Adam and Eve.'

'Adam and Eve! Who gives their children such names? It is cruel. Abominable.' Mrs Simpkins suddenly fixed Quinn with a startled look. 'It is not about that girl that you have come? You do not think my Felix had something to do with that?'

'You said your son has abandoned you. Do you mean that he is missing?'

'We had a quarrel . . . he will be back. He will come crawling back on his knees and hands, crying for his Mutter!' The pads beneath her eyes were suddenly glistening with dampness. She breathed in a noisy snort of air through her nose. 'I only hope he has not done a stupid thing.'

'What stupid thing do you fear he might have done?'

The tears suddenly got the better of her. She could only bat away Quinn's question wordlessly with one hand. Quinn waited silently until she was able to speak again.

'We quarrelled. It has not been easy for me, bringing him up on my own. A boy needs a father's influence.' Mrs Simpkins looked at Quinn curiously. 'Do you have children?'

'No . . . I . . . am not married.'

She tilted her head backwards, as if under the impact of this information. 'You are very wise.'

'Do you have any idea where he might be?'

'Oh, I have an *idea*! But I hope to God I am wrong.'

'Go on.'

'He said he would join the army! Can you imagine such a thing? Felix Simpkins a soldier!'

'You do not think he would go through with it?'

Mrs Simpkins merely made a contemptuous noise.

'Mrs Simpkins, when was the last time you saw your son?'

'He will be back! Don't you worry, he will be back.'

'You remember going to the meeting at the Baptist church with him? He was seen there that day with you. Witnesses have come forward who said that Eve Cardew spoke to him.'

'That girl! It is all her fault!'

'Why do you say that?'

'She gave him that awful feather.'

'And it was as a result that Felix said he was going to join the army?'

'Oh, he said it before! But would he do it? He would talk and talk and talk, but it is not the same as do, do, do. But when she gave him that feather, I saw it in his eyes. This time he would do it. I begged him, I pleaded with him.' The nervous energy suddenly left her, like air from a burst balloon. She sank back in her chair, out of Quinn's sight. 'How could he do this to me?'

Quinn pulled his chair forward and sat on the edge of it, leaning across as far as possible to keep Mrs Simpkins in view. 'When did he leave?'

'What does it matter? He is gone. And not a word to his mother. He is probably in France now. In uniform. If he is not dead already. A bullet through his brain. I would not be surprised if one of his German cousins fired it. This is what happens when our countries go to war. The Kaiser is King George's cousin, is he not?'

'Could he not be staying with a friend?'

Mrs Simpkins' eyes bulged incredulously. 'A friend? Felix?'

'A lady friend, perhaps?'

She snorted derisively.

'It's not so preposterous, is it? I hear that Eve Cardew was once quite smitten with him.'

'What is this?'

'Did you not know? When they were children, they were very close. Her brother has confirmed it.'

'It was not very friendly what she did, I think.'

'Perhaps he might be staying with someone from his place of work? Have you checked with his employers?'

Mrs Simpkins screwed her face up into a look of distaste. 'This is what he wants. People running around after him. Just ignore him and he will come crawling back, I tell you.'

'Sadly, madam, I cannot just ignore him. I have my work to do. Perhaps if you could give me his employer's details?'

She wrinkled her nose and relented. 'Griffin Mutual. That is where he works. It is in High Holborn. More than that I cannot tell you. He does not tell me anything, you see. I am only his mother. Why would he tell me?'

Quinn made a note. 'I wonder, do you have a recent photograph of Felix?'

The woman let out a heavy sigh. This was all, evidently, more trouble than it was worth. All the same, she hauled herself out of her seat and disappeared from the room. A moment later she came back with a print of a photograph in a cardboard frame. It showed about thirty men in straw boaters, posed for a formal group photograph. 'He had this in his room. It is him with his colleagues. I don't know why it was taken. Perhaps they went on an excursion. I don't remember.' There was no hint of enjoyment or frivolity in the faces of the men, but this did not necessarily contradict Mrs Simpkins' suggestion. She pointed to a figure standing at the end of the back row. 'There. That is Felix.'

Quinn tried to read the face of the individual she had pointed out. Whether it was due to the youthfulness of the subject, or the deficiencies of the print, the face he saw seemed to lack any distinguishing features. It was almost like an absence of face, a blank, white shape on the photograph, with the merest dots and blobs to indicate his eyes and mouth, and barely a smudge where his nose should be. Judging by the men he stood next to, he seemed to be of average height, though his build was somewhat on the slight side. 'May I take this with me? I will return it once we have concluded our inquiry.'

'I have no need for it. I think I know what my son looks like. And I have no wish to look at these other men.'

Quinn took the photograph and handed Mrs Simpkins one of his cards. 'Do you have a telephone?'

'I do not. But the Gardeners have one.'

Quinn frowned quizzically.

'The Gardeners live upstairs.'

'If you hear from Felix, please call me. It's very important that I talk to him. I need to eliminate him from our enquiries.'

'They do not let me use it. The Gardeners. They do not let me use their telephone, because once I complained about the beastly noise it made while I was in the middle of a lesson.' Mrs Simpkins gave her impression of a telephone ringing unanswered. 'On and on it went! Oh my, you would not believe it! How am I supposed to listen to my pupil play with that din going on?'

'Is there anyone else you can ask?'

'Oh, they will let me use it if I tell them it is to report my own son to the police. That is how much they hate me.'

'I simply need to talk to Felix, you do understand? It's possible that he may know something that may help us find Eve Cardew's murderer.'

Quinn stood up and nodded once with finality. But she showed no sign of stirring from her armchair. After a moment, he turned away and let himself out.

THIRTY-FIVE

There was no sign of Inchball back at the Yard, which put Quinn on edge. All around him, he sensed the hostile, suspicious glances of the other CID detectives. Coddington's men. Whenever he returned their gaze, they would look away, or more often than not, turn their backs on him.

He was aware that he had been away from his desk for

sometime. Almost certainly, his absence had been noted. Coddington was bound to have someone watching him, looking out for ammunition to use against him. Possibly, he had even been followed.

Quinn felt more alone than he had in a long time. Even in Colney Hatch, he had from time to time enjoyed the companionship of his fellow inmates.

He hung his ulster up on the shared coat stand. The other detectives' bowlers filled the hat pegs in a defensive ring, like the closely packed shields of Roman legionaries in the *testudo* formation. There was no space for Quinn to hang his, so he kept it on his head.

Everything about the place conspired to repel him.

At his desk, he picked up the earpiece of the telephone, and when the operator came on the line asked her to connect him to the Griffin Mutual Company in Holborn. He hung up the earpiece and waited. A moment later, the clatter of the phone's bells startled him.

Quinn identified himself to the speaker on the other end of the line and gave his business. After several fearful minutes during which it seemed that he had lost the connection more than once, he was put through to a man called Birtwistle.

'Hello?'

Quinn had the photograph of the clerks from Griffin Mutual on his desk in front of him. He tried to work out which one was the man he was speaking to. It was probably the heavily built man in the centre of the front row, his long face soured by a sneer. 'Hello, my name is Chief Inspector Quinn of New Scotland Yard CID. I wish to speak to one of your employees, a clerk by the name of Felix Simpkins.'

'Felix Simpkins is no longer with us.' It was hard to discern any real intonation in the voice that buzzed in his ear like a trapped wasp. But he sensed anger. Yes, it was certainly the fat man in the front row, Quinn decided.

'I see. He has left your employment? Do you know where he has gone?'

'I neither know nor care.'

'He said nothing about his intentions?'

'He said nothing. Not a dicky bird. In fact, he simply did not show up for work one day. Left me in the lurch and no mistake. I now consider his employment terminated. He had fair warning.'

'When was this, the day he first failed to show up?'

Birtwistle took a moment to make his calculations. 'That would have been Monday, the seventh inst.'

'If he does turn up, would you be so good as to let me know?' Quinn gave his name again and hung up.

Inchball still wasn't back and Quinn was itching to share what he had discovered.

Somehow, whether by habit, or drawn by some instinct of attraction, he found himself outside Sir Edward's office, standing over Lettice as she pounded away at her typewriter. It was several moments before she looked up. 'What are you doing here?'

'I need to talk to you.'

Lettice looked nervously around her. 'Not here.'

'Can you leave that? Meet me outside.'

'Now?' The question was incredulous, almost hostile. But when he nodded, she consulted a silver pocket watch. 'Let me see what I can do.'

Ten minutes later they were standing on Victoria Embankment. Quinn was carrying a large brown envelope. Neither of them had put on their overcoats, though Quinn was still wearing his bowler.

'What did you tell Sir Edward?'

'I missed my lunch break so I told him I was faint from hunger. He took pity on me as I haven't had a proper lunch break since this war began.'

It came as a startling revelation to him to learn that she was working under such pressure. 'Do you want to get something to eat? There's a Lyons teashop on Parliament Street.'

'Very well.'

He told her what he knew while they walked.

The Lyons teashop was filled with soldiers. Quinn was impatient to hear what she thought, but first they had to wait for a table to be cleared. Then she consulted the menu and gave her order – a toasted teacake – to the waitress.

She got straight to the point. 'So where is Felix?'

'That's a very good question.'

'The most likely explanation is that he has joined up.'

'It's a possibility.'

'Is he the soldier that Macadam saw?'

Quinn pursed his lips critically. 'Macadam was shot on Sunday the sixth of September. The day before, on the afternoon of

Saturday the fifth, Eve Cardew gave Felix a white feather. At that time he was not a soldier. It is possible, I suppose, that he could have gone straight to a recruiting office and enlisted on the Saturday afternoon. But if that's the case . . .'

'Why did he kill her? He would have answered the taunt of the white feather by joining up. There was no need to kill her.'

Lettice's teacake arrived. They looked down forlornly at it. Not so long ago, the creamy butter would have been pooling as it melted. Not any more. The toasted surface barely glistened. If there was any butter on it, it was the merest scraping of a knife that had perhaps once been shown the butter pot. She took a bite of the teacake and washed it down with tea.

'And then there's the white feather in her mouth,' she continued. 'Why put that there?'

'Exactly,' said Quinn, delighting in her eagerness and intelligence.

She answered her own question: 'To teach her a lesson. To say, look, I'm not a coward. I'm a soldier now.' She made short work of the first half of the teacake, and again rinsed it down with tea. 'You have to find Felix.'

He enjoyed watching her eat. She was utterly unselfconscious and, despite the skimpy buttering, was evidently relishing every mouthful. 'At least now we have a photograph of him.'

Lettice nodded towards the brown envelope that Quinn had placed on the table. 'Is that it?'

Quinn smiled. He took the photograph out and pointed at Felix. 'That's him.'

'He's just a boy.'

'He is evidently old enough to enlist. That's what his mother thinks he's done.'

'But he doesn't look like a murderer, does he?'

'What does a murderer look like?'

'Not like a sweet young boy.'

'Sweet?'

'Yes. He looks sweet.'

'You can't tell someone's a murderer just by looking at his photograph, you know.'

'I know that.'

Quinn looked down at the photograph. 'Is he sweet? I don't see it. But I don't see that he is a murderer either. I just see a blankness. Nothing.' Quinn stared fixedly at the image, as if he were willing more detail to appear where Felix's face was. 'I suppose if we prove him to be Eve's killer, the telltale features of a murderer will appear. After all, he was not a murderer when this photograph was taken.'

She held her teacup halfway to her mouth and paused to lick some food, a raisin perhaps, from her teeth. 'Are you laughing at me?'

'No, not at all. I often wish that I could.'

'What? Laugh at me?'

'No. Tell just by looking at them. But in my experience you cannot. Every murderer I encounter looks different from the last.' Quinn wondered whether this was true. Superficially they differed, for sure. But was there not some quality to their faces that they all shared? He would not call it a haunted look. After all, some of them looked decidedly blithe and careless. Nor was it a look of particular malice, an inner coldness, what you might call evil. Some of them were quite affable creatures, and were even kind-hearted in other respects than that they had killed. No, it was the mark of a line having been crossed. A look of knowledge, you might say. Of the most terrible knowledge there is. A burdened look. Was this the mark of Cain? If so, it would only become evident after the murder had been committed, and so his quip about the photograph had a grain of truth to it.

'Do you think the killer is Felix?'

'I don't know. But I think the fact that he has gone missing is telling. I would very much like to talk to him. Until I have, I cannot really say very much about him. It may turn out that he has a watertight alibi.'

'Then why run away?'

'You cannot read too much into that. It may be entirely unconnected to Eve Cardew's murder. It is dangerous to focus on suspects whom one cannot speak to. One is tempted to fill the gap with all sorts of speculations. But essentially, we have nothing. Until we can speak to him. For now, he remains simply someone we would like to talk to. If I were running the investigation, I would circulate his image in police stations and in the press. Someone will come forward with word of him eventually. However, DCI Coddington is in charge.'

'And he has arrested this German butcher?'

'William Egger is not German. He has – had – a German father. And if that is all that you look for in a suspect, then Felix qualifies on those grounds too. His mother is German.'

'I never realized there were so many Germans living amongst us.'

'Well, one tends to think more about that sort of thing now than one ever did before.'

She dabbed her mouth with her napkin. The teacake was eaten. 'Of course, it could be neither of them. It could be someone who has not come to light yet. A stranger whom she met on the day she was killed, right before she was killed. Just some man wandering about Wormwood Scrubs looking for a girl to kill. How can you catch someone like that?'

'There is usually only one way to catch such a perpetrator.'

'Which is?'

'To wait for him to kill again.'

Lettice's eyes widened in horror. 'Is that all you can do? It's hardly a foolproof method, is it! I mean, what happens if he does not, and obviously I hope he does not . . . But if he does not then you never find him. And if he does, well, that's worse, because someone else has died. And so you will have failed in your first duty, which is to protect the public.'

'We are not miracle-workers.'

'Well, I hope DCI Coddington has got the right man. At least then we know that the killer is behind bars.'

'And if he has not, the real killer is still out there.'

Lettice dabbed the crumbs from her plate with a damp fingertip. 'What will you do next?'

'There is very little I can do, officially. I am not leading the investigation. I am not even connected to it. I have asked Coddington to allow me to work with him on it, but he refused. If I were to go to Coddington with my theories, he would disregard them simply because they come from me. He has already disregarded the feather found in Eve's mouth because it does not fit with his theory. It doesn't incriminate Egger, so it is ignored. And probably it smacks of the kind of clue that I rely on, in his mind. A psychological clue. The only fact that would sway Coddington towards Felix Simpkins is his mother's nationality, and it is the least relevant aspect of the case. In fact, it is not relevant at all. But why should he swap a man with a German

father for one with a German mother? It makes no difference to
him which one swings for the crime, except that he favours the
former because he is already behind bars, whereas the latter is
nowhere to be found. A bird in the hand and all that.'

'It makes a difference to you, though?'

Quinn did not need to reply. He knew that she understood
him, and that was enough.

THIRTY-SIX

T axis were thin on the ground. Many had been requisitioned
for military purposes. It was the same with buses. And of
course, there were just fewer men to drive them. Whatever
the reason, Quinn had to wait quarter of an hour on Victoria
Embankment before he was able to hail one. In happier times,
if he needed to go anywhere urgently, he would have had
Macadam drive him there in the Model T that was allocated to
the Special Crimes Department. What had become of that? he
wondered. It rankled to think that it had been absorbed back
into the fleet of police cars that were under Coddington's
command. It rankled even more that no one had thought to tell
him.

The driver was one of those cabbies who like to chat. He
had two sons in the army, who were doing their bit for King
and Country. This information was offered almost as soon as
Quinn was in the taxi, in an aggressive, accusatory manner. As
if to say, 'And what are you doing not in uniform, you bloody
shirker?'

Quinn offered the gratitude of the nation, but that didn't seem
to satisfy the driver, who had served at Mafeking but was too
old for active service now, otherwise he would have been the
first in line at the recruiting office. Any man would, he claimed.
Any man with an ounce of honour in his bones.

The conversation dried up after that.

It was a relief when they at last pulled up on Hammersmith
Road, outside the West London Hospital. Once again, a convoy
of ambulances was parked up, with soldiers fresh from the Front

being taken out on stretchers or in wheelchairs. Quinn and the cabbie watched in respectful silence as the wounded were ferried inside. Even the garrulous cabbie seemed cowed by the sight. Quinn sensed the other man's dread, as if he expected at any moment to see his sons among the muddied and bloodied human wreckage. For Quinn, the spectacle was even more shocking than on his first visit. It gave the impression of the war being some endless and ruthless industry for the manufacture of broken men. Was this happening every day, every hour even? The immense scale and destructive power of the war struck home, and the sense of it being beyond the control of any human agency or government. Something monstrous had been unleashed, in the face of which there were no words.

In the corridor outside Macadam's room, he encountered the same matron he had seen on his first visit. She frowned at him critically. 'Can you people not leave the poor man in peace?'

It was unfortunate that he had not had the photograph of Felix Simpkins in time to give it to Inchball for his visit earlier, but that was the way it went with police work. Sometimes you had to go over the same ground twice. Besides, he wanted to look in on Macadam himself.

Quinn conferred with the MO5(g) soldier on duty. 'Anything unusual to report?'

The soldier stifled a yawn as he shook his head.

Macadam was propped up in exactly the same position as before, as if he had not moved a muscle since Quinn's last visit. A flicker of surprise opened up his face and he strained to sit up. 'Guv? I wasn't expecting you! Inchball didn't say.' His speech was breathless and wheezy. He winced at the effort of movement.

Quinn held up his hand in demurral. 'No need to get up, old chap.' He took a seat next to the bed. 'How are you doing?'

Macadam collapsed back with some relief into his former position. He closed his eyes to recover his strength. 'It's not so bad. I'm bored out of my skull is the worst of it. I'll go crazy if I have to stay in here much longer.'

'You can't rush these things.'

A smile tweaked at Macadam's lips. 'Next you'll be telling me I had a lucky escape.'

'It's true.'

Macadam's eyes sprang open, and Quinn saw a weariness there, a look of defeat almost, that he did not recognize in his sergeant. 'Maybe. But I'm no more use than a corpse lying here like this, am I?'

'That's not true. You're the only one who's clapped eyes on the chief suspect.'

Macadam pulled a face. 'Some use that was. You should have seen the sketch the artist did. I mean, it sort of looks like him, but then again, it sort of don't. It sort of looks like a thousand other blokes.'

Quinn took the photograph out of the envelope and handed it to Macadam. A new intent came into Macadam's eyes as he scanned the image, a purposeful energy. It wasn't long before a look of recognition lit up his face as if a flare had gone off. 'That's him! There!' He pointed to the last figure on the right of the back row.

'Are you sure?'

'One hundred per cent.'

'The quality of the photograph is not great.'

'Nevertheless, I'm sure it's him.' Macadam smiled and held on to the photograph as if he were reluctant to relinquish it. 'Who is he?'

'His name's Felix Simpkins.'

'How did you find him?'

'A witness, two witnesses in fact, came forward. They saw Eve Cardew give him a white feather at the Purity Meeting.'

'What does Coddington have to say about that?'

'I haven't taken it to him yet. I wanted to be sure. But at least it gives us a name. The next thing to do is to check with the Royal Fusiliers. Simpkins left home on Monday the seventh, the day after he shot you. He failed to turn up for work. So either he is with the regiment or he has gone into hiding. A telephone call to regimental headquarters should be enough to settle that question.'

'He won't be there.'

'In which case, we will put out his photograph and start a manhunt.'

'Can you do that without Coddington?'

'With your positive identification of Felix Simpkins, even Coddington must be able to see that he has the wrong man.

Especially if you are able to positively state that William Egger is not the man who shot you.'

Macadam pursed his lips. 'I wouldn't put anything past Coddington. He'd say I was mistaken, or I fingered this Simpkins chap to please you. That's how it works with his officers, so he probably reckons it's the same with us.'

Quinn held one hand over his eyes and drew the palm down slowly until it covered his mouth. He sat like that for a long time, as if forbidding himself from saying whatever was on his mind.

THIRTY-SEVEN

Back at the Yard, Quinn made a point of walking straight up to Inchball. Coddington was in his office with the door open. He had a clear view of most of the CID room, including Inchball's desk.

Inchball tensed nervously and looked over his shoulder, his eyebrows raised quizzically.

'I've just got back from seeing Macadam.'

'I thought I was doing that, guv? I got the sketch an' all. Took it to the regiment. They said it looked like every single blighter who's enlisted in the last month. Unless we have a name for them, they can't help us.'

'Felix Simpkins.' Quinn placed the photograph on Inchball's desk and pointed to Felix Simpkins. 'That's the man who shot Mac. Can you check again with the Royal Fusiliers to see if they had anyone of that name? A telephone call will suffice. We need to get this resolved as quickly as possible. Also, take it to the print office and get some copies made.'

'How many?'

'Let's say a thousand for now. Have them run up some Wanted posters while they're at it. *Wanted, Felix Simpkins for the murder of Miss Eve Cardew.* You know the sort of thing. We need to get his mugshot out to as many police stations as we can. And not just Metropolitan. He may have left the capital by now.'

Inchball nodded and picked up the receiver to the telephone on his desk. In this respect, CID was better equipped than the Special Crimes Department, where the three of them had had to share one telephone.

As Inchball spoke to the operator, Quinn heard the scrape of a chair and became aware of a flurry of movement out of the corner of his eye. There was a long, high-pitched shout, which seemed to get closer the more it continued. Quinn left it to the last possible minute to turn towards it, by which time Coddington was upon them.

Coddington snatched the receiver out of Inchball's hand and slammed it back in its cradle. His face was red with rage. Quinn could feel the heat from it as it was pushed right up to his own. He could smell the sourness of the other man's breath. An eighth of an inch closer and he would have felt Coddington's moustache tickle him.

'No, no, no, no, no! This isn't how it works! You don't tell my men what to do. You've gone too far this time, Quinn.'

'You don't understand, Coddington—'

'Oh, I don't understand, do I? Am I too stupid to understand? Is that it?'

'There's been a new lead. We know who shot Macadam.'

'I have him, the suspect, the prisoner, the guilty one, the villain, the . . . the . . . the . . .'

'Murderer?'

'The murderer, thank you. I don't need you to tell me the word, I know the word. The murderer. You don't get to be a Detective Chief Inspector without knowing the word for someone who murders.'

'You have the wrong man.'

'I have the wrong man! Of course I have the wrong man! Because I am stupid! Of course I am stupid. Because I am stupid DCI Coddington! Not ever-so-clever DCI Quinn. Yes, how stupid of me not to be you! But what would you say, DCI Ever-So-Clever Quinn, if I told you that he has confessed! Yes! Would you still say I have the wrong man?'

'You have a confession?'

'Yes, he has confessed! Put that in your pipe and smoke it!'

'To killing Eve Cardew?'

'More or less.'

'More or less? What does that mean? He has either confessed or he hasn't, surely?'

'He has confessed to wanting to kill her. That he had the intent to kill her.'

'It's not the same thing at all.'

'It won't be long before he goes the whole hog. He's working up to it. We just need a little more time with him. He'll crack soon. We'll get a full confession then. We have a partial one now, that's enough to show that we have the right man, all right.'

'Did you ask him about the white feather? Why did he put a white feather in her mouth?'

'Shut your fucking mouth about that fucking white feather. The white feather has nothing to do with this case! When will you get that into your thick fucking *head*!' To emphasize his point, Coddington struck Quinn loosely about the head. It wasn't a forceful blow but it was enough to knock Quinn's bowler hat on to the floor. There was a sharp intake of breath from the watching detectives, as if Coddington had finally gone beyond the pale. But he was not done yet. As Quinn's bowler spun to a standstill, Coddington raised his foot above it to bring it down with a deliberate stamp, crushing the hat under a massive boot.

The collective gasp that this provoked was even louder than the first. This was a department of bowler hat-wearing men. It was universally recognized that you do not mess with a chap's hat, let alone commit an act of violence against it, whatever your beef might be with him. If there was a moment when the group's sympathy swung away from Coddington and towards Quinn, this was it.

'DCI *Codd*-ington!' At what point Sir Edward Henry had entered the room, and how much of the scene he had witnessed, Quinn did not know for sure. But it was clear that he had seen enough. The small confirmatory nod from Miss Latterly, at whose desk Quinn had stopped off ten minutes or so earlier, said as much.

Coddington's mouth flapped uselessly beneath his walrus moustaches.

'In my office, now. You too, Quinn.'

Coddington's face burned red as he endured Sir Edward's roasting. Quinn kept his eyes down.

'Never have I seen such a disgraceful display of unprofessional conduct. It was worse than loutish. If I had witnessed it coming from a tyro constable, I would not have credited it. But to see one of my most senior officers, a man whose behaviour ought to be held up as a model for lower ranks, to see such conduct in him – it beggars belief. There can be no excuse for it. Of course, there will have to be a disciplinary hearing, but in the meantime, DCI Coddington, you are suspended from duty. Do you have anything to say for yourself?'

'I was sorely provoked, sir.'

'By DCI Quinn, you mean?'

'That's correct, sir.'

'I see. So what did Quinn do to provoke you?'

Quinn began to defend himself: 'Sir, I—'

Sir Edward held up his hand. 'You'll get your turn in a minute, Quinn. First I want to hear from Coddington.'

'He was trying to undermine me.'

'In what way?'

'He was talking to one of my officers. Sergeant Inchball. He was issuing commands to Sergeant Inchball and directing him to undertake investigative tasks. He was having Inchball make a telephone call.'

'Is this true, Quinn?'

'It is true that I was talking to Sergeant Inchball. I have just come from visiting Sergeant Macadam in hospital. I was telling Sergeant Inchball that I had learnt some important information from Sergeant Macadam. I had previously offered my assistance to DCI Coddington but he had refused it in no uncertain terms, so I knew that he would not be willing to accept it now. For that reason, I took the information to Sergeant Inchball, who is now a member of DCI Coddington's team, in order for him to bring it into the investigation. I was not seeking to undermine DCI Coddington but to help him.'

Coddington snorted incredulously and shook his head, as if he could not believe Sir Edward could be so easily taken in. This was clearly a mistake. It made him look like a petulant child. Not only that, he appeared to be disparaging Sir Edward.

The commissioner was not impressed. He glared at Coddington, before demanding of Quinn: 'What is this new information?'

'Macadam has been able to positively identify his assailant.'

'I see. Do we have a name?'

'Felix Simpkins.'

'And who is Felix Simpkins?'

'A young man who lives with his mother in Godolphin Avenue and who works for Griffin Mutual as a junior clerk. He has gone missing; possibly he is on the run, or he has enrolled in the army. Inchball was checking that out when DCI Coddington came over. The rest I believe you saw.'

'And is there anything that ties Felix Simpkins to Eve Cardew?'

By now, Coddington was muttering 'No, no, no!' under his breath.

'As I was trying to explain to DCI Coddington when he lost his temper, Simpkins was given a white feather by Eve Cardew at the Purity Meeting in Hammersmith Baptist Church. This was shortly before she disappeared. As you know, there was a white feather found in her mouth. It was because I knew that my assistance would meet with such a reaction from DCI Coddington that I chose to act through Inchball. I thought there might be more of a chance of Coddington taking it seriously if it came from someone other than me.'

Coddington could hold in his frustration no longer. 'Oh, I see what you've done here, Quinn! You and that floozy of yours.'

'Silence, Coddington. Whatever DCI Quinn has done, that is nothing in comparison to your misconduct. I do not expect my senior officers to settle their differences in this playground manner! In all my years, I have never seen anything like it. Not even in India. Do you hear that?'

'Yes, sir.'

'If, as it seems, you are allowing your hostility to DCI Quinn to cloud your judgement regarding the case, then you are not fit to be in charge, that much is clear. You will be informed of the date of your hearing. In the meantime, get out of my sight.'

Coddington's jaw trembled with rage as he saluted.

There was a moment of calm in his wake. Sir Edward seemed momentarily distracted, shaken by the ordeal of reprimanding one of his officers. Quinn noticed that his hands were trembling as he took the cap off a fountain pen and then stared at the nib of the pen as if unsure of its purpose. Finally, with a look of bewilderment, he replaced the cap on the pen and put it down. He then clasped his hands together and wrung them methodically. Finally, with an air of decision, he laid them flat on his desk.

'I'm putting you in charge of the Eve Cardew investigation, Quinn.'

'Thank you, Sir Edward.'

'Don't thank me. Just catch the bloody murderer.' Sir Edward glanced briefly up at Quinn. There was a flash of warning in his look.

PART VII
Release

17 September–18 September, 1914.

GERMANS AT BAY ARE HURLED BACK
BY BRITISH AND LOSE HEAVILY.

War Lord to Direct Campaign Against Invading Russians.

GREAT BATTLE TO CROSS THE AISNE.

*Daring Raid to Heligoland By British Submarine
Which Sank Cruiser.*

TWO TORPEDOES SEALED THE HELA'S FATE.

To-day brings the best of news.

The Kaiser, having failed to find his much-desired "place in the sun" on the west, has now transferred his attentions to the east.

There he will be the General commanding the German troops which hope to repulse the Russian millions.

Such joyful news must bring heartfelt relief not only to the German generals who had to face the Allies' plans and the Kaiser's criticism at the same time, but also to the invading Russians.

That the War Lord's presence will have the same effect in the east as it had in the west is not an impossibility.

Daily Mirror, *Thursday, 17 September, 1914*

THIRTY-EIGHT

The custody officer gave Quinn a look that he was used to. The one that said, *Are you sure about this?* But to give the man his due, he did not miss a beat. He reached into a drawer and produced a fat green ledger. Before anyone was going anywhere, a release form had to be filled in and signed, in triplicate.

As long as one of the higher-ups put his name to this madness, it was all the same to him. He just did what he was told, his expression made clear.

Quinn signed in the appropriate places, bristling at the man's infuriating condescension. After a while, the maintenance of scrupulous neutrality becomes offensive. And he was vaguely aware that something was going on with the fellow's eyebrows.

The custody officer was a lanky, languid individual with a long moustache that had the look of being much twirled. He took his time checking the paperwork, fingering that moustache of his all the while, as if it was in his power to put the kibosh on the whole thing after all.

'That seems to be in order,' he said at last, with a faint air of disappointment. He detached the top copy of the form along its perforated edge and handed it to Quinn. The first carbon copy beneath was also detached, to be sent in the internal mail to the central office. The third copy remained in the ledger. All this was executed with painstaking deliberation on the part of the custody officer, including the repositioning of the sheet of cardboard that prevented any writing on the top form imprinting on the forms beneath. He detached himself from his stool with the same meticulous care that he had used to detach the sheets of the form. He whistled through his teeth something that was very nearly a tune, while his face assumed an absent-minded look. Then he held up one hand to point decisively at nothing, before he turned to take down a set of keys from a hook on the wall behind him. The whole pantomime was done to make the point that as far as he was concerned this whole business of releasing prisoners went very much against the grain.

The custody suite was in the basement of New Scotland Yard. There was something satisfyingly symbolic about this. The whole weight of the law, in the shape of the very headquarters of the Metropolitan Police Force, was bearing down upon the individuals who were being held there.

The officer led Quinn to the cells, the doors of which were painted in a bottle-green enamel. *Who chooses the colours of these things?* It was the first time the thought had ever occurred to Quinn, even though he had been to the cells numerous times before. It was the first time, however, since he had himself been incarcerated inside a cell, although that had been in a lunatic asylum, not a police station. The experience had inevitably changed his perspective. This particular colour was no doubt chosen for its neutrality. It was intended to neither cheer nor depress, neither to uplift with hope nor oppress with despair, those who were brought to it. It was a colour that offered nothing, like the copper's face when Quinn had signed the form.

The key fitted into the lock with unexpected ease. Quinn had braced himself for a last minute impediment. But the key turned the mechanism with an impressive click. The heavy metal door creaked as the custody officer pushed it open, releasing a blast of fetid air from the cell.

Quinn had not seen William Egger since the day of his arrest. The young man lay on the narrow bunk, curled into a semi-foetal position with his back to the door. The rank smell came from a rusty bucket in the corner that served as Egger's latrine. A small cloud of delirious flies buzzed around it.

The light seeped in through the bottom third of a window, set high in the wall and cut off by the ceiling.

Such was Egger's apathy that he did not stir at the sound of the door opening. He had learnt to expect nothing from such intrusions, nothing except more questioning and whatever rough treatment Coddington had sanctioned in the interrogation. Quinn did not doubt that Coddington's men would have pressed Egger hard for a confession. They would have had scant regard for his rights. Quinn knew how their minds worked. This was war. Egger was an enemy alien in their eyes. He had killed a young English girl. And taken a potshot at a policeman. Possibly he'd also been spying on a sensitive military base. Therefore everything was permitted. Normal rules did not apply.

The fact that it made no sense would not have troubled them one iota.

'You're free to go.'

When even this did not succeed in rousing him, Quinn wondered if Egger was asleep. He approached the bunk and looked down. The one eye that he could see was wide open, staring blankly at the painted brick wall inches from his face, as if he was intent on reading the graffiti that was scratched there.

'Didn't you hear me? I said you can go. We have no more questions for you.'

At last there was some movement from the young man, though it was minimal: the closing of his eyes. Then his mouth opened and he seemed to say something, but Quinn didn't catch it. 'I beg your pardon?'

Egger opened his eyes again. He did not turn to face Quinn, did not move at all from the bunk. He addressed his remark to the wall. 'So that's it? You got no more questions?'

'That's right.'

Egger forced out a laugh. It was more a sharp expulsion of bitter air. 'So what was all that about, then?'

'I have not been involved in your case so far, so . . .'

At last, Egger rolled on to his back to look up at Quinn. 'Except you was the one what pulled me in.'

'It was the only option you had.'

'I trusted you. Quick-fire Quinn. He'll do right by me.'

'It wasn't down to me. If it had been, you would never have been arrested in the first place. We might have wanted to talk to you, but—'

'I know what your *talkin'* is!'

'No.'

'One man to hold me, two to lay into me with the rubber hose. You rozzers love a nice length of rubber hose, doncha?'

'I'm sorry to hear that you have been treated like that. If you wish to make a complaint . . .'

'Forget it.'

'If it's any consolation, DCI Coddington has been taken off the case. He has been suspended from duty pending an enquiry.'

'You coppers is all the same.'

'We make mistakes. A mistake was made here. I apologize for the distress you have suffered. It shouldn't have happened. I

am afraid these are difficult times. The war has made everyone
jumpy, and your . . .'

'What? Me being German? Is that what you're gonna say?
Only I ain't German. Me old ma's English. She was born in
Shepherd's Bush, same as me. I can't speak German, ain't never
been to Germany. That don't cut the mustard with you fellas.
You already made your minds up, aincha?'

Egger sat up on the edge of the bunk and rubbed his face with
the palms of both hands.

'The sergeant here will make sure that all your belongings are
returned to you.'

Egger looked down at his feet. 'I wouldn't mind my shoelaces
back.'

'Of course.'

'And the rest of it.'

The custody officer saw his opportunity to make it clear how
much he was a stickler when it came to returning effects, though
he might turn a blind eye to certain other things. 'It's all in the
safe. You'll get everything back you signed over.' Egger slapped
his thighs and shot to his feet at last. 'Ma'll be at her wits' end,
she will.' A wince of pain yanked his mouth in a wide spasm as
he took his first tentative step towards the door. He blew out his
cheeks and held a lingering look of recrimination on Quinn.

THIRTY-NINE

Quinn was under no illusions. He could expect nothing but
trouble from the Coddington loyalists left on the investigation. Men like Leversedge and his cronies. In the same
way that Inchball had been reporting back to him while
Coddington was in charge, he was sure that the traffic in information would be going the other way now. He may have won
the command, and in the process taken over Coddington's office,
but he could trust no one. Except Inchball. He could always count
on Inchball.

As for the bloody office, he didn't want it, hadn't asked for it,
but Thompson had insisted as soon as he had heard of Sir Edward's

decision. As far as Quinn could work out, the CID chief's intention was to make his life as difficult as possible. He knew that Quinn's sudden ascendancy would be unpopular with the men. By rubbing their noses in it, he would stir up even greater resentment against Quinn. Quinn would fail and Thompson's man Coddington would be reinstated.

It was a peculiar sensation, sitting behind Coddington's desk, looking out across the floor of the CID office towards the desk he had briefly occupied. He almost expected to see himself still sitting there, sorting through the sack of letters. He felt like an imposter, and yet it was Coddington who had for so long been the one who had passed himself off as Quinn, assuming his trademark herringbone ulster, as if that was all you needed to do to become a great detective: to wear a certain type of raincoat.

The case file pertaining to Eve Cardew's death was open on the desk. It contained little of substance. On the top lay a one-page confession to the murder which Coddington had drawn up in William Egger's name. It remained unsigned.

There was a diffident tap at the door, which Quinn had left open, just as Coddington usually did. He looked up to see DI Leversedge wearing an uneasy smile, his eyes shifting nervously about. He noticed for the first time how blue Leversedge's eyes were.

'May I come in?'

Quinn nodded, watching the other man carefully as if he might do something unpredictable and dangerous at any moment. Leversedge closed the door behind him.

'I just wanted to say, it's good to have you on the investigation, sir.'

This was such an unexpected remark that Quinn couldn't suppress an incredulous snort.

'No, I mean it. I know we haven't always . . . I haven't always . . . you may not have thought that I . . . because of my . . . you may have thought that I . . . that I was . . .'

'Coddington's man.'

'Yes. That. You may have thought that.'

'You aren't?'

'DCI Coddington and I go back a long way. But . . . he's not . . . well . . . he's not one-tenth of the detective you are.'

Quinn frowned. This was indeed a turn up for the books. But

then again, what alternative did Leversedge have? 'One-tenth? I wouldn't have put it so high as that myself.'

'It's hard to put a figure on it.' A smirk yanked up the corner of Leversedge's mouth.

'On what?'

'His incompetence.' Those blue eyes twinkled with the intoxicating allure of disloyalty.

'You know that he got the idea of his coat from me?'

'Oh yes. Everyone used to laugh at him behind his back for it.'

'Even you?'

'I'm afraid so.'

'I thought you were his friend.'

Leversedge shrugged. The blue of his eyes seemed suddenly very cold.

Quinn held up the unsigned confession. 'Did you have any hand in this?'

Leversedge shook his head with emphatic force. 'No,' he added firmly, so that there should be no doubt. So much denial could only mean he was lying.

'This is what your case hinged on?'

'Coddington was convinced. He just needed to get a confession.'

'He told me he had a confession.'

'Egger said he could have killed her, he wished he'd killed her, he wanted to kill her. But he never said he actually did it. It was driving Codders mad.'

Quinn flicked an eyebrow at *Codders*. 'Do you believe William Egger killed Eve Cardew?'

Leversedge shook his head.

'And yet you went along with this?'

'You know Coddington. You couldn't argue with him. Once he got an idea in his head, you couldn't shake it out.'

'But you raised your objections? They will be in the file?'

'I told him what I thought, yeah. But I didn't write it down. There was no point. He was my CO. I had to follow orders. You can't have men chipping away at your authority, undermining your leadership. You know that.'

'I value a frank exchange of opinions with my officers.'

'Yes, and then you tell us what to do and we get on with doing it.'

'You know that I have released William Egger?'

'I had heard.'

'Do you think that is a mistake?'

Leversedge shrugged. 'I heard you fancy someone else for it. So . . . it makes sense to let Egger go. Who is he, this other suspect?'

'His name's Felix Simpkins.'

'What put you on to him?'

'Witnesses saw Eve Cardew hand him a white feather on the day she was murdered.'

'What witnesses?'

'It's a woman called Mrs Ibbott and her daughter Mary. They came to me informally as they know me from—' Quinn broke off. It was excruciating to bring any detail of his private life into police work, no matter how innocuously. 'Mrs Ibbott used to be my landlady.'

'You trust them, then? They wouldn't be trying to fix this Simpkins fella up?'

'They have no motive to do that.'

'You can never be too sure.'

'And yet you arrested William Egger on the basis of the flimsiest of anonymous tip-offs.'

'It wasn't my doing, I told you. And if you want to know, I said the same to Coddington.'

'I'm sure you did.'

For a long moment Leversedge stood looking at Quinn without saying a word. The sarcasm in Quinn's remark was inescapable. Leversedge was calculating how to respond to it. Everything seemed to hang on what he said next.

'Look, you know what it's like in here. Or maybe you don't. You've been up in that attic of yours for so long. This is a tribe. These men, they're not clever like you, most of them aren't anyway. They don't think things through. They don't see the big picture. They've got instincts, that's all. That's what they act on. That's what drives them. Instincts. Emotions. Call it what you like. Now you may think DCI Coddington is a prize chump, but the men . . . the men liked him. He was one of them. Of their tribe. He was the chief of the tribe. The instinct here is loyalty.' The smirk returned to Leversedge's face, as if he was aware of the irony of him of all people talking about loyalty. Or perhaps he was simply laughing at the fools who placed such store by it. 'Now you, you're clever, you're a great detective, no one's disputing that. But the men don't like you. Sorry and all that, but that's just the way it is. They don't like you because they don't know you. As far as the tribe's concerned, you're an outsider. And the tribe doesn't like outsiders. They specially don't like outsiders who've done the dirty on the old chief so they can take possession of his hut.'

Quinn thought about challenging that 'done the dirty' but he was too interested in what Leversedge had to say. He nodded for him to go on.

'The way I see it, you need the men on your side. You can't bring this Felix Simpkins fella in on your own. Or not just you and Inchball. You need the men. And you need me to bring them over to you.'

'And how will you do that?'

'If I tell them you're all right, that's enough for them.'

'Why would you do that?'

Leversedge's expression became serious, almost sinister. 'One good turn deserves another, don't you think?'

Quinn felt a tight compression around his heart. It was the grip of corruption. There were days when he hated his fellow policemen and there seemed little difference between them and the criminals they pursued. It disgusted him to think that he might become tied to Leversedge in some loathsome bond of reciprocal favours. All the same, it was useful to know where one stood with these types. 'What particular good turn did you have in mind?'

'Listen, I want to help you, guv. I really do. I'm not interested in stirring up trouble. I'll deliver you the respect of the men. All I'm asking in return is that *you* show me a bit of respect. I'm not Coddington. I'm my own man. Let me in. Let me work with you on this. We'll get the bastard who killed that girl.'

'You were there when Sergeant Macadam was shot.'

'A regrettable incident. But I have to say, and it pains me to say it, Sergeant Macadam was acting without due authorisation from either myself or DCI Coddington. If he'd stuck to what he was told to do, he wouldn't have got hurt.'

'Did you see anything?'

'Do you think I would have let Mac go chasing after him on his own if I had?'

Quinn offered no answer to that.

'Now then, shall I gather the men together for a briefing? You can tell us all about this Felix Simpkins chap.'

Quinn could not help wincing at Leversedge's tone of easy familiarity, as if to say that everything was settled between them now, and on a mutually beneficial footing. The final twist of Leversedge's mouth suggested that he understood Quinn's discomfort completely.

FORTY

There were a dozen or so detectives in the room. Most of them looked like they'd been told to 'give the new guv'nor a chance' by a man who winked knowingly as he said it. There was none of the lively banter that usually preceded briefings, the snatches of gallows humour and facile ribaldry. They stood before Quinn in stony silence.

As for DI Leversedge, he managed to keep his face straight at least. He gave Quinn the briefest of reassuring nods, a sign of the new understanding that existed between them. If he had been playing Quinn, he would have been more effusive in his support. He was eager to make his mark on proceedings, taking control of the situation right from the start. He clapped his hands together to silence a room that was already dumbstruck. 'Right, you lot. That's enough of that. You all know why we're here. You may have thought we had little Evie's killer banged up, but it turns out we didn't.'

There were some grumbles of discontent, which Leversedge was quick to quell. 'Come on now, that's enough of that. I know you all thought the world of old Codders. We all did. We all do. But this job isn't about winning popularity contests. We're detectives. Our job is to detect. You know me and DCI Coddington were like this.' Leversedge showed them his two index fingers linked together. 'Which is why it gives me no pleasure to say this to you. Codders got it wrong. Fair and square. Lucky for us, we've got DCI Quinn here to put us right.'

This provoked a small chorus of half-hearted jeers, which

Leversedge met with a stern glance. Someone even called out 'Quick-fire Quinn?' derisively.

Quinn frowned, as if he was too deep in thought to notice the heckle. 'Thank you, DI Leversedge. The first thing I will say is that we don't, in fact, know who killed Eve Cardew. Not yet, we don't. But we do know who shot Sergeant Macadam.' Quinn nodded at Inchball. 'Sergeant Inchball, if you will do the honours.'

Inchball began to circulate the printed pages that he had had done up by the print office.

'This is Felix Simpkins, positively IDed by Sergeant Macadam as his assailant. When he shot Macadam he was wearing the uniform of a private in the Royal Fusiliers. Inchball?'

'I checked with the regiment. There ain't no soldier in the Royal Fusiliers by the name of Felix Simpkins. Definitely not one what enlisted on Saturday the fifth of September, which is the day he must have enlisted if he did – which he didn't – because we know he weren't no soldier before that date for sure.'

'How do we know that?' Quinn knew the answer to the question he was asking. But his purpose was to make sure that everyone in the room understood the significance of the next detail that Inchball would reveal.

'Because Eve Cardew gave him a white feather for cowardice that very day.'

'Those of you who have read the ME's report will know that a white feather was found in Eve's mouth.'

A young detective with an earnest face thrust his hand into the air, like an eager schoolboy. Quinn doubted he was a troublemaker, but there was something promisingly dogged about his expression that might get him into trouble all the same. He looked like he might grow into the kind of copper Quinn could work with. 'DCI Coddington said that wasn't nothing to get excited about. He said she could have just breathed it in. Just like she might have breathed in an insect.'

'Who are you?'

The young man looked about him uncertainly, as if he was checking with his colleagues whether he should answer. 'Detective Constable Willoughby, sir.'

'Well, Constable Willoughby, what do you think of that . . . *theory*?'

Willoughby's earnestness tipped over into panic, which he swallowed down in a single noisy gulp. 'Me? What do *I* think?'

'That's right.'

Most likely, the boy had never been asked his opinion before. It would have been drummed into him that he wasn't there to think, only to do as he was told. So this would be an uncomfortable experience for him, but it would do him good. Besides, he was the one who had brought it up. Not only that, Willoughby couldn't be much older than Felix Simpkins. Which would mean he was emotionally closer to the suspect than any other man in the room. Quinn waited for him to answer. 'DCI Coddington . . .'

'Forget what DCI Coddington said. What do *you* think?'

'I have swallowed an insect myself upon occasion.'

'And?'

'Well, they kind of fly in your mouth, don't they? Little tiny creatures.'

There were sniggers from around the room, but Quinn held up his hand for Willoughby to go on.

'But a feather's different, innit? Especially this feather what was in her mouth. According to the medical report, it was two and a half inches long. I don't see a feather that big just floating about on the breeze and accidentally blowing into the first open mouth.'

'You don't? What do you see?'

'I see someone putting it there.'

'And who do you think put it there?'

'The killer.'

'And why do you think he did that?'

Willoughby screwed up his face in concentration. 'He wanted her to eat her words.'

'Why?'

'Because she said something he din' like. Maybe she called him a coward . . . I dunno.'

'How would that make him feel? A young man insulted and humiliated by a pretty girl he once carried a torch for?'

'Angry.'

'He wants to make her listen, to make her understand . . .'

'But she just keeps insulting him.'

'Until the only way he can shut her up . . .'

'Is to put his hand over her mouth and hold it there until she stops.'

Quinn nodded approvingly at his young protégé's deductions. 'Obviously, our first priority is to find Felix Simpkins. We'll need a search warrant for his mother's house. DI Leversedge, get on to it. The address is 12a Godolphin Avenue. She says he hasn't been there since last Monday, but he may have left behind something that will give us some clue as to his present whereabouts.'

'Right, guv. Will do.'

'We'll circulate the posters to every police station in London and get the flyers in the hands of every detective. If that doesn't turn up anything, we'll spread the net wider. In the meantime, let's find out all we can about his relationship to Eve Cardew. I haven't seen anything in the case file about Eve's private life. No diary. No letters. Was nothing recovered from her home?'

'DCI Coddington didn't see the point, guv. Not once we got the tip-off about Egger. I imagine he didn't want to disturb the family any more than was necessary.' It seemed that Leversedge had a talent for disloyalty. It was not a likeable trait, even if the man he was turning against was a personal enemy of Quinn's.

'Sergeant Inchball and I will go to the house and retrieve any relevant evidence we can find. I am sure we can persuade the family to cooperate.'

The door to the briefing room opened. Quinn recognized Vernon Kell, the head of MO5(g), from that first meeting in Sir Edward's office. Kell, once again in khaki, gave Quinn a nod to continue and slipped discreetly to the back of the room. Quinn could hear a sound like sandpaper being drawn lightly and slowly across flesh. It was almost inaudible, but the fact that Quinn had heard it once before attuned him to it. Quinn couldn't help thinking that Kell's asthma must have been a disadvantage in his career as a spy. It was certainly distracting. The meeting was coming to a close, but Quinn felt the need to extend it for Kell's benefit. He also wanted to keep talking to drown out the sound of Kell's laboured breathing.

'So, to recap, Felix Simpkins is our prime suspect. However, we should not allow that to blind us to the possibility that there may be others involved, or that, despite appearances, Simpkins is innocent and it may be another party altogether. We must keep an open mind, in other words. There are several details that do not, as yet, add up. Simpkins wearing the uniform of a private in the Royal Fusiliers when he shot DS Macadam. But we now know that there is no one by the name of Felix Simpkins in the regiment. This leaves open several possibilities. Either Simpkins signed up under a false name, or he joined a different regiment and Sergeant Macadam was mistaken in identifying the regimental badge. I doubt that, but it's possible. The other possibility is that Simpkins is masquerading as a member of the Royal Fusiliers. That his uniform is fake. If that is the case, we have to ask ourselves why. And where did he get it? Where did he get the gun with which he shot Macadam? Any thoughts?'

Leversedge was quick with his, eager to impress the Secret Services observer. 'Perhaps he was involved in a wider conspiracy? A third party may have supplied him with the gun and uniform. The proximity of the crime scene to the base at Wormwood Scrubs may be the significant thing here. Do we know if he has any Germanic connections?'

Quinn was reluctant to feed this particular canard but he could not very well refuse to answer the question. 'His mother is German.'

There was a general stirring in the room, as if at last something of moment had been said. Quinn couldn't help being irritated, though quite possibly it was this detail that won them over to his side. It was as if something primal in them was being satisfied. If they had felt cheated at losing one 'German' as a suspect, they were being compensated now. As if the suspect's guilt or innocence was not what mattered to them so much as his nationality. You could swap one murdering Hun for another; it made no difference.

Quinn saw the same look of ugly satisfaction on almost all their faces, even Inchball's. There was little point trying to disabuse them. He resigned himself instead to using their prejudice to motivate them to find Simpkins. He would have to make sure that he kept a tight rein on them when it came to apprehending the boy. There were times, with certain vicious killers, when Quinn had turned a blind eye to the aggressively persuasive methods of interrogation that Inchball was skilled in. But he could not sanction such a procedure with Felix Simpkins. Whatever had driven that young man to kill Eve Cardew, if indeed he was her killer, it did not merit brutality. Something had snapped within him, perhaps. Quinn had the sense of Simpkins as a friendless, loveless individual. Even his own mother disparaged him. He was far more likely to crack and confess all if he was shown a little gentleness.

'We need to catch Simpkins before he does anything else stupid. The circumstances of Eve's murder were singular and specific. He may not even have intended to kill her. I certainly do not believe we're dealing with a ruthless multiple murderer here, and hope to God that events will not prove me wrong. I see Simpkins more as a frightened child. A number of witnesses have testified to his timidity. He appears to have been dominated by his overbearing mother. That is not to say he is any less dangerous. He has already fired recklessly at one of our own, endangering Sergeant Macadam's life. I believe it was fear that pushed him to that. Fear is a dangerous emotion, and it could cause him to lash out again, especially if he feels himself cornered. He may be a milksop mother's boy, but he is a milksop mother's boy with a service revolver. So be careful.'

Quinn gave a stern nod to dismiss the room. The men filtered out, grimly energized.

The soft, rasping sound of breathing signalled that one man remained. Kell advanced towards Quinn across the newly vacated space. Quinn saw that the other man had a rolled-up newspaper tucked under one arm. The sight of newspapers always made him apprehensive.

Kell waved the newspaper in Quinn's face. 'I hope you know what you're doing, Quinn.'

'I'm doing what I always do. Building a case based on evidence. It has not failed me to date.'

'You should take a look at this.' Kell thrust the newspaper out. It was a copy of the *Clarion*. Quinn took it gingerly.

He opened it out to read the main headline on the first page. BOSCH BUTCHER FROM BUSH FREED.

He scanned the report underneath. It was clear that the writer's view was that a terrible error had been made in releasing William Egger, who was described as the 'prime and only suspect in the murder of Eve Cardew'. The reader was directed to an editorial inside, which Quinn declined to turn to. He handed the paper back with a shrug.

'It does not concern you?'

'It concerns me that news of Egger's release got out so quickly. Someone must have leaked it. I have a good idea who.'

Kell took a few short breaths. 'This is not what I expected.'

'I can't control what's written in the papers.'

'Oh, but you can. You must.'

'My job is to catch criminals.'

'We had a criminal. You let him go.'

'He didn't do it.'

'How can you be sure?'

'I'm sure.'

'If you're proven wrong . . .'

'I won't be.'

'Do you know what your job really is, Quinn?'

'I just told you. To catch criminals.'

'No. That's what we in the espionage business call your cover.'

'I'm sorry, I don't . . .'

'Your real job is . . .'

Quinn hung on with bated breath as he waited for Kell to master his own breathing and finish his sentence.

'. . . to create the right narrative. How you *do* that is by catching criminals. But the catching of the criminals is not your ultimate objective. It is not the point.'

'It is not?'

'The truth is not as important as you may think.' Kell blurted this out quickly with a hot flash of impatience, as if he was answering some objection Quinn had raised.

Quinn said nothing, but made a mental note that it was not he who had brought up the truth.

'Who actually did or did not kill this girl is not important at all. What is important is that the police are seen to be swift and remorseless in resolving the case. Certainty is more important than truth, Quinn.'

'This is because of the war?'

'Of course it's because of the bloody war, you idiot! Everything you do is because of the war. In arresting the German butcher, we showed that we were in control. Certainty, clarity, decisiveness. Furthermore, we couldn't have asked for a more perfect villain. A German butcher, Quinn! His nationality and profession played perfectly in the national consciousness. Do you release what you have let slip through your fingers? Have you any conception what you have done? In place of certainty, clarity and decisiveness, you have sown confusion. You have confused your men. And now, with this . . .' Kell brandished the newspaper, 'you have confused the public. It will not end well. Well, at least this Simpkins chap has a German mother. I very strongly recommend that you find him and find him quick.'

'We are doing everything we can.'

'Are you, Quinn? I wonder.'

Kell shook his head and took himself from the room, which suddenly seemed very quiet without his ratcheted breathing.

FORTY-ONE

Millicent Jones stood on the corner of Goldhawk Road and Pennard Road. She saw the man watching her from the other side of the road. He was silhouetted in the muted glow from a nearby street light, its beam dimmed and narrowed so that it would not be visible from the air. There was something odd about his shape, she noticed. He seemed to be wearing a short cape, or perhaps a shawl around his shoulders. It was as if his body was formed in sections that did not fit together so well. His face was hidden in shadow but she knew that he was watching her and she knew what he wanted.

She knew too that she would give it to him. No, not give it. She would make him pay, of course. But he would get what he wanted from her, all right.

Why else would a girl be standing on a street corner at this time of night?

She had learnt early on that there was something men wanted that only women and girls could give them. She was eleven years old and the man who taught her the lesson was a 'friend' of her mother's she'd been told to call Uncle Pete.

She saw the looks that had passed between her mother and Uncle Pete. And gathered from the thrupenny bit she was given afterwards that more than looks had passed too.

And so she had learnt her second lesson. That this thing men wanted, they were prepared to pay for.

It was soon after that that her mother had put her out on the streets and told her not to come back until she had earned her keep.

'You know what to do, girl. I made sure of that,' her mother had said, as if it was something she should thank her for.

She also handed down to Millie all the essential trappings of the trade: the high-heeled sandals, the paintbox of cosmetics, the cabinet of perfumes and cures, the low-cut black dress trimmed with tassels, the string of black beads, or 'pearls' as her mother insisted on calling them, and of course, the bedraggled boa that made her sneeze and brought her out in a rash every time she wrapped it round her neck. Millie believed the feathers had once been white, but now they were a grubby grey and reminded her of wounded pigeons.

She looked again across the street. The man was still there, watching, an uncertain presence swaying in and out of the light. He was a shy one, all right. What was he waiting for? She could die of old age waiting for this one to make a move.

He should shit or get off the pot and that was the truth.

She fluffed her boa encouragingly and extended one leg through the slit in the side of her dress.

It was enough to stir him into action. Lord knew men were simple creatures. Like clockwork toys, they were. The glimpse of a girl's knee was enough to wind them up and set them in motion.

He stepped forward out of the cone of dim light and was swallowed for a moment by the inky blackness of the night. Millie could hear his footsteps as he crossed the empty street. Her body relaxed into a lolling posture as she waited for him.

And then he was there in front of her.

'You took your time, dincha, mate? Whatcha afraid of? I ain't gonna bite.'

The man said nothing in reply. He simply took hold of her arm at the bicep in a vice-like grip.

'Come with me!' His voice was as urgent as his actions now, as he dragged her along towards the alley where, by day, Shepherd's Bush Market was situated.

FORTY-TWO

Quinn stared at the telephone on the desk a split second before it began to ring. It was almost as if his look had provoked the remorseless clanging. More likely, the contraption had made a small noise, a vibration or a click, prior to ringing out in earnest, and he had subconsciously responded to that. The noise set his nerves on edge, but he was reluctant to answer the call. He was aware that this was not his office and therefore not his phone. He was afraid that he would be placed in a false position and obliged to account for himself with needless explanations. The imposter had made an imposter of him.

But there was also the possibility that it might be important.

'Quinn.'

There was silence at the other end of the line. Or rather, not quite silence. It was the crackle of wax melting in your ear after one or two drops of hydrogen peroxide have been administered.

Eventually, a thin, crumpled voice formed itself out of the crackles. 'Am I speaking to DCI Coddington?'

'No. DCI Quinn. I have taken over from Coddington.'

There was a pause as the voice took in this information.

'To whom am I speaking?' prompted Quinn.

'DI Driscoll here, from Shepherd's Bush Station. I think you'd better get over here.'

'Why? What's happened?'

'We've got another one for you.'

'Another what?' Even as he asked the question, Quinn knew what the answer would be.

'Dead body. Another girl, murdered. She was found an hour ago, in the market just off the Goldhawk Road. We think it might be connected to your case.'

'I'll meet you there.'

DI Driscoll shone his flashlight down on the body of the young woman slumped inside the arch of the railway viaduct. The beam flitted about before settling on the blood that had soaked into her dress. The quivering spotlight then zagged up to show the gaping wound in her throat where the blood had evidently come from.

The ground began to quake. The clatter of a train overhead momentarily drowned out what DI Driscoll was saying. But even without that, Quinn was finding it hard to take it in. He felt a creeping numbness come over him.

Driscoll directed his flashlight to the girl's face. Quinn knew that he always hoped for too much from the facial expressions of the dead. But usually what he saw there was only what he would expect, often less, as if death acted as an emotional mute. What might have been terror at the moment of demise somehow settled into an expression of mild surprise, or annoyance perhaps. Always, though, there was an element of defeat in the expression.

'One of the stallholders, a Mr Mills, who has the carpet and rug stall, found her when he was setting up. He thought it was a tramp at first, when he saw her feet sticking out. They get a fair few of them, so it was a natural assumption to make. I'll draw your attention to this object . . .' Driscoll led Quinn further into the arch. The flashlight beam lapped out like the tongue of an eager dog, hunting down clues. It settled on a glinting flash of metal. 'I had my men leave it where we found it. It's a meat cleaver.' Driscoll waited a moment for that to sink in. Then, not trusting that it had, added: 'The kind used by butchers. As you can see, the blade is streaked with blood.'

Quinn felt the ground tremble again, although there was no train passing over this time. He reached out to steady himself against the curve of the arch. The bricks felt cold and damp to his touch. The arch echoed with the constant, even drip of moisture, like the tick of a clock measuring out time. For one brief moment he imagined the slime covering the bricks to be blood. And the liquid he could hear dripping was blood too.

The new Shepherd's Bush Market had only been open a few months. It was hardly the most propitious beginning for the enterprise; first the war and now this. The stalls had sprouted up like brightly coloured mushrooms alongside the railway viaduct that ran between Uxbridge Road and Goldhawk Road. Some of the traders had taken over the arches, which gave them an air of permanence that the canvas stalls lacked. The market was uncharacteristically quiet today. Uniformed police blocked it off at either end. The traders busied themselves with grumbling, flashing resentful glances towards the police. They gave the impression of having been cheated out of something valuable, which they had – the morning's takings. One or two appeared determined to stay cheerful, or perhaps it was simply habit that had them whistling breezily only yards from the corpse of a murder victim.

'Do we know who she is?'

'Millicent Jones, a known prostitute.'

'What made you think this is connected with my case?'

'Well, the meat cleaver, of course.'

A white blur on the ground near the body caught Quinn's attention. He had Driscoll shine the beam on it. A cascade of dingy feathers formed in the gloom, some of them stained red with her blood. It looked like an exploded chicken.

'She doesn't seem the type for handing out white feathers,' said Driscoll.

Quinn thought back to his own recent encounter with the prostitute in King's Cross. He remembered the parasol with which she had attempted to entice him. These girls always liked to have some cheap prop to advertise their business. 'She wasn't. That's a feather boa.'

Driscoll lifted his head and looked at Quinn thoughtfully.

'Did you find anything in her mouth?'

'I beg your pardon?'

'Did you look in her mouth?'

'I did not,' Driscoll answered firmly, as if Quinn had just asked him to commit an act of violation.

'Would you care to do so now, please?'

'Is that not a job for the Medical Examiner?'

'If you are too squeamish, then please give your flashlight to me and I will look.'

'Squeamish? You think I am squeamish?' Driscoll prized open the dead girl's mouth and shone his torch inside. 'What am I looking for?'

'It should be obvious.'

'I can see nothing.'

'There is no white feather in there?'

'No.'

'Thank you. That's all I need to know.'

Crisp footsteps behind him drew Quinn around. Leversedge stood at the entrance to the arch looking in. The two men exchanged an uneasy glance. 'This is a turn-up for the books, wouldn't you say, guv?'

'It's not the same killer.'

Leversedge drew his mouth down in a sceptical moue. 'Bit too early to say that for sure, don't you think? Especially considering how close we are to the Eggers' shop. And what with you just letting him go, it doesn't look too good, if you don't mind me saying.' Leversedge held up his palms to fend off any objection from Quinn. 'I'm only saying what everyone's thinking.'

Quinn narrowed his eyes to consider Leversedge. 'The method is completely different to Eve Cardew's murder. And besides, do you really think that if William Egger were so stupid as to commit this murder so soon after his release he would do it so close to his home, with a butcher's meat cleaver which he would leave at the scene?'

'That all smacks of psychology, guv, if you don't mind me saying. There's nothing wrong with psychology, don't get me wrong. But in my experience, you can't base a whole case on psychology alone. It confuses the jurors. No, what jurors like is a bloody meat cleaver found next to the dead body. That's the kind of clue the jury can understand. The same's true for the general public. You don't need psychology to explain this. Fella's a monster, can't control his murderous impulses. He's German, after all, isn't he?'

'You don't believe that.'

Leversedge gave a non-committal shrug.

'Someone's set this up to incriminate Egger.'

'Why would anyone want to do that?'

'To throw us off the scent.'

Leversedge paused to think about what Quinn had said. 'You don't want me to pull Egger in again, then?'

'That won't be necessary.'

'We ought at least to dust the cleaver for prints, don't you think?'

Quinn studied Leversedge's face carefully for a moment before replying, 'If you wish.'

Leversedge's mouth assumed its downward curve again, although this time seemed to be communicating satisfaction.

FORTY-THREE

Mattilde Simpkins was dressed exactly as she had been the last time she had opened the door to Quinn. But there was something forlorn about her appearance now that Quinn had not noticed before. What had seemed mildly eccentric then now struck him as positively deranged. She was dressed for a performance that she would never give. He noticed a stale odour coming off her, imperfectly masked by a liberal dousing of lavender-scented eau de toilette. Her black evening gown was faded and frayed at the cuffs, specked with pale stains. The plaits of her hair hung stiffly. Almost overnight she had become frail.

But the change that had come over her was most evident in her face. It was not simply that she looked older and more haggard. The life had gone out of her.

Her expression had lost its elasticity. Her jowls sagged. Her mouth was slack and affectless. Her eyes, rimmed red from crying, stared blankly without registering what she saw. He had seen such faces in Colney Hatch. On occasion, his own face had stared back at him from a mirror in a similar way.

Her look of stupor alerted him to another possibility. He sniffed the air more carefully and identified a whiff of strong liquor in amongst her other odours. She swayed within the door frame as she squinted at him. At last he must have come into focus. 'It's you. You're the policeman.' There was a slow, tacky deliberateness to her speech, as if she was trying very hard to appear sober. She took in the three men who were there with Quinn. 'Are they policemen too?'

'Yes. This is Detective Inspector Leversedge, Detective Sergeant Inchball and Detective Constable Willoughby.'

'Have you found my son?'

'No. Have you heard from him?'

Whereas once such a question might have provoked a tirade of complaints, she simply shook her head blankly.

'Leversedge.'

At Quinn's cue, Leversedge held up a baffling piece of paper. 'I have a warrant to search these premises.'

It was as if a switch had been thrown. All the emotion that had been lacking from her responses so far surged to the surface. Her face contracted into a clench of self-pity and a wail like steel being lathed came out of it. 'Noooooo!' She turned her back on them and fled into the depths of the basement flat.

Quinn followed her in. 'Mrs Simpkins, please! We need to look in Felix's room. That's all. We need to find Felix, to make sure that he's all right. To help him. He may be in danger. That's why we need to find him, so we can help him. There may be something in his room that will lead us to him. Please be strong, Mrs Simpkins. If you help us, it will be better for Felix, I promise you.'

But she disappeared into a bedroom and slammed the door in his face.

Quinn turned and gave the nod to the other men, who set about peering into the other rooms with practised efficiency.

In truth, there weren't many doors to check, so it wasn't long before Inchball announced the discovery of Felix's bedroom with a quiet, 'Guv.'

The room was in a state of semi-disarray, like an argument that one party had walked away from. The mess made the room look even smaller than it was, and it was small enough to begin with. The single bed had not been made. Clothes were strewn across the floor and the bed, as well as draped over the back of a wooden chair. A culture of mould was flourishing in a teacup on the bedside table. The wardrobe door hung open. Each of the drawers in a chest of drawers was pulled out to a progressively greater extent, so that it looked like a small flight of steps. 'Evidently, he left in a hurry,' said Leversedge. 'And his devoted mother hasn't been in since.'

'That's good for us,' said Quinn. 'It means we're more likely to find what we're looking for.'

'What exactly are we lookin' for, guv?' asked Willoughby.

'We won't know until we find it.'

Leversedge hiked a bemused eyebrow at Quinn before turning slowly to Willoughby. 'A diary would be useful. Any correspondence, particularly from foreign nationals, by which I mean Germans. His mother is German, so he has German cousins and uncles, etc. If you could turn up a railway timetable, that would be most useful, particularly if it has one of its destinations underlined.'

'Underlined, you say?' asked Inchball ironically.

'Circled would be acceptable too.'

'I'll see what I can do.'

Inchball set to with a focused energy that verged on brutal. He pulled out the drawer from a small desk and tipped its contents on to the floor, then knelt down to pore through them. The drawer itself was discarded carelessly. Quinn stepped around him, placing his feet fastidiously like a cat, to get to the wardrobe. Leversedge turned his attention to the chest of drawers, while Willoughby looked under the bed. There was hardly enough space for the four of them in the room, so they were forced to move with an almost choreographed consideration for each other. The meaty smell of male hormones hung in the air, to which the policemen's exertions contributed.

Quinn rifled through the clothes hanging up, his fingers blindly probing the pockets and linings of every jacket and pair of trousers. It wasn't long before he found something. To the touch, it was a strange combination of opposite attributes: it was soft but also spiky, yielding but resistant too, if he allowed his fingers to approach it from another direction. Its core was firm but it seemed to dissipate quickly into fibres of nothingness.

From the pocket of Felix's Sunday-best suit jacket, Quinn extracted a white feather, about three inches in length. 'I think I've found it. The thing that we were looking for.'

The other men stopped what they were doing and turned to him eagerly. When they saw the feather he was holding out to them, their expressions clouded. 'This changes everything,' said Quinn.

Leversedge didn't look so certain. 'Does it tell us where Felix Simpkins is?'

'No. It tells us something even more important than that.'

'Do you still want us to carry on looking?' There was a note of disappointment in Inchball's voice, as if he was afraid he might be denied a privilege that he had been looking forward to.

'Yes, turn the place upside down.'

Quinn pocketed the feather and left the others to it.

He crossed the dark, narrow hall to the door behind which

Felix's mother had disappeared. He knocked gently and went in without waiting for a response.

She was lying on the bed, fully clothed, her back to the door, facing a window across which the curtains were drawn. A feeble light seeped through them. There was a stale smell in this room too, though predominantly of mothballs. It was tidier than her son's room, which was not saying much, but the tidiness had a sterility to it. The wallpaper was a watery yellow colour, with a mottled design to suggest marble perhaps, though it put Quinn more in mind of aspic.

'Mrs Simpkins?'

There was no sound or movement from the woman on the bed. Quinn wondered if she was asleep and walked round to look at her from the other side. Her eyes were open, staring blankly into space.

'Mrs Simpkins,' he repeated. She did not look up at him. 'It's DCI Quinn.'

Even that revelation did not produce a response.

'Can you hear me, Mrs Simpkins?'

At last she stirred. It was the merest upward movement of her head. Something like a dismissive snort sounded in her throat. For some reason, Quinn thought of his own mother. The movement was similar to a disdainful mannerism of hers that she had adopted whenever he tried to speak to her of his father after his death. A glacial bitterness had gripped her, more scorn than grief. At the time, knowing nothing of his father's longstanding affair with another woman, Quinn could not understand, or forgive, her attitude. She gave the impression that she knew something that he did not know, something that she could never be induced to tell him, though she hinted at its significance often enough. Whatever it was, this secret knowledge was supposed to justify her seeming lack of compassion, not to mention her self-pity. But such was his faith in his father that he was compelled to believe she was mistaken. Worse than that, he began to hate her for what he perceived to be her disloyalty.

In truth, his mother had maintained a scrupulous display of loyalty to her deceased husband, but Quinn had always suspected that that was done for the sake of appearances rather than because she felt his father deserved it. The last thing she had wanted was people gossiping about her marriage. The only complaint that she occasionally let slip was that her husband had abandoned her, which Quinn had always taken to be a reference to his death rather than anything else. And so, the truth had been suppressed, which had created that area in which Quinn's own obsessions could take root and grow, fertilized by his conviction that his father had been murdered by a mysterious conspiracy of malign forces.

'On my sixteenth birthday, Mumie presented me with the gown that I was to wear for my performance.' Mattilde's voice was deep and husky. It trembled with a sense of awe, as if she was struck not so much by the momentousness of what she was saying, but of speech itself. 'It came in a big box tied up with a silk ribbon, and layers and layers of tissue paper inside. I knew what it was, of course; there was no surprise, because I had been to Frau Ganz's atelier to be measured for it. She had a tiny room on the fourth floor of a building on Hausvogteiplatz. There was no lift. We had to climb the stairs. They smelled musty and damp and were very grubby. I remember thinking this is not very nice, not what you expect from a dressmaker who serves the cream of Berlin society. It was a long way too. But I did not mind really because I was so excited. I flew up those stairs, my feet barely touched them! Mumie chose the fabrics for me. The bodice was crushed velvet in midnight blue. The skirt was a cascade of black taffeta. The neckline was very low! Shocking! Though it was covered with a fine gauze of lace. "Mumie!" I said. "You are not a child any more," she said. "You are a woman now. You must make an impression when you walk out on to that stage."

'I loved that dress. Even though I had not chosen the fabrics, had had no say in its design, I loved it. I loved the feel of it against my skin as I plunged my arms into the box. I wanted to dive into it. To drown in it. I had never seen anything so fabulous. If I played well, Mumie said, I would get more gowns like this. As many as I wanted!

'I put the gown on and looked at myself in the mirror. I had become a different person. But it was the person I was always meant to be. I turned for Vati to see me. He looked me up and down, so slowly and strangely, like I had never seen him look at me before. And then I saw that his eyes were glistening. A tear, a single tear, ran out. But he was smiling too. "No," he said, "you are not Vati's little girl any more."

'The day of the concert came. I had such butterflies in my stomach. In the morning, I was sick. "It is a good omen," Mumie said. But I could not eat a thing all day. As I waited in the wings to go on, I held my hands out in front of me; they were shaking. Shaking shaking shaking. We had been told that a great impresario was in the audience. Herr Lieberstein was his name. I had heard Mumie and Vati talking about him with great excitement in their voices. This man had the power to make our fortune! But Vati came up to me and he said, "Forget about Herr Lieberstein. Forget about the audience. Forget about them all. Just play, just play for your Vati."

'At last it was time to walk out on to the stage and take my place at the piano. As soon as I held my fingers over the keys, the shaking stopped. I played as I had never played before. I did not play for the impresario. I did not play for the audience. I played for Vati.

'At the end, as I took my bow, the audience erupted in applause. They stamped their feet and cheered. Calls of "Brava! Brava!" I was even required to play an encore. They would not let me go without an encore! But Herr Lieberstein, we discovered, had already left. He did not stay to pay his compliments.

'After the concert, Vati kissed me tenderly on each cheek and told me that I had played exquisitely. Professor Friedrich Kiel himself described my interpretation of the first movement of Beethoven's Sonata No. 2 as a revelation. But evidently it was not good enough for Herr Lieberstein.' She swallowed heavily, momentously. 'There would be no more beautiful gowns.'

'Mrs Simpkins, there's something I need to tell you.'

For the first time she looked up at him. Her gaze was stripped of pretence, but also of hope. 'That day, the day of my sixteenth birthday, it was the best day of my life. There has never been a day to match. Nothing that has happened to me since then has made me as happy as the gown that my mother presented to me on my birthday. Nothing has moved me like my father's tears when he looked at me and saw me as a beautiful young woman for the first time. My whole life was ahead of me. I had so much promise. I was to play at the Stern Conservatory before an invited audience. The famous impresario Herr Lieberstein himself would be there.' All at once, her voice lost its wistfulness and grew as hard and sharp as a pointed stick. 'What did I do to deserve this? A son who is a murderer!'

'That's just it, Mrs Simpkins. I don't believe Felix killed Eve Cardew.'

'What does it matter? He has abandoned me. As his father before him abandoned me. I am alone in a foreign country. I have no one. He is worse than a murderer to me. He is a boy who does not love his mother.' Her voice wound itself up into a high-pitched, self-pitying whine.

There was a tap on the door. Quinn turned to see Inchball scowling distastefully at the woman on the bed. 'Got a minute, guv?'

It was a relief to get out of that bedroom. The atmosphere created by the yellow wallpaper, the dim light and Mattilde Simpkin's cloying nostalgia was suddenly unbearable to Quinn. The colour of the wallpaper particularly distressed him, as it put him in mind of a nasty medicine he had been forced to take as a child. He could not remember what it was for. Only how he had gagged when the spoon was held to his mouth.

Inchball held out a dog-eared sheet of paper, torn from an exercise book. It was criss-crossed with well-worn folds, along some of which it was falling apart. Large looping letters in a child's clumsy hand filled the page. 'I found it in that desk of his. Inside a *book*.' Inchball managed to imbue the last word with suspicion.

> *Dearist Felix,*
> *Meet me in the Scrubs at 4 o'clock. There is a plase near where the airships land where my brother and his pals have bilt a den out of branches and things. For we must run a way. A Great Evil has come in to my life you would not believe. I will tell you all later. You are my Saviour. We will live in a cottige with flowers and hens. I can do sewing. No one will find us. I love you and will love you forever. You are my only hope. If you do not come I will kill myself.*
> *Your Darlin Eve*

Judging by the handwriting, Eve must have been about eight or nine when she wrote it. Perhaps even younger. If that was so, it was a startlingly precocious letter. There was the odd spelling mistake but Quinn had seen more wayward efforts written by adults. For example, she had had no trouble with the difficult words 'Saviour' and 'believe'. Her father's influence, no doubt. There was a touching naiveté about the sentiments, but an unsettling intensity too. It had evidently made an impression on Felix Simpkins, who had kept it safe all these years.

Quinn folded the paper along its creases and handed it back to Inchball. 'Get the others.' He spoke quietly, without any urgency or excitement in his voice. But the steady gaze and barely perceptible nod with which Inchball greeted the command showed that he grasped the significance of the moment.

FORTY-FOUR

I t was strange to sit in the back of a Model T police car and be driven by someone other than Macadam. But Willoughby seemed a capable enough chauffeur, despite his youth, if a little heavy-handed with the horn. In fairness, Quinn couldn't criticize him for that. Macadam had at times shown the same tendency. If anything, Macadam was a more reckless driver, taking corners at speed and pulling out into oncoming traffic. Quinn had thought nothing of it at the time. But now, when he compared it to Willoughby's more cautious approach, it seemed a miracle that they had ever arrived at their destination in one piece. And yet it was now that he had the greater sense of being driven towards catastrophe.

The other vehicles on the road appeared lumbering and backward, like great mastodons that should have become extinct aeons ago. It was either that or they were engaged in a widespread conspiracy to frustrate Quinn at every turn.

As they drove along Wood Lane, the White City came into view on the left. It was like something out of a dream, a construct of imagination and wish-fulfilment. It reminded Quinn of an archaeological site, like the forum of Rome or the Acropolis of Athens, except that these were monuments of the future, not the past. Even so, there was an empty desolation to the site. The buildings there were not ruins, not yet, but seemed to hold within their shallow grandeur the ghost of their own dilapidation. The White City stood as a symbol of aspiration, but it was bereft of purpose. Except that now, like many buildings of uncertain status, it had been co-opted into the war effort. A space that had grown out of a vision of humanity coming together, of peace and harmony between nations, of the friendly rivalry of games, was now being used to plan and manufacture more efficient ways for one group of humans to inflict destruction on another.

It seemed ironic too that the site that had been chosen for it was so close to a prison, next to which there was a workhouse and an infirmary. These somewhat less noble buildings came briefly into view, as a sobering reminder of where you could end up if you failed to find a place in the great and glorious vision that had been decided upon for mankind's destiny.

Willoughby steered the car sharply towards the verge and pulled up. They were on Scrubs Lane, the road that ran between Wormwood Scrubs and Little Wormwood Scrubs, alongside the railway. The car gave a short squeal as Willoughby yanked the handbrake on, then shuddered noisily in the dying of the engine.

Quinn looked out at the fence that ran along the park perimeter. 'It was here, wasn't it, where Macadam was shot?'

'That's right, guv.' Leversedge avoided Quinn's eyes as he answered the question.

Quinn reached inside his jacket beneath his trademark herring-bone ulster and felt the cold, unyielding metal of the service revolver holstered there. He felt the constriction of the holster harness around his chest, as if it were a disease that limited his ability to breathe. He did not take the gun out yet. But something of its steely presence entered him and enabled him to get out of the car.

Leversedge led them into the park through a gate. Ahead of them was the giant hangar of the Royal Navy Air Service base. Quinn stood for a moment to take it in. The sheer scale of it pulled him up short. He felt a sliver of doubt enter him. Perhaps he had been too hasty to dismiss the possibility that the case had something to do with the war, after all. He felt a burning curiosity to know what went on inside that hangar. How much more keenly must the agents of the enemy have felt it?

The angry clacking of an agitated blackbird drew his gaze to a line of scrappy bushes. Leversedge armed a swathe of branches to one side, to create a way through. Quinn bowed into an enclosed space, hidden away from the main park. A sudden chill entered the air, which hung stagnant and bated, as if the ground was holding its breath. Quinn instinctively knew that this was where Eve had been killed.

Leversedge pointed wordlessly at the crude assemblage of wood and corrugated iron at the apex of the space.

Quinn reached inside his jacket, and this time he withdrew his service revolver.

They spread out into a fan, and paced with slow, noiseless steps towards the den, their bodies sitting lower than they would if they were walking naturally. There was something self-conscious about their gait, as if they were concentrating hard to perform the steps of a complicated dance. Their faces were grimly deadpan, grey with tense anticipation. If it were not for the fact that the man leading them in their dance was holding a gun, they would have appeared ludicrous.

Inchball was on Quinn's left; beyond him, Willoughby. Leversedge was on Quinn's right. As they approached the den, they drew closer together. Quinn drew a circle in the air with his free hand. The other men took up positions around the den.

The entrance to the den was a flap of tarpaulin covering a crawl hole low to the ground. Quinn sank to his haunches and began to edge the tarpaulin slowly to one side. The heavy cloth cracked at the movement. A cascade of dirt and debris fell from its rigid folds. Spiders scuttled out of the way, light-starved insects flexed their antennae. The precarious structure above shifted dangerously.

Quinn kept his head to the side of the gap he had opened up and peered inside. The first thing he saw were the soles of the man's boots, one on top of the other, right there in the entrance. He was lying on his side. His face was obscured by the focused gloom of the den's interior. Quinn could not be sure, but if he had to guess, he would have said that he was asleep.

He saw the glint of the gun lying on the ground in the lee of the man's huddle. He felt an aching tremble in his reaching arm as he stretched to retrieve it. He held the revolver behind him for one of his officers to take.

When that was done, he let the tarpaulin fall and holstered his own weapon. Then he pulled the tarpaulin all the way across and

shook the sleeping man by the leg. 'Come on, Felix, wake up.'
He kept his voice low and calm, as if he was a father waking
his son on a school day. The young man stirred groggily and
lifted his head, blinking. 'It's time to come out,' said Quinn.

Felix Simpkins sat up and rubbed the loose dirt from his hair.
His face was as black as a coal miner's, though streaked with
paths of stark white skin.

All at once Felix's body shook in a few short convulsions,
like a cat coughing up a fur ball. He burst into tears and new
streaks of white were washed away on his cheeks.

Quinn stood back and hauled him out by the boots.

The sorry spectacle stretched out on the ground was at first
difficult to decipher. As Macadam had described, he was dressed
in a khaki uniform, though his legs lacked puttees and his head
a cap. With his teary eyes and quivering lip, he did not look
much like a soldier.

He had made no effort to resist, not even scrabbled for his
gun.

'You damn well nearly killed one of my officers,' said Quinn,
with the tone of a schoolmaster chastizing a pupil.

'You mean he's not dead? Thank God! Oh, thank God!' Felix
began to blub again, but this time they were tears of relief.

'Get up!'

Felix scrambled to his feet and stood with his head hung in
shame.

'You'll be charged with attempted murder for sure, while we
make up our minds what else to charge you with.'

'Yes, sir.'

'What were you thinking, you bloody fool?'

'I . . . I . . . I'm not really in the army. I bought this from a
junk shop on the Goldhawk Road. I wanted to enlist, but I
couldn't go through with it. I thought I would but I still couldn't.
So I thought if I wore the uniform it would be the next best
thing. I . . . I . . . I'm sorry.'

'Eve Cardew giving you the feather pushed you into this, I
suppose?'

'I already had the uniform. But I hadn't worn it until she gave
me the feather.'

'You young fool. What were you doing here that day you shot
my detective?'

'I wanted to see her.'

'Why?'

'I don't know. I can't explain it. Once, I was meant to meet her here. But I . . . I let her down. I failed her. Perhaps if I had met her then, when she asked me to, she would still be alive and none of this would have happened. I suppose I wanted to put things right somehow. I thought if I could find out who killed her . . .'

'You were playing detective!' cried Inchball contemptuously. 'Fool.'

One thing was still puzzling Quinn. 'Where did you get the gun?'

'From the same shop. I wasn't going to buy it but the man there persuaded me. I didn't know it worked. I didn't think it would actually fire. I didn't even think I was pointing it at him. I meant to fire into the air.'

Was it plausible that the boy was such a bad shot that he had missed even when he had taken aim at the open sky? Quinn had seen more unlikely things with his own eyes.

'But at the last minute, my hand sort of slipped.'

'You shouldn't have been playing with the bloody gun in the first place,' observed Quinn sharply.

'I thought I'd get into trouble for wearing the uniform. And for being here.'

'Well, you would have done, but it would have been a damn sight less trouble than you're in now.'

'I'm just glad he's not dead.' Felix began to rock with sobs again.

'Oh, do stop crying!'

'Did you kill Eve Cardew?' The question was fired out by Leversedge.

The young man's look of appalled horror was enough of a denial. 'What? No! Of course I didn't. I loved her.'

'It's often the ones as say that what turn out to be the murderers,' observed Inchball darkly.

Felix flashed a look of mute appeal towards Quinn.

Quinn shook his head as he took in the boy's abject appearance. He was in a filthy state, that was true enough, but somehow he was not as physically ruined as Quinn might have expected. 'How have you survived out here? What have you done for food?'

'I . . . I have money.' But there was a flicker of disingenuous-ness in his eyes.

'You haven't been to the shops like that. You would have been seen. We'd have caught you before now.'

Felix gave a sullen shrug. His face darkened, a blush colouring the skin beneath the grime.

Quinn stooped down and looked back inside the den. He brought out a shallow enamel bowl and an empty milk bottle. He gripped the bowl by a handkerchief, while he had the upturned milk bottle loosely skewered on a stick in his other hand. 'Someone has been helping you.'

Felix was quick to deny it. 'No!' Too quick.

'Who?'

'No one. I stole the milk. From a doorstep. Sorry. I'll pay for it.'

Quinn held out the bowl. 'And this?'

Felix gave another shrug. 'I found it.' It was a child's lie, innocent in its complete lack of plausibility and logic.

'Take him in.'

Inchball and Willoughby grasped an arm each, vying to be the one who clapped the handcuffs on him.

'I've got him, thank you, DC Willoughby.' Inchball wasn't just pulling rank. It was his association with Macadam that gave him the right to make the arrest.

It looked like Felix was about to turn on the waterworks again. A pout bubbled at his mouth and his voice spiked into a high whine. 'I wasn't trying to kill him. I didn't know it would fire.'

'Tell that to the jury,' said Inchball. 'You coming, guv?'

Quinn was staring down at the enamel bowl. It was white with a blue rim; here and there the enamel was chipped away and scratched, evidently an old bowl, one that would not be missed, perhaps. It looked as though it had been licked clean.

'Guv?'

'I'll see you back at the Yard,' said Quinn. He held the enamel bowl out to Inchball as if it contained freshly picked cherries. When Inchball approached as if to take one, Quinn withdrew it and put forward the milk bottle instead. 'I want that dusted for fingerprints. I'll hang on to this a little while longer, I think.'

Inchball nodded to Willoughby for him to take the milk bottle on its stick off the governor. He had his own hands full with Felix.

'What do you want me to do?' asked Leversedge. Quinn suspected that he was angling to tag along. Perhaps Leversedge genuinely wanted to make himself useful, or was simply curious about what Quinn was up to. But Quinn could not forget that until recently Leversedge had been Coddington's animal, and so he could not dispel the thought that he wanted to stick with him so that he could report back to his master.

Besides, Quinn's instinct was that he wanted to be alone.

So it was a surprise even to himself when he said, 'You can come with me.'

FORTY-FIVE

And so Quinn found himself once again on the doorstep of the house in Wallingford Avenue. He still had hold of the enamel bowl, which created the impression that he had come round to beg for something to put in it, flour or sugar perhaps. He quickly hid it under his ulster and kept it there with his left arm held stiffly against his body.

On the way over Leversedge had shown commendable restraint. It was clear he had questions, but for some reason he preferred to keep them to himself. So the two men had fallen silently into step. Occasionally Leversedge had looked at Quinn as if he might ask a question, but thought better of it at the last moment. Perhaps he simply did not wish to show himself at a disadvantage. Alternatively, it was possible that he wanted to detach himself from whatever Quinn had in mind. The less he knew, the less culpable he was if Quinn turned out to have it spectacularly wrong. *Nothing to do with me*, he could always plead when Quinn was left with egg on his face. And if by some miracle Quinn succeeded in cracking the case, he was there by his side to share in the glory. It was a canny tactic; hedging his bets.

There was another possibility, of course. That Leversedge's detachment was the studied neutrality of an observer. He was watching Quinn and making mental notes, so that he could report back to a third party. Quinn was in no doubt who that might be.

Then, at the last moment, as they were waiting for the door

to be opened, Leversedge couldn't help himself: 'How do you want to play this?'

There was only one way to answer such a question. 'Let me do all the talking.'

Before Leversedge could object, the door was opened by the same gaunt woman dressed in black who had let Quinn in last time, her hair tied up as before, though now he noticed even more of those loose strands of grey, as if her derangement had progressed from the last time he had seen her. The whites of her eyes were clearer, but the same dark rings stood out from the exceptional paleness of the rest of her face.

'Is Pastor Cardew at home?'

'No.'

'Very well. May I then speak to Mrs Cardew?'

The woman's face clouded in suspicion. 'And who might you be?'

The question threw Quinn. 'Do you not remember me?'

'I have never seen you before.'

'I came here. You let me in. I spoke to Pastor Cardew and his son, Adam.'

Quinn was aware of Leversedge's agitated fidgeting beside him, prompted by the information that Quinn had been to the house before.

'Ah. You are no doubt mistaking me for my sister, Gwyneth. We are twins. Identical twins.'

'So *you* are Mrs Cardew?'

'Yes. Gwyneth was good enough to take care of the house after . . . after what happened to Eve.' A tremor shook her jaw. 'Gwyneth has gone now.'

'That's right. You were indisposed the last time I came to the house.'

Mrs Cardew averted her eyes as if flinching away from a blow.

Quinn took off his bowler hat and bowed his head. 'I am truly sorry for your loss. We are doing what we can.'

Mrs Cardew glared uncomprehendingly at Quinn, then turned her gaze on Leversedge. 'You are the police?'

Leversedge, perhaps remembering Quinn's prohibition, merely raised his eyebrows and nodded.

'I am Detective Chief Inspector Quinn and this is Inspector Leversedge. We are investigating your daughter's death.'

'You arrested a man and then let him go.' She gave the factual statement a steely, accusatory intonation.

'He was not the murderer.'

'Have you found the murderer now?' There was the same uncompromising edge to her voice.

'May we come in? I think it would be better to discuss these matters inside.'

Her eyes narrowed, then something shifted inside her, surrender perhaps, or possibly calculation. She stood aside to let them in.

Quinn had the impression that her resemblance to her sister was very close indeed. But then again, perhaps grief makes doppelgängers of us all.

The pallor of her face stayed with him even though it was turned away from him. He saw it now as a sign not of sickness, but of a kind of luminous energy. He would not go so far as to describe it as strength, but there was something thrilling – momentous, even – about it. She shone with righteous anger.

Quinn could imagine that, in happier times, she and her husband must have made a handsome couple.

She led them past the scriptural embroideries and Bible scenes, through into the same parlour where he had interviewed Pastor Cardew and Adam. The drapes were still drawn, though a fractured light spilled in from a gap in the curtains.

She gestured for them to sit down. Leversedge accepted the invitation with a solemn nod, but Quinn remained on his feet. He took his handkerchief from his pocket and produced the enamel bowl from his ulster, with what he recognized as a needless flourish. 'Do you recognize this?'

Mrs Cardew frowned and held out her hand to take it.

'I'm sorry. I can't let you hold it. There may be fingerprints on it.'

'It's a bowl.'

'Yes. What I am trying to establish is whether you possess such a bowl.'

'It looks familiar, yes. I should think they are very common. I believe we bought ours from Blackley's.'

'Where is it?'

'In the kitchen, I should think.'

'Would you be so kind as to fetch it for me?'

Mrs Cardew tore herself away from the sight of Quinn as if
he were some extraordinarily compelling spectacle.

They were left with the ponderous ticking of the grandfather
clock hanging the heavy seconds in the air between them like
an unspoken grudge.

They could hear the clattering of pots and pans from the
kitchen, growing more frantic and frustrated as the minutes
passed. Quinn watched the minute hand move three slow, arthritic
minutes and at exactly five past twelve, Mrs Cardew came back
into the room.

She was empty-handed.

'It appears to be missing.'

'This could be it, then?'

'Yes, I suppose it could be. Where did you find it?'

'The same place we found Felix Simpkins. Close to the spot
where Eve was killed.'

'Felix Simpkins? So *Felix* killed her? Is that what you're
saying? I don't understand.'

Quinn did not answer. He was more interested in studying
Mrs Cardew's confusion and incredulity. She sank down on to
a chair. Quinn sat opposite her to watch her face.

'You don't think he did?' Quinn said at last, his voice low and
throbbing with tense potential.

'Felix? I would not have thought him capable of such a thing.
Why did he do it?'

'I have not said that he did.'

She closed her eyes, revealing to him the fine, delicate flickering
of her eyelids. 'I am tired, so tired. My thoughts are all confused.
My heart aches. I cannot . . .' She snapped her eyes open again,
suddenly alert. 'Do you have children?'

'No, I—'

'Then you cannot imagine what it is like to lose one.'

Quinn waited for her to go on. When she did not, he thought
the time had come to ask the question that might destroy her.
'Did you know that Eve was not a virgin?'

She looked him steadily in the eye and swallowed. 'All those
years. All those years, I said nothing. I refused to believe. How
could it be true? But I saw the change that came over her. And
the way he looked at her. Did I turn a blind eye? Is that what
you will say? I turned a blind eye, as you might to a child dipping

his finger into the sugar bowl? No, it was not that. I did not turn
a blind eye. You don't know what it was like. You don't know
what *he* is like. I tried . . . I tried to stop it. I tried to tell him.
"It's not right! You mustn't! She's your daughter!" But you don't
know him. He is . . . when he is there before you, he is . . . it's
almost as if he is divine. His faith is so powerful. It sweeps away
all objections. *All* objections!' Her gaze was appalled and appalling,
stripped, raw, opened up like a gutted animal. Quinn could not
look away.

'He explained it to me. There is a word for it. Antinomian.
Have you heard of that word?'

Quinn shook his head.

'It is a real word. A real thing. He showed it to me in his
theological dictionary. Antinomian. Antinomianism. It means
that the true believer can do no wrong. Is beyond all legal and
moral law. It is there in the theological dictionary. Do you wish
to see it?'

'Perhaps later.'

'And besides, he said to me that the sin was not his, it was
Eve's. Eve was the sinner. She tempted him. And I . . . I . . . I
could not listen to him. I blocked my ears and closed my eyes
and I took to my bed. My head was in such pain. You cannot
know. I was so weak. I could not have stood up against him. He
had God on his side! I was just a weak, weak woman. We are
but weak vessels filled with sin. He has explained that to
me. What can we do?'

'When Eve went missing, after the Purity Meeting at the
church, both your husband and your son went out to look for
her, did they not?'

She closed her eyes again and nodded, her mouth drawn into
a grimace of anguish. 'And all the time I was thinking, what has
he done to her? What has he done to her? And still I said nothing.'

'You believe your husband killed your daughter?'

'I don't know. But Eve . . . was becoming . . . more unpredictable . . . wilder. She was dropping hints. She said to me once,
as we were coming out of church, "I wonder what his adoring
congregation would say if they knew what he was really like?"
To my shame – to my shame! – I reproached her! "What on
earth are you talking about, you silly girl?" Those were my very
words to her. I know that he heard her. I know that he heard her

say that. She threatened to ruin him. All of us. And she was the sinner. It was her sin that had caused all this.'

'Were there others? Other girls that he . . .?'

Her shock at the suggestion was unfeigned. 'I had not thought there might be others. I know that . . . well, the reason Gwyneth left in a hurry, I know that that was because of her sinfulness. But Gwyneth is not a child, not like Eve was. And so I never imagined . . .'

'We found another girl dead. Does the name Millicent Jones mean anything to you?'

Mrs Cardew shook her head, her look of shock deepening.

'Did she attend Sunday school at the church?' It was a long shot, considering the dead woman's profession. But she hadn't always been a prostitute, he supposed. Perhaps once she'd been a little girl who said her prayers and believed in God. An innocent child corrupted by the touch of a man she should have trusted more than any other. Who knew what paths had led Millicent Jones into criminality? Or perhaps Pastor Cardew had turned to prostitutes to satisfy his lusts, veiling his sinfulness behind a mission of salvation. It was not inconceivable that Millicent Jones had gone on the game while still a child. His connection to her could have gone back years.

'I don't know. It's so confusing. I have a terrible headache. I cannot think with all these questions.'

'Where is Pastor Cardew now?'

'He'll be there. At the church. That's where he said he was going.'

A sudden excitement – the chase closing in – energized Quinn. 'Is there something here that belongs to your husband that we may take? Something that only he handles?'

'What do you want it for?'

'It will help us to confirm whether or not he has handled this bowl and another item we found in the same place. That may suggest that he has been helping Felix Simpkins.'

'I don't understand. What does that signify?'

'The longer Felix Simpkins remained on the run from the police, the greater his guilt appeared. It was in the interest of the real murderer to keep Felix out of our reach.'

'You really believe he did it.' It was not a question. The words were a sign of her trying to come to terms with the new world that she found herself in, a world in which her husband might be the murderer of her child.

'We are still in the process of gathering evidence. It goes without saying that there are some questions I would like to put to Pastor Cardew.'

Mrs Cardew rose from her seat and crossed to a glass-fronted bookcase. 'Why don't you take his dictionary of theology? I don't believe anyone else in this house has ever had occasion to turn its pages.'

Quinn was on his feet too, as was Leversedge. The two policemen nodded to one another. That would do very well.

Quinn left it to Leversedge to extract the book without contaminating it with his own prints.

Her lips were tightly sealed as she showed them to the door, a long engrained habit that seemed to be her refuge. Then, at the very last moment, she blurted out, 'But what will I say to Adam? He knows nothing of any of this.'

She looked from one man to the other with a stark and desperate glare.

FORTY-SIX

They covered the one and a half miles to the Baptist church on Shepherd's Bush Road at a brisk trot. Leversedge was again subdued, either from the exertion or because he was still processing the information that he had just taken in. He limited himself to one question, which was not so much a question as an objection, but he gave it an interrogative intonation to soften it. 'You realize that even if his prints are on the bowl, it doesn't prove anything?'

'It will prove conclusively that it is their bowl. That it was taken from Wallingford Avenue and given to Felix. I realize that it does not prove that he was the one who took it there. But if his prints are on the milk bottle as well, it will be more incriminating still. I think it will at least be enough to persuade Felix to give him up. And if his prints are on neither, then he will be in the clear.'

This last point seemed to forestall any further questioning, though judging from his frown of consternation, Leversedge was far from convinced.

They gave themselves a moment to catch their breath before taking the fifteen or so steps up to the main entrance. For some reason, Quinn had expected the door to be locked, but it gave without resistance.

They saw him as soon as they were inside. In truth, it was impossible to miss him.

He was standing straight ahead of them, high up as if ascending to Heaven. It was a startling, incomprehensible sight until Quinn realized he was balanced on top of the balustrade of the gallery that ran around the church. His body swayed forwards and backwards as if subject to the buffeting of a strong wind. At first Quinn thought that he was engaged in some act of maintenance. Had he climbed up there to change a light bulb perhaps? But then Quinn noticed the rope. One end was looped around Cardew's neck, the other was tied to one of the balusters.

The sound of their entrance drew Cardew's gaze down. It was as if he had been waiting for them.

'Pastor Cardew, please, I beg you. Think of your son.' Quinn knew well the impact of a father's suicide on a son.

'Nearer, my God, to thee!' cried the pastor in a ringing voice, as clear as any sermon he had given.

And then he jumped the short distance to the jolting snag of eternity.

His body jerked and swung and spun. His limbs thrashed uselessly.

Quinn was rooted to the spot. Leversedge tore off at a sprint to find the stairs up to the gallery.

It seemed to take an age before the man on the rope was completely still. But it was not long enough for Leversedge to get him down alive.

PART VIII
The White Hart

18 September–21 September, 1914.

A THOUGHT FOR TO-DAY.

Times of general calamity and confusion have ever been productive of the greatest minds.

Daily Mirror, *Saturday, 19 September, 1914*

FORTY-SEVEN

D riscoll and his men were all over the church.
Quinn and Leversedge stood watching the activity. It
was that point in an investigation when police work
becomes little more than purposeful milling about.

'So that's it then?' asked Leversedge. 'We are to take his
suicide as an admission of guilt?'

'I would prefer a note,' remarked Quinn. He thought of the
letter his father had written that he had read in his cheap hotel
room in King's Cross. Would it be easier to read another father's
suicide note?

'If there's one here, these chaps will turn it up. I'll get some
other men over to Wallingford Avenue.'

'Thank you.'

'We'll also look back at the old registers for the Sunday school,
see if there's a Millicent Jones. I doubt it but you never know.'

Quinn shifted impatiently. He felt nervous acuity tingling
through him. 'Yes. Thank you for reminding me. I would like to
do that now.'

Leversedge held out a restraining arm. There was an uncertain,
almost wary, look in his eye. 'All in good time, guv. I'll have
Willoughby go through them. Eagle-eyed that boy is.'

Quinn frowned. He recognized the brimming of a manic energy
that he had not experienced since his own father's death all those
years ago. He breathed deeply through his nostrils. 'If you think
that would be better, then of course.'

'There is one thing I don't understand, guv.'

Quinn raised his eyebrows questioningly.

'The feathers. The white feathers. From the outset you were
convinced that the feather in her mouth was significant. When
Willoughby put forward his theory about the feather, you were
very taken with that, if I remember rightly. The feather was the
key, you said. But if the feather was so important, doesn't that
make Felix Simpkins the killer, not Eve's father?'

'The turning point was when I found the feather in Felix's

jacket. That proved that he had not placed *his* feather in Eve's mouth as I had originally believed. He had not made her eat her words. Therefore, he was not her killer.'

'So was the feather nothing after all, just like old Codders said?'

Quinn started in alarm at the notion that Coddington might have been right about something. 'No, the feather was significant. It must have been. But just not in the way we understood.'

'In what way then?'

Quinn frowned. 'I don't know. Perhaps if we find that note, it will explain it for us. Or maybe we shall never know.'

Leversedge's expression grew sceptical.

Quinn understood. He could not shake off a flat, empty feeling himself. It was not unusual in the wake of an investigation, particularly if the prime suspect insisted on dying before Quinn had a chance to take a conclusive statement. Although often, it had to be said, the death in question was meted out by Quinn's revolver, rather than being inflicted by the criminal's own hand. But even when the perpetrator was taken alive, he did not always provide the resolution that a good detective might hope for. Some of them would insist on denying everything and making life difficult for all concerned.

And so Quinn was used to loose ends that refused to be tied up, gaps that could only be filled with speculation. But a peculiarly tenacious sense of dissatisfaction nagged him now. True, if the pastor's prints were found on the bottle and the bowl, as he was certain they would, there would be one more piece of the jigsaw in place, but it would still not be a complete picture.

He would have dearly loved the opportunity to speak to Cardew one last time. But this final act, his suicide, was arguably the most eloquent statement he could have given.

Sometimes, you just had to close the file and move on.

Quinn narrowed his eyes and nodded decisively. It was the kind of look that passed between a senior police officer and his subordinate every day. It implied a degree of trust, mutual respect even.

Quinn turned sharply and, without further word, left the church.

As he stood at the top of the steps looking down on Shepherd's Bush Road, he wondered if he really did trust Leversedge now.

He remembered the old saying. Keep your friends close and your enemies closer.

He descended the steps to look for a taxi.

FORTY-EIGHT

Someone had left a copy of the *Clarion* on his desk. The front page was all about the action along the Aisne. The account was written in a jaunty tone that left a bad taste in Quinn's mouth. He had no doubt that it had been cobbled together from War Office releases and news agency dispatches sent down the wire by some journalist sitting in a cushy London office, someone who knew no more about what was going on at the Front than he did. He understood that the purpose of news now was to keep the nation's spirits up. In his own small way he sometimes shaped the news, and so he had his part to play in that, or so Kell would have him believe. But still, the writer's chirpy optimism struck a false note with him. It was unearned, to say the least. Every day now there were growing lists of casualties published. It was all too easy for journalists to pay tribute to the noble heroism of these men who had made the ultimate sacrifice for their country. Such platitudes rolled off the pen, or typewriter, or whatever it was these fellows used to write their jingoistic propaganda, all too easily. The deaths they catalogued in their addenda had no meaning for them.

Each death that Quinn had ever investigated, each death that he had witnessed, even the deaths for which he had been responsible, which had earned him his ridiculous moniker in the papers, each and every one of them had carried its own weight of emotion as it had snagged itself on to his memory. So that now he sometimes felt as though he were subject to a different gravity to other men.

And today another weight had been added to his soul. He imagined the deaths as lead weights suspended from his flesh by fish hooks. Such weights would not only slow you down, they would distort you. He was being pulled out of shape by them.

He had seen a man plunge to his death at the end of a rope.

Even if that man was in all probability a murderer and certainly an incestuous child-rapist, he could take no pleasure in even that death, could find nothing either glib or sententious to say about it. Could only wonder, with a kind of depressed dread, what newspapers like the *Clarion* would make of it, and how they would represent his role in it. He had not delivered the narrative that Kell had demanded. There was no German involvement in Eve's murder, after all. It was just a sad, sordid family tragedy, or so it seemed. And to make things worse, her apparent murderer was a pillar of the community who was well known for his patriotic support of the war. No, it would not play well with Kell at all, nor with Sir Michael Esslyn and his fellow War Office mandarins.

Perhaps only Sir Edward would appreciate his efforts. He had not delivered a narrative, that was true, but he had followed the evidence, even when it took him to places he had no wish to go.

Quinn turned the page. What he saw there did nothing to lift his depressed mood.

SECOND MURDER IN WEST LONDON.
BOSCH BUTCHER FROM BUSH RELEASED BY POLICE. BODY FOUND SOON AFTER.
QUICK-FIRE QUINN IN CHARGE.

The piece had been filed by the crime reporter George Bittlestone, known to Quinn from previous investigations. Of course, he did not blame Bittlestone for reporting the news of Millicent Jones's murder. But the implication of the crudely juxtaposed headlines was clear. William Egger was the murderer and it was Quinn's fault that he had been allowed to kill again. Quinn scanned the first paragraph of the account. Just in case anyone was still in any doubt, it was pointed out that a meat cleaver, similar to the kind used by William Egger, was found near the body. There was no mention of white feathers.

Quinn felt a sullen rage rise up in him.

Bloody journalists. If Quinn had his way, they would never tell them anything. Or at the very least, everything that was told to them would go through him. Because the only thing worse than journalists were the coppers who leaked information to them.

This had to have been fed to Bittlestone by someone on the team, someone who was trying to make Quinn look bad and reassert Coddington's interpretation of the case. Of course, it had been done before the suicide of Pastor Cardew had signalled his guilt. Events had taken over and disproved Coddington's theory more conclusively than Quinn could have. But still, the damage was done. His credibility was undermined. The public were stubborn as well as stupid. They would remain convinced that Egger was the murderer, especially as they had obtained no written confession from Cardew.

It could even be argued that Cardew had killed himself out of grief at losing his daughter, not because he was her murderer. And perhaps that was true. Was Quinn any better than Coddington? He had latched on to a theory and moulded the facts to prove it.

No. All his instincts told him that Cardew had killed his daughter because she threatened to expose him. The mask he presented to the world, of virtue and saintliness, was about to be ripped off. Yes, she was his daughter. And it was a terrible crime for a father to kill his own daughter. But he had committed horrendous crimes against her before. Quinn knew from what Cardew's wife had said that he considered himself above the law, above morality. As a true believer, he could do no wrong. That was all very well, that was something he could square with his conscience and his God. But for his congregation to find out what kind of a man he was, that was something else. That was something he could not allow. He would do anything to keep his secrets hidden.

It had to be. And yet there were loose ends that did not fit Quinn's theory either. For one, the bloody meat cleaver. Even if the Sunday school registers did turn up a link between Millicent Jones and Cardew, that did not prove that he had murdered her, or what his motive was. Perhaps Eve had confided in Millicent. Or perhaps Millicent had been subject to Pastor Cardew's perverted attentions too. It was possible that he had conceived the idea of silencing anyone whom he had molested. And that something had caused him to back away from this madness and take his own life instead. Even if you accepted all that, why was the meat cleaver there? Was it possible that Cardew had killed Millicent deliberately to direct the trail away from him and back towards Egger?

In that case, why did he kill himself?

Or was the meat cleaver simply irrelevant? A coincidence, dropped there by accident by God knows who? Now he really was turning into Coddington, disregarding the meat cleaver in exactly the same way Coddington had disregarded the feather in Eve's mouth.

No, the case wasn't over. It was natural to think that Pastor Cardew's death had brought it to some sort of conclusion. But there were still too many unanswered questions for that.

The candlestick telephone affixed to Coddington's desk – Quinn's desk now – burst into startled life. Quinn glowered at it as if he suspected it of playing a part in the conspiracy he was beginning to imagine aligned against him.

He grabbed the receiver and leaned forward to snarl into the mouthpiece: 'Quinn.'

'Oh, thank goodness.'

He heard a woman's voice, at once both intimately familiar and strangely unplaceable. It was always the same with the ghostly crackles that came to him down the telephone line. So much of what was essential to identifying the speaker was stripped away. You did not have the person in front of you. But you seemed only to receive a fraction of their voice too. All emotion was stretched out to an infinitesimal thinness that could be fitted inside the wires that connected one telephone to another.

Even so, the panic in the woman's voice was unmistakable. The words tumbled out of her, tripping over themselves: 'I've been trying to get hold of you all day. Your phone was ringing and ringing. And then I spoke to someone who was very rude. And then no one knew where you were. And when I told them what it was about they said I was not to worry, this sort of thing happens all the time. Happens all the time? It may happen all the time to other people but not to us. And how am I supposed to not worry? I'm going out of my mind with worry! My little girl! My little girl is missing. And then he said, this fellow I spoke to, a policeman it was too, if you can believe it, he said . . . well, I won't repeat what he said, but he made the most vile insinuations. Simply vile, I tell you.'

'Is this Mrs Ibbott?'

'Of course it is, who else would it be?'

'Mrs Ibbott, has something happened to Mary?'

'Yes. Yes, Mary. It's Mary. I don't know where she is. She went out this morning and didn't come back in time for lunch. I have called on all her friends and no one has seen her. And now Mr Timberley has taken it into his head . . . Oh, Mr Quinn, I'm dreadfully afraid.'

'What about Mr Timberley?'

'Well, it was in the newspaper, wasn't it? All about that butcher. Oh, Mr Quinn, what were you thinking?'

'What do you mean?'

'If he's the murderer, why did you let him go?'

'He isn't the murderer.'

'But they found that poor girl. And now my Mary has gone missing. Mr Timberley is convinced, convinced I tell you. And now he's gone too. "If Quinn won't do his duty, I will." That's what he said. Oh, Mr Quinn . . .'

'Where has Timberley gone?'

'To save my Mary, God bless him.'

'But where?'

'Oh, Mr Quinn, what have you done? He's got my Mary now, my poor Mary.'

'Who has?'

'That awful Bosch Butcher, of course! I only hope that Mr Timberley isn't too late!'

'Don't worry, Mrs Ibbott. Everything will be all right. Stay calm and wait at the house for Mary to return. She will come back, we'll get her back. I promise you that. Thank you for calling me. You did the right thing.'

Quinn nestled the receiver carefully back on to its cradle. The moment demanded action, but Quinn needed to think first. He pinched his bottom lip between thumb and forefinger. He had just made a promise that it was not within his power to keep. And worse still, that he had no idea how to go about keeping.

He rose slowly from his desk, unable to take his eyes off the telephone, as if it were a malign imp squatting on his desk to curse him.

FORTY-NINE

William Egger, it could be said, was a stubborn bastard. Despite everything that had happened, he put on his butcher's apron, his straw boater and went out to stand proudly in front of his family's shop. The door still had its fractured wooden panel over the broken pane. Unpleasant words had been daubed on the shutters, but that was all right because as he opened them up, he folded the words away.

Mum hadn't the heart to keep the shop going on her own, that was understandable. And she was reluctant to have him open the door to customers now. 'You know what happened last time,' she said ominously as he came back in.

'What you mean, last time?'

Mum didn't answer, except to look down at the sawdust on the floor. But he knew what she meant. The shop had been closed since the day of the riot and his father's death. William felt his lips compress at the memory.

At last his mother met his eye. Her look offered no comfort. 'It will be even worse now. Now they think you're responsible for that girl's death.'

'They ain't all bad. We still have friends. And people got to eat.'

His mother shook her head. She could be as stubborn as him in her own way. 'We'll have to sell up. There's no alternative.'

'Sell the business? Now? Are you mad? We'd have to let it go for a song.'

'There's nothing we can do about that.'

'We can carry on.'

'We've got nothing to sell. What meat they didn't steal I had to throw away because of the broken glass.'

'There's a carcass hanging in the cold room, ain't there? I can butcher that. Got some trotters we can put out. Pork knuckle. Tripe. Black puddings. There's liver sausage, bratwurst and salami. Ain't that what we're famous for, our salami?'

'And when that's gone?'

'We'll get another delivery.'

'Of salami? From Germany, I suppose.'

'All right. Maybe not salami. But we got suppliers in this country.'

'It's throwing money away, William.'

'What you talking about?'

'No one will come. Unless it's to steal it from under our noses.'

'No. You're wrong. We'll open up. Give them a second chance. It's what Dad would have wanted.'

'Did you read what they wrote?'

'Don't you worry about that. I'll get some paint.'

'And they'll write it again, as soon as you've painted it over.'

William felt the hopelessness of the situation wash over him. His bottom lip trembled as it had when he was a little boy on the verge of tears. Only now, his whole body began to tremble too.

The strain of the last few days suddenly hit him. He could barely get the words out. 'But if we don't . . . if we don't carry on . . . they will have won.'

William mopped the tears from his eyes and stood up straight.

His mother flexed a small wince and disappeared wordlessly into the back. A moment later she came back wearing her apron. She gave a terse, unsmiling nod that was his cue to take his place beside her behind the counter.

It was satisfying to feel once more the sharpened blade of the cleaver pass smoothly through the flesh of a pig. And comforting to be back amongst the smell of meat and blood. Perhaps others might find the smell cloying, but William had been brought up in the midst of it. It had infused his dreams since he was a baby in his cot.

It was the smell of home.

He chose to do the butchering in the shop. For one thing, he didn't want to leave Mum on her own. But it was also to show the world that it was business as usual. And he didn't want anyone to think that he was hiding away in the back.

He kept up a steady rhythm with the cleaver. It was delicate work, not what some might think. If you chopped and hacked, you'd be left with mangled fillets, not to mention butchered fingers. It was all in the sharpness of the blade. You had to let the blade do the work for you. It was natural to get into a bit of a rhythm. It was how his body responded to the task, to its repetition, as if making a virtue of its monotony, turning it into a game, or a song. Dad had always sung as he cut up chops. He didn't know he was doing it, or thought no one could hear him. But William and Mum would raise their eyebrows and smile a colluding smile to one another. Sometimes they couldn't contain themselves and would burst out laughing.

Dad would look up wonderingly and realize. 'Ah. And so. I was doing it again, was I? The singing?'

William and Mum would nod in unison, sharing the joke with any customers who might be in the shop. And Dad would go back to his chopping, trying hard this time to work in silence, but before too long he would be humming to himself, and then letting out a few tra-la-las or om-pom-poms, giving a sly wink to any child who happened to be in the shop with its mother, letting them know that he knew what he was doing all along.

Yes, it helped to get into a bit of a rhythm. Perhaps it was simply the difference between a natural butcher and one without talent.

And the product of the rhythm was consistency. Each chop took the same amount of time to cut, and every one weighed the same, to the nearest half an ounce.

The task became hypnotically absorbing. Which helped the time to pass more quickly. And God knew, it was dragging today. As Mum had predicted, there had been no customers. And so, when the shop bell rang at last, he lifted his head hopefully, ready to beam a welcoming smile towards whoever had just come in.

But something was wrong. Something was obviously wrong. Because as soon as the shop bell rang, Mum started screaming.

William's welcoming smile tensed into a rictus of fear.

But the man did not return his smile. His face was red and set in an angry, clenched grimace. He was advancing towards William with a gun held out in front of him. He stopped just in front of the counter, the arm holding the gun stretched out above William's chops, so that the barrel was only inches from his face. 'Where is she? What have you done with her, you brute?' The man's voice was high and strained. He wasn't exactly shouting. He was grinding the words out. His whole body was clenched, including his vocal cords. It was clear that he could hardly speak.

At some point, Mum must have stopped screaming. Because it was very quiet in the shop now. He could hear the man's heavy, laboured breathing.

'I don't know what you're talking about, mate. Where's who?'

'Mary!'

'I don't know no Mary, mate. You got the wrong fella.'

The man shook his head in three quick jerks. 'No! No, don't lie. You've taken her. I only hope for your sake she's still alive, otherwise I don't know what I'll do.'

'You deaf? Or mad? I don't know what you're talking about. I tell ya, I don't know no Mary.'

'Tell me where she is or . . . or . . . or . . .' The man swung the barrel of the gun towards William's mother. 'I shall shoot her, so help me I will.'

'Don't you go shooting Mum, now!'

'Then tell me where Mary is!'

'Mary! Mary! How many times do I have to tell ya, I don' know no bloody Mary!'

'You've got her back there, haven't you? The woman's in on this too. You're both German spies. Don't deny it! Well, I'm going to stop you. I'm going to stop you, I am!'

The man kept the gun trained on Mum. With his free hand he groped for the flap to the counter. His fumbling was to no avail. 'Let me in, or I'll shoot her. I will, I'll do it. I don't mind shooting a dirty German spy.'

William's mother began to make a half-keening, half-moaning noise.

'You leave Mum out of this, do you hear me? And don't you go calling her no names. She ain't even German!'

'Just let me in and take me to Mary.'

'How many times? There ain't no Mary here!'

'Let me in!'

'All right! Just put the gun down, eh, fella? That's fair, ain't it? Put the gun down and you can come back here and have a look. What you say to that?'

The hand holding the gun began to tremble. But the man did not lower his weapon. He merely turned it from William's mother back to William. 'I won't point it at her. But I'm not going to put it down. Not until you show me where you've got Mary.'

William didn't bother to contradict him now. He was getting

tired of the man's stubborn refusal to listen to reason. The time
for words was coming to an end. He felt his grip tighten around
the handle of the cleaver in his right hand. He kept it down low,
out of sight. With his other hand, he reached across and lifted
the counter. He took one step to the side to let the man enter.

The man's arm was shaking violently now. That gun could go
off at any moment. All it needed was for the man's finger to
tighten on the trigger in an involuntary spasm. And the gun was
once again inches from William's head. If he was going to act,
he had to act now, as the man crossed the threshold of the counter.
Leave it any longer and he would see the cleaver in William's
hand.

William gave a desperate, wordless cry. He did not know what
he meant by that cry. He hoped perhaps that it might serve as a
warning to his mother, that she might take it as her cue to run
into the back. Partly, too, it was intended to put the fear of God
into this mad fucker. He could tell from the man's trembling arm
that he was already scared. That made him dangerous, but maybe,
just maybe, it meant that he lacked the nerve to go through with
this terrible endeavour that he had set in motion.

At the same moment as he let out his cry, William pivoted
round and ducked his head down, out of the firing line. In one
fluid movement, he thrust the meat cleaver blindly out behind
him, towards his attacker, its blade angled up in the direction of
his thrust.

He did not know, or care, where the blade struck. He only
knew that it did, for he felt it meet a sudden resistance. He trusted
to the blade. Let the blade do all the work. It was a sharp blade,
after all.

There was a weak popping sound, not even as loud as a hand
clap. And the faintest possible smell of gunpowder. Something
light and tinny clattered to the wooden floor. Then there was the
heavy slump of the man going down.

William turned slowly, keeping his meat cleaver arm extended
protectively.

The man lay stretched out, his feet behind the counter, his
head in the shop. He had a hand to his throat. Blood bubbled
out through his fingers. His eyes swam desperately, searching
for something to focus on. Searching for his Mary still, no doubt.
He strained to sit up, but the effort was too much for him. His

lips parted, as if he was about to say something. But instead of words, he coughed a spray of blood into the air.

The shop bell tinkled once again, like a genteel death knell. William heard the door thrown open with some force.

He looked up from the body on the floor to see his shop fill with policemen.

FIFTY

Quinn covered his face with his hands. A deep groan rumbled in his chest and then vibrated in his throat, rising in pitch and intensity until it was a howl.

He dropped his hands and looked out of the window of the police car into which he had retreated after the discovery of the grim tableau in the pork butcher's. He could not remain in there with Timberley dead on the floor, William Egger in handcuffs and Egger's mother inconsolable and barely able to support herself. She had virtually collapsed into the chair that was brought for her.

He watched the small crowd that had gathered. It was amazing how quickly word got about. But really, this was too much. One of the uniformed coppers ought to have seen them off by now. This was a crime scene, not a bloody music hall.

A taxi pulled up and two men got out. One was carrying a camera and tripod. The other he recognized as George Bittlestone, the hack from the *Clarion* who had written the piece about Egger's release. Bloody vultures. All the same, Quinn had thought better of Bittlestone.

Quinn got out of the car and approached Bittlestone. 'This is on you, Bittlestone.'

Noticing the dark mood of the detective, the photographer scuttled away to set up his camera.

Bittlestone squeezed out a tense smile. 'A pleasure to see you too, Chief Inspector Quinn. What on earth are you talking about?'

'I saw your last piece.'

'You're only upset because I criticized your decision to release

Egger. As it turns out, I believe I have been vindicated in my criticism.'

'I'm upset because a young man is dead. You killed him, Bittlestone. As surely as if you had slashed his artery yourself.'

'No. The Bosch Butcher from Bush killed him, or so my sources tell me.'

'Ah, yes. Your sources.'

'I hope you're not going to ask me to reveal them.'

'I'm just warning you.'

'Warning me? Is that a threat?'

'Don't be a fool. I don't make threats. Whoever's feeding you information from the investigation, you can't trust them.'

'You would say that, wouldn't you?'

'They got it wrong. William Egger did not kill Eve Cardew.'

'So you say.'

'No. It's not just what I say.'

'What's this? Have you found her murderer?'

'Her father, Pastor Clement Cardew, committed suicide in his church today. We're not looking for anyone else in connection with his daughter's death.'

'My heavens! And when were you intending to share this juicy titbit with the public, Chief Inspector?'

'Things have happened very quickly. We don't have conclusive proof that it was Pastor Cardew yet. There are still a few loose ends to tie up. Be careful how you write it. You can cite an unnamed source close to the investigation.'

'Did he leave a note?'

'We haven't found one. But when we do, you'll be the first to know.'

Bittlestone narrowed his eyes and smiled coquettishly. Quinn was reminded that the man had certain proclivities which placed him on the wrong side of the law. But whatever his differences with Bittlestone, and whatever he wanted from him, he would never use that knowledge against him.

'You're suddenly being nice to me. It makes me very suspicious. When you first saw me you wanted to bite my head off.'

'Come to *me*, Bittlestone, always come to me. Don't go to anyone else.'

'I'm a journalist. I have to get my information from whatever source I can.'

'There are certain details in the Cardew case which I suspect will not come out officially. His standing in the community will serve to suppress them. As he is dead, he cannot be charged with any crime. He may not even be linked to his daughter's death.'

Bittlestone gave a wry smile. 'Intriguing. That *even* of yours is intriguing. You seem to be hinting at other crimes.'

Quinn raised his eyebrows and gave the most minimal of nods.

'I see. And you would be prepared . . .'

Quinn's nod this time was minutely more pronounced. Even so, it would not have been noticed by anyone watching.

'And in return for this, you would expect the name of my source? But you do understand, Chief Inspector, that places me in the most dreadful quandary. A journalist must never reveal his sources. You know that.'

Quinn gestured for Bittlestone to give him his ear. He leant forward and murmured into it. 'Another girl has gone missing. That's what this is all about in there. But Egger had nothing to do with it.'

Quinn straightened up.

Bittlestone regarded him thoughtfully. 'Her name. The name of the girl who's gone missing. You'd give me that first? Is that what you're saying? Is that how badly you want this?'

'Who is it? Who is your informant?'

Bittlestone winced. 'Oh, I'm so tempted, so tempted. Can't I offer you money, Chief Inspector? That's usually what you people want.'

'Is it DC Willoughby?'

Bittlestone made a gesture with his hand. *Higher.*

'Leversedge?'

Again the same gesture.

'Coddington?'

Bittlestone closed his eyes in an extended blink and then stared expectantly into Quinn's eyes. 'Well? Her name?'

'But Coddington was off the case by the time we found Millicent Jones and the meat cleaver?'

'Well, I don't know, he must have heard it from someone who was still on the investigation. What's her name, Chief Inspector?'

'Mary.'

'Don't you have a surname?'

It was Quinn's turn to wince. But soon it would be impossible to keep the information out of the news anyhow. He was just giving Bittlestone a head start on the inevitable. 'Ibbott. I, double B, O, double T. I'll write down her address. Tell her mother I sent you. Tell her I said it would help to find Mary if we put her photograph in the paper.'

'And the pastor?'

'We'll talk about him another time.'

The crowd suddenly livened up and Quinn saw that the door to the shop was opening, tentatively, as if whoever was coming out was unsure how doors operated. A uniformed policeman poked his head out and surveyed the crowd with a disapproving glower. 'All right, you lot. Hop it.'

But the crowd was not in the mood to hear such discouraging words.

''Ave you got 'im? 'Ave you got the Bosch Butcher?'

'Shouldna oughta let 'im ou' in the first place!'

This observation was met with laughter, which soured the copper's expression even more. 'Clear off, I say, or I'll haul the lot of you off in the back of that Black Maria.' As if to confirm his threat, the nearest horse stamped a hoof and lowered its head in a majestic nod. The crowd didn't exactly disperse, but it thinned out enough to satisfy the copper, who held the door fully open. A moment later, William Egger was manhandled out of the shop, his head heavy with shock, hands cuffed behind his back. He walked with stumbling step, partly because he was being pushed along by an officer behind him, and partly because he was unable to take in where he was or what was happening to him. The man was in a daze.

He only seemed to come to his senses when he caught sight of Quinn. Egger shuffled to a halt and stared uncomprehendingly into Quinn's eyes, as if he expected to find some explanation for what had happened there. 'It was a cap gun. I di'n' know it was a cap gun. Wha' was 'e doin' with a cap gun, the bloody fool?'

Quinn shook his head, but had no words.

The uniformed officers led him away and bundled him into the Black Maria.

A moment later Leversedge came out, ducking his head through the doorway and blinking in the sunlight like a troglodyte emerging. Quinn beckoned him over. Leversedge's expression remained wary.

'How did Willoughby get on with the Sunday school registers?'

'Nothing. No mention of Millicent Jones. There's nothing linking her to Cardew.'

Quinn nodded as if he had been expecting this.

Leversedge hesitated before going on: 'And another thing.'

'What?'

'I just had a word with one of my sergeants. We had the report in from the fingerprint boffins. On the meat cleaver that was found.'

Quinn felt a tightening in his chest. He tried to draw breath but there was nothing there.

'They found his prints on it. Egger's.'

'Who told him? Did you tell him?'

'What?'

'Did you tell Coddington about the cleaver?'

'No.'

'Someone did. He was the one who leaked it to the *Clarion*.'

'It wasn't me.' Leversedge spoke quietly, firmly, holding Quinn's gaze.

'So who did?'

Leversedge shrugged. 'Who says anyone did?'

Quinn angled his head as he took in what Leversedge was saying. He nodded for him to go on.

FIFTY-ONE

Leversedge looked up at the door of the White Hart pub in Bishopsgate as it swung open. A small rabble of squaddies burst in, bringing with them an air of hard-edged, defiant hilarity. They were on a pub crawl, evidently. Filling their last night in London with the noise of their unravelling swagger. Their eyes were urgent and hungry, latching on to every object that came into their line of sight as if it owed them something. You felt their sense that this might be not just their last night in London, but their last night on earth.

Before their entrance there had been an air of sullen

determination to the early evening crowd of regulars, who seemed almost professional in their focused dedication to the task of drinking themselves to oblivion. Solitary drinkers for the most part, or men who huddled together but had nothing left to say to one another.

There were two pots of pale ale on the table in front of Leversedge, so far untouched. And the seat opposite him was empty.

Leversedge consulted his pocket watch. It was five after seven. He felt a flurry of apprehension.

Then a familiar voice nearby made him look up. 'Thanks for the pint.'

'You're late.'

'You're late, *sir*,' Coddington corrected, as he slipped into his seat. 'I'm still your governor, Leversedge.'

Leversedge shrugged and picked up his own pint. 'Cheers.'

Coddington took a deep gulp of his beer, before wiping the foam from his moustache on the cuff of his herringbone ulster. 'You do realize you're breaking the law, don't you?'

'How's that?'

'The Defence of the Realm Act 1914 makes it an offence to buy a pal a drink.'

'Are we pals? I thought you were my governor?'

Coddington chuckled noiselessly. 'We can still be pals, can't we? Even if I'm your governor.'

'Well, you've still got the disciplinary to get through.'

'That won't be any problem. Once they see how Quinn's fucked up.'

'It doesn't look good for him, that's for sure.'

'So that explains it.'

'Explains what?'

'Why you wanted to meet. All that time, not a word from you, not a peep, not a dicky bird . . . then all of a sudden . . .' Coddington put on a high-pitched ingratiating voice which was evidently intended as an impression of his companion: '*Dear Codders, long time no see. How d'you fancy meeting for a pot of ale?*'

'You know how it is. I've been busy. With the case.'

'Busy fucking it up.'

'I was just doing what I was told. What else could I do?'

'I know you.' Coddington's tone turned nasty. 'Always looking for the main chance. What's best for DI Leversedge? That's all you care about. Threw in your lot with the new boss, didn't you? I can see it now. Nothing for your old pal Codders. When I needed you most, were you there for me? Were you buggery.'

'I had to be careful. Anyhow, I'm here now.'

'When it's all going to shit for you.'

'Not for me, for Quinn.'

'Trying to get back in my good books, ain't ya?'

'Why d'you bother coming if you're just going to give me grief?'

'Maybe I like giving you grief. Maybe it makes me happy, giving you grief.' Coddington was enjoying himself. 'Maybe I want to hear you say it.'

'Say what?'

'Sorry.'

Leversedge lifted the pot to his lips and muttered his apology.

'Didn't quite catch that.'

'I said, sorry.'

'Sorry what?'

'Sorry, guv.'

'Sorry, guv for what?'

'Sorry, guv, for . . .' Leversedge broke off and raised his eyebrows questioningly.

'Sorry, guv, for doubting you.'

'All right. Sorry, guv, for doubting you.'

'I can't wait to hear Sir Edward Henry say that.'

'You think you're going to get an apology out of him?'

'I'd better, or there'll be hell to pay.' Coddington stabbed an angry finger towards Leversedge. Remembering himself, he relaxed back into his seat. 'Nah, don't you worry, he'll be down on bended knee begging me to come back. After that fucking loony Quinn gets his comeuppance. That reminds me. You know why I like this pub?'

Leversedge shook his head.

'The old Bedlam Hospital used to be around here, di'n' it. Where they put all the mad bastards like 'im.'

'So?'

'Every time I come 'ere, I like to think of Quinn locked up

in the loony bin. He'll be back there soon enough, you mark my words. He'll lose his fucking marbles for good this time.'

'He's not happy, I'll tell you that much.'

'Music to my ears, that is. I'll drink to that. I'll fucking drink to that.'

'Still, he might just wriggle out of it.'

'What do you mean, wriggle out of it? He's fucking fucked, he is. You got the meat cleaver, di'n' you?'

'Yeah, but . . .'

'What do you mean, *yeah but*? That fucking proves it. That proves Egger's guilty.'

'The way Quinn sees it, a good barrister will argue it proves nothing. May even get it dismissed as evidence.'

'Dismissed? What you talking about? It's got Egger's prints all over it!'

'I wish. That'd make our job easier, I'm telling you. Nah, it's been wiped clean. No prints on it at all.'

Coddington's jaw dropped. 'You're fucking having a larf, ain't you? What you mean, no prints on it?'

'That's what I'm telling you. It's clean.'

'That's fucking Quinn what's done that, that is.'

'What do you mean?'

'Cleaned the Bosch's prints off it, didn't he?'

'Nah. Quinn's not the type. He's as straight as they come.'

'Straight? Quinn? Don't make me laugh.'

'I'm telling you, he's not the sort as tampers with the evidence. He believes in cracking the case. Fair and square. Find the killer and prove it. That's his way.'

'Bollocks. He's as bent as the rest of us.'

'What d'you mean? I'm not bent.'

Coddington gave another noiseless chuckle. 'If you say so.' His eyes scanned the pub quickly. 'You don't have to pretend with me. I know exactly what you're like. Not above planting the odd stolen necklace or bloody handkerchief yourself, are you?'

Leversedge stiffened. 'I only ever did what you told me.'

'No need to be like that about it, old chap. We did what was necessary. Sometimes you have to give justice a helping hand. She's a blind old bitch after all. That's how I know Quinn wiped the meat cleaver.'

'What do you mean?'

Coddington leant forward over the table and lowered his voice to a hoarse whisper. 'Because I know for a fact that the butcher's prints were on it.'

'How could you know that?'

'Because I took that cleaver out of the fucker's shop and put it there myself.'

'You? I don't understand.'

'For Christ's sake, Leversedge. Do I have to spell it out for you?'

Leversedge froze, his pint pot halfway to his mouth. 'For Christ's sake, you didn't?'

There was a burst of raucous laughter from the pub-crawling squaddies. It was Leversedge's turn for his mouth to hang open.

'Don't look at me like that. I had to, di'n' I? I had to nail that bastard Quinn. Nail him good and proper. He won't come back after this.'

'But you didn't kill her? You didn't kill Millicent Jones?'

Coddington cast a furtive glance about. 'Keep your fucking voice down. She was a fucking whore anyhow. They all are. She had it coming. They all fucking do.'

'Jesus Christ, guv.'

'You're not going soft on me, are you, Leversedge? We've all done it. We've all planted evidence to get the right result.'

'But this is more than planting evidence.'

Coddington beckoned for Leversedge to get closer. 'There's just two people know about this. You and me. So if even a whisper of this gets out, I'll know who to come for.'

At that moment, a man seated at the table behind Leversedge stood up. If Coddington paid any attention to him at all, it was to dismiss him as another drunk steadying himself for a stagger towards the bar. The man had his back to them. He was dressed in a Norfolk jacket with a workman's cap on his head.

The man turned around slowly to face Coddington.

A look of horror appeared on Coddington's face. 'What's that fucker doing here?'

'Albert Robert Herbert Coddington, I arrest you for the murder of Millicent Jones.' Silas Quinn lifted a police whistle to his mouth and blew one long, sharp blast. All the several doors to the public bar crashed open. Uniformed bobbies burst in to position themselves at every exit.

Suddenly the pub fell quiet. It took the raucous soldiers a moment longer than everyone else to realize what was going on, but eventually even they were subdued.

A snarl of disgust contorted Coddington's features. 'Fucking traitor.'

Leversedge met his gaze and drew himself up defiantly. Inchball appeared at his side, followed by Willoughby.

'You too, eh, boy?'

'It's over, Coddington,' said Quinn.

'Over is it, Quinn? Over, you say? Nah, it ain't over yet, not by a long chalk.' Coddington's hand disappeared into his ulster and came out clutching a revolver. He held the gun out in front of him, levelled at Quinn's head.

Coddington's hand shook violently as he squeezed the trigger. There was the sound of glass smashing and all around the pub men hit the floor, even the pub-crawling squaddies. Quinn alone did not flinch.

The smell of gunshot hung in the air. The weapon in Coddington's hand was oscillating wildly now, his arm pivoting like a mechanical part caught between two opposing magnetic fields.

The silence in the aftermath of the gunshot was profound.

Coddington glared incredulously at his enemy, still standing unscathed before him. A moment later, he caught a blur of movement out of the corner of his eye. His legs buckled as an unseen force crashed into them. The gun flew out of his hand and clattered away out of sight. Coddington looked down to see Sergeant Inchball's plunging back as he rugby-tackled him to the floor.

FIFTY-TWO

Quinn had never hated a murderer the way he hated Coddington.

Usually he felt some degree of fascination towards the men he was pitted against but with Coddington there was only hatred. Of course, he had hated the man before he knew he was a murderer, but with that discovery, he might have expected a grain of fascination to work its way into his emotions. But no, his hatred was pure and absolute. He could barely bring himself to look at him.

'What have you done with her?'

They had him handcuffed in the back of a moving Black Maria. Inchball and Willoughby were seated on either side of Coddington, Quinn and Leversedge facing him. The vehicle jolted and rattled as it raced along. It was not the ideal setting for an interrogation but there was no time to waste. The jaunty clop of the two-horse team reverberated in the dark drum of the interior, drowning out Quinn's thoughts. They were heading back to the Yard, but if they got any information out of Coddington on the way about Mary's whereabouts, they would divert.

'I don't know what you're talking about.'

'Mary Ibbott.'

'I don't know no Mary Ibbott.'

'Don't lie, Coddington. Things are bad enough for you already.'

Coddington gave a bitter laugh.

'I'll get it out of him,' said Inchball darkly.

'Guv, you've got to see,' said Leversedge.

'Don't *guv* me.'

'This is a chance for you to make amends.'

'What do I have to make amends for?'

'Murder.'

Coddington stared deep into the eyes of his former friend. 'You don't get it, do you? You never did. We make the rules. We are the law. We decide who's guilty, who's not. I did what I had to do. That's not murder. That's police work.'

'You're not police. You're a disgrace.'

'Just tell us,' said Quinn. 'Is she still alive?'

'How the fuck would I know? I told you, I don't know what you're talking about.'

There was a break in the interrogation. The relentless pounding of hooves filled in the pause.

Then Willoughby spoke up: 'I used to look up to you. Wanted to be like you. One day, I thought, one day, I might make it. Inspector, maybe even Chief Inspector. If I worked hard enough. If I kept my wits about me. If I could learn from the best. Learn from you. You've taken all that away from me. There's nothing left, nothing. Tell us where she is. It won't make it right. But there'll be one tiny little bit of you I can still respect.'

Coddington held a wince as he looked the young detective in the eye at last. 'I wish I could, lad. I wish I knew. But I'm telling you the truth, God's honest. On my life, on my mother's life, whatever's happened to this girl, I don't know nothing about it. I swear to you I don't.'

Back at his desk, Quinn breathed deeply and stared at the telephone on his desk for a heavy moment before picking up the mouthpiece.

'Mrs Ibbott . . .'

'Oh, Mr Quinn.'

'Silas, I thought we said you should call me Silas.'

'Oh, Silas. Have you found her?'

He could not imagine what in his voice had given her that idea. 'Not . . . yet.'

'Oh, Silas!'

'She was not there, at the butcher's shop where . . . where Mr Timberley had gone. And another lead . . . came to nothing. I'm so sorry.' Quinn broke off. 'Mrs Ibbott, I have to tell you something. It's about Mr Timberley . . . We were too late. There was nothing we could do.'

'What? I don't understand. What are you saying?'

'Mr Timberley is dead, Mrs Ibbott. I'm so frightfully sorry.'

'Dead? He can't be.'

'It was all really just a terrible accident. He had . . . well, the other man thought it was a gun, but actually it was just a toy. It was all so unnecessary. So stupid and unnecessary.'

'Oh, Silas. Whatever will we do?'

'Is there anything you can think of, anything at all, that could give us some clue as to where she might be?' But just as he asked the question, the answer came to him.

Quinn boarded just as the station master blew his whistle. He had to walk the length of the train, looking into every compartment for a vacant seat. Most of the other passengers were in khaki. And, as far as he could tell, most of them were drunk. It was the last train back to Colchester that night.

He found a compartment where one soldier had his feet up

on the opposite seat, which was otherwise occupied by his kit bag. Quinn could have chosen to stand in the corridor. Instead he slid open the compartment door.

The soldier opened one eye and glanced up at Quinn discouragingly. He made no move to sit up.

'Excuse me, do you mind?'

'Do I mind what?' The fellow spoke in a low, aggressive growl.

'Do you mind moving your feet? And your bag, of course.'

The other soldiers in the compartment regarded Quinn with hostility.

'Yes, I do mind, as it happens.'

'Well, I will move your bag for you, if you like, but you must move your own feet.'

'Don't you touch my fucking kit.'

'Listen, I don't want any trouble. It's just that I'm tired. I'm very, very tired. I've had a hard day. I've seen two men die and I'm trying to find a young girl who's gone missing. Here's, what, ten shillings for you to buy yourself and your mates a drink on me the next time you're out on a spree. Please, let me have that seat.'

It was a clever move to include the mates in the offer. The rest of the compartment seemed to be warming to the idea of the man in the herringbone ulster having a seat.

The soldier with his feet up stirred promisingly. 'Make it a quid.'

'Very well.' Quinn handed over the money. The soldier took it with a nod, then sprang up with sudden energy to heave his kit bag on to the luggage rack.

When he sat down again, he no longer seemed sleepy, nor threatening. 'You a copper then?'

'Yes.'

'Thought so.'

'What gave it away?'

'That coat, ain't it. None but coppers wears coats like that.'

Quinn's hand went up to remove a bowler hat that was no longer there. He remembered the wreckage that Coddington had made of it and ran his hand instead through his hair.

'You CID?'

'Yes, as it happens.'

'Thought so.' The soldier nodded eagerly to his companions, soliciting respect.

Quinn settled back into his seat. It was going to be a long journey.

The soldier wanted to know all about the case Quinn was working on. He seemed to be under the illusion that he could help him crack it.

'I regret I'm not at liberty to reveal the details of an ongoing investigation.'

The man seemed to take offence at this. 'Suit yourself,' he said huffily, before retreating into a resentful sulk. Before long, his head nodded forward heavily. Soon after that, he was snoring.

Quinn had telephoned ahead. There would be a police car waiting to pick him up at the station. And the military police at the garrison had been briefed. This shouldn't take any longer than it needed to. But as he had predicted, even without the soldier's tedious quizzing, the journey dragged. The train seemed to put in at every station along the way. More than once it clanked and groaned to a standstill in what appeared to be the middle of nowhere, the darkness pressing in all around, as if they were being held in the grip of an infinite night.

Each time, it was just as Quinn had given up all hope of ever moving again that the train would jolt into life again, like a slumbering soldier shaken from his sleep.

At last they drew into Colchester.

He was quick off the train, faster than the soldiers, who seemed reluctant to tear themselves away from the transient sanctuary of the compartment. Quinn had got the sense of how time for men at war is parcelled out into blocks in which they are safe, if bored, and blocks in which they might die. Who wouldn't be reluctant to leave a period of safety?

Quinn spotted the local detective sent to meet him. There might have been something in what the soldier had said, after all. He wasn't wearing an ulster – instead a belted raincoat – but he had the look of a copper all the same.

'Chief Inspector Quinn, I presume? I'm DS McKenzie from Colchester CID.'

Quinn shook McKenzie's hand. 'Pleased to meet you.'

Thankfully, McKenzie was a taciturn individual, singularly devoid of curiosity. He seemed inconvenienced rather than impressed by the arrival of a famous detective from Scotland Yard. He gave the impression that he had better things to do than act as Quinn's taxi driver.

Quinn looked out of the window of the car as they drove, peering through the darkness to try to form some impression of the town. But as in London, the street lights had been either switched off or obscured. If anything, it was darker here than London. The streets were certainly more deserted.

McKenzie drove slowly, as if he feared they might drop off a precipice at any moment. Quinn was half-hypnotized by the beams of the car's headlights, which seemed to form the way ahead just a second before it was needed.

'We have your man in here.' Captain Darcy cut an impressive figure in his crisp uniform and scarlet-topped cap. Just to look at him made Quinn want to say the word impeccable. His posture was as upright as a flagpole. His moustache was as precisely clipped as his vowels. Everything about him was an example to the men. He would talk a lot about standards, Quinn imagined, about the importance of maintaining them. All that had made him a willing ally in Quinn's plans. Darcy looked back as he led the way through the guardroom. In that brief glance, Quinn felt himself assessed, not critically, not dismissively, just interestedly; it was almost as if the MP had never seen a civilian policeman in close quarters before.

'Did you say anything to him about why you have detained him?'

'I thought it better not to.'

Quinn nodded approvingly. Surprise was always a useful advantage.

'Do you want me in there with you?'

'That won't be necessary.'

'I should introduce you, at least. Impress upon him the importance of cooperating.'

'There is no need for introductions. We know each other well enough already.'

The man was seated on the far side of a plain wooden table that was set perfectly square in the middle of the room. He sat beneath a bare electric light bulb that hung on a twisted cord. Colour flooded his face as Quinn came in. 'You!'

'Where is she, Hargreaves? Where's Mary?'

Corporal Hargreaves shifted warily in his seat. Quinn supposed that ordinarily Hargreaves would be reckoned a handsome man. He certainly carried himself like one. But now, something ugly revealed itself in his face. His eyes grew cold and cynical. His mouth spasmed into a sneer. 'You tried it on with my wife. Now you've come after my mistress.'

'I hope for your sake that you have not made her your mistress.'

'What if I have? It's not against the law.'

'Abduction. Rape. These are things that are against the law. Quite seriously so.'

'She came voluntarily. She's not a child, you know. Even though her silly mother treats her like one. She knows her own mind. I sent her the money and she came willingly. Like a shot. She wanted to be with me.'

'Her mother is out of her mind with worry.'

'Mothers . . . are generally tiresome creatures.'

'I have come to take her back.'

'You're welcome to her. Good riddance is what I say. It didn't turn out to be such a lark as I had hoped. She spends all the time crying when I am with her. And when I am not too, I shouldn't wonder. Where's the fun in that?'

'Where are you keeping her?'

'She's at the George in Colchester. I booked her in under the name Smith. Mrs Smith. Listen Quinn, if you're going to take her back, I ought to be compensated, you know. I paid out good money in this enterprise. There was the train fare, the hotel, not to mention all the stupid little things I had to buy her to shut her up. She came here with nothing, you know. Hadn't even packed a bag. Stupid bitch.'

Quinn lurched forward and grabbed the table, intending to hurl it out of the way so that he could get at Hargreaves. He discovered that it was fixed to the floor, as were all the chairs.

'Keep your hair on, old man. You know how it is. You of all people. It's not like you never let your feelings get the better of you.'

'I haven't raped anyone.'

'Oh, stop using that word. I didn't rape Mary, I tell you. She wanted it. It's not my fault if she spent all the time afterwards crying. The silly girl.'

'I shall make a report to Captain Darcy. What action he takes will be up to him.'

'Oh, he won't do anything. Old Darcy's all right. Once you get past the prim and proper exterior. All the chaps have mistresses, you know. The officers are the worst.'

'What about Mrs Hargreaves?'

'Cissy doesn't need to know about this, does she? I mean, what she doesn't know can't hurt her?'

'How on earth do you think you can keep it from her?'

'You owe me one, Quinn, after the liberties you took coming on to my Cissy that time. I'll let you off all that if you do the decent thing here. We're men of the world, after all, aren't we?'

'Decent? You don't know the meaning of the word.'

'Oh, don't get on your high horse with me. You haven't got a leg to stand on. You may not have succeeded, but you tried your damnedest to steal a wife away from her husband. You're guilty of attempted adultery.' Hargreaves smiled unpleasantly. He was evidently pleased with his choice of phrase. 'I'd say that hardly qualifies as decent behaviour.'

'We have nothing more to discuss here.'

Quinn turned his back on Hargreaves and strode towards the door.

FIFTY-THREE

Quinn left it until the next day to call at the George. He spent the night at Captain Darcy's residence, on a camp bed in the captain's living room. Darcy drove him into town himself, through a pleasant misty morning in which the smell of woodsmoke hung. The mist cleared as they drove, and a crisp sunlight glinted on Captain Darcy's brass buttons. His impeccable demeanour had been cranked up into a carapace of enraged perfection in response to Quinn's report of Corporal Hargreaves' transgressions.

The George was an old coaching inn on the High Street,

licensed to Mrs Gertrude Triscott, as the sign over the door noti-
fied him. A wrought-iron balcony decked with flower baskets
straddled the facade beneath the first floor windows. It was hard
to imagine a more English scene.

Mrs Triscott herself, a typical example of the hotel landlady,
sensible and stout in equal degree, greeted him with an arched
eyebrow and a defensive lean backwards when he showed her
his warrant card. 'I believe you have a Mrs Smith staying here?'

She showed him up to Mary's room. He noticed that she limped
as she climbed the stairs, favouring her right leg to take her
weight. The detail in itself was insignificant, although the fact
that Quinn focused on it, to the point almost of fixation, betrayed
his nervousness. He ought to have been thinking about what he
would say to Mary.

They came to a door on the second storey and Mrs Triscott
nodded. Quinn knocked. There was no reply. 'Mary? It's Mr
Quinn. Silas. I have come to take you home.'

He strained to listen. Something stirred inside the room. A
floorboard creaked. A moment later, the key turned in the lock
and the door began to open.

Mary Ibbott threw herself into his arms, hiding her face against
his chest, burying into him blindly, like a cat into a bed of catnip.
He held the quaking of her sobs close to him, absorbing her
tears, her shame, her misery and the gentle, convulsive buffets
of her forehead.

They travelled back to London in a mid-morning train that was
thankfully almost empty. Quinn had telephoned Mrs Ibbott
from the hotel, handing the earpiece to Mary for tearful confirmation that he had really found her.

Now they sat opposite one another in a compartment they had
to themselves. She avoided looking at him, keeping her gaze
fixed on the passing landscape. Her pale face was reflected in
the window.

From time to time Quinn saw her lips move as she murmured to
herself. Either she was working out what she would say to her mother,
or she was rehashing conversations she had had with her lover.
Admonishing him, perhaps, for his cruelty and heartlessness.

He did not press her for answers to any questions beyond the
one he had already asked her. 'Did he rape you?'

At that, she had burst into tears, closed her eyes and lowered her head, shaking out a denial.

Quinn might have suspected that she was lying, but without her cooperation, there was little he could do.

He did not press her for details of how Hargreaves had persuaded her to come to Colchester, or what passed between them while she was there, or why she didn't write to her mother to let her know that she was alive.

Nor did he tell her about Timberley's death.

He wondered whether this was cowardice on his part. He was afraid of the emotion it would undoubtedly unleash. But also, he could not imagine a way to break the news that did not involve some cruelty or even sadism on his part. He suspected that if he were to tell her, his motive would be to punish her.

It would be better coming from her mother, he decided.

As the train pulled into Liverpool Street Station, Quinn could see that the platform was already crowded with soldiers waiting to take it back to Colchester, commuters in the infernal business of war.

He was surprised that Mary wanted to take his arm as they walked along the platform. An embarrassed reserve had come over her after the spontaneous embrace of their initial reunion. But now her need for his support was greater than any other consideration. She pulled him to her. The presence of soldiers, and in such great numbers, seemed to have something to do with it.

Quinn patted her hand and held his head high.

As they neared the ticket barrier, he was surprised to hear his name called out. 'Inspector Quinn!' Adam Cardew, in the khaki uniform of a private in the infantry, came running with a faltering step towards them. 'I thought it was you.'

'Adam?' Quinn looked the young man up and down inquisitively.

'Yes. I did it.' There was a beat before Adam went on: 'I signed up. I . . . well, I didn't tell them about my gammy leg. Dosed myself up with aspirin before the medical and pushed on through. No one was any the wiser. Now I'm in, so there's nothing they can do.'

'Why?'

'Why not? There's a war on, isn't there?'

'What about your mother? She is alone now, now that your father . . .'

'She will go to live with her sister.'

'It's terribly sad. For her. For you.'

'Don't worry about me. I have every intention of taking a bullet to the head as soon as I am out there. I have positively made up my mind to make it happen.'

'Good God! Why?'

'Because it's what I deserve.'

'Why do you say that?'

Adam Cardew hesitated. He seemed to notice Mary for the first time. 'I say, don't I know you?'

Mary averted her gaze sharply, looking down at the ground in embarrassment. She seemed unable to answer Adam's question.

'This is Mary,' said Quinn.

'Mary? Yes! I do remember you, I'm sure. Didn't you used to go to . . . My God, he never did anything to you, did he? My father?'

Mary frowned in confusion and shook her head rapidly, still not meeting Adam's gaze.

'Is it because of what your father did? Is that why you said what you said? About deserving . . .' Quinn hesitated tactfully.

'A bullet to the head.'

'You're not responsible for your father's actions. You do not share in his guilt.'

'No. You're wrong. I knew. I saw. I saw what he did to her. Made her do. And I did nothing.'

Quinn breathed deeply, filling his lungs as if he feared the air was running out.

'Until it was too late. And by then there was nothing I could do for her, except . . .' Adam narrowed his eyes, as if to hold on to a vision that was fading before his eyes. 'She was . . . tormented. You don't understand. She could never have any peace. Never. Because of what he had done to her. She knew that. She was broken, damaged. That's why she was like she was. Why she tried to make everyone hate her. She tried to make me hate her. She said those things to make me hate her. Such terrible things. I just wanted her to stop saying such hateful things. I . . .' Adam broke off, a look approaching panic in his eyes.

'I tried to make her understand. But she wouldn't listen. I tried to explain. That I knew. I knew everything. I had seen them, you see. And I couldn't hate her. I had no right to hate her. She was my sister and I had let her down. It was all my fault. How could I hate her?'

Tears welled and broke to trickle down his face.

'I couldn't let her make me hate her.' Adam stared into Quinn's eyes, willing him to understand. 'I had to stop her.'

'I'm not sure I understand you.' Quinn had not been wholly attending to what Adam had said. He was anxious to get Mary back to her mother. But also, he was aware that he did not want to understand what Adam Cardew appeared to be saying. A door seemed to be opening; it would be far more convenient if it remained closed.

He was aware of a strange reluctance to probe. And yet despite it, he could not prevent a question from rising to his lips. 'How did you know where to find her?'

'It was our place. The place we used to go when we were children. Before . . . before he corrupted her. Before he spoiled everything. I thought if there was one place where she might be, where she would run to, it would be there. It was a place of innocence and happiness for us.'

'And she was dead when you found her?' He needed to hear Adam confirm this. And if he did, it would be enough for him.

Adam's head dipped sharply, his eyes skittering away from Quinn's. It could have been the confirmation Quinn was looking for, a terse, silent nod given because emotion had robbed the boy of words. Or it could have meant something else entirely.

Quinn chose to accept the first, easier, lazier interpretation. But still, he could not suppress one further question. 'Tell me, why do you think your father put the feather in her mouth?'

'Did he?'

'Who else? If he was her killer . . .'

'*If* he was.'

'You don't think it was your father who killed Eve?'

Adam ignored the question. 'Perhaps the feather is a little strange. But I think I understand why . . . why he would put it there. I think it was a gift. A kind of gift for her. He was giving her back something pure. He saw the feather as a symbol of purity. He was giving her back her purity. Restoring her to purity.

The feather, I think, must have seemed . . . pure to him. It must have reminded him of an angel's wings. Perhaps he hoped the feather would intercede on her behalf with God? It may not make much sense to you, but his mind, I think, must have been in some . . . derangement at the time. But if it had been me, I think that's what would have gone through my mind. That's why I would have done it.'

Another question began to form in Quinn's mind, but his solicitude for Mary prevented him from attending to it. But something else contributed to his strange reluctance to ask or even form the question. He knew that once it had been asked, it would be impossible to take it back. And if he could not take it back, he would have to follow it through to its natural conclusion.

'I'm going to war, sir. Have to get myself trained up first. But eventually, I'll take my place. And then, well, I don't imagine it will be that hard to get myself killed. I just have to stand up straight. They have snipers out there, I am told, who are picking off those of our men who are so careless as to let their heads show above the trenches. And so, I'll die a hero. Or a bloody fool. But not what I am. I don't care about any of that, of course. It's for my mother, you understand. I want to give her this. It's one way I can make amends. Will you let me go?'

'I know of no reason to stop you,' said Quinn.

Adam Cardew gave a brief nod of gratitude and turned away.

Quinn looked nervously towards Mary. He saw her bite her lip, uncertain of the meaning of what she had just witnessed, but somehow sensing its significance.

It seemed at first that Mrs Ibbott's face had been set to anger, and she had made up her mind to scold her daughter. But upon seeing Mary there on the doorstep, she was helpless in the rush of relief and joy and, yes, love that swept over her. The instinct to forgive, to hold on to what had been so nearly lost prevailed over the idea of reprimand.

Tears, there were tears of course, big, blubbering hot tears as she pulled her daughter to her and held her as if she would never let her go again.

Did she feel the change that had come over her daughter as she clutched her to her breast? Was she smaller, bonier, softer, more sinewy or more intractable in her arms? Or was it still, essentially, the same girl that she had always held? Older and wiser, perhaps, but such changes were not apparent to the touch.

The mother led the daughter into the drawing room and Quinn signalled that he would wait in the hall. Then the sharp, high, piercing wail behind the closed door told him that Mary knew about Timberley now.

This was not something that could be cried out quickly. More than simple grief, it would be grief compounded by guilt. Quinn knew that there is no more biting sorrow than that.

He thought about slipping away. But something kept him there. The sense that they needed him.

At last the door opened and Mrs Ibbott emerged. Her eyes were raw but she was composed and dignified. Her daughter's collapse had brought out her strength.

'How is she?'

'It has shaken her badly. She did not imagine that something like that might happen. None of us did.'

'Is there anything I can do?'

Mrs Ibbott braved a smile. 'I have kept your room for you, you know. And now . . . well, *he* is certainly not coming back here. I have made it clear to Mrs Hargreaves that she may stay, if she wishes. I consider her an equal victim in all this. But she has made the decision to leave. That is her choice, though I pray that she has no intention of joining that scoundrel. At any rate, with both of them gone, I see no obstacle to your return.'

'I would like that . . . very much.'

'That's settled then. Mr Appleby has gone now, you know.'

'Appleby?'

'Oh, yes, he's in the army now.'

'I see.'

'So, everything is changing. Nothing will be the same again. I think we should, those of us who are still here, I think we should stick together. Don't you?'

'Yes, Mrs Ibbott. I do.'

'Please, if I am to call you Silas, you should call me Edith.'

'Very well, Edith.'

'It will be good for Mary to have some stability in her life. You are something of a father figure to her, you know.'

'I?'

Edith Ibbott looked away from his embarrassment with a discreet, understanding smile. She held the door open for him to join them in the drawing room.

FIFTY-FOUR

The following Monday, as Quinn walked across the floor of the CID room, he was aware of heads lifting and turning to watch him on his way. It was always unnerving to feel yourself the object of other men's attention, but now, at last, he allowed himself to believe that the hostility and suspicion had gone from his fellow officers' gazes.

And if he still expected to hear passing references to Colney Hatch, he trusted that they might be made with a certain grudging respect, and even pride. As if to say, yes, our governor might be mad, but he's a damn good detective and he's our governor.

This much he had earned.

He was wearing his trusty ulster raincoat and a new bowler hat, which he had purchased that Saturday to replace the one destroyed by Coddington. Let them see him in that, restored to his former glory, as it were; and let them draw their own conclusions.

He hung the bowler and ulster on the handstand in the office that now belonged to him, and sat down at his desk.

A moment later, as if he had been waiting for Quinn to arrive, Leversedge came in, brandishing a brown folder. 'Do you want to see this?'

'I don't know. What is it?'

'It's the report from the forensics chaps. On the milk bottle and bowl found in Felix Simpkins' den. They rushed it through over the weekend.'

'What does it say?' But Quinn already knew, from Leversedge's fastidiously neutral tone. He was working hard to keep either glee or despondency out of his voice. Working hard to present himself as a loyal lieutenant.

Leversedge opened the folder and looked down at the report. It was a charade, of course. He knew perfectly well what it said. 'They found no match. Between the prints on those items and Pastor Cardew. And they were able to take definitive prints from Cardew's body. Of course, it doesn't prove that Cardew didn't kill his daughter. But it rather suggests that it wasn't him who helped Felix. They found Felix's prints, as you would expect. And one other set, as yet unidentified. So your instincts were right, guv. Just that . . .' Leversedge trailed off. But Quinn knew what he had been about to say. *Just that you got the wrong man.*

'Of course, with Cardew being dead,' continued Leversedge, 'this will never come to trial, so there's no danger of a defence brief blowing a hole in your case. The only question is, are you content to let it rest, or should we be looking for someone else?'

Quinn held out his hand to take the folder. 'As you say, it doesn't prove he didn't kill his daughter. There is enough other evidence to suggest his guilt. I'm content.'

Quinn did not look at Leversedge, but he could well imagine the moue of surprise that the other man was putting on.

'Can't help wondering whose the other prints are, though,' said Leversedge.

Quinn did not offer an opinion.

'So, Quinn, it seems you have done it again.' Sir Edward's brows clashed together like fighting birds let loose upon each other. The sternness of his expression contradicted the apparent compliment that he had just paid Quinn. Quinn took it as a compliment, at least. Sir Edward went on to voice his unease: 'It's never easy . . . never easy when one of your own turns out to be a wrong 'un.'

Quinn frowned at Sir Edward's uncharacteristic lapse into the demotic. 'The Force is better off without the likes of Coddington.'

'Indubitably. Indubitably. Even so, it would have been better for all concerned if that German butcher had been the culprit, after all.'

'Not better for him.'

'No? I suppose not.' Sir Edward made the concession with a regretful sigh. 'And so, you are satisfied that Cardew killed his daughter?'

'I am satisfied that Pastor Cardew was responsible for the death of Eve Cardew.'

'But there's no note, I believe? It would have tied things up nicely if you could have found a note.'

For one insane moment, Quinn contemplated forging a note and 'discovering' it somewhere in the Cardew's home or the church. If a note was what people wanted, if it was what they needed to accept that the case was solved, then he would give it to them. 'In my experience, suicides do not always leave a note.'

'Ah yes, I was forgetting . . .'

'If you are referring to my father . . .'

'I did not wish to bring it up.'

'In his case, there was a note.'

'Ah. I see.'

'Shame. Guilt. Remorse. Such feelings often play a part in the decision to take one's own life. And there are some acts of which one may be so ashamed that one baulks at putting them in writing, even in a suicide note.'

'I suppose you are right. You think this is the case with Cardew?'

'I am certain of it.'

'Well, yes . . . his own daughter.'

'He could not face the possibility of his crimes coming out. And now he does not have to.'

'Kell has been very impressed with you, you know?'

'Kell? Really? I am surprised. I have not delivered the outcome he wished for.'

'That doesn't matter to Kell. What matters is you stuck with it and cracked the case. You eschewed the obvious. You resisted the pressure that he put on you to go down a certain route.'

'He was testing me?'

'Everything we do is a test of some kind, is it not? You proved yourself impervious to such pressures. That makes you a man he can use, he tells me.'

'I see.'

'And so, Kell has proposed, and I agree, that we reinstate the Special Crimes Department, with you in command. Its terms of reference will be somewhat different from before. You will report to Kell rather than to me. In addition, I have approved an increase in resources. You may have two additional men.'

'May I choose them myself?'

'Whom do you have in mind?'

'DS Willoughby and DI Leversedge.'
'Interesting choices. Let me see what I can do.'
'Thank you, Sir Edward.'
'"In due season we shall reap, if we faint not." Galatians, chapter six, verse nine.'

Quinn recognized the note of finality that often came with one of Sir Edward's biblical quotations. The interview was over.

Quinn stood on Victoria Embankment, looking down at the restless surface of the Thames. The day was borne up on the river, crisp and clear-eyed, with a chill in the air that presaged autumn. Quinn studied the fleeting patterns made by the surge and play of the agitated peaks, willing them to form into a stable pattern that he could hold on to. He was looking for something to be revealed to him. A meaning, or perhaps a validation. But the river would not yield its secret counsel.

His body felt as if his internal organs had been replaced with stones. He imagined throwing himself into the river and sinking like a sack of stones to the bottom, never to be seen again.

He was thinking about Adam Cardew.

He now acknowledged that when Adam Cardew had approached him at Liverpool Street Station, he was trying to confess to his sister's murder. Quinn knew that he had sensed this at the time, but had refused to accept the confession.

Perhaps he had known all along that Adam was the killer. He was the one who had found Eve. He knew where to look for her.

Certainly Quinn had accepted that conclusion by the time of his interview with Sir Edward. The absence of his father's fingerprints had clinched it. And yet he had said that he held Pastor Cardew responsible for Eve's death. A clever distinction, worthy of a lawyer. Unworthy of a police detective.

There was a good reason for the physical depression he was experiencing. He had discovered some uncomfortable truths about himself. He was as bad as Coddington. Only moments ago he had actually considered forging a suicide note to silence his critics.

Once he had come to believe that Pastor Cardew had killed his own daughter he had blindly pursued a false trail, disregarding any evidence that was not consistent with his pet theory.

And the real killer had escaped justice.

Except that the penalty Adam Cardew could expect from the justice system – death – would now be meted out by a German sniper. Quinn had no doubt that Adam meant to carry out his threat of getting himself killed. Quinn accepted too that Adam had killed his sister out of love. That did not make it any less of a crime, of course, and it was not for Quinn to mitigate an offender's crimes. That was the job of his legal defence. A clever lawyer might be able to argue that Adam had not meant to kill her, but merely to silence her. Perhaps he might have got off on a charge of manslaughter. If Quinn had prevented him from boarding that train, he might have saved his life.

The ceaseless churn of the river tide continued.

'Penny for your thoughts.'

He turned to where Lettice was standing at his side.

'I was thinking where I should take you for our second . . .' Quinn hesitated as he tried to think of the correct word for what he was proposing. 'Outing.'

She wrinkled her nose at his choice of word. 'And where did you decide?'

'Do you like toasted teacakes?'

'You know I do.'

'Well then?'

He held out his arm. It was possibly a little bold of him, her angled head and arched brow seemed to suggest. But her smile as she took his arm lifted the weight from his spirit.